Critics Praise
MURDER AT SAN SIMEON

"Hearst and Biddle paint a fascinating look at life at San Simeon."

—Bobbie Hess, *San Francisco Examiner*

"[An] engrossing tale . . . The most powerful writing comes in the flashback scenes. . . ."

—Les Roberts, *The Plain Dealer* (Cleveland)

"Hollywood movie stars of the era abound in this fascinating novel of the excesses of money and power."

—Susan Rose, *The Snooper* (Belleair Bluffs, FL)

"Described with brio is the relationship between Hearst and his silent-screen-star mistress, Marion Davies, whom the publisher kept a virtual prisoner at the castle where she took revenge by throwing wild parties and having assorted, barely concealed affairs."

—*Publishers Weekly*

"For the film buff, the book is a treasure trove of famous names and gossip."

—Kathey Clarey, *The Fresno Bee*

"The book succeeds on every count: plot, characterization and certainly period detail. . . . Readers looking for glamour and excitement will not be disappointed."

—Robert A. Carter, *Houston Chronicle*

MURDER AT SAN SIMEON

PATRICIA HEARST &
CORDELIA FRANCES BIDDLE

A LISA DREW BOOK

POCKET BOOKS

New York   London   Toronto   Sydney   Tokyo   Singapore

This book is a work of fiction. Names, characters, places and incidents are products of the authors' imagination or are used fictitiously. Any resemblance to actual events or locales or persons, living or dead, is entirely coincidental.

"Heart Castle," "Hearst San Simeon State Historical Monument," "La Cuesta Encantada," and "The Enchanted Hill" are trademarked and/or servicemarked by Hearst San Simeon State Historical Monument™, San Simeon District, a Unit of the California Department of Parks and Recreation.

POCKET BOOKS, a division of Simon & Schuster Inc.
1230 Avenue of the Americas, New York, NY 10020

ISBN: 0-671-53402-5

First Pocket Books printing January 1998

10 9 8 7 6 5 4 3 2 1

A LISA DREW BOOK is a trademark of Simon & Schuster Inc.

POCKET and colophon are registered trademarks of Simon & Schuster Inc.

Cover art by Dennis Ziemienski

Printed in the U.S.A.

Thank You

THE IDEA FOR THIS BOOK BEGAN TO EVOLVE SLOWLY over the last three years. When I was growing up, my family rarely discussed my grandfather and never mentioned Marion Davies. Their relationship was a subject that simply wasn't raised, and I reached adulthood knowing remarkably little about William Randolph Hearst.

I finally decided that I owed it to myself and my children to learn about my famous grandfather, and began reading every biography I could find on the Hearst family.

While I uncovered numerous memorable accounts of W.R.'s exploits, tales of my grandfather's involvement in the death of Thomas Ince fascinated me—one of the great Hollywood mysteries—and I started thinking of the event in terms of a novel and *Murder at San Simeon* began to take shape.

There are several people I have to thank for helping to make this book a reality. First is Cordelia Biddle. She added her brilliant vision and scrupulous attention

Thank You

to period details to this story. I will always be grateful for her patience, hard work, and extremely understanding husband.

Many thanks to Alan Nevins for introducing me to Cordelia. Not only did we manage to finish our novel on time, but we are all still speaking to each other.

Of course, there is Lisa Drew—my once and future editor. What a great privilege it was to work with her again! Her commitment to this project (not to mention her prime-time definition of a "complete manuscript") was an inspiration to us.

And a special thanks to Roddy McDowall. His suggestion that I watch "show people" led to the serendipitous discovery of all of Marion's Hollywood friends on film.

Finally, I am especially grateful to my husband, Bernard. Without his love, support, and inspiration this book would not have been possible, and it is to him that *Murder at San Simeon* is dedicated.

—PATRICIA HEARST

MURDER
AT
SAN SIMEON

Prologue

November 1924

MARION GLARED AT THE FRONT PAGE OF THE *DAILY Examiner*. The newspaper lay on the floor, a defenseless blob of black and white. For good measure, she gave the paper a second angry kick, sending it scuttling under the bed where she jabbed it with her toe. Then she brought the full weight of her shoeless foot onto its inky pages.

The folded newsprint was slippery and cool; it felt good under her silk stockings. Not as nice as walking on the beach, but beggars couldn't be choosers. The image of herself reduced to poverty produced a wry smile that was part self-pity and part iron determination. In her twenty-seven-year existence, Marion Davies, ex–Ziegfeld girl and now star of the silent screen, had learned a thing or two about survival.

She gave the daily one more vengeful stab, then turned and studied her bedroom, part of her suite at San Simeon, La Cuesta Encantada, "The Enchanted Hill," William Randolph Hearst's vast mountaintop pleasure palace—the 250,000-acre estate he often referred to by the folksy title of The Ranch. The fury

1

on Marion's face disappeared in a complacent grin. She seemed on the verge of laughing aloud.

Belying La Cuesta Encantada's homespun nickname, the suite, like the rest of the house, was an elaborate blend of medieval, Renaissance, and rococo art and artifacts, a crimson-hued, gilded, and brocaded extravaganza stuffed to its fifteenth-century Spanish rafters with priceless antiques: heavy silver candlesticks from an Italian monastery, a seventeenth-century inlaid walnut chest of drawers, doors that had once hidden Spanish confessional stalls, a hanging Florentine lamp of silvered bronze, a brooding, brown-toned painting entitled the *Mystic Marriage of Saint Catherine,* and the pièce de résistance—a French Gothic bed, swathed in bloodred velvet hangings and gold tassels the size of muskmelons.

For the decidedly blond and vehemently blue-eyed Marion, the color scheme was startling—not to mention the ecclesiastic nature of the decor.

Although some of them early popes had mistresses, she reminded herself with a sly grin. That's what W.R. told me anyways. And those holy guys were supposed to be celibate—even in the Dark Ages. I know that much, at least. No flies on this girl, and that's the damn truth.

Marion sashayed across the Persian carpet. Again, the pervading hue was red. A scarlet woman, she decided while her eyes leveled on the room's single blue object: a sixteenth-century majolica inkstand in the shape of St. George slaying the dragon. The knight's lance was the pen; jabbed downward it became the reptile's destroyer.

Both the hero and his steed were the same ultramarine as Marion's eyes, while the dying serpent was a lustrous olive green flecked with gold. The inkstand was the only artwork Marion cared for, and she spent a good deal of time stroking the horse's shiny flanks and gazing at the saint's unseeing stare.

The Renaissance jewel cabinet sitting nearby, she didn't like, even though W.R. had stuffed it with plenty of diamond and platinum goodies. The box reminded her of a miniature mausoleum with its prissy Limoges medallions and tiny black urns. The damn thing gave her the creeps, if you wanted the truth. She didn't care how much it had cost.

If I owned this room, Marion told herself, I'd have it done over in blue. Aqua and turquoise and sapphire and lots of frilly chiffon and lace. But I'd have to be the house's owner, instead of its . . . what? What's that word W.R. taught me yesterday? Come on, you dope, think! Pops will be mad as the dickens if you can't even learn one new word. Especially after the dough he spent on those damn speech teachers, and that fancy-pants private secretary he just hired me—her with her dumb finishing-school manners!

But Marion's quick wrath at San Simeon's most recent employee was quickly supplanted by a vision of herself disappointing her Popsie. He'd get that sad-little-boy look on his wrinkled face, and he'd seem even more ancient than he was. And sixty-one wasn't a spring chicken in anybody's book.

Then maybe he'd get serious about going back to his wife in New York. A villainous look darkened Marion's face; she'd never met the hoity-toity Millicent, but she'd read all about her society goings-on—even in the Hearst-owned newspapers that filled San Simeon's library. "Mrs. William Randolph Hearst," the stories enthused as if a lowlife like Marion Davies couldn't possibly exist.

"Chatelaine!" Marion burst out with her kinetic giggle. "Chatelaine of San Simeon! That's what Pops said I was! Yessir, that's the t-ticket!"

3

But the stutter that had plagued her professional life caused her face to crumple. Chagrin mingled with frustration creased her forehead. Her blue eyes became dull, and her blond hair turned drab. It was as if someone had drained the life out of Marion Davies.

"Never could get it right," she stammered. "Flo Ziegfeld—he almost fired me 'cause of my speech. Wouldn't have been nowhere without those Ziegfeld Follies. And sometimes, I wish I wasn't!"

Marion began to weep here, a little-girl-lost sound totally out of keeping with the high-minded rooms or her marcelled and peroxided hair.

Old Pops, she told herself miserably, I don't know what he saw in me. I wasn't nothing but a teenage kid in the pony chorus. In the back of the chorus, if you want the truth. . . . Chu Chin Chow's phony-baloney "Ballet"—how's that for a laugh and a half? It was my big sister that was the real knockout. Mama Rose always said so. Even when we was still settled out in Brooklyn. Little Marion Cecilia Douras—a no-account Irish kid from the burgs!

Marion's sobs grew louder, then ceased with an alarming alacrity. "Anything," Marion corrected herself with a steely smile. The stutter had miraculously vanished:

" 'Wasn't nothing'—that's not proper English. I've got to remember that. I gotta show Popsie I can behave."

Her throat went tight with this last sentiment, but the underlying emotion was slammed shut. Her situation with W.R. was tenuous; it always had been. Even when he swore he'd divorce Millicent, Marion recognized the words as a ruse. He was a guy you couldn't quite trust, and because of that he was scary.

Out of habit, Marion cut short her examination of life with W.R.; there was no point fretting over situa-

4

tions you couldn't change. Instead she returned her concentration to the bedroom, to the coffered ceiling from the fifteenth-century Marchino castle in Cordova, Spain, the chaste and heavy confessional doors; even the window frames had been imported piecemeal from some French convent. W.R. liked his religion where he could admire it.

"Aw, nuts!" she sniffed with forced bravado. "Just take it on the chin, kiddo! Or like Miss Prim and Proper Secretary says—'A stiff upper lip!' That girl should know what she's yammering about!"

Marion roared at her private joke, then strolled past the bank of windows and stared at the view of California's majestic Central Coast. The arched windows were stone and encrusted with golden Gothic beasts climbing pillars wrapped with vines; W.R. had liked the motif so much he'd ordered his architect to repeat it on the sill and ceiling. The result resembled an enormous picture frame, as if the hills and sky belonged to a painting: the tawny and undulating mountains of the Santa Lucia Range, the cobalt sky, the grizzled-green hint of chaparral, the clusters of oaks nestled deep in the darker valleys, and the glint of the great sea beyond. There wasn't a human being as far as the eye could see.

"Who cares about pals anyhow?" Marion boasted. The stammer returned, turning her streetwise talk into a childish swagger. "I like a little P and Q now and then. Those Hollywood parties can get awful wild. Specially when they start passing around the junk. That heroin stuff will kill ya, sure as shootin'."

Marion smirked at her pun, then opened an elaborately carved drawer of her walnut dresser, rummaged in the back of her lingerie collection, and pulled out a bottle of bootleg gin.

"Here's to ya!" She winked at the gilded mirror's

reflection after she'd poured out a healthy dollop. "Miss Movie Star! Ex–Little Marion Cecilia Douras with her acrobatic chorus-girl stunts! Nobody, but nobody, could do a split like this kid."

The gin was warm, but like everything else at San Simeon the booze was the finest money could procure. Marion knew she wasn't risking blindness as she might with Mexican contraband. This stuff wouldn't give her stomach cramps or send her to the hospital; and it definitely wasn't lethal, no matter what the papers claimed. W.R. wasn't a drinker himself, but he liked to give his guests the best—despite that stupid regulation known as Prohibition.

But the hooch definitely needed ice. "Gotta remember to store the bottle in the toilet tank," Marion told herself. "At least, the stuff would be chilled. Can't have my kickers tasting like mother's milk! Not Mama Rose's milk, leastwhiles! My mama's idea of 'maternal' would sour any puss."

"Marion?" The voice on the other side of the bedroom door almost made Marion drop her glass. She stared down into the drawer stuffed with crepe de Chine camisoles and step-ins and carefully set her drink on a nearby silver tray. It would be a sin to ruin her expensive underthings. And she couldn't very well slip into W.R.'s bedroom reeking of stale gin.

"Hiya, Pops!" Marion made every effort to control her stutter; forced cheer seemed to translate itself into the hallway in spite of the door's ornate paneling.

"Are you all right, Marion?" W.R.'s curiously high-pitched voice sounded even more ethereal when worried. It reminded Marion of piano wires strung too tight. There wasn't any resonance to the tone, just a kind of eerie vibration.

"Sure, Pops. Just getting dressed for supper is all. Like to look my bestest for my bestest boy!"

6

"I thought I heard you talking in there. I thought perhaps you weren't alone, and as I passed your secretary on the stairs, I assumed you had some other visitor."

Marion's heart did a quick flip-flop. What could that damn spy have told him? A girl couldn't have a life if she didn't have one or two little secrets.

"Who would I be gabbing with? The only people up here work for you, Chief. You aren't jealous of Neylan or Joe Willicombe, now, are you? You know those fellas aren't this girl's dish!" The attempted joke flopped to the floor like a very dead fish.

"I'm not jealous, Marion. Unless you give me cause to be."

Marion heard the threat, and W.R. heard it, too, although he did nothing to rescind it.

"No more private dicks, huh? Like that time in New York? You know, after you handed me my first diamond bracelet? 'Member, Popsie? I was gabbing with that swell from Philadelphia? College kid with a gold-plated name?" Marion tried for a happy-go-lucky giggle, but the required smile stuck to her teeth like cheap lipstick. "I'll be downstairs in two shakes of a lamb's tail, I promise." She heard W.R.'s shambling body begin to relinquish his post outside her door.

"I wouldn't hurt you for anything in the world, Popsie," Marion stammered in a frantic gush. "You know I wouldn't."

"As you say, Marion," the squeaky voice acknowledged, but the sound seemed unrepentant. W.R. was used to getting what he wanted. And when he wanted it, too. Inadvertently, a long shudder climbed Marion's spine.

But I wouldn't hurt him, she assured herself as W.R. finally moved down the candelabra-lit hall toward the baronial Refectory and dinner. That old man's given me something no guy ever did. He made me feel important. He made me feel like I was worth something. A chatelaine, like he said. Kind of like a queen. And if that busybody secretary tells him any different, those'll be the last words she says! You can bet your bottom dollar on that!

Marion took one more quick pull on her gin, then flushed the rest down the toilet and headed for her room-size, cedar-lined closet. She wasn't a clothes-horse, although some film critics sniped that her career would be nothing without Cosmopolitan Pictures and William Randolph Hearst's lavish "costume dramas."

She picked out an ice-blue satin evening gown with a jewel neckline and gauzy sleeves. The color accentuated the blue of her eyes. " 'Cause that's what Mama Rose taught me," Marion crooned. Warmed by the gin, her words took on an almost hysterical energy.

"Mama Rose taught me how to please a man. Being a showgirl was just one of her neat, little tricks!"

Marion executed a neat two-step and a quick bump and grind.

"Danced for the best of them. Block and Deering and Pops and all his pals. Sang 'em Eddie Cantor's big Follies hit, 'That's the Kind of Baby for Me!' And boy, did those old stiffs eat it up! Every single word!" Marion snatched up a blue satin slipper and jammed it on her toes.

The matching shoe was nowhere to be found, however. Marion's wardrobe was often as jumbled as her emotions; and she didn't retrieve the slipper's mate until she'd stripped her overstuffed settee of a rust-colored pair of riding breeches, a houndstooth hacking jacket, and a white flannel tennis skirt. Blouses, silk stockings, even the man-tailored gabardine trousers Popsie had ordered for her from Brooks Brothers went flying.

The missing shoe was under the bed behind the offending newspaper. Marion inadvertently pulled out both at the same time.

"The funeral," she mumbled, glaring at the forgotten newsprint. The fact that W.R. hadn't allowed her to drive down to Hollywood for the funeral still rankled deeply.

The lead story of the Hearst-owned Los Angeles *Daily Examiner* covered the entire front page, and Marion glanced at it silently, mouthing words she'd already memorized.

THRONGS PAY FINAL RESPECTS TO FILM WORLD LEADER, blared the headline, while the follow-up story trumpeted:

"Funeral rites today drew forth such motion picture luminaries as Charles Chaplin, Douglas Fairbanks, Mary Pickford and Cecil B. DeMille. . . . Stars shared their grief with extra girls as all mourned a man they'd once called 'friend.' . . .

"Flags flew at half-mast, and the sets of Hollywood studios were deserted as producers and players alike gathered to eulogize one of their own. . . . John Garrigues of the United Lodge of Theosophists delivered the moving funeral oration. . . ."

Marion's face had become as fixed as one of W. R. Hearst's Gothic statues. Even her eyes were cold and wary. Whatever fear or anger had passed behind them were carefully guarded now.

"Recognized as a 'pioneer' in the industry, the deceased's recent works included this past spring's successful *The Marriage Cheat;* negotiations to film rights for Kathleen Norris' novel *The Hungry Heart* have kept gossip columnists buzzing. . . . His wife had no comment on the latter's status."

"I'll just bet she didn't!" Marion swore. "That lady's as clueless as—!" Marion nipped off the tirade, then turned to page two, opening the paper with slow determination. She'd been through this pantomime a hundred times since morning, each time letting her eyes drift across the words as if she suspected secrets of hiding there.

But the second page remained as bland as the first. There were the familiar accounts of Mrs. Warren G. Harding's failing health, the saga of a showgirl who was trying to bilk Cornelius Vanderbilt Whitney out of $1 million for a broken marriage proposal, and the blackmailing tale of a "British Beauty and Her Hindoo Sweetheart." RAJAH DENIES RUMOURS, the headline screamed. Marion knew every line by heart.

Next came a half-page ad for Marion's own film, *Janice Meredith;* "The Greatest Cast the Screen Has Ever Assembled," the ad touted, listing players "W. C. Fields, Harrison Ford, Tyrone Power as well as 8,000 OTHERS." Then came an installment from a serial entitled *The Discontented Wife,* while buried in the back section was a small addendum to the cover story:

"The cause of death was attributed to acute indigestion, perhaps brought on by ingesting bad liquor. . . ."

The report never varied no matter how many times Marion reread it.

She crumpled the newspaper and heaved it onto the floor. "Acute indigestion." She smiled. "Bad liquor. Cops! If those crumb bums only knew!"

1

The Present

QUILMAN BROTHERS MORTUARY HAD LONG SINCE lost its reputation as undertaker to the stars. Established during the luster years of silent films, the funeral home, in a venerable Spanish-styled building with tile roof, broad windows, welcoming, palm-shaded lawn, and large, discreet car park, had laid out the cream of the crop. But the decades following the Roaring Twenties had not been kind. The city had grown one hundredfold; newer establishments had muscled in, raising ever more lavish buildings that reflected the metropolis's increasingly luxurious tastes. Quilman Brothers had become "slightly stodgy," then "quaint"; finally it was "Not that old relic! I thought Rudolph Valentino was the last body to grace its chapel!"

Stuck in its original home at the now busy intersection of Pico Boulevard and Euclid Avenue in Santa Monica, an area dense with cinder-block apartment complexes whose stuccoed facades were painted either a dreary tan or an unpleasant hospital green, Quilman Brothers had become an anomaly.

11

Its front lawn had been chopped in half sometime during the late 1960s, and the mortuary's tall royal palms sold off to a developer building a condo complex in Marina Del Rey. A few years later, the reduced acreage was further decimated until it was no more than a strip of devilishly resilient Bermuda grass—the type every gardener wants to kill.

The interior of the funeral home was equally passé. The wall-to-wall carpeting was dusty brown, the mismatched leatherette chairs a dingy shade of mahogany, the curtains a mass of ocher-hued vines, while the permanently positioned "floral tributes" were a compilation of taupe and putty-colored camellias and lilies—colors you'd never find in their natural-born counterparts.

Wrenching open the heavy front door and immediately banging it shut against the gale-driven onslaught of autumn's first serious rain, Catha Kinsolving Burke took one look at the place and decided she'd never purchase another piece of brown clothing as long as she lived—even if the color did complement her hair.

Then she dutifully shook out her umbrella, rewrapped its sodden tie, slipped off her soaking raincoat, and stomped her drenched feet. In the minute and a half it had taken her to lock her rented car and race across Quilman Brothers' cramped parking lot, Catha had been wet through. Unsure where to set her dripping things or even what was expected of her, she hesitated by the room's grimy picture window, gazing at the unfamiliar street and the rain that continued its monsoon-size assault on the helpless city. Ever since her arrival at the disconcertingly named LAX airport the night before, the rain had pounded Los Angeles with a fervor that seemed somehow human.

"You're Miss . . . Burke?" Catha heard a voice behind her murmur. Despite the trained modulation of the tone, Catha recognized the speaker's hesitation. Self-doubt was her own worst enemy, and she had immediate sympathy for others who suffered from it.

"Your mother was . . . ," the voice continued, obviously wrestling with some unforeseen dilemma. Funeral directors and their assistants were taught to whisper condolences, not make snap judgments about titles.

"Or would you prefer to be called *professor?*" the unseen presence struggled while Catha pulled her eyes away from the sodden street and cruel rain.

"*Miss* is fine," she answered cordially, then was about to explain, I'm not a full professor yet, only an associate—in history and political science, which sounds a lot more formal than it is—when she realized the speaker was a very young, very short, and very round woman draped in a flowing black dress smothered in layers of rickrack, jet beads, sequins, and lace. Except for the color, the garment reminded Catha of the holiday skirts you stuff around the base of Christmas trees.

"I'm Fawn, Mr. Quilman's assistant."

Of course, Catha thought, but didn't dare say. Instead she smiled, extended her hand, and shook Fawn's round and clinging fingers.

"Catha Burke, but please call me Catha."

"Such a shame about this dreadful weather, Miss . . . er"—Fawn was definitely not a first-name person—"you being from back East and all," the wheezy gush continued, then Fawn stopped herself in a panic of self-criticism. "I mean . . . I mean, a funeral is saddening at any time . . . but the rain . . . well, we're not used to it in southern California, not like the northern part of the state . . . and especially not in mid-November. That's unheard of.

"Besides, it's so dangerous, you know, and it gets

everyone so darned depressed. Some of our older residents . . . well, they just can't take it. We get a lot of suicides at this time of year. Mr. Quilman, he says those are the hardest types of services to perform, because . . . you know . . ."

Fawn's mournful voice trailed off, but she continued to stare up at Catha as if she'd just divulged the raciest details of some movie star's sex life. Obviously, Fawn had her own peculiar ideas about what made hot gossip.

Looking down at the earnest face and ample dress, Catha experienced an absurd temptation to laugh. The entire atmosphere seemed suddenly ludicrous: a funeral parlor filled with fake antiques and liver-colored flowers, a young woman whose black-penciled eyes glowed at the mention of suicide, and a deluge of November rain.

The rain kept Catha on track, however. The rain that rushed the storm gutters, pounded pedestrians, and locked automobile brakes served as a reminder Catha couldn't ignore. She was in California to oversee her mother's funeral.

"I understand," Catha said softly. She'd never hurt the Fawns of this world if she could help it. "I'm sure you and Mr. Quilman are a great comfort to the survivors." Then, excusing herself with as much grace and dignity as she could muster, Catha walked into Quilman Brothers' dingy chapel.

There she sank wearily into a chair, staring blindly at a wall as she struggled to sort through the events of the last twenty-four hours. When she'd left her home in Middletown, Connecticut, the afternoon before, Catha had tried to persuade herself that her mother's death was for the best, that daughters and mothers often remain strangers, that the past is better left unexamined. Now those carefully rehearsed argu-

14

ments were beginning to crack, exposing holes Catha would have preferred to ignore.

Louise Burke, Catha thought, picturing the brooding face that had seemed more comfortable with scorn than pleasure. Catha hadn't been part of her mother's life since graduating from college ten years earlier. And after Louise Burke had decided to "return" to California, even that paltry communication had been curtailed. There'd been a once-a-year visit during summer recess, bimonthly telephone calls that ended too quickly and expressed too little, a birthday, a Christmas gift: there was precious little in Catherine Kinsolving Burke's life that bore a trace of her mother.

The two hadn't even resembled each other. Where Louise Burke had been stocky and stolid, Catha was tall and slender; and the dark, wavy hair that had been the unruly bane of her teenage years had been in striking contrast to her mother's short, oatmeal-colored locks. Even their personalities were different. Louise Burke had been a silent, bitter woman, full of secrets she'd never reveal. Catha, on the other hand, found it hard to repress a laugh. And when she smiled, as she often did, her oval face and moss-green eyes almost glittered.

At those moments the true Catha Burke would pop out. She might have been driving her mother to the nearby Santa Monica Place Mall or strolling the landscaped bluffs of the Ocean Avenue Park when some odd incident—the hot sunlight glinting across the pristine blue of the Pacific Ocean, a delicate, night jasmine–scented breeze, even the squeal from an improbably shiny flamingo-pink car—would cause Catha nearly to burst with emotion. At those occasions, Louise Burke would eye her only child with a combination of dismay and censure, mixed with something resembling regret.

What that tenuous and buried emotion had been,

Catha had never had a clue. Just as she'd never known the identities of her father or grandparents. Her mother had been an orphan. She'd been raised in a Protestant-run school somewhere on the California coast, moved East during her brief and disastrous foray into matrimony, and been left an early (and relieved) widow with an infant daughter to raise. That was the sum total of Catha's knowledge of her mother's life.

Louise Burke's pragmatism was the one trait her daughter had inherited. It was what had drawn her to study history. Catha Kinsolving Burke liked to believe that the proper compilation of facts could explain away any mystery.

"Excuse me . . . Miss Burke, is it?" another voice intoned from the chapel's purple-and-lavender darkness. Where Quilman Brothers' reception room had been done up in dingy brown, the chapel resembled the mammoth orchid corsages worn at ladies' club teas.

"Catha," she corrected him lightly. This speaker was clearly more comfortable than Fawn, and the emotion transmitted itself at once. Catha felt relief slip over her shoulders; the sensation was like wrenching off a heavy coat.

And I am relieved, aren't I, Catha realized. It's not just this man's easy tone. Relief was my first reaction when I heard that Mother had died. I stood at the kitchen phone and told myself that whatever Mother's unhappy secrets had been, how they'd affected her life, and what damage they'd done, was finally a thing of the past.

"Call me Catha, please. Miss Burke sounds so . . . so . . . old." Catha found herself smiling despite the moment's solemnity.

"Well, it does now, doesn't it?" the minister chortled in response. He was silver haired and silver bearded, and he moved through the chapel's darkness with proprietary ease. "Certainly no one your age would want to be considered old."

"Heaven forbid." Catha grinned. "I mean—"

"Oh, you can mention heaven in my presence. You just can't add any—how shall I put it . . . critical qualifications? I'm Arnold Tiernan. I'll be officiating. We have the ashes prepared, as you wished. And I must say, I agree with your decision. The open casket can be needlessly maudlin. Death should be a rebirth, a celebration of life eternal—at least that's what the Episcopal Church tries to teach."

Catha liked the man. He wasn't at all what she'd anticipated. "You didn't know my mother?" was out of her mouth before she'd had a chance to think the phrase through.

"No, I did not. That is, not till the very end. She wasn't a regular at Saint Andrew's by the Sea. I don't think our congregation was strict enough for her. But that's fairly typical of most of our transplanted Easterners. Especially the older generation. They like the traditional fire and brimstone—"

"That sounds like Mother, all right."

"The Book of Common Prayer from the 1920s, too, if you can believe it."

Catha smiled again. Remnants of an Irish lilt filled Father Tiernan's voice with homey comfort; for a moment she yearned to be back in her cozy apartment, gazing through her kitchen's bay window at the stately Greek Revival homes that dotted Wesleyan's campus. She pictured herself with a cup of her favorite Darjeeling tea, her faded university sweatshirt hugging her back and a sheaf of uncorrected papers spread on the table before her.

But that vision dragged forth a memory of Win, the

17

arguments he'd been too reasonable to permit, the "intellectual" silences that were their substitute and that had occurred with increasing regularity during the past year. Winslow Reid, tenured professor in Eastern religions, an accomplished teacher and author, authority on the Yemen, and the former lover of Catha Burke.

Without intending to, she sighed noisily, then thrust her thoughts back into the present.

"My mother was critical of a great many things— me included," Catha said as offhandedly as she could. "She once told me she wasn't attending church because her priest had become 'minister to the stars.' "

"That wasn't me, I'm afraid," Father Tiernan laughed. "Although I wish it were!" Then he eased his way back into an all-business mode, and his voice became deliberate and wise.

"Have you decided how to dispose of your mother's remains?" he asked, and Catha was about to try to explain the lack of communication between mother and daughter when Fawn waddled forward to express concerns that the service proceed as quickly as possible.

"We've got another . . . ," she concluded limply, "I mean, well, this is a busy time of year here at Quilman Brothers," then tried to atone for this lapse in etiquette by adding ponderously, "I asked your mother's mourners to sign the guest register in the reception area. Mr. Quilman believes in the healing powers of mementos for the bereaved."

Fawn's register contained only seven names, although Catha was relieved to find any mourners at all. She hadn't known whom to call or even if her mother would have approved the "fuss and bother." All she knew was that her mother didn't want to be "buried in the ground—not with all those trees and roots." It had been a lifelong and almost hysterical desire.

"Your mother was a fine woman," a fiercely blond and red-taloned checkout "girl" from Von's supermarkets hissed in a tobaccoy growl after the service was finished. "She never bought frozen. Always fresh. And she didn't go in for prepackaged, neither. Not like some of these others! I don't know how they can face themselves in the mirror. Buying empty calories on food stamps and God knows what other government benefits—"

"Thank you for your condolences," Catha interrupted as quickly as she could. "And for coming," she added, although she wondered if the checkout lady didn't attend every funeral she could sink her magenta claws into.

"Bless you," the handyman from her mother's apartment complex said. He was Russian, Catha guessed, or perhaps Ukrainian, and of an age and shape and color so innocuous he looked as though he were wearing a disguise. "Mrs. Brit, she was a very generous person."

Burke, Catha was about to correct, but instead murmured, "Thank you for coming. I'm sure my mother would have appreciated it." A statement Catha didn't quite believe.

If the checkout lady's pet peeve was money squandered on frozen dinners, Catha's mother's had been unnecessary celebrity. She'd abhorred fame of any sort, from the inconspicuous do-gooder thrust into the limelight to the latest in filmland gossip. Louise Burke had never attended movies or watched television, and she steadfastly refused to distinguish one actor from another.

"All this playacting," she'd barked one day in an uncharacteristically revealing tone, "it comes to no good in the end." It was as if Louise Burke had a personal vendetta against the entire film industry.

Knowing this made the last two visitors seem a shock. A man and a woman of a "certain" age, but with decidedly regal bearing and fashionably elegant clothes, stepped up to Catha as soon as the other mourners had shuffled away.

The woman was impeccably white-coiffed; not a single, shiny strand was out of place. Her navy Chanel suit was no doubt the real thing, and her handbag echoed her patent leather–accented pumps with an effortlessness Catha had always found disconcerting. Confronted by such obvious panache, Catha felt like a total hick; she wished she could toss her soggy, knockoff Burberry raincoat into the nearest and darkest corner—but then realized she'd still be left with the all-purpose corduroy skirt, flat heels, and nondescript French braids that were the uniform of her tweedy New England existence.

"I was Lita Grey's last assistant," the woman's modulated tone soothed. "At the agency, you know . . . Lita Grey Chaplin." Seeing no spark of recognition in Catha's quizzical stare, the voice pushed ahead. The accent was something Catha couldn't quite place; it had either once been British or wished it were.

"Lita Grey was Charlie Chaplin's second wife. She was *much* younger than he, of course." The way the woman emphasized the word *much* made it sound as though Lita had been a child of five when she'd married.

What on earth did Charlie Chaplin have to do with my mother? Catha wanted to ask, but she didn't have a chance because at that moment the equally polished man took his turn.

"Mr. Barrymore's final instructions were that we

should continue to . . . to . . ." His meticulous (and truly) British lexicon failed him momentarily.

"Look after your mother," the woman interjected.

"Look in on!" the man corrected with punctilious insistence.

What's going on here? Catha wanted to burst in. Who is this Mr. Barrymore? What are you two talking about?

The pair prattled on, seeming to have forgotten Catha's existence. "Mr. John hardly suggested I care for Louise," the dapper man argued with surprising force. "I'm a gentleman's gentleman, not a nursemaid, after all."

Lita Grey's assistant continued to assert her own: "He wanted to atone for the damage done. Those were his specific orders. And Lita's, too—as you well know—"

"Who is Mr. John, if I might ask?" Catha finally interjected, and was met by two nonplussed stares.

"I'm sorry to interrupt." Father Tiernan came to the rescue. "But we do have to decide where to dispose of your mother's ashes, Catha. I know she didn't wish them buried. In fact, she was quite adamant the one time she discussed it with me. Did you have any other instructions?"

Catha thought she might have imagined it, but the three appeared to share a look. "No," she answered reluctantly. "I'm afraid I didn't know my mother terribly well. She had a life in California—as well as a prior history here—that she never chose to discuss with me."

Again, there was a distinct impression of a secret passed among the circle. "Perhaps one of these two guests has an idea. They appear to know more about Mother than I."

The elegant woman and dapper man did nothing to

refute the statement. Instead a silent conference passed between them.

"San Simeon," the man dictated, taking the lead with a methodical nod.

"Off the pier that's now part of that charming state park," the Chanel-suited woman added with a tone that brooked no dissent. "You don't want to charter a boat in this quirky weather. And it's worse in the Central Coast area. It always has been. The most violent storms can develop in mere hours."

"Well . . . ," Catha stalled. She hadn't the slightest idea what the pair were up to, but she definitely felt railroaded. She looked at her watch inadvertently, and again her thoughts turned to Win. Only this time, he wasn't sitting at their shared desk, engrossed in a contemplation of Islamic practices among the *qabili* of northern Yemen; this time he was packing his bags.

I thought I'd be on a plane to Hartford tomorrow, she told herself with an inward groan. I thought I'd be home in time to see Win off on his sabbatical. Shake hands and wish him luck and tell him there's no hard feelings. "I don't know . . ." Catha glanced from face to face. "How far is San Simeon?"

"Oh, just up the coast," the woman answered with a breezy smile. "A tad north of Santa Barbara. It should be a perfectly delightful drive. Now that we've had all this glorious rain. The hills up that way turn the most luscious green . . . almost a kelly green, if you can believe it."

"San Simeon is a good deal north of Santa Barbara," the natty man growled. "I should know, if anyone does."

"Well, what are a few extra miles when one is carrying out one's mother's final wishes!" was the overbright response. Catha decided that if the words had been armed with pistols, the man would be riddled with holes.

"I see," Catha sighed. She hadn't meant to let the sound escape. She'd wanted to appear competent and mature—an adult capable of determining her own course of action.

"I'm sure you won't regret it, dear!" Lita Grey's former assistant sang out, and the two turned on their heels and hurried away before Catha had time to protest.

But where were their raincoats? she wondered in a sudden pique. Or their umbrellas? They couldn't have sauntered out in this deluge. In her mind's eye the perfectly tailored woman and the immaculate "gentleman's gentleman" had turned into the twin demons of a fairy tale. Catha almost wondered if the pair had existed at all.

"I suppose you were in on this little scheme, too, Father Tiernan." She tried for a teasing tone, but the suspicion of being forced into the scheme lingered. "If you'll give me the urn or whatever the container's called, I'll drive up to San Simeon tonight."

"Oh, I couldn't let you do that." Father Tiernan's answer was priestly dismay.

"Why not?" Bewilderment and the day's tangled emotions were beginning to take their toll. Catha could feel her temper rising.

"I wouldn't be doing my job," was the implacable response. "The ministry is called to heal in times of trouble. I can't very well let you make that journey all alone."

Catha moaned silently. The four-hour ride would be spent in the company of Fawn or someone just like her. "I hardly knew my mother, Father Tiernan. You needn't concern yourself about belated grief—I promise."

"I'll make a pact with you, Catha Burke. I've got a young assistant, a recent seminary graduate who's going up to San Luis Obispo to assist the chaplain at the prison nearby. His name's Esteban Gonzalez. If you drive him up, I'll give my permission."

Catha could do nothing but acquiesce. This is what Mother wanted, she reminded herself. If I can't leave tomorrow, I'll go the day after. Maybe Winslow won't have left yet; maybe we can say our farewells in a dignified fashion. I owe Mother this much, after all.

24

2

THE NEXT MORNING SHOWED A MARKED IMPROVEMENT in the weather. The rain had continued to pummel the city during the night (Catha had gotten up twice to check for flooding on her rickety motel-room balcony), but toward dawn, the winds and driving rain had begun to abate, and by first light the sky was drawn with extravagantly whorled clouds while the scent of washed eucalyptus trees scudded down the streets of the quiescent city.

Standing on the tattered carpeting of her narrow balcony and watching the high, dramatic sky, Catha lifted her face to the fragrance. The smell was the cleanest she could imagine; it made her feel resilient and alive.

Beyond the motel's asphalted grounds, she could see Ocean Avenue with its gracious double aisle of royal palms framing the Pacific. It's mid-November, she remembered, maybe I'll finally spot a migrating whale.

Catha's mother had claimed to have seen a whale breach off Santa Monica beach, but Catha had never been so fortunate. She'd once caught a glimpse of dolphins gamboling along a line of breaking waves, and she'd counted plenty of bark-brown pelicans, but the migratory whales had eluded her.

I wish Win could have seen this with me, Catha thought reflexively, then realized that no amount of Pacific Coast magic could have changed the way Winslow Reid viewed the world. The two of them had been disparate souls from the beginning.

Catha jerked herself back to the present. "Time to get moving," she announced with a brisk smile. She'd asked Esteban Gonzalez to be ready at seven sharp in order to beat Friday's rush-hour traffic. It would never do to be late.

The ex–seminary student had the tall, gangly body of a youth who'd grown too fast—all elbows and knees and stretched-out neck. He was also surprisingly blond with a tanned face that turned white near the hairline—a weekend athlete who never bothered with sunblock. Catha had imagined the name belonging to someone of Spanish descent, but here he was, a fair-haired kid loping down the broad stone steps of Saint Andrew's as if he'd just been invited to join a game of pickup basketball.

"I've got your . . . ," he called as Catha stopped the car. "I mean, I've got the . . . the . . ." Esteban Gonzalez became embarrassment personified. "Right here under my raincoat. I didn't want it to get wet."

Esteban pulled out his prize: a box of nondescript tan-gray that looked no different from a package sent parcel post. My mother's ashes, Catha told herself, but that was as far as she allowed her thoughts to travel.

"You've never done this before, I take it?" she asked with a quiet smile. She was determined to be pleasant, and truthfully, the young priest's earnestness

26

and breezy manner made the task easier than she'd thought.

Esteban began settling his angular frame into the car's less-than-roomy front seat. The rentals at the Los Angeles airport were never simple models such as sedans or station wagons; the car companies seemed to feel that visitors to southern California wanted race cars and coupes, and Catha had given up arguing for more conservative vehicles long ago. The particular brand assigned to her this time was low-slung, fire-engine red, and unnervingly peppy. Catha had no idea which manufacturer had built it.

"Sorry about the cramped quarters. It's a rental." She'd intended the statement as an apology, a way of distancing herself from a car-mad culture, but the priest's response was an admiring whistle.

"Really," he gushed, drawing the syllables out. "It's a sweet machine."

If Catha didn't know better, she would have assumed the speaker was still in his teens: a friend's kid brother asking for a lift to the beach. She almost expected a surfboard to be part of his baggage.

"Oh, there've been two mud slides. Father Tiernan said to tell you. He said you might not have turned on the radio. There's been a minor one near where Ocean Avenue turns into Channel, and a larger one on the PCH just north of Temescal. If we retrace our steps slightly and take the California Incline to the Pacific Coast Highway, then head north, turn inland on Temescal, and follow Sunset till we get back to the water, we should be right as rain."

"Not a very apt analogy," Catha couldn't help observing. The words were tarter than she'd intended; she disliked men who deprecated a woman's driving ability—even if the man was no more than an over-grown boy.

27

"I'm comfortable driving in ice, fog, and snow," Catha boasted. "A little mud never hurt me."

In spite of herself, Catha took Esteban's advice and started down the California Incline. The wide Santa Monica beach spread across her view, and beyond it the storm-gray ocean and the battered, restless clouds. It was a sight Catha loved.

"Sorry about barking at you back there," she began while Esteban blurted out a sudden:

"Look! There's Marion Davies's beach house. Or what's left of it. They turned the north guesthouse into the Sand and Sea Club, and I guess the wrecking ball tore away the rest. The original mansion had over a hundred rooms, you know, and bathhouses that could accommodate a thousand lockers . . . and a swimming pool with a marble bridge." With his nose pressed close to the windshield, the priest might as well have been panting with excitement.

"You mean Marion Davies the silent-film actress?" Catha followed the priest's goggle-eyed stare.

"You bet!" Esteban nearly woofed while he spun his face back toward her. "I can name all her hits: *Little Old New York, When Knighthood Was in Flower, Janice Meredith*—"

"You're a wonder, Father," Catha laughed. "I would never have taken you for a vintage-film buff."

Esteban blushed until the roots of his pale hair glowed. "I love the old movies. I guess they're kind of like an addiction."

"I've heard of more dangerous habits," Catha joked as she gave Marion Davies's former mansion another glance; what little remained of the three-storied, Corinthian-columned colonial gave the term *beach house* new meaning.

"You know what Charlie Chaplin said about the

house?" Esteban mused. "The whole thing, I mean, not the part that's still standing?"

The famous actor's name gave Catha a peculiar sensation, a jolt in her stomach that was half-fear and half-caution. She had a quick vision of the mysterious woman who'd once served as Lita Grey's assistant. Lita had been "much younger" than Chaplin, the woman had announced. The words still had a sinister ring.

"He said Marion's house had more columns than the Supreme Court building in Washington. I like his movies—in spite of some of the things I learned about his personal life . . . sleeping with his leading ladies and all that other messy stuff. . . . I mean, he could be a really funny man. *The Gold Rush* is my favorite of his pictures. It's the one with that weird little shack. . . . I also like *The Idle Class*—you know, where he plays both a tramp and a fop? . . . Lita Grey was a maid in that one."

Again, the odd click of apprehension. Catha took a final peek at the once grand residence.

"Anyway, Marion's home was called Ocean House back then, and the road was Beach Palisades Road, not the Pacific Coast Highway. She had parties you wouldn't believe . . . even built a special ballroom for one gala, and when Norma Shearer arrived in a huge Marie Antoinette outfit and couldn't get through the front door, she told Marion to cut a hole in the brand-new wall.

"Of course, there was a lot of heavy drinking—even during Prohibition. John Barrymore and Errol Flynn nicknamed the place Cirrhosis by the Sea . . . and John Gilbert tried to commit suicide there because he was so upset about his love affair with Greta Garbo. He staggered off into the sea, but some screenwriters fished him out . . . at least that's what I read.

"Anyway, all sorts of famous people visited. George Bernard Shaw went there with his wife, and Lindbergh and old Joe Kennedy . . . he was a young man then, of course—"

"Sounds like quite an illustrious crowd," Catha interrupted as she pulled ahead of a purple low-rider truck and dodged into the fast lane. She kept a steady lookout for black-and-white patrol cars while she pushed down the accelerator. Catha was a secret speed demon—and she prided herself on never getting caught.

"Oh, it was!" Esteban enthused, but his tone then turned unexpectedly perplexed. "That's because . . . well, you know . . ." Bashfulness overcame him, and Catha finally understood her passenger's personality. He was a young man caught between two worlds, the product of a traditional religious education crashing full bore into the mores of the late twentieth century.

"Because of what?"

"Well, you know . . . she was Hearst's mistress . . . William Randolph Hearst, the publisher." The blond face was fiery pink.

"Oh, I don't believe that was much of a secret!" Catha grinned.

"Really? Not even back then?" Esteban pondered Catha's statement, and his loose-limbed body slumped. Catha found his dismay profoundly touching.

"Is that so terrible?" she asked gently.

"He was married!" The admission seemed too much for the young man. "Adultery's a sin, you know!" he managed to add.

"That was probably the least of his transgressions." Catha laughed. She hoped her tone would cheer her passenger; she couldn't remember when she'd met a person as good-hearted and honest. *He'll make a good* priest, she told herself, if the world doesn't stomp on him first.

"I think we should try an exchange," Catha continued in the chattiest vein she possessed. "Your knowledge of film lore for my academic specialty, which is American history. What do you say?"

"Okay." Esteban's answer was relieved. "But I think we should stay clear of any facts the church might disapprove—"

"Okay. History with the *Good Housekeeping* seal of approval. . . . William Randolph Hearst—Marion Davies's supposed 'friend'—started out working for the publisher Joseph Pulitzer in New York.

"Young Willie had been kicked out of Harvard for giving his professors chamber pots with their names inscribed on the insides. The final straw in a long line of similar stunts.

"Of course, he had more money than God—" Catha emended her analogy, substituting hurriedly, "I mean, than goodness knows.

"Mama was doting. Papa was made of money—a rough-and-tumble miner turned politician who'd discovered the biggest silver strikes in the world, the Anaconda and Homestake mines. Anyway, Willie decided he wanted to be a newspaperman. So off he trots to New York City and gets a job at Joseph Pulitzer's *New York World*."

Catha stopped her steady stream of information, reminding herself that she wasn't giving some poor freshman a quiz.

"You've heard of Pulitzer, haven't you?" The tone was coaxing and kind.

"As in the Pulitzer Prize?"

"It's the same name, but what I was going to describe has nothing to do with literature or investigative reporting. Do you know what yellow journalism is?"

"Well . . ." Eagerness suffused the young man's face. "I've heard the phrase."

"The term *yellow* originated with a cartoon character that appeared in Hearst's own newspaper, the *New York Journal*. This is obviously well past the period in which Hearst was subservient to Pulitzer.

"Anyway, competition escalated between the former employee and his boss over control of New York's popular press. Pulitzer hired his own cartoonist, a man named George Luks, to create a duplicate 'Yellow Kid' series—"

"But isn't there . . . I don't know . . . something bad associated with the name *yellow journalism?*"

"You're right. The term has a very nasty connotation. Pulitzer's specialty was sensationalism; Hearst bettered his onetime mentor at his own game. Murder was a popular subject, and so were stories of the occult and, of course, sex.

"When the architect Sanford White threw one of his notorious bachelor parties, the 'Girl in the Pie' story that ran in the *World* described a model stepping from an enormous dessert 'covered by the ceiling and nothing else.' The article was accompanied by a lurid and suggestive drawing.

"I suppose this particular brand of publishing has become old hat, but the style was new back then."

Catha continued to gun the car up the PCH, glancing at the multimillion-dollar homes that teetered precariously on the shale bluffs in Pacific Palisades' exclusive Huntington section. The houses seemed to slide closer to the abyss each time she visited; yards of shiny black plastic stretched over disappearing gardens, giving each property a woeful appearance as if it were screaming for help.

"Want to continue the history lesson?" she asked, dispelling the spirit of doom.

"Okay. But you've got to turn here at Temescal Canyon, and—"

"I know. You don't have to tell me again. Follow Sunset north till we rejoin the PCH." Despite her rule about male interference, Catha found herself smiling.

Driving inland past Pepperdine University on the winding and often rock-strewn Malibu Canyon Road, Catha began to truly relax. She'd only followed the route twice before: once in a misguided effort to get her mother to purchase a car at one of the auto malls along the Ventura Freeway—a road more commonly referred to as the 101—and the other time on an excursion to Santa Barbara, a mini-vacation Louise Burke had steadfastly refused to enjoy.

But both drives had filled Catha with unexpected exuberance: the twisting canyon drive switchbacking along the ravine's edge, the ragged depths falling away from the car's hurrying windows, sea-breeze-borne clouds climbing inland, and finally, passing the tail end of Mulholland where Malibu Canyon turns into Las Virgenes Road, there was the wonder of the vast arterial freeway itself.

"So, I guess I'll begin with Ferdinand Lundberg's *Imperial Hearst*," Catha said as she entered the on-ramp, then zipped forward, leaving an overpampered white Porsche in the lurch. "It was a book first published in the thirties. I assigned it to a class last spring. We were playing around with the idea of imperialism as an American incentive—"

"Such as?" Esteban interrupted.

"Expanding trade markets . . . clandestine alliances of financial interests." Catha knew she was hedging, but she also realized some of her views might be considered radical—especially by a young man who'd chosen a life within the bastion of the church.

"Wars could be looked upon as the culmination of our commercial desires," she ventured, trying to find a way to bring the conversation back to the safe subject of William Randolph Hearst. His wholehearted commitment to the Spanish-American War was a lot easier to discuss than the country's involvement in Kuwait or Somalia. "Take our role in the Spanish-American War, for instance—or our creation of it, I should say."

"I don't know when that was."

Catha smiled reassuringly. "I bet most of the students who enter my classes don't know either—and when they graduate, the information's promptly forgotten. The Spanish-American War occurred at turn of the century—1898, to be exact."

"But that's ancient history!" Esteban protested. He was obviously anxious to get on with his share of the bargain: a description of silent-film stars and their lives.

"Sort of, but it's got a lot to do with Marion Davies's friend, Mr. Hearst. He was the man who started it."

3

"WHAT DO YOU MEAN HEARST STARTED THE Spanish-American War?" Esteban demanded as the car continued northward. His voice was edgy with mistrust, as if his faith in a divine power were being challenged.

Catha carefully chronicled the disastrous "war" from the *New York Journal*'s first banner headlines screaming CRUISER *MAINE* EXPLODES IN HAVANA HARBOR, WARSHIP SPLIT IN TWO BY SECRET ENEMY MACHINE, and ENTIRE COUNTRY THRILLS TO THE FEVER OF WAR down to the now famous AVENGE THE *MAINE*.

She lighted on the publisher's infamous telegram to the Havana-based *Journal* illustrator, Frederic Remington: "You furnish the pictures and I'll furnish the war." She included the shameless invention of a bogus "Cuban Joan of Arc," the pretty eighteen-year-old Evangelina Cosio y Cisneros, daughter of a rebel leader, whose incarceration in a Cuban prison was intended to rally what the *Journal* referred to as "the ladies of America."

Catha next recounted the young woman's rescue

from her captors and safe delivery to a rather confused New York City—all much heralded by Hearst's daily press; and she concluded with the newspaper's exhortations to "write to your Congressmen! Urge them to action! We must protect our women at all costs!"

"Wow!" Esteban gawked when the story was over. "I can't believe Hearst could have done all that stuff. I mean, I can't believe anyone could be that powerful. To convince the president of the United States to declare war and everything, and all to sell more newspapers than the other publishers."

"You'd better believe it. The same thing's still happening today."

"Wow," Esteban repeated. "That's a lot of muscle." Then he grew silent for several long minutes. "All this history-collecting you're involved with—do you have another life outside of work?"

The question took Catha by surprise. "Sure I do," she started to mumble. "I mean, I used to."

"Used to?" Esteban's tone had turned serious.

Catha considered her options. She could continue in the same vein as before, hiding her emotions behind a facade of intellectual bravado—or she could address the truth. "No one likes to admit they've got problems, Father."

"Sometimes the most capable and industrious people are the ones most in need."

Catha turned to stare at the young priest, and before she knew it, a flood of personal revelations about her failed relationship with Win had spilled out of her mouth. "But he's extraordinarily bright," she found herself concluding as she struggled to put the past into perspective. "I don't think his mind can quite cope with the mundane things the rest of us find important."

"Such as?"

"Oh, friendships, having coworkers over for supper, that sort of thing. And he's definitely against what he refers to as 'foolishness.'" Catha tried to laugh, but Esteban saw through the effort.

"What did your mother think of Win?"

"My mother?" The name startled Catha into silence.

"Did she approve?"

Catha couldn't come up with an answer. The complex push and pull of her situation with her mother was too painful to explain. Catha was quiet for a long time.

"You don't have to talk about this if you don't want," Esteban finally offered, and again Catha was struck by his perceptive and understanding tone.

"It's really a matter of not knowing my mother well enough," she admitted after another long pause. "I mean, never connecting with her. We weren't at all alike, and I guess . . . I guess neither of us made much of an effort."

Esteban let Catha's words die out. "A lot of people feel guilt when a loved one dies." The statement was intended as a guide rather than a question.

Catha pondered the words. "I'm not sure what I feel yet. Confusion mostly . . . and I guess I blame myself for not being sadder. My friends who've lost their mothers—it takes them a long time to get over it."

"Each of us grieves in our own way," Esteban said gently. "My guess is that you've been an adult so long you've forgotten how to be a child."

"That's not what my mother would have said." Catha tried to grin.

At that moment the offshore oil rigs of Santa Barbara came into view—huge metallic platforms and rigs that sat atop the ocean as if they'd been grounded in cement. They seemed more permanent than the Pacific itself, stretching across the horizon like a robot army waiting to storm the shore.

"I hate those things," Catha announced in an attempt to return the conversation to safer parameters. "They give me the willies. I've only seen them once before, but from the looks of it their ranks are growing. Everyone claims the environmental movement is all-powerful in California, but you can't convince me. Not if they let these monsters sit here, just waiting to befoul the water."

"I guess we'll have to pray that doesn't happen." Esteban followed Catha's lead while she surprised herself by suddenly reverting to their earlier discussion. "You're right," she said softly. "I guess my mother meant a lot more to me than I want to believe."

The journey continued, winding along the coast and then turning inland to pass Buellton, Los Alamos, and a vast stretch of uninhabited turf before the road again descended seaward to Pismo Beach. Hawks flitted overhead casting vibrant shadows on the silent land.

"This is a beautiful part of the world," Catha murmured, and she and Esteban drove on in contemplative silence until they reached their destination: William Randolph Hearst State Park in the almost nonexistent beachside community of San Simeon.

The brief burial service was nearly finished, and like all momentous occurrences, the event was less anticlimax than a whirl of images so brief they might have belonged to a dream.

" 'O Lord Jesus Christ, who by thy death didst take away the sting of death . . . ,' " Esteban read while he and Catha stood at the end of the long wooden pier connected to the state park. The park and its sister retreat, the mansion and museum known simply as Hearst Castle, were divided by Highway 1, a quiet stretch of asphalt traversing softly rolling hills, shaggy bluffs, and pastureland dotted with cattle.

" 'Thou shalt show me the path of life.' " The words were taken from the 1920s edition of the *Book of Common Prayer* that Louise Burke had insisted upon. Catha smiled ruefully remembering her mother's refusal to acknowledge the newer "standardized" version.

" '. . . in thy presence is the fullness of joy . . .' " Catha heard the prayer, but her brain refused to concentrate, inadvertently conjuring up memories of her mother, then of Lita Grey's assistant and the man who claimed to have been John Barrymore's valet. Catha searched her thoughts, but Louise Burke's orderly existence yielded no further clues to these exotic connections.

" 'Unto Almighty God we commend the soul of our sister departed and we commit her body to the deep . . .' " Catha willfully turned her thoughts to her surroundings.

The pier she and Esteban stood upon was solid and wide, long enough to berth an oceangoing freighter— or Hearst's 220-foot steam yacht, *Oneida*. Built as San Simeon's private dock, the place was now used by commercial fishing boats. But November was well past the season, and the pier was deserted except for Catha and Esteban and a flock of curious seagulls who'd settled themselves on the dock's high railing—noisy spectators with a decidedly proprietary air. Catha followed their lilting movement and saw, through a swirl of mist and melting fog, the castlelike residence that had once belonged to William Randolph Hearst. San Simeon, La Cuesta Encantada, "The Enchanted Hill," seemed to glow on its distant mountaintop, a place of towers and turrets like the lost kingdom in a children's fable.

" '. . . in sure and certain hope of the Resurrection unto eternal life . . .' "

It's over, Catha told herself, Mother's really gone.

Daughter and priest walked the length of the pier, heading for the eucalyptus grove and Catha's rental car.

"And now, Miss Catha Burke, what do you think you'll be doing?"

The words startled Catha. Esteban had reverted to his gym coach persona without skipping a beat. "You're going to make an excellent priest," she said. "You know when to be professional and when to become that simple soul known as a friend." A momentary awkwardness followed the statement, but Catha covered it with a brisk and purposeful: "I'm driving back to Santa Monica. Hopefully, I can catch an evening flight from LAX."

Worry creased Esteban's face, and his hair fell topsy-turvy onto his tanned forehead. "If you think that's wise . . ." He hesitated. "This hasn't been an easy couple of days. . . . I could return with you, you know. I'm sure the prison chaplain can dispense with me for another twenty-four hours. . . . Or you could stay overnight in Cambria. It's a pretty village. You can go home tomorrow. One day more won't cause any harm." He hadn't added that perhaps she should allow herself time for contemplation, but they both knew that was the subtext of his words.

"You're a good person, Esteban Gonzalez. I'm glad to have met you—"

But Esteban was already expanding his plan. "You know what you can do?" he interrupted with a boyish gush. "Go and visit the castle . . . San Simeon! You know so much about the man who created it, and maybe it'll help . . . seeing the house, I mean. Maybe it'll help with that course you're planning . . . on imperialism. What did you call it . . . back there in the car?"

" 'The Impulse to Imperialism'?"

"That's it!" Enthusiasm spewed out of the young man. He might as well have been jumping up and down as his team scored the deciding point. "They give you a guided tour. . . . But maybe you could sneak away and find some old manuscript in a secret drawer . . . something about that war you were telling me about!"

"I somehow think historians have combed the place already," Catha chuckled. "I don't believe there are any more skeletons remaining in San Simeon's closets."

"Oh, well . . ." Esteban hesitated. "I didn't mean . . . well, you know, anything sacrilegious . . . or illegal."

"Just kidding." Catha laughed, then decided on a sudden whim to take the young priest's advice. An extra day away from her students at Wesleyan wouldn't kill anyone—least of all the members of the freshman crew team who'd stumbled into her class hoping it was a "gut course." And if Win's flight had left by the time she returned, so be it. They'd already said enough good-byes.

What I need in my life, she reminded herself, is less regimentation and routine.

The tour bus was packed by the time Catha climbed aboard. She'd opted for tour number one, an overview of Hearst's vast estate with a glimpse at several of the public rooms and a tantalizing visit to the lavish Roman-inspired outdoor and indoor swimming pools.

Purchasing her ticket in the cavernous, modern staging area at the foot of the mountain, Catha had convinced herself that her knowledge of history would give her an edge over her fellow tourists, and she'd felt slightly smug, as if she alone were privy to secrets about the castle, its quirky creator, and his role in shaping America's destiny.

Now that she was faced with a packed and noisy busload of people, the feeling of exclusivity vanished. The only available seat was beside the bulging rear wheel well. In front of Catha sat a middle-aged couple with two sullen teenagers in tow. The girl alternately glared out the bus window and flicked her over-moussed hair; the boy adjusted the volume on his Walkman so that the noise spilled onto the surrounding seats while the parents affixed leaden smiles on their furious faces.

The row behind Catha was no better. A hefty man and an alarmingly similarly featured woman had squeezed themselves into the twin seats. Catha guessed the two were brother and sister; she also surmised that the tweed-coated and talkative sister was from out of town—probably an East Coast resident like herself—while the brother with his voluminous turquoise-and-purple-striped jogging suit was a definite West Coast stalwart.

As the bus's air compressor released the door with a wheezy moan and the tour lurched upward toward San Simeon's long and winding drive, the public address system began cranking out tinny renditions of Prohibition-era tunes while a recorded voice laboriously explained the rules for visiting the museum mansion.

I can't believe I did this, Catha argued with an inward sigh, then gritted her teeth against all possible enjoyment. You wanted to be irresponsible and impulsive; now look at the results. Catha might as well have been mimicking one of her mother's many injunctions. The words *I told you so* clanged uncomfortably in her ears.

Finally, the loudspeaker's obvious regulations ("Don't chew gum"; "Stay on the carpets designed for tourist traffic"; "Keep up with the group") faded into a re-creation of Hearst's own words—a youthful letter he'd written to his beloved mother. Purchased by Hearst's father, the property was originally known as Piedra Blanca Rancho, and it was a favorite retreat for the San Francisco–based family. They visited whenever they could.

"I love this ranch," Catha heard a facsimile of the voice of young William Randolph Hearst explain. "I love the sea and the mountains and the shady places in the hollows. I would rather spend time here than any place on earth."

Catha glanced out the steamy window, suddenly touched at the passion behind the sentiment. Imagine, she told herself, imagine having as much money and power as that man had, and being able to indulge yourself completely.

Hearst took the place he loved the most in the world, and he built his dream house on it, plunking down gardens and walls whenever he chose, attaching a zoo and a mile-long covered bridle path. He was living every child's fantasy.

A cluster of Barbary sheep came into view, calm descendants of animals imported for the largest privately owned zoological garden in the world, and Catha stared at them as they raised their curlicued horns and gazed imperturbably back.

The bus jolted around a sharp bend in the road, and another broad sweep of land came into view. Small but steep ravines pitched away from the drive, and within them were indeed the "hollows" and "shady places," the oaks and fertile springs, while the hilltops held rustic shelters for the roving animals: the zebras, bison, llamas, giraffes, and kangaroos that had once wandered W. R. Hearst's park unobstructed.

A magic world, Catha told herself, watching the narrow road zigzag its way up the mountainside. No other house was in sight, no one for miles and miles. Catha could almost imagine herself a guest at the fabled San Simeon—or Marion Davies motoring north to the "ranch" after a grueling schedule of filming in Los Angeles. What perfect freedom any visitor would feel, Catha thought, alone on 250,000 acres.

At that point, the garishly clad man behind Catha twisted around in his seat with a violence so sudden, Catha's seat was shoved forward. She turned around to protest just as the man shouted to his sister:

"There! That's the place! Just like the old guy said! A big old oak in the middle of a ravine and all those thorny bushes bunched around it. That's where the woman's car must have crashed. The one that murdered that Hollywood big shot back in the twenties. What was her name? God knows I've heard the old guy blabbing about her long enough. . . . Oh, yeah . . . Kinsolving. That's it! Abigail Kinsolving!"

4

CATHA FELT THE BLOOD DRAIN FROM HER FACE. What had that man just said? Murder? A murder connected to someone named Abigail Kinsolving?

"Excuse me?" Catha scarcely managed to whisper. Was this Kinsolving woman part of her unknown family? Catha twisted around in her seat until her torso felt as if it had been unscrewed from her legs.

"Excuse me!"

But the man was not to be dissuaded from his monologue. He jammed his beefy shoulders against the bus's window, craning his neck backward as the ravine jounced out of sight.

"The very place," he proclaimed while Catha struggled unsuccessfully to distract his attention. "Same as the old guy said. That's the kind of juicy stuff they should include on these tours. Marion Davies and Charlie Chaplin, Rudolph Valentino and Greta Garbo, Mary Pickford and the rest of the gang. There were some pretty wild goings-on up here. The Roaring Twenties! And boy, did those people know how to live it up—"

45

"Excuse me!" Catha almost shouted. "What were you saying about Abigail Kinsolving?"

"Huh?" The fat man stared while his sister snickered a high-pitched but not unfriendly:

"Oh, Donald! Don't be such a dummy! That woman you were just gabbing about! The one that got herself killed down in that ravine."

Donald became suspicion personified. "I might have got the party's name wrong," he mumbled into his purple chest.

"Please!" Catha begged. "My middle name's Kinsolving. I've never known why my mother chose it."

"Is that a fact?" Donald's friendlier sibling seemed genuinely concerned. "Imagine that!

"Why, just think, Donnie! Just think how we'd feel if Momma didn't keep blubbering about all our 'ancestors' and where they'd lived in the old country!"

But Donnie wasn't about to relinquish his superior position. "Mightn't be so bad," he insisted. "I've never seen sunny Napoli, and from the looks of it I never will."

At that moment the tour bus ground to a halt, and the door wheezed open as the passengers simultaneously burst from their seats. The smells of aged vinyl, frozen hair spray, and plasticized floor matting perfumed the suddenly cooling air. Everyone except for Catha, the ubiquitous Donald, and his chatty sister seemed determined to be the first to alight on San Simeon's hallowed grounds.

"All ashore that's going ashore," Donnie announced in a take-charge manner. "Got everything, Toots? Purse? Collapsible umbrella? The point-and-shoot?"

"My name's not really Toots," Donald's sister confided with an indulgent giggle. "It's Dottie—short for Dorothy."

Catha shook the woman's hand. "Catha Burke."

"You mean Catha Kinsolving Burke." Dottie smiled, then swatted her brother on his broad striped back, ordering, "Oh, go ahead, Don, tell her. It's probably just some loony story the old guy invented.

"You know how folks stuck in nursing homes get . . . pretending the world used to revolve around them. To hear our uncle Bert describe it, he single-handedly recaptured the Anzio beachhead.

"Come on, Don! Be a sport." Dottie winked conspiratorially to Catha. "Tell the lady the story."

But by then, the tour guide had begun his scripted spiel, and the group clustering close around him hushed the trio before Donnie had a chance to share his news.

Catha could do nothing but wait. But she hovered close to the brother and sister, studying the estate spreading before her until the scene nearly eclipsed her curiosity about the shadowy Abigail Kinsolving, and what, if any, connection they had.

Tall garden lamps in the shape of Greco-Roman road markers guided the eye toward a long flight of gracefully curved marble stairs. Hearst's evening guests must have been greeted by the lights' alabaster brilliance, Catha told herself. They stepped out of their chauffeur-driven limousines right where I'm standing, then they moved up the steps: the ladies clad in the flimsiest of chiffons, jet beads, silk stockings, the racy, helmet-shaped bobs of the rebellious flapper era. There would have been music, too, strolling violins sifting through the lime-flowered air or the sudden, gramophone squawk of a brand-new Al Jolson recording.

Imagining those glory days, Catha trailed the guide and his flock up the steps that led to the Neptune Pool.

The oval pool seemed vast, the blue of its water an impossible azure as if it were lined with turquoise-tinted mosaics instead of liquid, while the formal grid-and-key design crisscrossing the watery depths shone black as polished ebony.

"No, ma'am. The Roman-inspired design only looks black," the guide was telling the mother of the two disgruntled teenagers. "Actually, it was executed in green serpentine, a material known as verde antique."

Her son merely stared, but he turned down the volume on his Walkman.

"And the structure facing you is, of course, the much-photographed facade and pediment of the ancient Neptune Temple. Mr. Hearst acquired it in Italy in 1922. As you can see, the Roman artwork became the inspiration for the pool itself."

The guide's voice and delivery were kindly, if a bit didactic, and his compact, guard dog body appeared to take the measure of his charges, as if trying to decide how best to marshal such a disparate group. Catha knew the feeling herself: opening day of freshman classes.

"The double colonnade flanking the temple is a much later creation. In fact, the columns, capitals, and entablatures were carved right here at San Simeon, although, naturally, in an exact replication of the Roman style. Mr. Hearst was never one for halfway measures.

"The marble was imported from Carrara, Italy. The statues in the large alcove were the creations of the French sculptor Charles Cassou. Mr. Hearst commissioned the work especially for the space and entitled it *Naissance de Venus*. That's 'birth of Venus' for those folks who don't speak French.

"Any questions, please feel free to speak up. This is your tour, remember. You're the ones who'll decide how we proceed. If there's something you don't understand, just give a holler."

But none of the visitors said a word. They couldn't take their eyes off the brilliant blue of the pool and the many-columned glitter of its setting.

A few stray storm clouds that had threatened to rumble over San Simeon's mountaintop suddenly dispersed, allowing a staggeringly bright sun to strike its way through the air. Light glanced off the glimmering water, off the pristine white of the marble, off the fuchsia, magenta, and celadon green of the bougainvillea vines. The sight was almost too perfect to believe.

"Part of *Spartacus* was filmed next to the Neptune Pool," the guide oozed while the watchers gaped. "Laurence Olivier was standing right over there talking to Tony Curtis."

Every head spun, including Donnie's and his sister's.

"I'll be," Catha heard Dottie murmur. "Tony Curtis! Wow!"

"Many stars of the so-called silents were visitors to San Simeon as well. The well-known performers Charlie Chaplin and Rudolph Valentino were often guests of Mr. Hearst and his good friend the actress Miss Marion Davies."

Donnie gave his sister a playful if overly forceful nudge, but the guide overrode the interruption.

"The temple was dedicated to Neptune—or Poseidon as the ancient Greeks called the god. Prior to that time, the pool was a smaller, four-lobed affair. Pretty, to judge by the photos, but nothing compared to the magnificence that now spreads before you. Oil burners kept the pool at a constant seventy-five degrees. Mr. Hearst didn't like his guests to be uncomfortable. And that went for luminaries like John Barrymore and—"

"What happened to the earlier swimming pool?" the teenage boy suddenly demanded, and Catha realized he'd dispensed with his headphones entirely. They and the Walkman were crumpled into an over-stuffed pocket of his grubby, teal-colored parka.

"Mr. Hearst had it dug up!" the guide almost smirked. "Telephoned his architect, Miss Julia Morgan of San Francisco—the castle had a real fancy switch-board in those days—and said, 'Get down here right away, Julia! I've decided I want something bigger and grander. Something to match my newest art acquisi-tion.' He was always doing that. Whatever he wanted, he got. How would you like that, son—if any little thing your heart desired could be yours for the asking?"

The boy gawked, and Catha felt momentary pity. Even the most extravagant vision produced by a mod-ern teenager paled in comparison to what William Randolph Hearst had been capable of conjuring up.

"Right this way, folks. I'm going to take you up the famous 'hidden steps' so you can get a view from our lovely North Terrace before we proceed through the sculpture gardens and on to Casa Grande—the main house where Mr. Hearst and Miss Davies used to entertain.

"There'll be plenty of time for photos after we have a quick gander inside one of the guesthouses, Casa del Sol. If you want to check out the interiors of the other guesthouses, Casas del Mar and del Monte, which, trust me, are truly lovely, you'll have to come back and join tour numbers three and four.

"Would you believe it, but the tourists who pass through San Simeon every year pay for California's entire park system? That's right! You folks are keep-ing the entire state alive!"

Shuffling like chastised sheep, the group crept up a second set of marble stairs, there to gaze back at the wonder of the Neptune Pool, the buff-colored moun-

50

tain range that spread behind it as though a set designer had placed it there, and a shimmer of distant ocean basking in the warming sun.

Marion Davies certainly lucked out when she met Mr. William Randolph Hearst, Catha told herself while Don and Dottie sidled over with the intention of finally sharing their well-kept secret. Donnie dragged his size-fourteen feet every step of the way.

"Now, don't take my word for it," Donald began by insisting. "I could have got the name wrong, like I said. But Dottie, she won't stop pestering me till I tell you what I know."

While Dottie moved away to join the rest of the tour, Don continued obediently. "Okay, so this Kinsolving dame was someone who worked up here at San Simeon. Or maybe she was a friend. All I know is that the old guy down at the convalescent home where I work gets bent out of shape whenever he talks about her. He's like a water valve you can't shut off. Most of it doesn't make much sense, but Dottie insisted I tell you. So there you are.

"But, like I said, I could be wrong about the last name. It could be Kesselring or—hell, it could start with a *Ch* instead of a *K*. All I know for certain is that the gal's first name was Abigail."

Catha decided to backpedal. Something was troubling Donnie; he had the nervous appearance of a man who believed he'd said too much. His eyes shifted from the path to the rose garden; they never once met Catha's glance. She wondered if Donnie was hiding something or if his reaction was simply the age-old fear of becoming too involved.

"Do you know how old this Abigail was when she came here? Or even where she was from?"

"Nope."

"Oh, Don, come on! Don't be such a killjoy!" Dottie called as she reemerged from the Casa del Sol. "Spill the beans! You know the old man said more than that. Tell the lady about that famous Hollywood big shot, the one this Abigail person killed!"

"Did this supposed murder happen here at San Simeon?" Catha interrupted. "The one you believe Abigail committed?"

But that was the last question she had time to ask because by now the tour was being hustled along the formally planted esplanade toward Casa Grande, the massive and twin-towered main structure Catha had seen dominating the landscape when she and Esteban Gonzalez stood on the sun-dappled pier. That moment seemed ages ago. Catha had the impression she'd been tossed backward and forward through time as well as space—like a pole-vaulter who refused to relinquish his grasp.

Mexican fan palms took up their stately places among espaliered rosebushes festooned with buttercup-yellow, peach-hued, or vermilion blossoms, while now and then the funereal formality of a Roman sarcophagus offset the floral array. A rose-colored Byzantine column surmounted by stylistically carved lions added to the juxtaposition of serious museum and garden ramble.

"Now, I bet you're all noting that Casa Grande looks a lot like one of your Spanish cathedrals." The guide deftly corralled the strays, ushering them forward at an ever-quickening pace.

"The inspiration for the house is the Cathedral of Santa Maria la Major in Ronda, Spain. Of course, that structure only has one puny tower and we've got two. Mr. Hearst, he liked to do things in a big way. The towers were completed in 1924, but those aren't the beauties you're looking at today. Remember I told you folks how the Neptune Pool was dug up and rebuilt?"

All heads silently nodded.

"Well, right after the original towers were finished, Mr. Hearst had another and better idea—so down came a couple of years' hard work and up went a new pair of towers."

Catha stared skyward. Despite her prejudices against big business, and the venality of the very rich in particular, she was beginning to like this guy Hearst. He'd created a marvel. Who wouldn't do the same if they could? The illusory Abigail Kinsolving and her involvement in an equally mysterious murder began fading into the background.

"Now, as we step up into Casa Grande, remember, folks, stay on the guest runners. The carpets they're protecting are priceless, and I don't think anyone wants to go into hock to repair them."

Adjusting her eyes to the muted interior, Catha stared. It seemed impossible to imagine that this great, soaring edifice, the double-height Assembly Room with its gigantic and deeply coffered ceiling could be the creation of an American—and the son of a silver miner, at that.

"The ceiling is Italian Renaissance, folks. Look up and you'll spot the crest of the Martinengo family of Brescia, Italy, in the central coffer. That gargantuan stone mantel bears the coat of arms of the French family who owned the Château des Jours. Please note the intricate carving of the overmantel and the superb display of Flemish tapestries on the walls.

"Woven in Brussels in the sixteenth century, the tapestries covering the long walls depict the deeds of Scipio Africanus, the Roman general who defeated Hannibal, while the tapestry in the north alcove, the

Triumph of Religion, was designed by Peter Paul Rubens."

Oohs and aahs accompanied each of these parcels of information, and heads and shoulders swiveled accordingly, but no one strayed from his allotted spot. The room was simply too awe-inspiring to tangle with.

"Keep in mind that the Assembly Room is just one of many public rooms found in Casa Grande; the structure contains one hundred rooms, including basements and so forth. It also houses thirty-seven bedrooms—twelve for servants—forty-one bathrooms, fourteen sitting rooms, and a kitchen and pantry that would rival any hotel's.

"The measurement for this modest cottage is over seventy-three thousand five hundred square feet; that's approximately one and a half times the size of a football field."

No one made a sound. Most had merely left their mouths hanging agape.

"Now, if you'll give your attention to the dark wood carvings lining the lower third of the walls. You'll notice small seats protruding at regular intervals. Those are choir stalls purchased from Renaissance churches all over Italy. When Mr. Hearst said take a pew, he meant it."

This time the guide's tired attempt at humor failed to bring his listeners back to earth. Each person was enmeshed in his own private world, trying to fathom the wealth, obsession, and vision that had produced this space. In Europe, the accumulation of property and artwork was somehow comprehensible; centuries as well as countless generations were involved; families intermarried; wars were fought and booty carted home. But this man, Hearst, had done it all himself. And he hadn't begun to build his masterpiece until his mother died in 1919.

"Remember, folks, San Simeon stands on the very spot Mr. Hearst used to visit as a boy. His parents took him camping up on this mountaintop, though it wasn't the kind of camping you might imagine. No, sir, old George Hearst, he ordered up generators to light all the tents.

"Why, the several sleeping tents were as big as modest-size houses; each had a sitting room and two bedrooms. George didn't want his young wife, Phoebe, or their only child, Willie, to be uncomfortable in the slightest.

"Now, if you'll follow me, we'll move on to the Gothic Refectory—that's the dining room—and you'll see how those old camping days were re-created. In spite of all the silver and gilt—and believe me, the house has a ton of it—Mr. Hearst insisted on having his ketchup and mustard bottles on the table in full view. And paper napkins, to boot!

"Right this way. Dinner at San Simeon was always served promptly at nine o'clock. Cocktails started at eight on the dot in the Assembly Room. But Mr. Hearst, he didn't partake. He might have taken a medicinal whiskey now and then, but he wasn't a drinker. Didn't really approve of the stuff. Insisted on a two-cocktail limit for his guests, too, though he did supply them with the best booze money could buy. And this was during the Prohibition era, folks! Good gin was well nigh impossible to come by.

"Now, some of you may think that his stern views had to do with religion, but Mr. Hearst wasn't a religious man—just liked to collect the trappings of it. And we're about to walk right through one of them—a four-hundred-year-old convent gate—"

"Before we go, could you tell us something about the chairs?" This was Dottie speaking, the first challenge to the guide's steady monologue since entering the main house, and Catha turned to study her. Dottie had been transformed by the house. She was no longer the giggling out-of-towner in awe of her big brother, but a woman with a mind of her own.

She'd distanced herself from Donald and was gazing intently at the overstuffed sofas, armchairs, and club chairs that dotted the vast room. Each piece was enormous, designed to meet the requirements of a person of both height and girth—as Mr. Hearst had been. But despite the furniture's well-padded, chintz-ruffled size, the room dwarfed the lot, making each grouping appear as incidental as seats in a hotel lobby.

"Are they antiques as well?"

"No, ma'am. Mr. Hearst, he ordered those up from a furniture store in San Luis Obispo. Practicality was what he liked, and as I've said, comfort. See those fat little cupids covering the fabric? And all those bunches of posies?"

Dottie couldn't help but notice the design. Putti carting garlands of ribbon and blossoms swam over each chair back, seat, and pillow while the wide, comfy sofas were awash in rose, Delft-blue, and peach-hued renditions of the smiling god of love.

"Yes, I do . . ." Dottie's answer was tentative, like a student fearing a scholastic trap.

"Well, I like to tell myself Miss Marion Davies chose that fabric especially. She was what you might call the doyenne of San Simeon, though she and Mr. Hearst never married."

And with that discreet nod to an unusual relationship, and a broad, knowing smirk from Donnie, the group trooped into the Refectory, where the polished medieval table was set as if a dinner for twenty-four fortunate guests were about to begin.

* * *

"Dottie," Catha whispered while the guide began cataloging an endless array of Flemish and Mexican silver candelabra, a huge Queen Anne wine cistern, English warming plates, Irish serving dishes, and a deeply chased parliamentary mace from Dublin.

Sienese banners fluttered high overhead, their jewel-like colors catching the light beaming through the clerestory windows. The room had a festival air. Catha half-expected French horns, tambours, and troubadours or a minstrel calling the throng's attention to the intricately carved musicians' gallery.

"Dottie . . ."

Dottie didn't turn. She was enthralled by the silver littering every surface of every gleaming table.

"Dottie, may I ask you something?" Catha repeated with as much force as she dared.

The silver caught the sunlight sweeping through the windows, splattering the scarlet, gold, and cobalt blue of the banners with shards of light as sharp and bold as cries of surprise.

"Dottie?"

Dottie jumped. "Oh, jeez, Catha!" She blushed. She'd obviously forgotten where she was.

"Do you think I could talk to the elderly gentleman your brother knows? The fellow at the convalescent home?" Catha hated the manipulation in her voice. She knew she sounded gushy and insincere, but she realized Dottie was the only route past Donald's dubious interest in her plight. Without intending to, Catha also began copying Dottie's breathy speech.

"I mean, I'd really like to hear what he has to say about this Abigail lady. She might be a relative, an aunt or something I never knew I had. And . . ." Catha was about to explain that her mother had recently died, that her last wish was to have her ashes brought to San Simeon, and that the visit was proving as perplexing as the dead woman's final desire. But Catha didn't know where to begin. And she wasn't certain Dottie would understand even if the right words could be found.

As if those complex questions were visible on Catha's face, Dottie's answer was quick and compassionate: "Sure, honey. I'll see what I can do."

By now the tour was being urged toward the Morning Room where the medieval decor of the Refectory continued. A heavy-timbered Spanish ceiling and a fourteenth-century marble archway created a castlelike fastness while sanctuary lamps from Spain and Italy dangled a repoussé wonder.

Rich in detail, the deftly hammered silver and gold sprinkled light toward the corners of the stone-walled room, which was smaller in scale than the Assembly Room or Refectory. Catha could easily imagine the Morning Room in its heyday. She could almost see the guests in their tennis whites or hacking jackets sauntering through the Gothic doors.

She looked in Donnie and his sister's direction, but they were deep in conversation.

After they'd passed down the corridor into the Billiard Room, Dottie finally approached. She waited until the guide had concluded his description of the millefleur French tapestry.

"*Millefleur* means a thousand flowers," he'd explained with a now familiar drone, "and you can see the reason this Gothic design was given its name. The scene depicts a stag hunt. Lots of little details comprise the storytelling aspect of this magnificent hanging. Trees have been chopped down, and a pregnant dog is among the huntsman's pack of hounds. See her master giving her a nice ear-rubbing? As to the riders' medieval clothing . . ."

Catha had found her attention drifting. She felt nearly stupefied with information, and her thoughts kept wandering to Abigail Kinsolving—if such a person had even existed. Would Abigail have walked through this room? And if she had, what was her connection to the lord of San Simeon?

". . . There's only one other tapestry in the world similar to it. People ask how much an art object like this is worth, but as with everything else in Mr. Hearst's collection, the answer is, it's priceless.

"Now, before we bid adieu, I want you to take a gander at this French jewel cabinet. It's dated 1562, and rumor has it the piece used to grace Miss Davies's suite. Be sure to take a moment to look it over."

"Catha?"

Catha spun around while Dottie beckoned. Donnie had lagged behind the milling crowd while his sister stood to one side, ready to act as intermediary.

"Donnie's got something to tell you."

"Name's Ethan," Don announced abruptly. "Ethan Purnell. Claims to have been a sheriff or marshal during the twenties. Maybe deputy sheriff. I never been too sure."

Donnie stared at Catha, waiting for a response. But Catha, for once, kept her mouth shut.

"I don't know precisely what his line of work was, but it had something to do with law enforcement. Well, you should see the old gent. Must be ninety years, if he's a day. But straight as a rod. Not an ounce of fat. All sinew and grit, you know, like those guys in the old outwestern flicks. A real cowboy type, if you get my drift—"

"Don . . ." Dottie's whisper was a gentle reminder.

"Oh, yeah, well, Ethan and me, we've gotten to be

kind of friendly down there at the home. I'm his nurse, see. They hired me 'cause I'm pretty big as well as strong. I can help those old guys when they start to fall or something. Besides, some of them real ancient gents are totally bedridden." Don glanced at Dottie for approval, but the stare she returned sent him hurrying back to his story.

"Anyway, like I said, Ethan gets to be a regular fountain when he starts yakking about this Abigail person. That's how come I know she died up here—and also about her killing that Hollywood type. But like I said, that's all it is. Just weird old stories . . . kind of mixed-up, like. I mean, sometimes you catch him in the mood. And sometimes he does dumb as a horse.

"Besides, like I told you, I can't be certain of the name. Probably doesn't have anything to do with you."

"But if I could talk to him myself . . . ," Catha interposed.

"I don't know." Donnie wavered. "The old coot can get pretty paranoid. I mean, murder is a frightening thing when you think about it."

Or even if you don't, Catha thought, but didn't say. "I wouldn't stay five minutes, and you could be there the whole time if Mr. Purnell wanted." She shifted her feet anxiously; something told her the convalescent-home attendant was about to relent.

"I don't know . . . Maybe . . . I'll see what I can do. But, look, if I do let you come on down to the home, you can't tell old Ethan where you heard the story. It's supposed to be, like, you know . . . a confidence or something. I mean, if he was, like, law enforcement, I guess he shouldn't be blabbing—"

"Thanks!" Catha began to gush, then Donnie burst out with his formerly bombastic tone.

"Just don't tell him you heard it from me, that's all. If what Ethan claims is true and there were two deaths at San Simeon, then maybe all the other stuff is the genuine article. Maybe the whole affair was hushed up, like he says. Maybe there was some scary monkey business going on up here."

5

FOLLOWING DON AND DOTTIE'S POD-SHAPED, TUR-
quoise minivan down Route 1, Catha wondered if Californians chose cars to match their clothes or vice
versa as she began to bombard herself with questions.
It was a trick she used to get to the root of academic problems.

What was Mother hiding? she demanded. Did she
know this Kinsolving woman? Could they have been
related? Was that the connection to San Simeon—why
she wanted her ashes brought here? And if so, why
the secrecy? But the answers remained elusive. Catha
tried to pay attention to the road, but found herself
driving like an automaton.

"Two days," she murmured. "That's all it's been.
Thursday was Mother's funeral. That was yesterday. I
flew in the night before. It was raining horribly."

The normally soothing repetition of facts failed to
achieve its goal, however. Catha felt more jittery than
before. Another wild-goose chase, she decided angrily.
I don't know what I'm looking for. Whatever Mother
and I didn't share—and there's plenty to choose

from—it's too late now. And if this Kinsolving person turns out to have been a relative, well, she's dead, too.

By now the autumnal sun was setting; red-gold light poured across the roadway, lengthening the shadows of pine trees, traffic lights, and automobiles alike. Every object had a darker mirror image: some raced ahead; some remained stationary.

Inexplicably, Catha remembered a frigid winter morning the year before. She'd driven Win to the airport in Hartford before dawn—he'd been scheduled to deliver a speech in Chicago that morning—and it wasn't until her return trip to Middletown that the sun had finally made its tentative February appearance.

An ice storm had blown in the night before, and each tree, each bough, each blade of grass along the highway, had been encrusted with the crystalline substance. As the sun rose, its rays had illumined every glassy shard, turning it all a glittering pink. Fields and woods had fallen behind the hurrying auto, the scrunch of tires on salted asphalt, the swish of snow flung to the highway's shoulders: those comforting sounds had been supplanted by the sight of the rosy world. Catha thought she'd never seen anything as wondrous.

"Oh, great! Now I'm daydreaming!" she warned herself, jolting back to the present. "Daydreaming and tearing off after some goofy old guy in a convalescent home. My head's not screwed on straight; that much is certain."

Thoroughly regretting her visit to the nursing home, Catha decided to make her interview with Ethan a brief one. Whatever specious reasoning or misguided hopes had led her to this folly would soon be thrust aside.

True to Donnie's description, the nursing home had a magnificent view of the twin smokestacks of a power plant that dominated the crescent-shaped beach of Morro Bay. The tall, brick monstrosities outshone the peaceful harbor, the fishing wharfs cuddling close to shore as well as the restaurants, shops, and tidy two-bedroom homes that the seaside community comprised. Belching out a viscous, white cloud that seemed capable of glowing, the otherworldly creations even dwarfed the imposing black bulk of Morro Rock, the 578-foot conical mass that rose from the Pacific's shoaly waves.

"My God," Catha gasped. "Talk about destroying the environment! What's a power plant doing in the middle of a beach?"

She followed Donnie's van into the nursing home's parking lot, gazing at the embarcadero as the lights of the sleepy town came alive. What a pretty place this must have been, she realized, before man decided to intervene.

Donnie watched Catha's glance return to the smokestacks as the three climbed out of their vehicles and clustered on the pavement. "You get used to them." He shrugged. "I mean, after a while you don't even see them anymore."

I'll bet, Catha nearly said, but stopped herself in the nick of time. Donnie was doing her a favor, even if it was one she no longer wanted.

"This here is Ethan." A starchily white-haired old gentleman stood ramrod-straight, and neither beside the putty-colored wall nor too far away from it. In fact, the stucco seemed like a prop, and Ethan appeared to be a cutout, cardboard doll.

Catha imagined Ethan coming equipped with a variety of paper costumes: Confederate general, carpet-bagging politician, antebellum judge. Snip along the dotted lines; watch out for the tabs; add buckskin gloves or a set of law books. It was the white thicket of carefully groomed hair that caused the resemblance—that and the determined stance.

The vividly coal-dark eyes were another matter; they bore into Catha and then seared their way across the crowded room, incinerating wheelchairs and their aged occupants, deaf old men in dressing gowns huddled beside the TV, and the two lime-green-clad nurses gabbing at their station. Ethan's eyes might as well have been on fire.

I wouldn't have called him a "cowboy type" at all, Catha told herself while she boldly stuck out her hand and said, "Pleased to meet you, Mr. Purnell. I'm Catha Burke."

But Ethan didn't speak or move. In fact, he didn't give the slightest impression of having heard Donnie's introduction. A too-large and snow-white shirt collar rustled across his throat as he breathed. The sound was as scratchy as newspaper being balled up for a fire, but that was the only noise.

"He gets like this sometimes," Donnie mumbled in apology. "Like I told you back at the castle, he can be a regular windbag or he can go dead as a ghost."

Although this was delivered in a whisper, Catha could have sworn Ethan heard every word. The black eyes flared with renewed heat as though contempt and irony were staging a pitched battle.

"Well, I'm happy to make your acquaintance, Mr. Purnell," Catha repeated. After that she let her hand drop. There seemed nothing more to say.

"Oh, isn't that the cutest!" Dottie, at the nurses' station, was gushing over a knitted layette set—a gift for a soon-to-be ex-employee of Morro Bay Convalescent Center.

Again, Catha was aware of the heat sparking in Ethan's eyes. She tried to imagine what he was seeing, turned her head to stare, even stepped slightly to one side in an attempt to fall in with his line of vision, but nothing in the long and L-shaped room seemed remotely arresting.

Empty custard cups littered a Formica-topped table. The residue of cherry-toned Jell-O clung to the Pyrex sides, and several dollops of the gelatinous goo had mounded on the table's phony oak-grained surface. The color and consistency reminded Catha of a child's finger-warmed crayon—and the stuff probably tasted no better.

Ethan closed his eyes, then snapped them open again and returned his viselike gaze to Catha. His proud, wizened chest heaved, giving the impression that somewhere within the depths of spotless broadcloth and brittle bone thoughts were struggling to find expression. Catha wished with all her soul that she'd never met Don and Dottie or listened to their foolish prattle. This old man with his confusing maladies and troubled brain was too complex to cope with.

". . . and the color's just adorable." Dottie's voice drifted to the fore again, impervious to her dismal surroundings or the sense of doom that seeped through the cheerless room.

"What do you call that shade of angora you used to edge the booties? Salmon?" Dottie rattled along while the clock tapped out an irregular tick, and two cars swished by on the sea-sprayed roadway. After that, the vacuum of silence returned.

"Can I get you anything, Mr. Purnell? Would you care to sit—"

The coal-fired eyes cut short Catha's query. She looked to Donnie for help, but he was already trying to scuttle away. For all his braggadocio, Donald was unequal to Ethan's military bearing.

"How would you like to join the other gents for a

game of Go Fish?" Donnie was nearly shouting. "I know each and every one of you is an ex-cardsharp! Besides, it's only the evening news on the tube."

Ethan didn't open his mouth; the promised speech didn't rumble forward; he scarcely seemed to blink. Catha wondered if he'd become catatonic, and she was about to confide this suspicion to Donnie when the wretched attendant whirled away in a flurry of false excitement.

"Well, let me go shuffle that deck of cards and call the other pistol-packing varmints!"

Pain creased Ethan's ancient eyes, effacing their brilliance.

Murdered, Catha reminded herself. Someone was murdered at San Simeon, and the story claims it was Abigail who committed the crime.

"Donnie and I met at Hearst Castle," Catha began, realizing, even as the words tumbled out of her mouth, that the effort was futile. "He told me you've always lived in this area . . . and that you might have some information on the place . . . stories that never made the newspapers."

With each lurching start and quivering stop, Catha knew she was losing the old gentleman. She glanced at the bulbous and institutional clock spilling neon-bright numbers over the grungy wall: 5:53. If she left right this minute, she could reach LAX in time for the midnight flight to Hartford.

"I'm a history teacher," she added, "at a college back East." Why on earth, she wondered, would a speechless resident of a California convalescent home care about a course entitled "The Impulse to Imperialism"?

Catha glanced desperately in Donnie's direction, but he avoided her gaze with singular determination. I'm carrying out my end of the bargain, she groused soundlessly. Why can't he help me get the old guy talking? All I want is to determine whether this Abigail woman was named Kinsolving. For the first time since her arrival on the West Coast's less than sunny shores, Catha felt wholly inadequate.

"It's a small liberal arts college," she resumed with a polite smile. "The name may not be as well known out here as Yale or Harvard or Princeton, but we give our students an education equal to those larger institutions. Better, sometimes."

Oh, damnation, Catha told herself, I might as well be discussing the Monroe Doctrine or the Hay-Pauncefote Treaty. Maybe Ethan has the right approach. Never open your mouth.

"Well, I suppose I'll be pushing off now. . . . I'm pleased to have met you." Catha pulled the strap of her shoulder bag closer to her raincoat collar and began tying the garment's tan twill belt. Despite the nursing home's hothouse heat she felt suddenly cold. Her feet, still encased in the rain-spattered shoes she'd worn for the past two days, seemed chilled and wet, as if she'd just slogged through a series of sleet-covered puddles.

"I guess I'll be leaving then . . . Connecticut's a long way away."

"I know." The words rumbled volcanically in Ethan's hollow chest.

Catha beamed encouragement, but what she got in return was a smile so sorrowing it seemed ready to dissolve. Without thinking, she grabbed Ethan's paperweight hand.

"Why don't we find someplace to sit down and talk," she suggested, but Ethan's dismissive scowl made her reassess the idea of a quiet tête-à-tête.

"On the other hand, we could just stand here . . . that is, if you're comfortable."

For an answer, Ethan drew himself up straighter than before. If the initial impression had been that of an old soldier unwilling to die, the new demeanor was commander in chief.

"Catha Kinsolving," he said with a voice that rang as loud and clear as a gong.

"Burke," Catha began correcting automatically, but Ethan's self-assured tone cut short the effort.

"Catha Kinsolving! I knew you'd find me. Sooner or later, I knew we'd have to meet."

6

IF EVERY ONE OF THE RESIDENTS OF THE CONVALES-
cent home had started shouting simultaneously, Catha
wouldn't have heard them. Too many sirens, whistles,
and snare drums were clamoring inside her ears. She
felt as if she'd suddenly been released from the claus-
trophobic downbeat of an after-hours, alternative-
music club. She breathed in the air brushing past her
face; perfumed as it was with disinfectant, denture ad-
hesive, stewed tomatoes, and canned green beans, the
breeze seemed peculiarly fresh.

"How do you know me?" Catha murmured. The
question was deceptively simple. Half of her anticipated a cantankerous " 'Cause Donnie told me,
missy!" The other half almost dreaded Ethan's answer
would meet her expectations.

"You're Abigail's granddaughter. That's how I
know who you are." Sure in his regimental spit and
polish, Ethan became quarrelsome with impatience.

"Recognized you the minute you walked through
this door. Same hair, same green eyes, identical face.
You and she could have been twins, though, of course,

70

you don't have one ounce of her gumption. Abigail wouldn't have stood around here namby-pambying with an idiot like Donald! Or his sister, neither. A pair of dummies, if you ask me. But then, I can't take care of myself anymore, and that's a fact."

The unexpected avalanche of verbiage momentarily exhausted Ethan's supply. He glared at the nurses' station and then at the feeble old men clustered close to the TV. Again, the glance seemed to encompass more than the room. Ethan was confronting a lifetime of years: enemies, acquaintances, lovers, and friends.

"I heard that Hearst fellow kicked off just like those poor, drooling sots over there. Heart attack and everything. Failed, the doctor here calls it, as if youth were a choice a fellow's too ornery to grasp. Every time I hear that fool expression, I want to yell, 'What's the failure? A body gets old, that's all there is to it. It's not like you've gone to the dogs on purpose. It's not like choosing a life of crime.' "

"What about Abigail?" Catha started to interject, but Ethan, once released from his self-imposed exile, was like a gas jet with a broken valve. He'd talk as long as the supply lasted.

"Course the less said about that old cuss, the better. Hearst didn't make it easy on any of them, and that's a fact. Not even Marion—and she could stand up to him. She had some mouth on her, and she liked to use it. Course, Marion's language might seem tame nowadays. It took Abigail some getting used to, I'll tell you that."

Catha pricked up her ears. "Was Abigail a regular guest at San Simeon?"

"Huh!" Ethan snorted. "Shows what you know!"

But that's the point, Catha wanted to protest. I don't know anything! Until five minutes ago, I wasn't even aware I had a grandmother. She didn't voice these complaints, however. Faced with Ethan's appraising gaze, she lost what remained of her inherited "gumption."

"Or did she work up there? Was she a maid?"

"Maid!" Ethan raged. "A beautiful, educated girl like her being a maid! What are you thinking of Miss Catha Burke? Abigail was Marion Davies's private secretary. Hired by old man Hearst himself. I guess he hoped some of Abigail's East Coast breeding and class would rub off on that dizzy, floradora flapper girl.

"And I guess it would have, all right, if things had worked out, if that Hollywood fellow hadn't gummed up the works by getting himself killed."

Catha could see Ethan was struggling past a bog of tears and regret. She yearned to reach out and offer support, but knew her youth was regarded with suspicion.

"She didn't do it, of course." The simple statement restored Ethan's equanimity. His eyes glared; he seemed to dare contradiction. "Not that your mother ever believed me. But Louise always was a pigheaded woman. And a stubborn little girl before that—almost from the minute she could walk."

Leaving Morro Bay Convalescent Center, Catha was convinced she knew less now than before her visit to Hearst Castle. With the second big shocker, Ethan's statement that he'd known her mother, the old man's mouth had angrily clamped shut. Silence had overtaken him as if his mind had deserted its earthbound body. Even his fierce, black eyes had lost their glimmer.

"Mr. Purnell?" Catha had prodded. "Mr. Purnell? Can you tell me more about Abigail or the infant she named Louise—or the murder at San Simeon?" But the effort had been hopeless.

Donnie had scurried forward in the nick of time, urging Ethan's tall, weary frame toward a chair and swaddling the now motionless legs and shoulders in a pair of flannel blankets. The cloth had once been baby blue, but age had turned it a sickly yellow-gray. Catha thought she'd never seen a sight so pathetic.

But Donnie had redeemed himself from this ignominious act, scribbling down the address of Ethan's closest of kin—a nephew named Lucas Purnell with a law degree and an office in L.A.'s swanky Century City.

"I'll bet he can help you out. He's a nice, young fellow. Environmental lawyer, but no tree-hugger, if you get my drift. Visits regular-like. Handled all the paperwork when the old guy was admitted, and if you swear you won't breathe a word"—Catha had quickly nodded assent—"the old coot's stored some 'official report' with Lucas. You can't tell him I told you; I wasn't supposed to listen in on their conversation, but I was passing Ethan's room with a load of clean towels when I happened to overhear the two discussing the stuff."

I'll bet, Catha had told herself, but she'd put on her most understanding and sympathetic expression and hadn't uttered a sound.

"Anyway, I think that box of letters and whatnot contains clues to that murder he was investigating . . . you know, the one I mentioned up at the castle." Then Donnie had stopped himself and a vast grin had flushed his face.

"Say, you know what I'll do for you, Catha Burke? I'll get old Ethan to give Lucas a call . . . sort of warn him you're coming. Seems like the old gent kind of knows your family already . . . at least that's what I guessed when I heard you two yakking."

After appropriate words of thanks, Catha had

walked out of the nursing home and climbed into her car. Her mind was whirring, a morass of unanswered questions that seemed to add a new unknown at every turning: a grandmother Catha had never heard mentioned, an unsolved murder, and now an elderly gentleman who claimed to have investigated the crime.

A visit to Lucas would mean another delay in her plans, but Catha knew she had to get to the bottom of this peculiar story.

Century City is a steel, glass, and brass-plated heaven. Take the newest, shiniest, and most extravagant architecture of any American city and plunk it down on wide and beflowered boulevards; add a shopping mall with outdoor cafés, Italian market umbrellas, three "nuclear," high-end clothing stores, a trendy bookshop, caverns of underground parking, an eight-screen movie complex, and boutiques devoted entirely to luxuries like Scottish cashmeres or Pratesi pillows. Throw in pricey hotels, banks devoid of customers, and black marble office towers; give the streets names like Avenue of the Stars or Constellation Boulevard, and while you're at it, stage a klieg-lighted film opening to attract that aforementioned and exotic species— and you'll have Century City.

At least, that's how Catha saw the place as she swerved her car along busy Santa Monica Boulevard, turning right on Century Park and left on Constellation. Lucas had described his particular edifice as "a smoked-glass facade with chrome accents," but the buildings all looked alike. Worrying where she'd park on these meterless streets, she did a surprise U-turn and headed back toward the mall. She'd leave the car there and walk. It would be a novel experience: walking in southern California.

* * *

The reception area of Lucas's office was everything Catha had feared it would be. Mocha, suede-covered, sleek Italian modulars; burled-walnut end tables; and an étagère added to the look of casual wealth, while the dove-gray carpeting felt as thick and soft as a bed of sea sponges. Catha wondered how anyone could negotiate the stuff in high heels.

"I see they make you work on Saturday," she tried, smiling at a cool young woman who took her name and then relayed it into the hushed and private ether of a wand-thin charcoal phone.

Glancing about the room and at its less-than-gracious inhabitant, Catha knew her smile looked out of place. It was too wholesome, too New England, too ordinary. As were her clothes, and her damn French braids. At twenty-four, twenty-five at the most, the receptionist was decked out in a black spandex skirt, neon-green, body-hugging jacket, and shoes whose heels looked like water slides at an amusement park. Her nails were acrylic talons of Chinese red. Catha reflexively hid her own fingers.

"Mr. Purnell can see you now." By her icy tone, Catha surmised that Ethan's nephew hadn't met with the Malibu Barbie's approval either. Turning down the corridor that led to the lesser offices, Catha decided she was going to like Mr. Lucas Purnell.

She stopped, drew a breath, and stifled an admonishing sigh as she entered the office. Lucas was motioning her forward while he kept a steady clasp on a cordless phone and maintained an in-depth and technical conversation.

With his rolled shirtsleeves, horn-rimmed glasses, and chiseled cheeks, Lucas must once have been every college girl's dream. Catha recognized the type immediately. Men like Lucas had made a hash of her under-

75

graduate days—her graduate studies, too, if you wanted the truth. And if they could, she knew they'd barge their broad and brainy shoulders into her professorial life as well. Just because these demigods were no longer captains of the track team or presidents of the student body didn't mean they'd ceased being heartthrobs. Catha had made it her rule to resist them. If you didn't learn from past mistakes, what good was the lesson?

Amused eyes looked Catha over, registered the practical clothing and the wilted raincoat she'd been too insecure to leave in the reception area. He nodded toward a chair as tawny curls whisked around perfect ears.

Catha sat, or rather, she dropped into place. The raincoat clung to her arm, and she rolled it into a ball and stuffed it on the seat beside her. Her neck and arms were damp and uncomfortably warm with embarrassment, and her toes scrunched up in her shoes.

"The approach on the wetlands project will have to be preemptive, Stephen." The briefest wink gave Catha to understand she'd have her host's attention as soon as this pressing business was resolved. The glance was filled with playful self-assurance. Catha wanted to dislike it, but found she couldn't.

"No, we'll have to strike first. If we leave key issues to the developers' discretion, then we're cast in a defensive role."

Catha gritted her teeth. She felt as if she'd been consigned to the hell of her college dating years. She crossed her legs, but the expanse of taupe stocking reminded her of an old lady's elasticized support hose. She drew her ankles in, then realized the pose looked alarmingly prim.

"I've got to go, Stephen." Another slight wink and

a nod in Catha's direction. Behind the glasses, Lucas's eyes were a piercing gray-yellow. Like a lion's eyes, Catha told herself. A young lion in his prime. The slightly rumpled hair matched the description, and so did the muscular shoulders in the cream-colored shirt.

"I'll call you back this afternoon. . . . I know it's Saturday. . . . Well, this evening then. . . . But think about what I've said—a preemptive strike. We'll get the grassroots organizations out there at the site. Call a press conference. God knows we've got enough star power to attract the cream of the fourth estate. I can get Jayni on the case as soon as you say the word. We all know what she's capable of. . . . Meryl, too, if you want. . . . We might as well come out with all our guns blazing."

"I guess you must work seven days a week," Catha ventured as Lucas returned the portable to its cradle. As an opener, she realized the banter sounded incredibly lame, but at the moment, she seemed incapable of a wittier effort.

"I'd work eight days a week if I could." Lucas smiled. "When you're trying to save the world, you need every minute." Lucas's leonine eyes never wavered, and Catha realized he meant what he'd said. His seriousness piqued her curiosity but also heightened her discomfort.

"Uncle Ethan told me you wished to examine his effects."

"That's right."

"May I ask why?"

Catha paused. Confronted with Lucas's direct gaze, the story she'd fabricated seemed flimsy and obvious. On the other hand, confessing to Abigail's possible involvement in a murder case was impossible—especially to a total stranger. Catha had experienced enough difficulty facing the fact herself. "I'm considering a course on the imperialistic incentive," she began, hoping Lucas wouldn't notice her nervousness. "I'm not certain your uncle was aware of that fact. . . . Unfortunately, I didn't have time to fully explain my intentions. . . . I'm hoping to entitle the course 'The Impulse to Imperialism.' "

Catha cursed herself while the words tumbled out. She'd always been a failure at lies. "Keep it simple," she'd heard over and over. "Don't extrapolate. Don't expand. If they want more information, they'll ask." The warnings had applied to university hierarchies— and not necessarily deceit, although Catha sometimes found the two disconcertingly similar.

" 'The Impulse to Imperialism'—that's quite a mouthful." The way Lucas wrapped his lips around the words made them seem like open seduction.

Catha forced herself to return his stare, but her own effort seemed waxy and thin. Inadvertently, her eyes returned to her appearance: all-purpose corduroy skirt, no-nonsense pumps, and the ridiculous, industrial-strength hose. What passed for a "business outfit" in Middletown looked the height of dowdiness in Los Angeles. Catha hated herself for the judgment, but there it was—a woman with a mission reduced to quibbling over clothes.

"And how could Uncle Ethan's papers help your research, Miss Burke?"

"Catha. Please. I'm sure you and I are about the same age." Catha had no idea where that bit of nonsense had dropped from. With great effort, she managed a broader smile, faking a serenity she didn't feel.

"Your uncle investigated a murder that occurred at

San Simeon . . . a murder that took place during the early twenties. As you know, William Randolph Hearst was an extraordinarily vocal proponent of certain aspects of U.S. intervention—"

"I'm sorry, Catha, but I don't understand the connection between Hearst's politics and my uncle."

Catha recognized the flaw in her argument immediately. She sighed inadvertently, then folded her hands in her lap and tried to regroup while Lucas continued in the same self-assured manner.

"You could ask me what happened to Twentieth Century–Fox's famous movie lot, for instance, and I'd be happy to describe the developers' war that occurred when studio finances failed after the filming of *Cleopatra*.

"I could tell you how the tire industry lobbied for the end of Los Angeles' trolley system, and I could detail the nightmare occurring this moment in Marina Del Ray on account of a proposed misuse of sensitive wetlands. I could discuss storm drains, and the heavy metals found in Santa Monica Bay, but those issues are matters of public record.

"What I don't understand is my uncle Ethan's involvement with our nation's expansionist tendencies, and so I'm sorry, but I'm afraid I'll have to refuse you access to his private effects."

"My grandmother was accused of murder. Your uncle claims she didn't do it!" Catha blurted in spite of herself.

Lucas paused while the words took effect. "I see." His tone was new and not at all what Catha had anticipated. A softness had entered his voice, and a quiet hesitation that sounded like sorrow. "Uncle Ethan told you this . . . this disturbing piece of information? He knew your grandmother?"

"Oh, it's not what you think," Catha hurried ahead. "It wasn't a robbery or anything like that. I mean, your uncle Ethan led me to believe the crime had another motive altogether."

"I didn't imagine it was simple larceny, Catha. You don't look like the granddaughter of thieves." Lucas's smile was so understanding, Catha didn't know what to do. She shifted in her chair, recrossed her legs, flicked an invisible wrinkle from her skirt, and blushed. It was a reaction she hated above all others— and she had an entire catalog of inappropriate responses to choose from.

Lucas pretended not to notice her dismay. "What were the particulars of the death, insofar as you understand them?"

"I haven't a clue, other than the fact that the supposed crime occurred at William Randolph Hearst's estate, San Simeon." Catha's words were needlessly defensive, and her jaw jutted forward slightly. "I wasn't aware of Abigail Kinsolving's existence until yesterday. My mother was orphaned as an infant. Of course, I realized she'd had a mother, but no name was ever mentioned."

"And your mother can't supply you with the information?" Again, the tone was so kindly it took Catha by surprise. Every drop of protective anger deserted her.

"My mother's dead," she answered with a subdued voice. "That's why I'm in California. I drove up to San Simeon to oversee the disposition of her ashes. It was happenstance that introduced me to your uncle."

"I see," Lucas repeated, then stood up and walked to his office's panoramic window. By now, the sun was directly overhead, and it sent down molten rays of light that seemed to squash every building in sight.

"Just think what we've done to our planet," Lucas almost whispered. His back was to Catha, and his voice was pensive and weary. Catha considered attempting a clever rejoinder, but knew she'd never manage it. Her emotions were too tangled, like a jumble of torn and color-coded telephone wires. "Mother" was printed on one; "Grandmother—murderer?" was written on another; while a frayed and supremely tattered line bore the scratched-out image "Winslow Reid and other mistakes."

"You know, Catha," Lucas was continuing in the same thoughtful tone, "I wish I'd seen this city when it was a simple village of orange groves and dirt lanes, a few sparse haciendas on the hillsides. Sunset Boulevard was a broad and dusty country road back then—ankle-deep mud during the rainy season and hard-baked clay when the weather turned dry. . . . And the water in Santa Monica Bay! It's difficult to conceive of how pristine this spot must have been. Uncle Ethan told me that one time he—"

The name seemed to jolt Lucas back to the present. He turned away from the window to face his guest, and the smile he attached to his lips became as smooth as any mannequin's.

"I keep most of my uncle's papers here." Whatever private concerns had troubled Lucas were now completely masked. He'd become the bright, young environmental lawyer once again, the glib confidant of stars and Hollywood moguls alike. Catha regretted the change, but told herself the transformation was just as well. If she found the handsome, ex-jock Lucas dangerous, how much worse would his sensitive alter ego be?

As if he'd read Catha's thoughts, Lucas grinned

again. He needed another persona to hide behind as much as she required hers.

"I realize it seems odd to store a collection of probably worthless papers here." He smiled. "A law firm isn't exactly a manuscript repository, but Uncle Ethan's always been a little peculiar about the safety of his artifacts. I expect he has his reasons; he was familiar with most of the residents of Cambria and its vicinity. He lived there a very long time . . ."

Lucas left this tantalizing thought unfinished as he opened cabinet drawers and retrieved a brown-and-black banker's box marked with red, block handwriting that spelled an elderly but determined ETHAN PURNELL.

"I don't expect you'll find anything earth-shattering or inherently dangerous in Uncle Ethan's so-called treasure trove. Just old letters, news clippings, antique police notes, and a few faded photos, from what I remember. I'll have the secretary make copies of the originals.

"I've only looked in the box once—years ago, when he first requested I keep it. But he questions its whereabouts periodically, and I find it easier not to lie. I know deceit is supposed to be stock-in-trade for attorneys, but I find I'm not much good at it."

Catha blushed until even her collarbone burned flaming red. "Do you suppose I could borrow the originals instead of Xeroxes? Sometimes the way ink dries or paper creases gives off clues copies miss."

Lucas pondered the request, battling his sense of professionalism. "I guess Uncle Ethan would want me to help in any way I can."

Alone near the bank of elevators in the office building's deserted hall, Catha felt her skin begin to prickle. Her palms were wet with apprehension as she juggled the unwieldy carton and pushed the DOWN button. Thank God that's over, she promised herself. I'll read Ethan's papers, and then I absolutely swear I'll go home. I'll go back to my cozy nest in Connecticut, pull the quilts over my head, and forget everything about California.

7

Back in her motel room, Catha dumped the contents of Ethan's box on the bed. Yellowed and brittle news clippings, letters penned in ink that had faded to an almost illegible heliotrope-gray, scribbled words on shards of crumbling paper, typewritten pages the years had limned with crusty brown, and three badly mangled photographs spilled across the glossy expanse of a king-size, burgundy bedspread.

Catha stared at the photographs; the black had paled to sepia while the white bloomed over the faces as if sunspots had attacked the lens—smiling faces clustered in groups and not one recognizable. I need a magnifying glass, she told herself as she began racing her fingers over the rest of Ethan's collection. She riffled the age-speckled clues as if she were scattering the pieces of a jigsaw puzzle. It was an uncharacteristic gesture. Catha was ordinarily neatness itself, but impatience created another persona. She felt compelled to get to the bottom of this mystery.

In the past, her historical research had often felt like a treasure hunt; newly uncovered facts or linked ideas had made her want to whoop aloud, and she'd stood beside some musty library shelf or stared at the wobbly lines of microfiched newsprint until her eyes had positively blazed.

But the stakes were raised this time. This time the protagonist was her own grandmother. "Abigail Kinsolving," Catha murmured, "Abigail Kinsolving, private secretary to Marion Davies—or so old Ethan Purnell insists. A young woman hired by William Randolph Hearst himself. Hired to teach his mistress how to be a lady."

This last statement was a question mark. Catha couldn't verify the information. In fact, when she paused to make a note on the yellow legal pad that accompanied all her scholarly quests, she was forced to admit the entire foundation of her inquiry was suspect. She had only Ethan's word to go on.

Separating the newspaper clippings from letters she assumed Abigail had written at her boss's behest (Marion's florid signature was accompanied by a tiny, discreet "A.K."), then dividing Ethan's scrawled notes from the scrupulously typed police reports, Catha struggled for professorial detachment but found it difficult to attain. This is my grandmother, she kept repeating silently, the unknown link to a past I never understood.

With building excitement, she started reading the newsprint, becoming increasingly cautious when she realized how fragile the collection had become. Then she took a few preliminary notes, summarizing the information that underscored her investigation. What Ethan had chosen to save was going to prove crucial.

"April 11, 1924. The Los Angeles *Daily Examiner*. The film *The Marriage Cheat* is previewed at a Benedict Canyon residence. A dinner dance follows . . . much society buzz about this, descriptions of the house, etc. . . . The British author Elinor Glyn's controversial drama *Three Weeks* commences its run in Los Angeles . . . photo of actress playing lead—femme fatale pose . . . previous novel of same name was banned in Boston. Too much overt sensuality, paper reports . . .

"April 18. Same year. L.A. *Examiner* again. Marion Davies broadcasts to England via radio. She becomes the first American woman to do so. Lots of congratulations and other politico palaver from both sides of the Atlantic. . . . Davies photographed wearing a cloche hat and plenty of lace. . . . She's referred to as the 'Queen of the Screen' . . ."

"Hmmm," Catha found herself muttering while she wrote QUEEN OF THE SCREEN in block letters on her legal pad. "If I were unaware of Marion Davies's existence, then perhaps the epithet was created by an excess of Hearst propaganda—a challenge to the rest of the filmmaking community." This last query was summarized by an underlined Propaganda? as well as an arrow pointing toward the previous entry. Then Catha gingerly unfolded another piece of fragile history.

"October 26, 1924. A fleet of new V-63 Cadillacs for the Ince studios in Culver City. . . . Photograph of a proud Thomas H. Ince with his business and production managers beside the aforementioned vehicles . . . discussion of an incipient contract between the producer/director and William Randolph Hearst's Cosmopolitan Pictures . . . as of writing, all still very hush-hush, but reportage seems overly coy. . . ."

Catha digested these facts while making furious notes. Thomas H. Ince, she wondered, who in the world is he?

"November 18. Same year. Ditto paper. A one-inch headline screaming: HEARST SUIT RESCUED MERCHANT VESSELS." Catha scanned the story and the attached editorial extolling the same patriotic action. "???" she scribbled on her pad, then dashed a quick follow-up: "Save for class on imperialism—look into story later!"

Catha shifted slightly on the bed; her toes were beginning to tingle and her elbows felt slightly numb, but she refused to relinquish her position.

"November 20 and 21," she read as she spread out two more of Ethan's stored clippings. "A serialization of the story of *Janice Meredith*. Quote states: 'The great Cosmopolitan Pictures film starring Marion Davies.' Photo of the actress surrounded by a bevy of admiring men—all in Revolutionary War dress. . . . Half-page advertisement of the same, trumpeting that 'Miss Davies gives a better performance than in *Little Old New York*.' . . . Actors include 'W. C. Fields, Tyrone Power, and 8,500 others' . . ."

Catha glanced across her motel room, recalling Esteban's descriptions of the silent-screen stars. He'd said that Charlie Chaplin and Lita Grey had been regular guests at both Ocean House and San Simeon, and that John Gilbert, Greta Garbo, and Barrymore had visited as well. But Esteban had also suggested that Hearst had been unhappy when Marion spent too much time alone in Hollywood—that he'd kept her under lock and key at San Simeon as often as he could.

Catha stared at a patch of nondescript motel wallpaper until it turned into a grainy, beige blob. She had a peculiar sense of straddling two disparate worlds: a glamorous 1924 full of silent-screen stars and showy tycoons, and a present oppressive with worry.

Nineteen twenty-four, she told herself. The United States was at her glory. We'd escaped the ravages of the First World War, the Depression hadn't yet wreaked its cataclysmic vengeance, and WW II was only a mote in Herr Hitler's eye. Our nation was giddy with power, a leader diplomatically and economically, and as far as our industrial capacity was concerned, none could match us.

The year witnessed the introduction of the eight-hour workweek, and passage of the Immigration Act; it was four years after women had finally gained suffrage in 1920—the year that also heralded the beginning of Prohibition. In 1924, Robert Frost won his first Pulitzer Prize for poetry, while Stalin succeeded Lenin as the Soviet communist leader.

Catha raced through this litany of facts, feeling somewhat better equipped to deal with the unknowns in Ethan Purnell's collected artifacts. Then she returned to his horde.

"November 22," she stated while scratching out rigorous notes. "Banner headline and accompanying article clipped from several pages of the *Daily Examiner*. . . . Seems as though an important section is missing. . . . Headline reads: THRONGS PAY FINAL RESPECTS TO FILM WORLD LEADER. Photos beneath, identifying Charles Chaplin, Douglas Fairbanks, Mary Pickford, and Cecil B. DeMille.

"Two newsclips list the deceased's previous film work as well as a 'planned production' that remains in limbo. . . . Hollywood 'studio flags' fly at half-mast . . . a 'moving funeral oration' is delivered by one John Garrigues of the United Lodge of Theosophists, but the dead person remains curiously incognito. . . . Perhaps the name was so well known it was only used once or twice?"

Catha turned the remnants over and over in her hand. They were featherweight with years and so frail one slight misstep would send them to oblivion. Who died, she wondered suddenly, and how? If this was the murder victim, then wouldn't there be some mention of foul play? But if the dead person succumbed from natural causes, why did Ethan bother to preserve the clippings?

She placed the clippings to one side, then began searching for the vanished scrap of newsprint she hoped would clear up the mystery, but there were only more ads for *Janice Meredith*, and further serializations of the same—all centering on Marion Davies surrounded by an adoring crowd. Hearst seemed to have done everything in his power to make his mistress a star.

Catha glanced away. There hadn't been a single mention of murder; the clippings had begun to seem like a definite dead end. She noted this on her legal pad, creating circles of question marks that resembled clouds.

"Amorphous," she mumbled, "that's what this process is—like fog I can't see through. I know there's a shape out there, something looming and ominous, but my senses aren't acute enough to discern it."

"Eyes not good enough," she dashed out in the legal page's margin. The note would serve as a reminder. She'd have to start reading between the lines if Ethan's information was going to make sense.

Then she picked up the letters, hesitating at first, afraid that the elegant and educated hand might reveal stories she'd rather not confront. This was my relative, after all, Catha reminded herself, the woman my mother refused to acknowledge or claim. I'm not certain I feel comfortable exposing her secrets. If she was accused of killing some so-called Hollywood big shot, perhaps she had a motive.

Catha took a breath and allowed those conflicting emotions to do battle. The detachment of the professional historian was being rapidly supplanted by a fear of learning too much. When Catha had begun her quest, Abigail Kinsolving had seemed no more than a spunky ghost, a young woman with a strange story to tell, and Catha had felt an odd kind of kinship. But what if Ethan was wrong? What would happen if Abigail wasn't the heroine her granddaughter imagined? Catha stared at the letters, and a new kind of resolve took hold. "You get nowhere by running away," she reminded herself. "Studying life isn't the same as living it."

Catha began to stack the collected stationery: lavender notepaper gone a fusty peach with years, ecru pages engraved with the San Simeon letterhead, embossed invitations to "Weekend Retreats," "Birthday Celebrations," and "Costume Extravaganzas" as well as lined sheets that resembled guest lists.

Visitors had been added and crossed off, seating arrangements reorganized time and again, even room assignments painstakingly cataloged. All were written in the boxy, self-assured script of a young woman who'd been raised and educated at a finishing school on the East Coast. Catha had seen countless examples of similar writing. It remained the handwriting of choice in girls' schools from Massachusetts to Maryland.

"Show Pola Negri and Rudolph Valentino to Casa del Sol," one notation vehemently underlined, while a circle was drawn around the name of Ernst Lubitsch, removing him from the duo altogether. "Casa del Mar—NOT del Sol" was printed in black, block letters under the director's name. The lesson was clear; Abigail had nearly made a heinous mistake.

"She must have had a hard time figuring out some of those peculiar pairings." Catha laughed while she gently flattened messages she believed Marion had dictated to Abigail. The handwriting had the same

90

genteel downward strokes and the spelling was flawless, but the text was a bubble of unguided thought:
a true joint effort between Marion Davies and her
secretary.

"Dear little Lita," one such note began, and Catha
jumped involuntarily.

"Lita Grey!" she scribbled with ferocious speed. My
God, I've come full circle. She took a quick, hard
breath, then realized her eyes had glazed over with
something that felt remarkably like tears. "Abigail?"
she whispered. The watermarked and heavy linen
paper was a tangible connection to the past, as potent,
almost, as touching that unknown person's hand.

*Can't tell you how jazzed (well, not like that,
you silly cluck!) I am about you and old Charlie
coming up next week. Really miss the studio chat
now that Janice is ancient history.*

*Bring your tennis togs—no, you'd better not,
kiddo—but tell the old man to pack his. Or Koko,
or whatever the hell that smarmy manservant of
his is named. Coo-Coo? Ok-ko? Well, you know
who I mean.*

*If your lord and master forgets his whites, we'll
supply. You know my Popsie. Trunks of clothes
and a tailor, too. I swear this house is better supplied than a Ziegfeld show.*

*Tell the old man Incie's coming too (with his
wife this time!!!!) and John (natch) and Jack with
her nibs. (She still has my gall-darned slippers!)
Elinor's bringing the man-eater. Tell Charlie. I
know he'll get a hoot out of it. I seem to remember
some oddity in Mexico—on your honeymoon?!
You and bonny Prince Charlie and Elinor in a
cozy nest for three!! The little birds blabbed!!!!*

If we can drag Monsieur Artiste out of his latest

funk, I think we'll have a regular Ascot—or is it Wimbledon?

Kisses and hugs, Maid Marion

Catha put down the letter; an entire picture had begun to take shape: the house and its mistress and a man obsessed. The dross was spinning into gold.

8

October 1924

ABIGAIL HURRIED ALONG THE LENGTH OF THE ESPLA-nade, passing trellised lemon trees and sculpted rose-bushes. A profusion of brightly tinted blossoms fanned out in all directions: a yellow as fat as ripened corn and a red as shimmery as blood. The scent of each flower was different, too: the peach-hued blooms smelled spicy; the white petals were candy-sweet; while the rare tangerine-tinged buds reminded Abigail of cinnamon cookies cooling on a windowsill.

She wished she could stop and sit on one of Mr. Hearst's many marble garden benches and just enjoy the place, but she knew she didn't have time. Tomorrow all the guests were arriving, and by her own count, Abigail had at least 5 million chores left to do.

She almost ran up the white and pebble-strewn path, her long, brown curls blowing backward in the sunny wind, and the discreet mauve print of her Liberty of London dress sliding over her lithe, tanned legs. She was all motion, all brisk determination; even the strands of her seed-pearl choker seemed energized into action.

"Slow down, Miss Abigail! This ain't no fire, you know," Nigel Keep, the head gardener, called out as she passed, but Nigel was one to talk. He and his team of undergardeners were forever dynamiting elephant-size holes in the ground—and then burying the roots of full-grown trees.

"If Mr. Hearst wants a full-fledged arboretum here, it's up to me to make it happen," Nigel's craggy, sun-burned face yelled almost daily while he pushed his crew toward newer and more improbable tasks. "No amount of reasoning's going to stop him. You might as well face facts, Miss Abigail. Mr. Hearst's a driven man. And he's not a patient one, neither.

"He brought an entire shipment of mature trees down here from an estate near San Francisco. Shipped directly to his private dock, they were. Me and the boys had a devil of a time carting them up that misera-ble five miles of winding drive.

"Had to use chain-driven Mack trucks; and even then the damn things slipped backwards. Each root ball weighed several tons. Felt like we were back in the days of the pharaohs, I can tell you. Excepting for the whips and slaves.

"And that live oak he wanted moved eight feet? The one in front of A House—Casa del Mar? The tree that had the nerve to knock off his hat one day? Well, don't get me started on that miserable job. We had to build a concrete tub to transport that gnarled old beauty."

Abigail grinned at the recollection. Who would have thought I'd end up here? she wondered. "Private sec-retary to Miss Marion Davies" sounded so refined when I applied for the job, but here I am in the midst of all this hurly-burly: masons, carpenters, painters, bricklayers, specialists in gilding and fresco work. Sometimes I feel I'm in the middle of one of those film sets D. W. Griffith constructs—Babylon in all its splendor!

"Watch out behind you, Miss Abigail!"

A huge wooden crate was wheeled past. It was followed by another, then a third and fourth and fifth. The carts' thick wheels scrunched along the pebbly path; when they were out of sight, the noise continued to rumble backward. Even the earth seemed to shake.

Abigail guessed the boxes contained the limestone surrounds of the enormous fireplace in the Refectory. The mantel was a full twenty-seven feet tall and had been purchased from a destitute French family, who, in a fit of ancestral pride, had eradicated the coat of arms before allowing the upstart American to ship it home.

Even without its regal crest, the fireplace created a medieval air in a room that already seemed haunted by long-dead knights and priests and princes. Dinner parties at the Refectory's long table should have had troubadours installed in the musicians' gallery and ceremonial trumpets heralding the guests to their banquet.

The gallery had seen its share of modern performers, though. Marion liked to chuckle about the many times Al Jolson had slipped up the hidden stone steps and belted out his signature tune "Mammy" to the startled throng. Of course, Abigail had never seen that exciting spectacle; she'd only been at San Simeon two weeks, and this was her first full-scale party.

"Guests!" Abigail forced her thoughts back to the work at hand. "I've got to find Marion and go over these room assignments. This weekend's got to be perfect!"

She sprinted up the steps that curved around the Egyptian Fountain: four enormous black granite sculptures representing the lion-head deity, Sekhmet. The seated female figures were the oldest members of Mr. Hearst's collection. Their stares were impassive, although Abigail secretly wondered what the goddesses were thinking as they surveyed the California countryside after their countless centuries in Egypt.

But she didn't have time for further reflection because by now she was on the majestic Main Terrace, and suddenly there it was: Casa Grande! No matter how many times Abigail had hurried along this same path or flew up any of the connecting garden walks, the sight of the main house filled her with awe. The imposing facade with its twin towers and vast entry door, with its fierce "wild men" Gothic statuary, its heraldic beasts, limestone gargoyles, escutcheons, half-columns, and its myriad of Italian, French, and Spanish windows was an architectural wonder.

The building reminded Abigail of photographs she'd seen of European cathedrals where the styles had changed over the centuries as additions were made or the old parts reworked. There was no doubt about it: Mr. Hearst was creating a masterpiece—one of the wonders of the modern world.

Scaffolding on the twin towers had recently been removed, but the hammering, sawing, scraping, and tumbled orders spilling from the mansion's rear wings nearly muted other noise. But not quite. Work on the Neptune Pool was taking precedence today.

"Tomorrow!" Abigail almost wailed. "Tomorrow everyone's arriving! Mr. and Mrs. Chaplin and Mr. Lubitsch and Mr. and Mrs. Fairbanks and everyone! Oh, gosh, I still have so much to do!"

With her light, strong feet tapping across the Main Terrace, Abigail fairly flew.

When she found her boss and the Chief, they were on the North Terrace and engaged in a conversation she devoutly wished she'd never interrupted. But with all the shouts and creaks emanating upward from the Neptune Pool, she was beside her employers before she realized her mistake.

Hammers and tongs rattled the air; masonry saws whined through marble and limestone; drills hacked apart concrete; a derrick dangled a full-grown cypress tree over a recently dynamited hole; while clouds of marble dust billowed skyward, covering the workers' faces, arms, and backs in a pall of purest white.

"But I don't want to wear my sweater! Honest, Popsie! I'm not cold!" Marion's stammer had the singsong stubbornness of a five-year-old, and her blue eyes were drawn into stormy slits.

Abigail stood stock-still, a faraway smile fixed on her face, and a noncommittal haze guarding her eyes. Her brown curls fell silent; her patterned skirt ceased rippling; even the gentle glow of her necklace seemed to check itself. During her brief employ at San Simeon, Abigail had become adept at playing statue.

"Look! Abigail's not wearing a wrap, and you don't say boo about her!" The tone had turned petulant, although Abigail could hear cold fury within the words—and the rage wasn't directed exclusively at "Popsie."

Abigail held her breath while Marion scuffed at the marble tiles lining the North Terrace. Her white plimsolls kicked a plume of dust over the man-tailored trousers the Chief liked his mistress to wear. Marion's shoes slapped the tiles again, raising another cloud of grit.

"I guess you think Abigail's grown-up enough to make her own decisions. Little Miss Prim and Proper! Little Miss Finishing School Education!"

Abigail hoped Marion wouldn't choose this particular moment to have one of her "jealousy attacks"—

not outside with an army of stonemasons, carpenters, and gardeners keeping watch. And not within such close proximity to starchy old Miss Morgan, either.

Abigail realized that petite but redoubtable lady would be bustling up the esplanade's broad steps any moment. She'd have her newest architectural drawings clenched in one hand and a question perched on her resolute lips. Responsible for much of the rebuilding of San Francisco following the devastating earthquake of 1906, Julia Morgan was impatient with "lesser intellects."

William Randolph Hearst was the only mortal she considered her equal. He was her employer and patron saint rolled into one, the sole creature on San Simeon's high hill who actually made her smile. Oh, maybe Thaddeus Jay, her assistant and chief draftsman, but that was a very different relationship. Thaddeus reported to Miss Morgan, as did every other artisan on the site. The tiny woman with her stern tweed suits, shapeless slouch hats, and owlish eyeglasses ruled the lives of a good many men.

But Marion was beyond Miss Morgan's jurisdiction, and by extension, the film star's secretary. Marion and Abigail could dawdle the afternoon away while Mr. Hearst and his architect dreamed up some new and impossibly lavish scheme for Julia's staff to execute.

That's what the two of them were doing now, in fact, tearing apart a perfectly lovely swimming pool and replacing it with a larger and far more costly one—and all because Mr. Hearst had purchased a Roman temple with statues of Neptune and his steeds carved into the pediment.

Of course, the swimming pool with its elaborate heating system was the last to face new construction, and time was running dangerously low. Mr. Hearst liked providing Marion's visiting Hollywood friends with all sorts of improbable luxuries. He loved hearing the golden girls and boys ooh and aah when he showed them around.

But now everything had to be finished extra fast because tomorrow Marion was staging another "week-end extravaganza" and a whole slew of motion-picture stars would be arriving in Mr. Hearst's private fleet of Cadillac limousines. The stonemasons, carpenters, gardeners, and painters would work the whole night through, if need be. And Julia Morgan would be there urging them on. No feat was impossible when Mr. Hearst commanded.

"Please, Popsie-Wopsie! I don't want to wear a sweater. I'm not going to take a chill. Honest!"

Marion's voice had become a little-girl wheedle; she puckered her glossy red lips and crinkled the corners of her enormous blue eyes. Abigail knew the Chief would momentarily capitulate; that particular behavior drove him crazy with joy.

Marion reached up and ruffled the shaggy, white head for good measure; and the old man froze, blinking down at his bouncy mistress, allowing her to run her fingers over his hair and dip them behind his out-size ears. The picture was that of an aging circus bear transfixed in the arced light of center ring. A muzzle was in place, and maybe a funny felt hat, but rip away the steel imprisoning the long-toothed snout and let the five-inch claws do more than entertain kiddies, and the monster could turn lethal in a second.

"Him's got all sloppy," Marion purred. "Him's got to have his Marion fix him up!"

Abigail wished she could tiptoe away, but she knew the movement would attract attention. Instead she clasped her competent fingers in a pose of duty and respect and waited.

"I'll sit on your lap when we go inside."

"Whatever you say, Marion." The squeaky voice was breathy with desire. For a moment, Hearst and his mistress were lost in their secret world. Even the creation of San Simeon disappeared. "But you'll have to wear your sweater."

"And nothing else?" Marion's giggle was raucous and lewd; she winked in her secretary's direction, but Abigail didn't dare blink back. "What would those olden-days nuns have thought of that nasty idea? The ones that said their prayers behind those big black doors in my room?"

"Hush, Marion. You're a very naughty girl." A decidedly priggish tone had entered the Chief's voice; he shot a furtive glance in Abigail's direction as if he believed he could disguise his relationship with his mistress.

"Tell me how bad I am, Popsie."

"Hush now, Marion. Remember, we're not alone."

Abigail looked away, shut her eyes briefly, and for some inexplicable reason thought about mosquitoes. The memory was from childhood—a penniless but upper-crust girl whose immediate family had come apart at the seams. One day there'd been the three of them: mother, father, and eleven-year-old daughter; the next, the family had been reduced to a grieving widower and his very perplexed child. Then the burden of parenthood, or living itself, had taken its toll; Abigail was orphaned before she turned twelve.

One grudging relation after another had taken on "the child," insisting that a Kinsolving must have "decent manners if nothing else." Pennsylvania to New Hampshire with two stops in Rhode Island for good measure: the cycle of adoptive homes and schools had spiraled downward, but the insistent whisper of the mosquitoes remained—reminders of summers that had never been as free or glorious as they might.

Finally, Abigail Kinsolving had entered the world on her own; an aborted finishing-school education, a choker of seed pearls, and two pairs of white cotton gloves completed her résumé. Apparently, those sparse attributes had satisfied Mr. Hearst.

"Well, what do you think of my new swimming pool, Marion?" W.R. had removed Marion's curly head from his breast, but the two continued to stand so close they appeared intertwined.

"Oh, I like it, Pops! I like it fine! It's looking just swell! All those Roman statues and everything. Don't you agree, Abigail?" Sure in her position as mistress of W.R.'s house and heart, Marion burbled her famous warmth, and Abigail smiled in spite of herself.

One blond and compact, the other taller and decidedly dark, the two women seemed unlikely compatriots or friends. Marion's twenty-seven years were worn with the casual world-weariness of her Ziegfeld Follies days; Abigail's twenty-three seemed naive by comparison. Marion had taught her companion a lesson or two. The first was "Don't take any guff from people you don't like"; the second, "There's no such place as easy street."

At that moment Julia Morgan hurried up the steps. Framed by her long, old-fashioned skirt, her dowdy jacket, high-buttoned blouse, her sketch pad, notebook, a sheaf of rolled drawings, and an umbrella to ward off the sun's sly rays, the woman seemed the quintessential boarding-school matron.

"Mr. Hearst—a word, please!" Urgency wasn't a tone of voice where Julia Morgan was concerned. It was a way of life.

"It's looking grand, Julia. Simply grand . . . although, I'm still not convinced we've got Casa Grande's towers right . . . there's something a little 'off' about them both."

W.R. didn't like direct answers; they weren't compatible with his sense of power. When a question was put forth by one of his minions, his own secretary, Joe Willicombe, say, or John Francis Neylan, Hearst's right-hand man in all business and publishing deals, the Chief hedged his bets by discussing seemingly random details until the time was right to pounce.

But Julia Morgan was aware of her benefactor's quirks. She had to be. She'd been working on San Simeon since its inception. Construction was begun, then the plans were changed. The pool itself had gone through more metamorphoses than she cared to count: drawings altered, foundations redug, concrete hacked apart and repoured—and now the Chief was casting his critical eye on the main house's twin towers! And just after the scaffolding had finally been disassembled!

Julia decided to dodge that problematic question. "I don't know if I can have the pool reopened in time for tomorrow's onslaught." Marion's motion-picture cronies were treated with contempt by the lady who'd been the first female to graduate from the École des Beaux-Arts in Paris. "The statuary is finally in position as are the colonnades, but the rest is out of my hands."

"Oh, but it has to be ready!" Marion turned a dismayed face from Julia Morgan to the aging W.R. "Pretty please, Pops!" The stammer reappeared; the word Pops sounded like a baby's first effort at speech.

"Well, of course, it's going to be ready, Marion. I know you want everything nice for your friends. That funny fellow Charlie Chaplin's coming up again, isn't he? And that pretty, pregnant little wife of his?" W.R.

might as well have been dangling a peppermint stick in front of an unhappy child.

"Incie's coming, too, Pops . . . and Greta and Jack and Doug and Mary and everybody! I just know they'll want to take a dip. The hill is so darn hot this October, and the beach is too far away. Besides, you promised!" Marion was so upset she could barely get the words out; nearly every consonant was a tangle of stammered repetition.

W.R. smiled indulgently while his mistress struggled with her recalcitrant tongue. "There you are, Miss Morgan," he announced. "Marion has spoken."

Julia Morgan glared. The look would have frozen water, but Abigail doubted Marion noticed. Another of the film star's mottoes was "Don't give a fluff about what people think. Or what they say."

"I'll see what can be done, Mr. Hearst. If you'd remember to pay your outstanding bills, perhaps this new construction could have occurred in a more timely fashion."

The gauntlet was down, but W.R. refused to accept the challenge. "Very good, Julia! You got me with that one!" His wide belly shook with laughter, and his leathery face creased itself into a beatific grin. "Got to remember my creditors. Got to take care of the little guy." The private joke almost knocked him flat, then he returned to business with a speed so startling it seemed as if the jovial host had been replaced by another man.

"By the way, Julia, did that ceiling from the Zagal Palace in Spain arrive intact? I told the dealers I wanted it shipped directly from Madrid to my warehouses here. No more needless stopovers in New York."

"The acquisition Arthur Byne and his wife were brokering?"

Marion fiddled during this exchange. It wasn't a discussion of antiquities that bothered her; it was the names of Arthur and Mildred Byne. They were collectors and art dealers, a scholarly couple W.R. depended upon. He'd used their services as long as Marion could remember, ordering up pieces of Spanish castles and monasteries, portraits, statues, altar screens—all sorts of expensive objects. The trouble was that the Bynes were married, and they served as a continual reminder that Marion was doomed to remain single. At least as long as the socially acceptable Millicent Hearst had her way.

"I haven't had time to check them myself, sir," Julia continued. "But I can leave the construction site and drive down to the warehouses immediately. You have well over a thousand crates stored there, but I'd recognize any newcomers instantly." The tone was newly meek, and the squirrel-bright eyes gentle. "Besides, I'm equally anxious to see that handsome ceiling. Thaddeus's recent drawings have precisely the appearance you and I have been searching for. Installed in Casa Grande, the alternating panels of pale green and gold will create a magnificent vision—"

"Miss Davies," Abigail cautiously interrupted, "about tomorrow. Who do you wish me to house in Casa del Monte—and who in Casa del Mar and del Sol?"

But Marion wasn't listening; her eyes were on the distant hills, and her thoughts had traveled with them. Something wet shivered on her cheeks, perspiration, perhaps, or a splash of fountain water. Abigail knew she'd have to wait.

That was the morning's last moment of peace, because John Francis Neylan chose that particular second to hurry to his Chief's side.

"Abe Lincoln with offices on Wall Street," someone had once quipped, and the description stuck. The only man ever to dare criticize the Chief, the former *San Francisco Bulletin* reporter turned personal attorney was scarecrow tall, and his long face had the word *conservative* stamped all over it.

It was rumored Neylan thought five times before he opened his mouth, and he rarely appeared without a charcoal-gray suit or somberly striped necktie. Urged to go horseback riding with his boss, or shooting or fishing or some other outdoor activity, Neylan's response was to exchange the dark gray gabardine for brown. He never went so far as to don twill riding breeches or a leather-patched hunting jacket, although once in a great while he might attempt a tattersall huntsman's cap. The result inevitably failed.

Marion believed Neylan slept in gray pajamas tailored to resemble a business suit, and she'd confided her suspicions to Pops. The idea had made him roar with laughter, but then Marion was good at tickling his funny bone. And her jealousy over Neylan was almost as comical as her jests. Marion could get as cantankerous as a dislodged snake when complaining about John Francis Neylan. W.R. would tease her till his belly shook. The Chief liked to keep his worshipers off guard.

With Neylan were the two Muller brothers, Karl and Freddie. The Mullers tried to emulate their older and more illustrious companion, although their twin suits were a shoddy navy blue. The Mullers had originally been Chicago boys, but they'd run afoul of the law during that city's "distribution wars"—a pitched battle in which pathetically young newsboys had been beaten and killed.

Charged with using "excessive" force (.45-caliber pistols, to be precise) in insuring Hearst's *Chicago*

American made it to the top of the heap, Karl and Friederich had needed a respite from the Windy City's judicial system, and their employer had decided San Simeon was an excellent retreat.

Like Neylan, Karl and Freddie were city folk. They favored dark jackets with lots of padding; they were as out of place among the balmy palm fronds dotting San Simeon's gardens as a pair of white Maltese puppies in a dank back alley.

The Mullers gave Marion the creeps, and she'd allowed as much to Abigail. Her words had been decisive: "Those boys are nothing but two-bit hoods. They're cheesier than the private dicks Pops hired to tail me once upon a time in New York City. The sooner they slink back to the stockyards, the easier this girl's going to breathe." On that instance, Abigail hadn't bothered to correct her boss's wayward vocabulary.

"Good morning, Marion." Neylan's sonorous speech remained studiously polite when speaking to his boss's mistress, although Abigail heard irony weighing down each syllable. "Miss Morgan. Abigail. Good morning to you, ladies."

"Good morning, Mr. Neylan," Abigail responded hesitantly. She knew she was balancing a narrow line. By being overly polite to Neylan, she'd incur Marion's wrath; by ignoring him, she'd make a more dangerous enemy.

"Chief, I have a few questions about your acquisition of the *San Antonio Light*. The former management isn't terribly happy." Neylan never beat around the bush when it came to business. He assumed the rest of the world was on his wavelength. "And there've been additional problems with Horace Glendenning."

Neylan's hollow cheeks looked as gray as granite while the Chief burst out with a healthy chortle.

"What's that young fellow griping about now?"

"You, sir. And this time I believe he means to publish his criticism."

"A woman scorned . . . How does that adage go, Neylan? You know the one I mean . . . hell and vengeance and all that biblical bunk. These idiot reporters don't know a good thing when they've got it. Glendenning isn't the first of his breed, and I doubt he'll be the last. I expect to be attacked as long as the world produces its share of spiteful men.

"Like that damned Ambrose Bierce. I gave him a fine job when I started out. Money and more flexibility than the fool deserved. But I wanted my editorial staff satisfied, and I had the cash to indulge their whims. Some of those fellows were real souses, but I never criticized. Just sent them home to sleep it off.

"That was when I owned only one newspaper, the *San Francisco Examiner.* Bierce was a real swashbuckler in those days; he could create or destroy a political career with the stroke of his pen. Carried a pistol on account of the threats."

The Chief had begun warming to his reminiscences. Wasn't he the man who'd entered the world of publishing and immediately outstripped the competition? Hadn't he declared "newspapers are the greatest force in civilization," that they "control legislation and declare wars"? And hadn't his words paid off in spades?

"Why, you know, I'll never forget my first meeting with 'Bitter' Bierce. I was nothing but a pup, back then . . . in my twenties, don't you know. . . . Well, I marched out to his house and banged on the door. I needed his brand of rabble-rousing on the *Examiner* staff.

"So I rattled the door and the great man appeared. Told him I was from the *Examiner,* and he looks me over and demands, 'You were sent by Mr. Hearst?' 'I *am* Mr. Hearst,' I crow back, and that sealed our bargain—till the day I couldn't stomach his meanness anymore. . . . Guess he hated me as much as I hated him. Course, he's no longer around to vent his spleen."

W.R. laughed louder, although this time the sound had a peculiar hollowness. It reminded Abigail of a pebble falling into a black and bottomless well. The journalist Ambrose Bierce had "vanished" in Mexico; there had been rumors he'd run afoul of "revolutionaries," but no body had been recovered, nor had any group claimed a blow against "Yankee imperialism." Abigail carefully shifted her weight from one foot to the other; she scarcely dared breathe.

"Horace Glendenning intends to excoriate your business practices as well as your political ambitions, Chief," the judicial Neylan continued. His delivery was unhurried. He was accustomed to analyzing problems until the solution became obvious. "He's threatening to rehash the difficulties you had with Al Smith and the Democratic Party—certain 'favors' you did for the Tammany mob. Claims he'd resisted exposing you out of deference to your mother's memory, but feels the time is now ripe."

The mention of W.R.'s beloved mother, Phoebe, made him stiffen momentarily. Neylan saw the reaction and so did Marion. Abigail watched her boss absorb the information. The ex-showgirl's sapphire eyes were anything but sympathetic; she hated to be supplanted—especially by a dead woman.

"Let him," the Chief growled. "Let him run to *The New York Times* if he wants. It's been done before. Hell, Al Smith, himself, was behind one of those scurrilous attacks. What tripe did the *Times* print then? Do you remember, Jack?"

Neylan did, of course. He remembered everything

that concerned his boss: who was managing editor of each of Hearst's twenty-two dailies and fifteen Sunday newspapers, what the circulation was, how many employees were collecting salaries—and which enemy was likeliest to attack. But he chose not to tip his hand.

"Glendenning is claiming you used the press to further your presidential aspirations and, when that dream failed, you retreated to San Simeon. He's also questioning your patriotism during the war, insisting you were pro-German. He also sent this. It arrived this morning. I think you'll recognize the source."

Reluctantly, Neylan handed over a wrinkled page of newsprint. Abigail was certain W.R. had seen the cartoon and accompanying editorial before, but he read each word as if confronting it for the first time. The drawing depicted an unfurling American flag out of which protruded a reptilian creature with a big-eared, Hearst-like face. The caption read, "Curled in our sacred flag—Herrr Hearssssst," while the article stated that the "pro-German Mr. Wurrsst" should be "burned in effigy."

Hearst didn't speak, and neither did anyone else. They stared into the distance or at the ground or their feet and waited. Finally, the great man opened his mouth:

"Let Horace Glendenning say what he chooses." A steel crowbar lying on icy turf would have been warmer than these words. Abigail felt an involuntary chill slip down her spine.

"He's unimportant, Neylan. An impotent, pathetic runt. Men like him turn my stomach." The rage in Hearst's voice was so subtle, the uninitiated might have mistaken it for reason, but not one member of this group would have made that error.

"You get my drift, Jack? I no longer wish to hear Horace Glendenning's name!"

Neylan knew better than to answer, but Marion was well equipped for these scenes. "Cut off his doodads!" she announced. "That's what I'd do if I was you, Popsie." The mood on the terrace changed instantaneously.

"Ouch!" W.R. chuckled, then added immediately, "Now, Jack, what do you think of my Neptune Pool?"

The gnatlike voice was back on track. As far as the Chief was concerned, ex-employee Glendenning had ceased to exist. Abigail wondered if, like "Bitter" Bierce, this new thorn in the Chief's side would wind up missing and presumed dead in Mexico.

"I think it's costing you a good deal of money, sir."

"That's all you ever see, Jacko." Hearst's laugh had become self-satisfied and relaxed. "Not that I don't respect you, but you've got to let your soul loose once in a while. Long after we're gone, San Simeon will remain."

With that, conversation ended. The lord of San Simeon gave a brief and imperious wave to the workers scuttling over the Neptune Temple's scaffolding, then clapped Neylan on the back in a gesture at once shy and domineering.

"Make sure the pool's operative by tomorrow afternoon, Julia. I don't want to see Marion disappointed." Then the Chief turned from the group and strode toward Casa Grande with Neylan and the Mullers gliding behind like evening shadows. Julia Morgan hustled away, and Abigail and Marion were left alone.

The air grew still; the noise of construction seemed to cease; the birds didn't chirp or the lizards scurry over the path. The lack of movement was so disconcerting, Abigail felt as if she'd been thrust into the eye of a hurricane.

"Should I put Mr. Lubitsch in Casa del Monte with the Chaplins?" she began. "And should Mr. Ince and his guest share quarters with Mr. and Mrs. Fairbanks?"

Whether it was the mention of Mrs. Douglas Fairbanks—Mary Pickford, "America's Sweetheart" and Marion's rival—or whether the source was more complex, Marion lashed out at her secretary with astonishing venom.

"You know what to do, little Miss Prim and Proper! We've been through this goddamn drill before. Why the hell do you keep these prissy lists if you come crying to me every second? I've lived on my own hook since I was in my teens, and I didn't go whining about it, neither. If it weren't for Pops, you'd be history, my girl. You'd be minced-up dog meat! And don't you ever forget it!"

9

ABIGAIL WOKE WITH A LURCHING START. HER BED shook with the violence of her movement, and she stared around her tower bedroom trying to remember where she was—and what had disturbed her sleep. Patches of sickly moonlight meandered across the stone walls; alternately imprisoned and released by a fickle covering of clouds, the pale shadows jounced over the low beamed ceiling and into the corners, creating an illusion of automobile headlamps spinning circles in the courtyard below.

Are they here already? Abigail wondered, then told herself, No, Marion's guests don't arrive until tomorrow. And even when they do appear, they won't be racing limousines up the garden path.

She slipped out of bed and walked to the window. Unlike Marion's suite or W.R.'s rooms or the compound's many guest quarters, Abigail's bedroom was spartan in its furnishings: one department-store twin bed, ditto one chest of drawers, a nightstand and a lamp with a buff-colored parchment shade, a sturdy ladder-back chair, and a table that doubled as a desk.

On first viewing her San Simeon home, Abigail had been surprised at the similarities between it and a college freshman dorm.

The single window didn't match the room's boxlike simplicity. The design was Gothic with two high-pointed arches and a crescendo of loops and vine leaves chiseled into the gray stone. The window was a copy of an original on a lower floor, and the carving had been distressed to bear the traces of age.

Abigail considered the replication perfect, although she wished she had its ancient mate instead. She thought she'd enjoy leaning against the mullions of an artifact that had existed in fourteenth-century France. She imagined the stone might have a few wicked secrets to share.

All at once, a terrible screech ripped the night, and Abigail jumped backward involuntarily. The howl was followed by another and more fearsome one, and then by something that sounded like a roar.

"Mr. Hearst's new panther," Abigail whispered, forcing herself back to the window.

The panther was the most recent addition to San Simeon's private zoo; he'd been living in his concrete-walled cage on the hilltop only slightly longer than Abigail had been ensconced in her third-floor room of the servants' wing.

Suddenly, the panther's bellowing snarl was accompanied by a prolonged shriek of the zoo's solitary mountain lion, which was then joined by the bugling yip of penned coyotes.

Abigail gave an involuntary shudder, but remained at the window. She wondered how the black bear was faring with all the racket. Whenever she visited the newly constructed cages, he seemed the saddest creature of the lot, snuffling at the barren concrete walls and pawing the sterile floor. Loneliness seemed to hang around his dusty head, and a sense of longing for the wild places he'd never roam again. The zoo pens were within walking distance of the house, but Abigail visited as little as possible—and then only as a guide for Marion's guests, although Mr. Hearst usually took those duties himself.

The zoo was one of the Chief's greatest pleasures, and he enjoyed pointing out the native species along with his more exotic specimens. He liked boasting that the mountain lion, bear, and coyotes were all local residents, creatures you might spot if you went for a horseback ride in the hills.

After displaying the predators' cages and giving strict warnings—"No one's allowed to tease my animals. They have right of way at San Simeon. Anybody bothering them gets thrown out on the spot!"—W.R. would pile his guests into touring cars, and they'd rumble down the long drive to admire his zebras, Barbary sheep, kangaroos, llamas, fallow deer, pronghorn antelope, great-horned elk, emus, ostriches, and his latest pets: forty head of lumbering, brown bison.

"Cost me one thousand dollars each!" Mr. Hearst would yell above the clamor of car engines and squealing surprise. He liked throwing around big figures like that. He loved the responses he received from some of Marion's younger actress friends.

Abigail listened as the unhappy panther roared again, then all at once, she was aware of noise closer to home: footsteps thundering down Case Grande's curved staircase, the slap of new leather hitting the stone steps and then bouncing across the carved-block walls. The Muller boys were on the move.

There were words after that, a garbled frenzy of orders that Abigail only partially heard.

"No, the guards have no idea how he snuck past the checkpoint."

"Do you mean to tell me that with all of Mr. Hearst's extensive security . . . ?" This was Joe Willicombe, the Chief's private secretary, the man who controlled San Simeon's many underlings.

"Look, boss, I'm just reporting the facts."

Then there was quiet as if a huddled conference were taking place. Abigail imagined bodies bent forward, the glare of the electrified Renaissance torches tossing bladelike shadows over the stairwell and across the worried backs. Karl and Freddie's dark jackets would sop up the light like desk blotters soaking up ink.

"Well, we've got to catch the goon before the Chief finds out. . . . This time it might be something really nasty."

Abigail recognized their consternation. W.R.'s provocative editorial policies had garnered a good many enemies. She'd been warned about possible attempts on his life when she'd first taken the job.

"You mean like a murder—"

But the conspirators were interrupted before they could finalize a plan. W.R.'s voice broke in upon them. "*Political assassination* might be a better term." Like his outburst on the North Terrace earlier that day, the Chief began his remarks with deceptive calm.

A scurry of nervous answers greeted the lord of San Simeon. Abigail heard apologies, excuses, and a confusing jumble of subterfuge. The Muller brothers' and Joe Willicombe's words tumbled over each other in an effort to save face.

"I see, boys," the Chief finally announced. "At least I see what you're trying to tell me. But I still don't understand why you three gentlemen are pussyfooting around here. It seems to me the time would be better spent searching the grounds. That is, if you intend to apprehend this unwanted guest." Abigail could picture the icy smile that would accompany this statement; W.R.'s expression would have all the benevolence of a cobra about to strike:

"And furthermore, gentlemen, I suggest that your several means of livelihood may be in serious jeopardy if you fail to find the interloper!"

The three employees bolted from the stairwell and banged out a side door. Abigail heard silence echo inward as the last massive teak panel sealed out a turbulent night. For a moment, the house was eerily still, then the ponderous rumblings of an old man in love with his home began creaking through the dark. Lights were switched on, and window latches tested. Abigail listened as a series of metallic clicks moved deeper into the house.

"Where's my mousie?" she finally heard W.R. croon softly in the semidark. "Where's my little mousie who lives inside the flowerpot? I've brought you your special evening treat. But don't you dare tell Marion."

Why would anyone feed mice? Abigail wondered. Especially inside a house?

The next morning was as fair as any California could offer. It was cloudless and mild and spectacularly blue. Abigail stood at her window, reveling in the beauty of the sight. The view was as integral to San Simeon as the statuary and gardens—as if Mr. Hearst had ordered up the picture specially, a pretty composition for his castle windows to frame: cobalt ocean, sagebrush hills, and in the foreground vibrant splashes of color surrounded by a dense and liquid green.

"Got to shake a leg," Abigail reminded herself while she dragged her sleepy body away from the window. "Today Marion's guests arrive. It's my chance to finally prove I'm worth my keep!"

Marion was ensconced in her suite in Casa Grande, and in a far better mood than she'd been the evening before. In fact, she was almost too cheerful—a state of mind Abigail immediately noticed, and then, as rapidly, regretted. The room stank of alcohol despite the wide-open windows and sun-warmed breeze.

"Sweets!" Marion called the moment her secretary stepped into the sitting room. "The top o' the mornin' to my new right-hand gal!" This cozy epithet was followed by a succession of words like *Cutie pie! Hon!* and *Doll!* while Marion beamed woozily and beckoned her newest employee forward with expansive and overly rehearsed gestures. Abigail guessed her employer had been nipping at her secret bottle of bootleg gin for some time.

But Abigail was nothing if not determined, so she fixed a pleasant smile on her face, marched to the writing desk that had once graced a sixteenth-century Moorish castle, pulled out a fountain pen and sheaf of lined paper, and reminded herself that the secret to a successful career was acting the part.

"Oh, hon, I nearly forgot . . . what about the costumes?" Marion stammered, spinning around the room in a sudden daze of worry and dismay. Her blue eyes had turned violet with concern, and her marcelled hair sprang out in coils that seemed electrified by a case of hostess's nerves. "Did we get the costumes ready? I mean, in case some of my pals leave their fancy duds behind? 'Cause . . . I mean . . . Well, I sort of forgot . . . I've had so much on my mind the past couple of days."

"We took care of that problem earlier this week," Abigail answered with a reassuring nod, "and I reminded each visitor when I made the follow-up telephone calls. I pointed out the invitation stated Saturday's entertainment was to be a costume extravaganza. Your guests seemed quite excited, Miss Davies. I mentioned that you'd decided to keep the party small and intimate in order to make the competition more intense.

"And, yes, I did inform them that you have an extensive collection of additional disguises should the need arise, although I can't imagine anyone leaving their masquerade finery behind. . . . With the exception of Mr. Barrymore," Abigail added after a thoughtful moment while Marion continued to career around her antique-laden suite, yanking open a priceless seventeenth-century chest of drawers and then slamming it shut, knocking clothing from the chaise longue, even ransacking the satin sheets on her massive French Gothic bed, and peering behind her Renaissance jewel cabinet.

Abigail guessed her boss was hunting for another hidden bottle of booze, and she had a momentary impulse to ask if Marion needed help with the search, but then reminded herself that the offer might be considered an impertinence. Marion's excessive drinking was supposed to be a secret. Even Mr. Hearst usually pretended to ignore it.

Besides, the actress's threats from the afternoon before still smarted in Abigail's ears, and the fear of losing her job loomed terrifyingly real. There'd be no returning to those frosty New England relatives if she failed in California; her distant relations had been only too happy to rid themselves of a "girl" they deemed "too impecunious for marriage." Abigail was on her own.

"Oh, you shouldn't pay any attention to what John says, sweetie!" Marion said, laughing, although her mind was clearly elsewhere. "He can be such a lush sometimes! I swear! I've seen him more stewed than a potful of hot tomatoes!"

Abigail pinched her lips; she didn't know what the proper response to that particular quip might be. Instead she answered, "Mr. Barrymore complained that his filming schedule might not allow enough time to invent a costume, but he assured me that in that case he'd 'hornswoggle' one from Warner Brothers. He also suggested that he was bound to win any 'competition for fancy dress'—whether you chose to invite five hundred guests or fifteen."

"Typical John. All peacock and swagger," Marion snorted. "But I thought he'd do better than jazz some poor, little seamstress—though I guess they like having sex as much as the rest of us. I know I'd certainly hate to give it up."

Again, Abigail didn't dare open her mouth.

The day continued in the same crescendoing frenzy. Luncheon was served alfresco on the North Terrace, where the panicky construction of the day before had miraculously ceased. There wasn't a workman in sight; even Nigel Keep's stalwarts had been ordered elsewhere. San Simeon looked as though it had never been buffeted by a single storm.

The scaffolding on the Neptune Temple had vanished, and the water glistening in the pool below sent an azure reflection washing up over the Roman columns. The tint on the marble was as fragile as a robin's egg. Abigail wondered what had transpired with the mysterious prowler, but when the interloper wasn't mentioned, she began to wonder if she'd dreamt the midnight conversation.

The Chief appeared just in time to dine with Marion, although Julia's place remained empty as did Neylan's. The lovebirds were allowed to remain at peace today. Abigail tried to squeeze herself into an inconspicuous package. She stared at the damask-clothed table, at the prosaic paper napkins fluttering their waxy edges, at the ketchup bottles and mustard jars sitting defiantly among the silver and gilt of the serving dishes.

"So, like I was saying, Popsie, he told Doug he might fly his Spad up from Beverly Hills," Marion's slightly boozy gush of words broke Abigail's reverie.

"That's where I met him, you know . . . at Doug and Mary's. He was a pilot in the war . . . a member of the Lafayette Flying Corps. . . . Got heaps of decorations . . . came home with the cutest little limp . . . though I think he exaggerates whenever a pretty girl comes around." Marion hiccuped here, but then turned the involuntary sound into a smug, little giggle. Marion might as well have been preening in front of a mirror.

"I guess he thought I was that pretty girl. . . . Well, you know how these flier boys get when they see a film star."

"I was not aware you had visited the Fairbankses' house by yourself, Marion." W.R.'s voice was a monotone growl, but Marion obviously decided to ignore the threat. Her preluncheon snorts of "mother's milk" had left her feeling pretty cocky. She'd promised herself that nobody could order her around—and that included her Popsie.

"Oh, you know how it is, Pops! . . . Down there in Hollywood, I mean. . . . It was one of those days when we'd been filming late. . . . You know how things get with us working stiffs . . . 'all work and no play' and all that other hokum." Marion began creeping her fingers up her Popsie's herringbone jacket.

"I mean, shooting those photoplays can really be a

drag . . . those flickers are all baloney, you know, Pops, no matter which way you slice it.

"Anyways, I guess Doug must have sent out a general invitation to the studio . . . nothing special, you know." The childish fingers crept farther along W.R.'s woolly forearm.

"You never told me you'd gone to Pickfair alone," W.R. repeated. His tone turned steelier by the second, and he kept his arm rigidly motionless under Marion's silky caress. He'd obviously smelled the gin on his mistress's breath, but was biding his time.

Abigail wanted to look away, but a fascinated horror kept her glued to the scene. She wanted to warn her boss, but there was nothing a mere secretary could say.

Unaware of the trap she was laying for herself, Marion's fingers continued to tiptoe up her Popsie's tweed jacket, then she giggled seductively, batted her eyelashes, and rattled off the most audacious non sequitur Abigail had ever heard.

"So Bill . . . Bill Wellman's the fellow's name, Pops . . . Anyways, he told Dougie he might just fly up here and drop in on our fun and games . . . you know, this weekend when all the other kids are up here. . . . The head chef can handle an extra guest, don't you think, Popsie? Pretty please, Popsie-Wopsie-Wopsie?"

Popsie didn't say a word, but the muscles of his jaw grew as rigid as iron.

According to Marion's instructions, the servants flanked the main entry to Casa Grande, uniforms starched and smiles in place. She'd seen a photo of a similar welcome reproduced in a British magazine, and she wanted to replicate the grandeur of a country-house shooting party.

Arranged by Abigail's diagram, the head chef stood beside the assistant chef, who was in turn accompanied by the French pastry chef and the four cooks. The head butler, second butler, head housekeeper, and assistant housekeeper were trailed by three waiters, four maids, three houseboys, and the lowly members of the dishwashing staff. Even Mr. Hearst's valet had been forced to stand at attention.

Black gabardine and taffeta (the maids were in their formal evening costumes) contrasted with white pima cotton and lace-edged organza (the maids' dinner aprons) that had been boiled in starch and then ironed until each shirtfront, cap, or apron gleamed. There wasn't a hint of color among the group. Except the smiles, of course, and the round and rosy faces. Mr. Hearst paid decent wages; the ruddy smiles were genuine.

The assembled honor guard of household help heard the hum of the limousines first, the fleet of black Cadillacs that had carried the guests from Mr. Hearst's private railcar—on the train from Los Angeles to San Luis Obispo—then a cavalcade of gleaming automobiles motoring up the coast toward the pleasure dome of San Simeon.

The engines grew louder and a scrunch of rubber tires meeting pavement began interrupting the steady throb of the perfect motors. Then the tires took over, crushing pebbles and twigs and eucalyptus bark in their determined climb. Finally, the first attenuated hood swung slowly into view. The visitors had arrived.

10

"WELCOME, WELCOME, WELCOME!" MARION SHOUTED
to the world. She threw her arms wide and smiled so
broadly her teeth twinkled. Marion was delighted with
the entire universe.

"I'm glad to see all of you guys!" Only then did
she realize she was still in the man's trousers Pops
had chosen for her morning attire and not in the blue
crepe de Chine teadress she'd picked out for herself.
The discovery slowed her momentarily. She peered
into the first car to see if it contained Greta Garbo
and John Gilbert, but when Charlie and Lita Chaplin
stepped out, she knew she was safe. Pregnant Lita
looked as listless as a bowl of leftover soup.

"Charlie, my boy!" A big, lingering smooch on the
lips greeted her favorite. Marion wasn't permitted to
kiss her leading men when the studio cameras were
rolling. W.R. had decreed the habit "unsanitary" as
well as damaging to her reputation, so she took advantage of every "nondramatic" opportunity—at least
when Popsie wasn't looking.

"And little Lita. How nice." The hand Lita proffered

was damp and pudgy; the child hadn't lost her baby fat, and yet here she was about to produce a miniature Chaplin. Well, Charlie always liked them right out of nursery school, Marion told herself. Just the same as my Popsie. You can't teach an old wolf new tricks. Her joke made Marion laugh aloud.

"Thank you for inviting us, Miss Dav—I mean, Marion," Lita stammered, mistaking the cause of her hostess's good humor. "And thanks for your letter. Charlie read it to me."

Her husband gave her a quick jab in the ribs that made the girl blanch and spin around to search his face. Marion spotted this brief display of marital discord. Something's rotten in the state of Albuquerque, she decided. This is going to be one hell of a swell party!

"Abigail, here, will show you lovebirds to your suite. I've bunked you and John Barrymore and Doug and Mary in Casa del Monte—but you can call it B House; everybody does. I thought you married couples would be a good influence on John . . . especially Mary, she's so . . . so . . ."

"Angelic?" Chaplin said with the remnants of a cockney accent, then turned on his rogue's smile, instantaneously shifting character. The comedian became his alter ego: a satyr ogling a nymph instead of a humble do-gooder sacrificing all for the girl of his dreams. Without the mustache he used in his film roles, Chaplin's expression turned almost evil.

Fascinated, Abigail stared, but the metamorphosis vanished, leaving a proper gentleman dressed in a blue-and-white-striped jacket, white flannels, a straw boater, and gold-tipped cane. Wavy, graying hair added stature to a still-youthful face; Charlie Chaplin looked as harmless as an ex-Etonian attending a rowing regatta.

"Perfect!" Marion roared. "Mary Pickford . . . angelic! I wouldn't have been so nice!"

"You're a very naughty girl, Marion, my love," Chaplin said, beaming while he took her hand and raised it to his lips. "And that's why I adore you." Then he turned his considerable charm on his hostess's secretary, grabbing off his hat with one quick swoop and holding it over his heart.

"*Enchanté,* madame—or is it mademoiselle?"

Marion had warned Abigail about Chaplin. She'd declared that his reputation "with the ladies" wouldn't "suit a dog." That's why the weekend's sleeping arrangements were so complex. Charlie had once been jilted by Pola Negri, who was now involved with "Rudy" Valentino. Ernst Lubitsch had been Negri's director back in Germany ("Onstage as well as off," according to Marion, who had knowingly smiled), but then he'd been brought to Hollywood by Mary Pickford, who, in turn, had dumped him.

Then there was the famous British author Elinor Glyn and the actor John Gilbert and his most recent lady love, the mysterious newcomer Greta Garbo. The young Swede was already turning the film industry upside down, and she'd provoked a hornet's nest of envy. There were rumors she only slept with other women, and gossip that she was a man in disguise—while Glyn was bringing a female friend whose name on the invitation list was simply Principessa.

Marion had topped off this gossipy litany by describing some peculiar entanglement between Chaplin and Glyn, which had brought the hostess and her secretary back to where they'd started. Abigail prayed she could keep the stories straight.

"I'm very excited to meet you, Mr. Chaplin," she mumbled.

"Excited, dear child? How very flattering!"

"How about a little libation?" Marion came to the rescue, grabbing Chaplin's hand and slipping it through the crook of her arm. "Or a dip in the Neptune Pool? The water's toasty warm! Popsie doesn't want his little girl to get her tootsies cold!" Marion's stammer was a joyous gush of fits and starts that seemed no more troublesome than a hostess's case of nerves.

"Where is the old duffer?" Chaplin inquired, slipping his hat back on his head at a rakish angle.

"Oh, you know Pops. Hiding out in his office or someplace. Gets all jittery when you kids arrive. I swear! Sometimes he's as bashful as a little boy."

"Not in the bedroom, I hope." Charlie hooked his cane under Marion's wide trouser leg. "Little boys aren't my cup of tea. Unless, of course, they have lips like yours."

"Stop that!" Marion howled, laughing so hard she almost fell over. "That's dirty talk, Charlie boy, and you know it! You'd better not let my Pops hear you cozying up to me like that. Why, he'd have a hissy fit! Lips like mine!"

"And I know whereof I speak," Chaplin crooned. For a moment, these two had eyes only for each other; impervious to the other guests, they moved closer as if something physical were pushing them together.

"Please, Charlie!" Lita whispered. "Can't we go to our rooms now? I'm awful tired."

"The mother-to-be. How can I have forgotten?" Chaplin's tone suddenly turned scathing.

"I'd be happy to show Mrs. Chaplin to her quarters, sir," Abigail interceded. Then she took Lita's hand and gently led her away from Casa Grande's entrance.

Abigail knew everything about the couple's complicated history. Lillita with her sad, dark eyes and oval face was descended from the state's early Spanish settlers; she'd caught Chaplin's attention when she was only twelve, and he'd become so obsessed that he'd commissioned a large oil portrait—fittingly titled *The Age of Innocence*.

After several years of persistent wooing (with time out for Pola Negri) Charlie finally made her his wife and then his leading lady, but during filming of her first star role in *The Gold Rush*, Lita Grey had been replaced. She'd had the temerity to get pregnant. That's what Marion had said during one of the weekend's planning sessions. "Charlie'll stick it to you every time," she'd murmured, then added as an afterthought, "That's why I'm crazy about the son of a bitch." At the time, Abigail hadn't understood what her boss meant.

A trio of voices followed Abigail and Lita as they walked toward the red-tiled roof of Casa del Monte: Elinor Glyn with her authoritative British accent, a husky drawl that could only belong to Greta Garbo, and the lovelorn murmurs of John Gilbert.

Marion had said "Jack" had even tried committing suicide over the ingenue's seeming indifference. He'd thrown himself into the surf near Marion's beach house in Santa Monica, and a group of writers working on one of Marion's photoplays had pulled him out. Apparently, no one involved had taken the incident seriously.

"Do you like Greta Garbo?" Abigail asked while she and Lita moved along the rose walk. The path was surprisingly private despite the circus exploding in front of Casa Grande's main entrance. "Miss Garbo, I should say."

Abigail knew she was pumping Lita for information, but Louis B. Mayer's new discovery was all the rage, and Abigail only had Marion's conflicted tales. One moment her boss was full of awe, talking about "this . . . this mystery face, dead until the cameras start rolling, and then, oh, brother, what life!" while in the next breath she'd start grousing about "borrowed" bedroom slippers or some other infraction on the Metro lot:

"Greta Louisa Gustafsson . . . that phony-baloney Swedish princess! I don't know why Mr. Mayer dragged the bitch over here. But he'll get her number, and she'll be out on her snooty noggin!"

Marion's invective would range over every disturbance Greta had created. The sets at Metro-Goldwyn-Mayer were either too hot or too cold; she didn't like the toilets; she refused to rehearse; she hated visitors on the set, but insisted on "dropping in" on her fellow actresses—and she never had a kind word for their abilities. "I am artist," she'd intone with her rotten English. "The rest is nothing."

"From what I hear, Miss Garbo's pretty swell," Abigail tried again. "But Miss Davies and some of the more established stars . . . I guess they're not convinced yet . . . about Garbo, I mean."

"Oh, you can call her Greta when you're with me," was Lita's no-nonsense response. "I don't count for much, you know. I'm just a kid—at least that's what Charlie tells me.

"I hadn't met Greta till the train ride up here, so I guess I don't know her any better than you do. Charlie doesn't like me to go out in society nowadays. And . . . well . . . before all this happened"—Lita stared down at her belly with a bashful shrug—"he didn't like my 'mingling' with his acting buddies, either. He said it wasn't right . . . me being only fifteen, and all. He said actors were like hyenas, ready to snag the young ones from the flock. I'm sixteen now, so I guess that's why he let me come."

By now they'd reached the door to Guest House B.

Abigail knew she should hurry back to her duties, but she hated to leave Lita on her own. She seemed like a child tricked up in women's clothing. Despite her protruding belly, she'd been squeezed into a formfitting, cherry-colored dress. It was the kind of outfit only the most brazen flapper girl would wear. Abigail could tell Lita was scared to death—and it wasn't just her peculiar clothes.

"You and Mr. Chaplin have the guest room on the right," Abigail soothed, as much to assuage her own feelings of helplessness. "Miss Davies thought you'd like the pink satin. . . . These bells on the wall are to call the servants. This one summons beverages, the other's for food."

"Wowie. That's what Charlie said. 'Hot and cold running servants'—he says funny stuff like that all the time."

Abigail didn't know what to answer; her finishing-school education was no match for the young bride's problems. Instead Abigail bustled Lita around the suite, pointing out the view, the radio set, the private bath with its unheard-of novelty—a shower—and finally the clothes closet in the hall.

"It's a convenience Mr. Hearst invented. That way, if you have a gown to be cleaned or pressed, one of the maids can attend to it without disturbing your privacy."

"Boy, Marion sure got lucky when she hooked up with him!" Lita whispered.

As Abigail climbed the steps leading to the Main Terrace, the first words she heard were Marion's querulous "What do you mean he wasn't on the train?"

The answer was an inaudible hum. Probably delivered by the head chauffeur, it clearly bore no weight with the angry Marion.

"Well, he would have called if he was going to miss my party." The tone was so self-involved Marion seemed capable of forgetting her other guests.

Abigail rushed up the steps, bolting them two at a time, then stopped in her tracks and stared at the group clustered in front of Casa Grande. All these film stars strolling amid all this perfect, white statuary! Rudolph Valentino and Pola Negri, Greta Garbo and Jack Gilbert, John Barrymore, Douglas Fairbanks, and Mary Pickford! The sight was almost too fabulous to comprehend.

The ladies wore picture hats, transparent silks, and reed-thin, high-heeled shoes. The men were costumed in natty English hunting boots and tattersall plaids; they looked as though they anticipated riding to hounds. Abigail took a deep breath. These are ordinary people, she tried to convince herself, they're no different than I am; there's no point in being nervous. Repeating those futile phrases, Abigail stepped toward the group.

"Is anything wrong, Miss Davies?" The secretary's voice quavered despite her promise. She also blushed, snagged her skirt on a rose thorn, and then stumbled over a wayward pebble. "I mean, can I be of some assistance?" Abigail was certain her nose had turned rosy, and her earlobes crimson.

"Incie and Nell weren't on the train! At least this bozo didn't see them!"

"But Mr. Ince would have phoned, I'm sure, Miss Davies." Abigail struggled to find intelligible speech as she cast pleading glances in the chauffeur's direction. But the man merely held his cap against his tunic and stiffened his legs inside his jodhpur trousers. He resembled a mounted policeman who'd heard every complaint in the book.

"That's what I've been telling this dumb cluck! He

didn't look hard enough . . . and now all the Caddies are here on the mountain, and none of the drivers are waiting at the station in San Luis."

A buzz of concern greeted this news, and the other guests pressed closer—much to Abigail's chagrin. She was convinced every one of the celebrities was staring directly at her.

"I'm certain Tom was planning to come, darling Marion. I spoke to him three or four days ago, and he said he'd see me at San Simeon." This was John Barrymore speaking as he strode forward. John Barrymore! Abigail was certain she was going to keel over and die on the spot.

"Where the deuce is he then?" Marion's tone was streetwise tough, but the affectation didn't mask genuine anger. Abigail could feel two blue eyes boring into her neck. "Do you think somebody here goofed with the invites? Somebody hired to write them?"

"You mean your delightful handmaiden? I sincerely doubt it."

Then the great John Barrymore took Abigail's hand, and she was forced to look up into the most perfect face she'd ever seen. She blushed with renewed vigor; this time even her lips turned hot.

"Absolutely charming," Barrymore murmured while Abigail warned herself to keep breathing.

"Simply give him a ring, Marion." Elinor Glyn's advice burst in as she paraded toward her hostess. The famous author of the notorious *Three Weeks*—a novel banned in Boston and many towns in her native England—had masses of orange-red hair and skin as translucent as alabaster. She was also a good deal older than she appeared; facial treatments so painful the novelist's arms had to be strapped to her sides maintained an aura of dewy youth. As a young woman

Glyn had been considered a "great beauty," a fact she never forgot.

A lifetime of flaunting convention had made her an authority on love, marriage, and the potent, sexual magnetism she'd deemed "it"; with those tricky topics well in hand, Glyn had recently been hired to write a column for the Hearst newspapers.

"That's what I'd do under the circumstances, wouldn't I, Principessa? I'd simply telephone the man. There's no standing on ceremony these days."

The statuesque Principessa nodded agreement. Well over six feet tall, her long hair sculpted into fat, yellow waves, and her eyebrows painted in extravagant arches, Principessa was swathed in a Chinese-style red dress whose side slits rushed up her bare thighs. The silk looked as if an upholsterer had stitched it in place.

The neckline was high and tight, but where one enormous embroidered dragon crawled toward her heart, a large triangle was cut in the fabric, creating a dangerous décolleté. Each time Principessa bent down, her generous breasts threatened to come tumbling out:

"You should listen to Elinor, Marion." Principessa's accent was as far from Italian as chicken soup is from *zuppa di scaròla*. "What she says makes sense. Track the weasel down. No one wants to see you unhappy."

"I'm not calling Tom Ince," Marion retorted crankily. "He should have phoned me. Besides . . ." Marion stopped herself. Something more severe than Ince's callowness was bothering her.

"Personally, Marion darling," Barrymore interjected with his Shakespearean diction, "I believe the trouble was in bringing Nell. She's his wife, and we know what that means to Tommy Ince—at least I assume the ladies do!" Loud guffaws greeted this verdict, but Barrymore overrode the interruption. "Or perhaps the difficulty was that he didn't want to face your lord and master yet. I've heard the two are working on a hush-hush deal at Cosmopolitan Pictures . . . maybe our friend Tom's gotten cold feet. The so-called maker of stars is afraid of doing an honest day's work!"

"As if we all don't work our you-know-whats off!" Douglas Fairbanks chortled. "I certainly do. Look at those stunts I had to perform for *The Thief of Bagdad.* Just ask Mary!"

"We're not interested in your bedroom antics, Doug. Everyone knows you swing from chandeliers." Barrymore's jest caused the other stars to laugh loudly and gleefully.

"Booze!" Ernst Lubitsch shouted above the melee. His thick German accent turned the word into a jeer more suitable for an umpire during a baseball game.

"Boo!" the crowd joined in. "Boo to Tom Ince for standing us up!"

The renowned director from Berlin chomped his ubiquitous cigar and mangled a protest. "No, I say *booze* . . . drinking . . . schnapps . . . I am not criticizing . . ." The remainder of the sentence became a tangle of German with a smattering of French. Lubitsch's face turned pomegranate red as he searched for an English translation.

"Booze," he insisted, to louder laughter. "Hooch." His checkered jacket and plus fours became lumpy with exertion, and one woolly, brown knee sock curled crookedly across his calf. Then he began chortling at the mess he'd made.

"I'm not being no fashion plate," he admitted, "and that is the sad truth."

Mary Pickford, "America's Sweetheart," raised her delicate eyebrows and strolled toward the garden, her face suffused in a seemingly winsome smile.

"She's an Irish spitfire," Marion had once confided. "Started United Artists in 1919. Her and Doug, and Charlie and D. W. Griffith himself! That woman's got balls—and more dough than God! She fired Ernst Lubitsch, for pete's sake! What other actress has that kind of power? . . . And she did it in public, too."

Mary Pickford's girlish curls and heart-shaped face seemed to belie the iron-lady description, but Abigail trusted her boss. After all, Marion was a Hollywood veteran.

"Rudy, my love, *querido* . . . Rudolpho Alphonso Guglielmi di Valentino d'Antonguolla, what is everyone saying?" Pola Negri was murmuring. Abigail couldn't hear Valentino's response, but Negri's answer was vehement.

"So stupid! This Prohibition! In Berlin, in Bavarian Film days, we drink as much as we wish. The state don't dictate. The state is our friend."

Negri's vamp eyes flashed. Only Lubitsch would have ventured another opinion, but he wouldn't have crossed "Polita" for the world. His eyes swept longingly over her till they came to rest on the elegant Valentino. Then the director sighed a gloomy, Germanic moan while Negri tossed her sleek, black helmet of hair and coiled a sinuous hand across Valentino's arm. Pent-up energy quivered in her body; her screen-siren dress shook, and the gold beads covering the bronze brocade clattered noisily.

Principessa warbled a line from "How Ya Gonna Keep 'Em Down on the Farm," following it up with a raucous:

"Anybody feel like dancing? This kid's an ace at the Black Bottom! . . . John, honey? What do you say? You and me paired up swell that time in Pasadena," while Elinor Glyn moved close to her pet, whispering words Abigail thought sounded like "My Tigressa."

"Elinor," Chaplin chuckled, breaking up the tête-à-tête. "Did you bring your tiger-skin rug with you this time?"

"Of course, Charles." Elinor turned coquettish in an instant.

"And are they still repeating that dirty limerick about you in London-town?"

" 'Sinning with Elinor Glyn on a tiger skin'? I prefer to think of the poem as sensual, Charles."

Chaplin laughed indulgently. Glyn was clearly one of his "ladies," while Principessa appeared undecided as to which part she should play: Glyn's current lover or a conspiratorial female friend urging the novelist toward a weekend flirtation.

Abigail watched the interaction between the three, fascinated and a bit in awe. But if she'd expected a feud to break out between Chaplin and Principessa, she was wrong. The comedian's mercurial face was wreathed in a genuine smile, and so was Principessa's; in fact, the two seemed to be eyeing each other as possible bedmates, a novelty not lost on the triumphant Glyn.

"Darling Gritzko!" she then sang out dramatically, hurrying to John Gilbert's side and dragging him away from Garbo's magnetic aura.

"No, Jack," Abigail heard Garbo mumble in her Swedish accent. "I will not discuss. Not now. Not never." But by the time this brief speech was finished, Glyn had taken center stage with her newest prize. The actor's brooding face flushed and the saber-deep creases in his handsome cheeks intensified.

"Darling Jack played the cossack Gritzko in *His Hour*," Glyn announced, while her eyes consumed every inch of Gilbert's body. "A film adaptation of the sequel to *Three Weeks*. . . . The scene where you strangled the gypsy girl was sublime, dearest Jack."

Principessa turned away with a throaty laugh, and John Barrymore was beside her in a flash.

"Oh, not much, princess," Abigail heard his mellifluous voice protest. "Filming *Beau Brummel*, actually . . . no cast of thousands for this deprived thespian—just one starstruck scissor girl."

Abigail felt a horrible sensation of betrayal. If she could have plunked herself down and wept, she would have. I'm being stupid, she tried to reason. That's how picture stars behave. Barrymore didn't think I was special; he was just being nice. Nonetheless, disappointment reigned supreme. Abigail couldn't look at her hero again; instead she walked disconsolately toward Louella Parsons and Doug Fairbanks.

"Where on earth can Tommy be?" the rotund and purple-clad woman was demanding. A lilac hat bounced on wiglike, black hair while a tenacious and toothy jawline quivered. "You'd think he'd put in an appearance. An invitation to San Simeon is a command performance, after all. Besides, Tom's about to sign an extremely lucrative agreement with W.R. No more oaters for Mr. Thomas Harper Ince."

Fairbanks's laugh was wholesomeness personified. "I'm surprised you don't know where Ince is, Lollie. Snooping is your stock-in-trade."

"The biggest snoop of all, Doug, you handsome devil! Ever since I told W.R. that Marion was being buried alive in those 'costume dramas' he keeps producing, he's given me carte blanche. I know secrets no studio will admit.

"I know who's on the junk and who isn't—and I don't mean merely heroin and cocaine. The dealer who hauls in supplies is a contract player at Mack Sennett's studio, if you'd care to pay him a visit."

"That poison's not for me, Lollie, you know that. I'm the husband of 'America's Sweetheart.'"

"And that means you're above reproach?"

"That means I'd better be." Doug grinned.

"All right, gang. Quiet!" Marion shouted. The chit-chat died down immediately. No one could forget they were guests of William Randolph Hearst. House rules took precedence over everything else.

"This here's Abigail, my right-hand girl. Popsie wanted someone to handle my correspondence and stuff like that. Now she's going to take you to your rooms, and I don't want any switching around, neither. I know what some of you Sneaky Petes are up to, don't think I haven't been watching—"

"You have letters, Marion?" Garbo interrupted. Her smoky accent was decidedly hostile. "Is this what you Americans call 'the fan mail'?"

"Did you remember to bring my slippers by any chance, Greta honey?" Marion's expression was deceptively sweet; her stammer had vanished entirely.

Sensing an incipient confrontation, Louella slyly pulled a notebook from her handbag. She's going to catch it if Mr. Hearst finds out, Abigail thought. Everything that happens at San Simeon is off the record. But all of a sudden, Abigail wasn't so certain. Louella Parsons had achieved a good deal of power in a very short time.

"Excuse me—*slippers?* What is this word, please?" Guttural *r*'s collided with half-swallowed *s*'s.

"The ones you 'borrowed' from my bungalow at the Metro lot, honey lamb."

"You are calling that house a bungalow, Marion? A fourteen-rooms villa? Mr. Mayer, he don't do like that for me."

"Please, darling," Jack Gilbert murmured, while John Barrymore bellowed a lively: "Boo!"

"Booze!" Ernst Lubitsch joined in, while Mary Pickford giggled noisily, "Did I tell you all that President Coolidge visited our set last week?"

"What did he say?" Barrymore immediately quipped. The four short words painted a complete picture: "Silent Cal," twirling his hat in his nervous hands and staring awkwardly while the latest screen temptress went through her lascivious paces.

"The president?" Pickford shot back. "Oh, he didn't say a word! Remember, darling, it's all in the eyes. That's what D. W. Griffith keeps telling me!"

The group laughed, and the atmosphere on the Main Terrace changed as rapidly as a storm blowing out to sea. The veneer of jaded sophistication vanished, and the crowd turned schoolyard happy. Film gossip shot through the air. Everyone had a story to share:

". . . Who remembers working on the orgy scene in *Intolerance* . . ."

". . . 'For shame, Mary!' Those were Belasco's very words. 'You've been a very naughty girl. You've been out in California making those flickers' . . ."

". . . So I told King Vidor, 'No, I never read the script. You're the director. You do the work . . .'"

Suddenly Marion raised her arms above her head and clapped her hands together loudly. "Marching orders, boys and girls! After Abigail shows you to your rooms, we'll rendezvous poolside. The rest of the afternoon is free. Riding at the pergola, tennis, a visit to the zoo . . . you name it."

An appreciative hum greeted the speech. Hatboxes were snatched up and jewelry cases and Pullman bags.

"Hold on there, fellas. I've got to read off my rooming list: Casa del Sol! A House! Greta and Jack, Rudy and Pola, and Louella!

"Casa del Monte! B House! Charlie and Lita, Doug and Mary, and John B . . . you reprobate. I want you to behave yourself this time!

"C House! Casa del Mar! Elinor and Prin . . . Prin . . ." Marion hadn't been able to pronounce *Principessa* from the beginning. Abigail considered stepping in, but knew it wasn't her show.

"Elinor and guest. Oh, and Ernst, you're in C House, too. Be careful of those cigars! You can't go igniting any surprise fires in the bedrooms!

"Dinner's the usual: cocktails in the Assembly Room at eight, dinner in the Refectory at nine sharp. . . . Pops won't invite you back if you're a slowpoke. . . . And tomorrow we've got our costume party; I only invited the best of you hams 'cause I want some real tough competition. . . . It's not going to be one of those big bashes like the ones down at Ocean House, so you'd better be extra inventive. . . . Oh, and Bill Wellman might show up. He said he'd buzz by in his Spad . . . if he's finished that flying flicker he's been shooting."

"What about Tom Ince?" Barrymore asked. "Where are you going to house him, if and when the great director shows his smarmy face?"

"To hell with Thomas Ince," snarled Jack Gilbert. The tone was so vicious everyone stopped and stared.

"He can eat bullets for all I care. Three stagehands died on Ince's set—or maybe you've forgotten. That's what actors are supposed to do, isn't it? Forgive and forget? Well, I don't forget, and I'm telling you, I hope someone finally had the guts to kill that son of a bitch."

11

"BLOOD EVERYWHERE, DARLINGS, AND, OF COURSE, the police had no idea who committed the crime!"

Elinor Glyn had her morning audience spellbound. Chaplin was already lounging poolside, and so was Doug Fairbanks, but their wives were absent; so were the two lovebirds, Negri and Valentino, as well as Ernst Lubitsch. Louella was probably skulking around, trying to dig up dirt—at least that was Marion's opinion. As for Barrymore, well, everyone knew he wouldn't appear until the "hair of the dog that bit him" had worked its way through his hungover veins.

Dinner the night before had been the usual San Simeon extravagance: roasted quail and ranch-raised venison, bluepoint oysters imported from faraway Long Island, artichokes straight from the estate's many gardens, and a steady complement of wines, champagnes, and ports only the most expert bootlegger could procure. Mr. Hearst rightly claimed that his wine cellar was unparalleled—despite that inconvenient stricture known as Prohibition.

The host had maintained his habitual abstinence,

but his guests were now suffering the results of overindulgence, and that in spite of W.R.'s supposed "two-cocktail limit."

"You simply won't believe how dreadful the entire experience was, darlings!" Elinor was continuing. "Imagine! Shot to death! And, you know, they say a dead person's eyes hold an image of the murderer for quite a long time."

"What did Principessa think?" This was Charlie's lazy question. He'd stripped off his San Simeon–supplied terry-cloth robe and was lying in his black bathing trunks on a pillowed deck chair while he alternately gazed upward at the electric-white brilliance of the Neptune Temple and down into the cerulean waters of the pool.

The morning of the costume extravaganza had dawned hot and cloudless; an unusually warm mid-October that might have been the height of flawless summer for the sunbathers beside the pool. Steam had wafted from its heated ripples during the cool mountain night; the oil burners had churned away admirably. Even at 4 A.M., the water was a gentle seventy-five degrees.

Not that anyone had ventured in for a dip; what with the booze and the chat and a midnight romp through Casa Grande during a hilarious game of "squashed sardines," there'd been no time for a swim.

"Principessa wasn't with me, you naughty man. I was alone at the Ambassador Hotel, and the man fell dead at my feet. I've never seen so much blood in all my life—it was on the walls and the carpet, even the ceiling. I'll never forget the sight as long as I live.

"And you know what the chief constable of Los Angeles said, darlings? 'One more death to add to the city's roster. Crime on the rise, and witnesses refusing to step forward.' He told me that more murders are committed in Los Angeles in one month than occur in an entire year in France! Can you imagine such an appalling fact? And this country in its teetotaling virginity."

"Speaking of virgins," Chaplin murmured without opening his eyes, "I'd still like to hear your luscious friend's reaction. I'm trying to picture her discussing homicide, but my mind is reduced to a vision of that potent red dress, and her breasts tumbling out like melons in a basket."

"Has anyone seen Greta or Jack?" Doug interrupted from the depths of his own lounge chair. Clad in impeccable tennis whites, he acted the part of the ideal guest. As master of his own lordly manor, Pickfair, Doug recognized the perfect moment for an innocuous remark. "Jack promised me a match on the tennis courts this morning. Said he'd picked up some pointers from Bill Tilden. But if he and Greta are going to play hide the sausage all day, I'll change out of these togs and take a swim before ambling down to the pergola for a ride."

The comments were intentionally soothing, but no one responded. It didn't seem strange that an international tennis champion like Bill Tilden would be giving lessons to celebrities, but Chaplin's quixotic mood was beginning to pall.

Glyn gave the comedian the briefest of glances. "I believe I made it quite obvious, Charles, that Principessa was not my companion at the Ambassador," she announced.

Marion offered in conciliation, "I thought you liked virgins, Charlie," then Fairbanks drawled, "Oh, he does all right, sweetie, but only in his own bed."

Posed by the water's edge, Marion looked as if she were performing in an advertisement for the newest bathing costumes.

"Who else does Goldilocks screw?" Chaplin groused under his breath.

Fairbanks, who was the only member of the group to hear him, answered jocularly, "Come on, old man, what's gotten your goat today? Your pretty little lady's pregnant; you should be on top of the world."

"Oh, screw you, Mr. Douglas Ullman," Chaplin grumbled. "Mr. Ullman, born in Hicksville, Denver. Doug the heartbreaker, a goddamn, yodeling Swede. What do you know about my marriage?

"What's the only thing dumber than a dumb Irishman?" Charlie sang, simultaneously leaping to his feet. Comedic energy galvanized the man; he looked as if he were caught up in a creative frenzy. Elinor smiled as did Doug. Charlie was merely being Charlie.

Sucked into Chaplin's high jinks, Marion shouted in return, "I don't know, Charlie! Tell me! What is the only thing dumber than a dumb Irishman?"

"How's that, Marion? I didn't hear you!" Chaplin almost yelled. He assumed a vaudeville stance, too— although, being cockney born and raised, he would have called it a "music-hall routine."

Marion's early training rose to the occasion, and she fairly screamed, "I said, what is the only thing dumber that a dumb Irishman?"

"A smart Swede!" Chaplin bellowed, and the hilarity in this rote response caused him to prance across the marble tiles while Elinor gasped, "Goodness, Charles!" and Marion stammered, "Aw shucks, Charlie. That's not nice. Doug's a nice fella. Besides, he's your friend." Then she turned to Fairbanks with a contrite smile. "So, Doug, you think Bill Wellman's flying up today? I can't wait to see his Spad again."

"And what else does Billie Boy let you see—up there in the blue, just you two?" Chaplin wasn't about to relinquish his vindictive tone, but Marion slapped him teasingly on the arm with her towel before he was halfway through his question.

"You hush, you old reprobate. That's all you ever think about! Just sex, sex, sex! No wonder Lita looks so scared."

Unfortunately, W.R. chose that moment to materialize, striding down the North Terrace steps in a dark brown jacket and plus fours that looked more suited to a day's grouse shooting than a sunbath by an opulently blue swimming pool.

Marion leapt away from Chaplin's side, covering her belted black bathing costume as if she'd been caught stark naked. "Hiya, Popsie!" she whimpered with a stutter so marked it was difficult to discern distinct words.

"Good morning, Marion," was the accusatory response. If a glance could have incinerated Mr. Charles Chaplin, W.R. would have turned the comedian to ash on the spot. "I trust you and your friends are not taking a chill."

Chaplin's answer to his host's stare was to turn toward Elinor Glyn and rekindle their interrupted conversation.

"A murder, Elinor?" The competition between the two men became suddenly palpable; every member of the group felt it.

"And at the Ambassador Hotel?" Chaplin continued, feigning indifference to the building tension. "How very odd."

Hearst appeared on the verge of setting both Chaplin and Marion straight, but instead stared at the pediment of the Neptune Temple. A sigh rippled across his stolid stomach. It was one thing to invite George Bernard Shaw and his wife to visit or have Winston Churchill sit on the veranda and paint, but Marion's insistence on a friendship with Chaplin was something else. The man was a low-brow lowlife, a former street urchin from the London slums; the Chief knew he could do better. Every one of those emotions trickled past his eyes: fury to disappointment to pathos to self-pity.

"Have you seen Julia?" W.R. finally asked. "I've made up my mind about those towers on Casa Grande, and I want to start the wrecking crew right away. There's something peculiar in the way they match. I'm not certain what the problem is, but I'm sure Julia and I can find a solution."

"You're not going to take the towers down till after the party, are you, Popsie?" Marion quavered.

"No, Marion," was the slow answer. "We'll postpone work until you say so." The voice was that of an old man who realizes he's made one mistake too many.

"Oh, and Marion," W.R. announced in a seemingly innocent aside, "what did I hear you and your friends discussing as I came down the North Terrace steps?"

"I don't know, Popsie." Fear increased the stammer. Marion felt as though she were choking on something sticky and hot. "Old studio stories, I guess."

"No we weren't, snookums," Charlie countered. "We were discussing the relative virginity of Principessa's handsome pelt. Prior to that, Madame Glyn expounded on some heinous murder at the Ambassador Hotel. She never did say if she knew the victim."

Chaplin totally ignored his host's mountainous shadow. Kick me out, you old windbag, the actor seemed to dare. Toss me off the mountain. I'll have some stories then—and you can bet I'll use them.

"Aw, Charlie," Marion protested. Panic, in the form of tears, blurred her eyes. She wanted to blink, but knew her wet cheeks would betray her. She didn't dare look at Popsie, and neither did Doug. Only Elinor braved the elements, and she did so with the time-trusted movements of a handsome and self-assured woman. She lifted her surgically sculpted jawline to the light while a tumble of radiantly red hair drifted across her shoulders.

"I was at the Ambassador for a lecture, Mr. Hearst. After you kindly hired me to write those articles on romance for your newspapers, I've been besieged with requests—"

But W.R. was having none of Elinor's interruptions. "I won't have the word *death* mentioned in this house, Marion!" his high-pitched voice boomed. "You know the rules. It's a bad luck word, and I won't allow it."

Glyn's playful banter was ground to dust. She started to protest, but the rage in W.R.'s tone cut her short.

"Got it, Marion?"

"Yes, Popsie."

"And what is my little girl going to do?"

"I'm going to remember all the rules."

Marion, being Marion, quickly shook off any residual feelings of humiliation or awkwardness. Tonight's the masquerade party, she reminded herself with a sudden grin. Tonight we're going to have ourselves some fun! Pops, too—if he'll let down his hair!

Soon she and Abigail were racing from Casas A to B to C with supplemental costumes in case any guest needed a last-minute change. There were doublets and hats, dresses, swords, outlandishly long beards, Civil War regimental regalia, Antony and Cleopatra costumes complete with rubber asps, Louis XVI wigs, antebellum hoopskirts, and an entire getup that resembled a crazed hobo with a live head poking out of a bag. Marion was a great one for practical jokes, and she trailed Abigail, modeling the bizarre outfit for each guest.

"Look!" she'd squeal with her breathless stammer. "It's my head the no-good bum's got in his sack. The guy's a dummy! Really! Except he's using my legs!"

Lita hated the spectacle and crept behind her Charlie, murmuring, "Make it go away. I shouldn't look at evil things like that. It's not good for Baby."

But Charlie and Marion had a high time with the prank; they broke into Barrymore's bedroom on the pretext of bringing him a much-needed highball and caused even his sturdy stomach to do backflips while Marion wiggled her supposedly severed head.

Abigail had accompanied them on this foray. Faced with the sight of a tousled John Barrymore wearing only a pair of silk pajamas, she became absurdly nervous, barged into a sixteenth-century walnut table that served as a nightstand, and almost knocked over the Chinese jade statuette lamp.

Her clumsiness had a chain reaction. First she stumbled against the massive Cardinal Richelieu bed, grabbed futilely at the carved swags that covered the bed's dark sides, then lunged toward the ponderous headboard itself.

The sorry spectacle lasted a few seconds only, but they seemed to Abigail to have composed her entire lifetime. Thrown finally against the salmon-colored damask of the bed's hangings, she couldn't bring herself to look up into Barrymore's face. Instead she stared at the patterned silk and memorized every thread in its gold-etched design. All the nightmares in the world—death by starvation or a landslide within a mile-deep tunnel—would have been preferable to this misery.

Recovering a tiny particle of her composure, she managed to mumble, "May I bring you some breakfast, Mr. Barrymore? Some toast perhaps, and a three-minute egg?"

"Or me on a platter?" Chaplin cackled while Marion spat with surprising ferocity, "Can it, Charlie! Leave the girl alone."

Doug Fairbanks and Jack Gilbert did play tennis, after all. Negri watched from the shade of a courtside table, and Rudy Valentino sat beside her under the broad umbrella. They sipped iced lemonade from tall Lalique glasses, and their faces were luminous with reflected sunlight. If a studio cameraman had been present—D. W. Griffith's indispensable Billy Bitzer, or the Russian wizard imported by Alla Nazimova to return her middle-aged skin to radiant youth—all play would have been curtailed as technicians scurried around trying to imitate this magical light.

Valentino knew all about Nazimova's cinematic tricks. He'd been her leading man in *Camille;* and his two wives, the former Jean Acker (reinvented as a more glamorous Jeanne Mendoza) and Winnifred Shaughnessy (aka Natacha Rambova), had been the sinuous Nazimova's protégées—as well as her lovers. For the "great Latin lover," the choice in bedmates was confusing.

His first marriage hadn't survived its wedding night, while the second existed only in publicity stills staged for *Photoplay* magazine. Valentino took his recreation with bachelor friends, inciting gossip about his homosexual tendencies, while Negri waited for the love of her life to make up his mind.

"Querido," she now murmured, *"querido,* you are so distant. What can you be thinking about?"

Rudolpho Alphonso Guglielmi di Valentino d'Antonguolla didn't speak. His beautiful falcon's eyes hardly flickered; even the scar, slanting across his right cheek, remained enigmatic and immobile.

It was a typical Valentino pose, electric with untapped energy. The seduced heroines in his screenplays knew all about this look—as did most of the women in America. Danger was what brought them running to the theaters, and they could recite lines from *The Sheik* that made their hearts palpitate and their palms turn hot with desire.

"*Querido?* Rudy?" Negri tried again; her voice was less sure this time, and her Polish accent thickened in compensation. "We can't go on like this, *querido.*"

"You mean *you* can't, Pola," was Valentino's almost inaudible answer.

"Rudy . . . please. I do anything you ask. I don't mind about your wife. I don't mind about the other . . . the other . . . things."

"What things are those, dearies?" Louella waddled into the shade cast by the courtside umbrella. "Mind if I join you lovebirds?"

Without waiting for permission, Louella dragged out a white cast-iron chair and plopped herself down. "How's your wife, Rudy?" She smiled while her broad backside rummaged around in the chair.

"Natacha is well, thank you." The response sounded translated, an affectation Valentino found useful. Out of habit, he offered Louella his left profile, shielding his scar in half-shadow.

"No bambini yet?" Lollie prodded. She knew, as did all of Hollywood, that the first marriage had remained unconsummated—and supposedly the second effort was faring no better.

"No, we have not been so blessed."

"Well, that Natacha's a busy gal . . . designing those productions for Alla, the Russki, and her all-girl gang. . . . I guess you two don't get much of a home life."

"We are both professionals." Rudy was composure itself. In the four short years he'd been a star, he'd learned on which side his bread was buttered.

"And now Natacha's back in New York . . . designing another of Alla's productions."

"That is correct . . . Lollie," Valentino added the name after a moment, sweeping the columnist's face with a hungry stare until even Lollie lost her composure.

"You're certainly a good-looking boy," she finally mumbled.

"Good shot, Jack!" the threesome heard shouted from the tennis court. "You aced me fair and square, old man."

"Fairbanks!" Valentino growled between his flawless teeth.

"Is there a problem between you two?" Louella wheedled.

"Pardon?"

"Between you and Doug. . . . I'll rephrase the question: A professional rivalry, perhaps?"

Even with the upper hand, which her job afforded, Louella squirmed in Valentino's musky presence.

"Doug has the good fortune to have his own studio," Rudy answered with guarded courteousness. "United Artists permits him control of his productions. I have not been as fortunate. The public wishes to see only one facet of Rudolph Valentino, and the studio acquiesces."

"Are you saying you're dissatisfied?"

"What do you think I'm saying?" The delivery was identical to his famous line in *The Sheik:* "Are you not woman enough to know?"

"And now, Louella, Pola and I must forsake your

most illuminating company. We promised Marion we'd sample her costumes."

Lollie decided to make one last stab at toppling the golden idol. "I've heard it was Elinor Glyn who penned that racy 'advice column' you did for *Photoplay*."

If the question took Valentino by surprise, he didn't show it. "It is true Elinor consented to advise me. I am an actor, Louella, not a writer. . . . And with the opening of *Blood and Sand*, my producer felt such 'advice' would be timely. As you know, I dressed on-screen in the film. Women fainted in theaters throughout the country; the distributors had to hire trained nurses to assist them."

But Lollie had heard all the publicity palaver. Mass hysteria always ensued when Rudy appeared. "What about the advice to lay a smooch on a lady's palm instead of the traditional back of her hand? Was that your idea or La Glyn's?"

"I have kissed many women during my career, Louella. I am considered an expert. But, really, we must leave you. We are here at Mr. Hearst's gracious behest. We do as he commands."

Lollie wasn't about to be bested, however, especially by what she assumed was a cheap reference to her own rapid rise as a columnist. Let them whisper W.R. hired me to write raves for Marion, she decided. Let the film world snicker that without the great W.R.'s backing I'd still be scribbling wedding announcements for a small-town press; I'll have the last laugh in the end.

"Perhaps later then, Rudy," Louella said, fairly beaming. "Besides, I only had one more question . . . about an Indian brave . . . a guy named Black Feather. I saw pirated studio stills . . . naked chest, braids, the whole primitive man bit. They tell me he's your 'inspiration.' "

Valentino's gaze narrowed. He seemed about to respond, then stopped himself. Rudy was a tougher man than Louella could ever guess.

"Pola? Shall we go? We have finished with Miss Parsons, I believe."

152

12

Marion had wanted torches. Flaming torches
to light the guests along the paths leading to Casa
Grande. She'd thought the effect would complement
the medieval appearance of the compound—sparks
flying upward in the night, and the revelers' faces lit
by fire. But the idea of burning embers zipping toward
San Simeon's teakwood eaves had turned W.R.'s
face ashen.

"You can't be serious, Marion," he'd gasped. "The
hills around here are like tinderboxes this year. You
know that. Fire on the hilltop! No, we'll use the electrified Roman mile markers. If those lamps are good
enough for me, they'll certainly pass muster with our
guests."

Following that brief and one-sided discussion, the
two had continued their masquerade party preparations in silence. Both were in W.R.'s Gothic-furnished
suite on the third floor of Casa Grande. The low, bar-
rel-vaulted rooms with their medieval appurtenances,
liturgical manuscripts, and statuary depicting saints
and prophets had an almost celibate formality that

contrasted with Marion's own raucously rococo and Renaissance nest. Her suite lay discreetly across a small sitting room and hall—an illusion of propriety no guest believed.

Marion had squirmed into her Anne Boleyn outfit while W.R. yanked on a pair of short breeches, a red-and-black-slashed doublet, and silky crimson hose. Underwiring had thrust Marion's breasts upward in the low-cut neckline almost exposing her rosy nipples. W.R.'s attire was a good deal more complex, but it lacked Marion's sexiness as well as her youth.

"You know what, Popsie," the actress had finally offered as she'd finished fastening the tight bodice and adjusting her capped sleeves. "I didn't mean . . . You know . . . I don't care about torches. . . . I mean, fire is a scary thing."

Marion had attempted a winning smile. At the back of her mind was the omnipresent threat of W.R.'s society wife, Millicent, and the nearly grown sons who seemed to loom up like angry ghosts, threatening to destroy Marion's tenuous hold on their father. "Because I love this place as much as you do, Popsie. . . . Honest, I do. . . . More, maybe. It's so peaceful up here on the hill!"

In the gilded lamplight that illuminated the suite's stone walls, Marion's black velvet bodice and pale, creamy skin had suddenly reminded Hearst of a Holbein painting, and he'd been momentarily distracted. In fact, he'd started wondering why he didn't own a Holbein—or a Vermeer or a Georges de La Tour, for that matter.

And so he'd stared at his mistress trying to envision her as a model for those great artists. Hans Holbein the Younger had died with a portrait of Henry VIII unfinished. W.R. was in the midst of assuming King Henry's guise, and the leap from reality to fantasy had been accomplished in a second. W.R. had begun studying Marion as if he were considering commissioning a likeness from a Flemish master.

But Marion had mistaken W.R.'s focused gaze entirely. "It's a cute outfit, isn't it, Pops? Shows I got what it takes. . . . Maybe you'd like me to give you a little quickie. . . . Maybe in that new elevator you had installed . . . the one that used to be a confessional stall in some old-time convent or monastery or something. . . . I know it's a teeny-tiny place, but I don't mind. Besides, I'll betcha that little room's seen a whole lot of kneeling."

"That is most inelegant language, Marion." Dragged back to the present and deflated by Marion's crass suggestion, W.R.'s tone had been censorious. "Besides, we have guests—in case you'd forgotten."

The rebuke had defeated Marion completely. "Guests, yeah, right," she'd stammered. "How can I be such a silly so-and-so? Well, maybe some other time. I'm always available, you know . . . no appointment necessary!"

And with this feeble joke, she'd affixed her royal crown, stuffed her feet into queenly slippers, and hurried from the oppressive suite. The vision of the rightful Mrs. William Randolph Hearst hadn't left Marion's brain for an instant.

In the hall leading to the new elevator, Marion made the evening's first mistake. Charlie Chaplin suddenly appeared, still in his afternoon apparel and sauntering serenely across the wine-red Persian carpet.

"So how's the old man?" he said, and winked conspiratorially. In the dimly lit hallway, Marion's near-naked bosom appeared the color and consistency of pecan ice cream—and every bit as tempting. "Everything hunky-dory with our lord and master?"

In response, Marion giggled uncertainly while Chaplin's coarse fingers darted out and began fondling her half-exposed breasts.

Marion glanced in the direction of W.R.'s suite, made a quick decision, and touched Charlie's lips with a very wet tongue.

"Popsie's gonna be jealous as heck if he finds out," she murmured gleefully.

"He won't hear it from me," Chaplin answered.

Marion's lack of response wasn't reassuring. The comedian realized his filmland friend was plotting some minor revenge, but he didn't consider the problem for long. Instead he simply took advantage of the situation and slipped the velvet bodice toward Marion's waist.

"You know what we can do, Charlie?" she whispered while keeping an eagle eye on W.R.'s closed door. "There's this cute little elevator Popsie just put in."

"The famous medieval Spanish confessional stall he's been telling us about?"

"That's the one!"

"Do you have something you want to confess to your chaplain?"

"Oh, you're such a funny guy, Charlie! You always make me laugh!"

"A commodity in short supply on this exclusive hilltop."

Marion didn't know what to answer. Her thoughts were ricocheting back and forth like words emblazoned on competing billboards; SECURITY and MONEY stood boldly on one side; LOVE and UNDERSTANDING teetered nearby; while LONELINESS and POVERTY seemed to repeat their message endlessly.

"You're right, Charlie, my boy," Marion finally replied. "They're pretty ritzy digs for a kid from Brooklyn." Then she grabbed Chaplin by the buckle of his alligator belt and dragged him toward the elevator.

"Are you going to kneel, Marion?" Charlie said, laughing.

"You just watch me, mister," W.R.'s mistress boasted with a seductive growl. "And I ain't no goddamn nun!"

By the time Henry VIII and his nubile, second wife, Anne Boleyn, entered the Assembly Room, the clock showed a precise five minutes before the start of cocktail hour. Relations between the king and his queen were more strained than they'd been in W.R.'s suite. Neither spoke; their thoughts were too occupied with recent events.

I must remind Abigail to teach Marion more graceful speech and manners, W.R. told himself, while the actress's blue eyes flicked to every mirrored surface, checking to make certain her costume and makeup hadn't been set awry by her encounter in the confessional stall.

W.R. mistakenly assumed his mistress's humbled silence connoted a new acquiescence, while Marion herself began yielding to an incipient rage. I'm young, she argued silently, why shouldn't I have a good time? I don't want to be stuck in the boonies all my life. I'm a sexy gal; fellas like me; why can't I act a little wild now and then? And if Popsie finds out, well, so much the better. It'll make him realize how much I'm worth!

The smile Marion turned on W.R. was docile and submissive, however, and the nod he returned showed how masterful he believed he'd become.

He glanced across the vast room to make certain the many lamps were lit, that the cushions were plump and inviting, and that the fire within the sixteen-foot-tall Château des Jours mantel had a stack of wood to keep it blazing long into the night.

Then he gazed upward at the wondrously coffered ceiling with its intricate wood panels. The antique treasure from the Palazzo Martinengo in Brescia, Italy, couldn't have had a greater showplace than San Simeon. The same was true of the gigantic Rubens *Triumph of Religion* tapestry, and the Giulio Romano–designed tapestries depicting the heroic deeds of Scipio Africanus, woven by Flemish craftsmen in 1550.

The lord of San Simeon glanced from one marvel to the next, from the regally proportioned sixteenth-century Italian table to a neoclassical Venus, from a voluptuous silver oil lamp to a pair of red granite columns, from the Carrara marble medallions to a Renaissance Madonna in a thick gilt frame. His proud eye took it all in: the burnished choir stalls lining the walls, and the heraldic banners embroidered in silver and gold.

Satisfied that his home looked as beautiful as any on earth, W.R., in his kingly costume, in his ermine and silks, his gilded chains and square-toed slippers, breathed a sigh of purest contentment.

"I sure do like that new elevator," Marion cooed. Then she sashayed a path toward the majestic hearth, snagging a glass of champagne as she passed. The usual phalanx of servants would parade in momentarily, but for a second or two she and her Pops had the place to themselves. The fire warmed her shoulders and nearly naked bosom, and she wriggled provocatively in the heat.

"Do you think any priests did it in that little box, Pops?" Marion drained her glass and strolled back for a second. "Them Middle Ages monks, I mean."

"That's a very naughty idea, Marion." W.R.'s critique wasn't as forceful as it might have been. The steamy luxury of the room was affecting him as well, making him feel expansive and slyly virile.

"You bet it is, Popsie!" she chortled. "But you know your little Marion! She's always good for what ails you!"

With a false sense of security bolstering her shaky ego, Marion was just about to ask W.R. his opinion of the fabric on the overstuffed sofas and club chairs—a decorating experiment she'd recently been permitted to attempt. The matched sets were covered in a cupid motif. Gods of love rollicked over chair backs and cushions, sprawling pudgy pink bodies in uninhibited glee.

But Marion didn't have time to direct W.R.'s attention to the cupids' salacious pranks because Neylan marched in at that moment—followed by the Muller boys.

"Come in, boys, come on in!" the Chief cackled. "Looking mighty handsome Jack, and you, too, Karl, and you, Friederich."

W.R. took a perverse pleasure in reminding his minions of their German ancestry. It kept them mindful of their Chicago days; besides a "conflict of opinion" with the city's law-enforcement agencies, anti-German sentiment during the Great War had made the Mullers' lives decidedly uncomfortable—a prejudice W.R. had experienced firsthand. He'd never once referred to Friederich Muller as Freddie, and he never would.

"Quite a getup you've got there, Jack. May I ask what you're supposed to be?" W.R.'s teasing tone sought out Marion, although she maintained a firm distance from the men. "And no gray suit! However did you manage such a feat? Do you see what we've got here, Marion? Jack's dispensed with his business attire."

"I'm Hannibal," Neylan's long face mumbled.

Under his short, pleated tunic and a breastplate formed from papier-mâché, Neylan's white, hairy legs looked as spindly as a spider's.

"And you've got quite a set of gams to match! Let's see, Jack. Stand next to my Flemish tapestries there—the ones showing Hannibal's defeat by General Scipio Africanus—and we'll see how you measure up to your model.

"And Karl . . . you and your bother are . . . ?"

"Roman centurions." Karl's answer was an embarrassed mumble while Friederich/Freddie didn't open his mouth.

"Ah, you're taking the opposing side! What do you think of that, Jack? Meet the enemy. The stalwarts guarding the empire from foreign upstarts like you."

Karl and Freddie eyed Neylan with newfound distrust, all the while shambling their huge sandal-clad feet and rattling bronze-toned cardboard shields.

"Jeez," Marion hissed under her breath. She wished her other guests would show, and that Pops would dispense with these lamebrain clowns. She tossed back the few drops remaining in her champagne flute, yearning to grab another, but reminding herself of Popsie's two-cocktail limit. She'd have to wait till he wasn't looking to snag some extra hooch.

"What do you mean you haven't found him yet?" Marion heard the Chief demand. Pent-up rage leaked out with each word, raising the register to match the speaker's wrath. "I've got all those goddamn cowboys riding the ranges, checking the cattle and zebra and bison and whatnot, and you mean to tell me this buffoon's disappeared. Disappeared without a trace! And for nearly two days? What did I hire you people for?"

The Mullers' and Neylan's answers were inaudible, but Marion could tell from the Chief's vindictive "Well, get moving then! I'm not paying you goons to dress up in skirts!" that the response had been less than adequate.

Whatever the problem, it would remain a secret because at that moment the entire group of guests burst through the Assembly Room door, bringing with them the cool air of a mountain evening and the brittle scents of cloth of gold and velvet embroidered with silk. Thick, beeswax candles flickered in the ecclesiastic candlesticks, and the fire leapt with renewed life as if someone had tossed a bundle of pinecones into the hearth.

"Hiya, everybody!" Marion cheered. "Come on and belly up to the bar!"

Chaplin was dressed as Napoleon; Lita was his Josephine. The casting was spectacular because Charlie bore an uncanny resemblance to the diminutive emperor, and Lita with her olive-hued skin and wide, doe eyes looked as fresh and unsullied as any girl from Martinique; even her pregnancy was disguised by the high, Empire waist.

Barrymore was clad in a brass-buttoned, gold-braided, skintight uniform from his film *Beau Brummel*. The parade-ground soldier made a deep bow to Lita/Josephine. "I see your Caribbean pigeon has something cooking in the oven, Bonaparte. Let's hope it's a son. Empresses are failures if they don't produce heirs to the throne . . . although between you and me and that marble statue over there, I've heard Josephine is mighty good in the sack."

Lita opened her mouth, trying for a clever retort that didn't materialize, while Chaplin smiled an easy "I couldn't very well dress up as a tramp! Not after the rumor Lita and I heard while making our way through Mr. Hearst's garden."

"What rumor?" Elinor Glyn demanded, crowding

close. Her long, silk charmeuse dress was printed in a tiger-stripe pattern while draped across her back was the real thing—head and claws and tail and all.

"What rumor?" she repeated. "If there's a problem afoot, your friends need to know. This beast is no protection for a lady."

"Yeah, Charlie!" Marion echoed, wriggling her plump breasts.

"Nan Bullen!" Charlie crowed as if her costume had taken him by surprise. "As I live and breathe. The young woman who would be queen! And where's that terror, his royal highness?"

W.R. finally struggled forward, his terrible shyness transmitting itself to each of his guests. He didn't speak, but grinned at a blur of faces; and his smile had the sickly self-consciousness of a child finding himself braving a gathering of adults.

No one teased their host on his costume, however; no one mentioned that Anne Boleyn's days had been numbered, or that her downfall had been an ill-timed romance. No one joked about divorce or beheading or poor Henry's travails with an unyielding church. No one remarked on the royal girth or Henry's appetite for young females. Privately, each guest ran down a list of possible quips and found each dangerously close to the truth.

"Welcome," W.R. managed after an embarrassed moment. "You're all looking mighty nice."

Marion barked loudly, "Have a drink, folks! Champagne for the snobs. Something stronger for anyone with a stomach for it . . . that should leave you out, John."

Marion led the group toward the fireplace, and a matching set of silver butler's trays covered with highball and champagne glasses, ice buckets, tongs, seltzer dispensers, and every known variety of booze.

162

"I see Abigail's brightened your outlook considerably, John. I'll have to sample her wares myself." Chaplin's remark caught Barrymore off guard. A brief display of anger flickered across the famous profile. Despite the actor's seemingly indifferent approach to life, he was a loyal friend.

"Leave her alone, Charlie. She's a good kid."

"Touché, Don Juan. And you can take your eyes off my wife's tits while you're at it."

"And when did holy wedlock become so important to Mr. Charles Spencer Chaplin?" Barrymore countered, then backed off and drawled to the room in general, "Speaking of mammary glands, where is our lovely Principessa?"

A matador in a formfitting "suit of lights" (Valentino) stared uncomprehending at a veiled gypsy girl (Negri); a cigar-chomping and velvet-pantalooned Romeo (Ernst Lubitsch) gaped at a tunicked and canvas-putteed doughboy (Jack Gilbert from his upcoming hit *The Big Parade*). Garbo (Mata Hari) studded with jewels from her oriental headdress to her gauzy harem trousers gazed at a resplendent Turkish pasha (Doug Fairbanks in a costume borrowed from *The Thief of Bagdad*), while Lollie Parsons, done up as a chunky Dutch girl with a stiff lace cap and flaxen curls, turned her own quizzical glance on Mary Pickford.

Pickford was the only star who'd chosen to imitate a rival actress. She was dressed as Lillian Gish in D. W. Griffith's epic chronicle of the French Revolution, *Orphans of the Storm;* her clothes were in tatters, and her long hair tickled her waist. Pickford looked so woebegone she seemed on the verge of tears—something she believed to be Gish's stock-in-trade and a very cheap shot.

"Oh, no!" Pickford now wept. "Where is the princess? Not carried away to the guillotine!"

"Oh, no!" the other guests chortled in unison. "Where is our noble princess? Not another victim for the fearsome tumbrels!"

"Principessa will be joining us later," Glyn answered with a coy smile, then refused to add another word.

Abigail arrived at that moment and with her, Julia Morgan. Julia hadn't dressed up for the event, nor did she intend to dine with the rowdy crowd. She was putting in an appearance out of courtesy only—then she'd retire to her tower suite and have dinner sent up on a tray.

She tried to exchange a look with her Chief, but he was surrounded by Garbo in her midriff-baring, odalisque outfit and Louella wobbling in her wooden clogs. The reassuringly pragmatic presence of Neylan had vanished.

Julia marched over to Marion, mumbled something about "revising Thaddeus's architectural drawings," and fled.

"Who in God's name was that?" Beau Brummell laughed. "Did your old man assign you a duenna, Marion? She'd certainly freeze my . . . Oh, excuse me, Abigail, I didn't see you standing there."

Feeling miserably self-conscious with this illustrious crowd (Abigail was costumed as a demure Revolutionary War–era maid from Marion's newest film, *Janice Meredith*), the secretary merely curtsied.

"Any word from Tom Ince?" Alcohol had transformed Marion's manner as well as untangled her tongue. The sound was the purr of a large and dangerous cat.

"No, ma'am. Neither Mr. nor Mrs. Ince have telephoned or cabled." For good measure, Abigail dropped another curtsy.

"Well, if—and when—that jackass shows, I'm tempted to give him the boot," Marion growled.

"Put Karl and Freddie on his case, my dear," Barrymore grinned. "I'm sure they've got boots to spare."

For better or worse Abigail was forgotten. She hovered near the twosome, but then dinner was announced, and she followed the parade of stars as they moved from the Assembly Room to the Refectory.

Candlelight cast otherworldly shadows, flickering across the banks of fifteenth-century Spanish choir stalls that lined the Refectory's stone walls until the color of the tracery turned as rich as melting chocolate. This same flamboyant Gothic motif continued with the enormous dining table, the "Dante" chairs with their gold-tasseled seats, the silver candelabrum, wine cisterns and warming plates, the sixteenth-century tapestries (one depicting the prophet Daniel in the court of Nebuchadnezzar), and the mantel, whose intricate carving climbed a full twenty-seven feet on its way to the ceiling. Passing from the Assembly Room through low-beamed portals of blackened oak, the visitors might have imagined themselves magically transported to medieval Spain or Italy or France.

The food itself contributed to this sense of timelessness. There were bisques and clear turtle soups, lobster meat in cream sauce, baby lambs, standing rib roasts, and vegetables plucked from San Simeon's kitchen garden, while washing it all down was a collection of wines as extensive as any European castle could boast: clarets and burgundies, Rieslings, Madeiras, and several types of champagne.

It was the middle of the third course, or was it the fourth? Abigail had begun to lose track. There'd been so much high-spirited gossip, filmland rivalries, private jokes that weren't private at all, even a shouting match about Louis B. Mayer's proposed changes for *Tess of the D'Urbervilles* (he wanted a happy ending), that Abigail's head was spinning.

She was seated beside Ernst Lubitsch at the end of the table. The director's Romeo outfit was now looking as rumpled as his daily wear—a fact Abigail found endearing. It brought the famous man closer to earth. "Charlie works to become a tramp," Lubitsch had confided. "Me? I'm a natural!"

Greta Garbo monopolized on the director's left; beside her was Doug Fairbanks, while Negri took the next chair. Pola had the place of honor at her host's right hand.

Marion and her lord sat opposite each other—centerpieces in the midst of the table's length—and the place cards ranging beside them displayed Marion's devilish streak. The only exception to the rule was Louella; she'd begged to be placed in her "host's illustrious shadow" and Marion had acquiesced. Lollie could make a demonic enemy.

At the columnist's left was John Barrymore (Marion believed John could give "the battle-ax" her comeuppance). Next to John was Lita; beside her loomed an empty chair. Marion still hadn't given up on the Thomas Inces or Bill Wellman, although Abigail wasn't certain the Chief would permit them entrance at this advanced hour.

Marion's side of the court sloped off in two unoccupied seats. Mary Pickford, who'd won the costume prize for "most vicious and mean-spirited impersonation of a fellow performer," sat glumly beside an empty chair while Elinor Glyn was placed on her right. The joke, of course, was that Marion had intended this jibe at Pickford all along. Charlie came next—a presitgious position at his hostess's left, while Jack Gilbert (in a gesture intended to challenge "that ingenue

Swede") took the place of honor on Marion's right. The absent Principessa would be seated at Jack's other side, while Neylan, in his Hannibal outfit, guarded the third empty chair.

Abigail couldn't see all the guests, but she could hear their voices: jovial, buoyant, and above all, proud. If anyone had told her that she'd not only survive the screen stars' visit, but actually begin enjoying their company, she wouldn't have believed it. But here she was, having the time of her life.

"We should have minstrels up in the gallery," Barrymore was bellowing. "Or Will Rogers—like the last time. . . . Remember, Marion?"

"Eddie Cantor!" Doug Fairbanks added. "Or Jolson . . . he's always amusing. What was that routine you did with him, Marion?"

"What about you, you old ham?" Barrymore countered. "What's wrong with homegrown entertainment? You could leap from the gallery to the chandelier and then onto the sideboard—"

"He's performed that trick enough at my house," Chaplin burst in. "Broke an entire set of Baccarat when he smashed into the bar with that damn fencing foil of his."

"I was the life of the party."

"Yes, he was, Charlie. You said so yourself." Mary was devoutly loyal to her husband.

"I'm the life of every party!" Charlie boasted, to which every actor and actress at the table shouted deafeningly, "Boo! Boo! More booze!" Even W.R. joined the act.

"Children," Ernst confided to Abigail, then added mock seriously, "Don't ever become a director, young lady. Better to be a nursery maid."

"I'll remember your advice." Abigail smiled.

The chat had continued in that vein, skating past

sensitive issues and hurrying over potentially hurt feelings. The stars were determined to enjoy themselves, although now and then there were darker elements at work.

"Oh, but you must remember Mexico, darling," Elinor's voice invaded a momentary lull. "When we were forced to share the same bed? I've had fond feelings for the country ever since." Abigail watched Elinor's halo of hair shroud both her own and Chaplin's faces. The two had disappeared into a private world.

Lita, at the opposite end of the table, witnessed the same scene. "Charlie?" she quavered, while Abigail scowled at her plate. I wouldn't let any man treat me like dirt, she promised herself, no matter how much of a celebrity he was.

Jack Gilbert lost this curious exchange altogether, but then he was having a difficult time. Stuck with Principessa's empty seat and Neylan's austere shadow, the actor's nervous eyes flashed. He'd unbuttoned the neck of his doughboy uniform and appeared thoroughly drunk. "Where's that cretin Ince?" he muttered, but everyone politely pretended not to hear.

Marion's sudden, inebriated giggle broke the ensuing silence. "No, you silly billy, that was *Little Old New York!* The flicker where I dressed as a boy . . . you remember!" Having wrested Charlie away from Elinor, Marion was cuddling close to her favorite.

Despite an evening ripe with innuendos, the sight of the hostess and the comedian in an intimate tête-à-tête made the other guests stop and stare. Everyone knew the rumors; when Marion was alone in Hollywood, Chaplin was her frequent "guest."

Fully aware of the spectacle she'd created, Marion gazed defiantly across the table.

"Pops loved it, didn't you, Popsie? He had Victor Herbert's orchestra play at the premiere, and bought the Cosmopolitan Theater in New York City, and printed up fancy programs with gilt edges.

"Then he produced *When Knighthood Was in Flower*." Marion's tone carried more than a hint of a threat; she seemed to be daring the great man to rescind his financial and professional support. Despite the champagne, and God knows how many glasses of wine, Marion's blue eyes had turned as hard as crystal.

"We had sets designed by Josef Urban. He used to do Flo Ziegfeld's scenery. . . . That's when I was hoofing it with Eddie Cantor and Will Rogers . . . the Ziegfeld Follies of 1917 . . ." The speech ended with a lonely sigh that masked an unladylike belch.

"That's right!" W.R. added, trying to get his mistress back on track. "*Knighthood!* Now, that was one stupendous film. I spent a fortune producing it. . . . Used real antiques . . . embroidered satins and laces . . . a perfect re-creation of merrie olde England . . . better than the real thing.

"When anyone tells me there's a lot of money in the picture-making business, I say, 'You're right. And most of it's mine.' Marion's talent deserves the finest!"

No one spoke after that, and the Refectory became a self-conscious clatter of silver and porcelain, crystal goblets and salt cellars lined with cobalt-blue glass. The candles flickered, spitting droplets of wax onto the ornate Spanish candelabrum and the mirror-bright wood of the table while the glass panes of the clerestory windows rattled, hurling puffs of intrusive air toward the guests' unsuspecting heads.

"What is keeping Principessa?" Elinor muttered, while Marion shivered and mumbled plaintively, "Someone just tiptoed across my grave."

Everyone heard the gaffe; the forbidden word *death* hadn't been mentioned, but *grave* made a decent substitute. Voices rushed to fill the void.

"So what do we all think of these new talking motion pictures?" Doug asked with a nonchalant smile.

"Talkies won't last," was Chaplin's immediate response. "Audiences want pantomime, not bungled words. There's no art involved when sound comes into play. Anyone investing in talkies is going to lose his shirt."

"That's rot, Charles, and you know it," Barrymore laughed. "Why do you suppose audiences pay to see actors onstage? Shakespeare must be spoken; it can't be reduced to phony sighs and batted eyelids."

"Another medium altogether, John. When you've been making films as long as I have—"

"I disagree, Charlie," Doug interrupted. "I think John may be on to something. Talkies are going to give us a run for our money. We'll have to learn to adapt—"

"Like hell!" Jack Gilbert suddenly raged in words that had turned mushy with alcohol. "Everyone knows what photoplays are like. A lot of useless words. Blah . . . blah . . . blah . . . Just give me the basics, I tell my directors. Don't muck it up with verbal drivel."

"Jack, dearest, that's terribly cruel!" Glyn protested, while Chaplin announced:

"Talkies won't work. It's as simple as that. Film actors aren't intended to speak, and that's all there is to it!"

"But you're talking now." W.R.'s delivery was alarmingly simple. Only a fool would have ignored the warning. "Aren't you, Charles? Or is there something you do better than talk?

"My little girl over there insists you're 'one of the sweetest guys in the world.' Can you tell me what she means by that interesting choice of words? I see no evidence of 'sweetness' tonight, but then, of course, I don't know you as well as the former Miss Douras does."

"Hey, Popsie, knock it off." Marion tried to laugh, but Hearst's innuendo hovered in the air, and the other guests ceased speaking or cutting their dinners or even chewing.

"Charlie and me, we're just funning, you know? That Hollywood gab is just studio gossip, is all. . . . They like to get us stars all bollixed up, who's screwing who. . . . It's a bunch of malarkey, really."

Silence followed these desperate remarks. Secretly, every guest was longing for a little excitement, something to add spice to an already entertaining weekend. Suddenly the door leading to the butler's pantry blew open with a crash that rocked the dinner plates, shivered the tines of the silver forks, and set the wineglasses bouncing on their crystal stems. Three men scrambled through the low-ceilinged entry, booted forward unceremoniously by a glowering Karl and Freddie.

13

D ARLING!" ELINOR GLYN SHOUTED TO ONE OF the newcomers, while Marion simultaneously roared, "You sleazy-eyed son of a—" The rest of the table erupted in confusion; everyone started talking at once while the three unknown intruders slouched near a silver-strewn sideboard, tan trench coats askew and steel-gray hats jammed over their ears.

"We found these two sneaking around by the Neptune Pool, Chief," Karl and Freddie boasted together, marching their quarry to their master's chair.

"The third piece of scum was weaseling around C House. Looked like he was working the front door. Robbery attempt is our guess, the dirty—"

"I explained what I was doing!" the third gentleman protested.

"Says you, you goddamn pansy!"

"Gentlemen!" another voice called from the door. The guests' necks spun around as if they were spectators at a rugby scrimmage. "Watch your language in front of Mr. Hearst."

Joe Willicombe made a move to drag the Mullers

away, but W.R. stopped him. "Let the boys have their say, Joe. As bloodhounds, I couldn't ask for better."

The Chief grinned at his stalwarts. "Go ahead, boys. Tell us how you rounded up these ne'er-do-wells." W.R.'s pudgy cheeks were now wreathed in smiles. For the first time since Marion's friends had blown through the Assembly Room door, the old man seemed genuinely happy. Even Charlie Chaplin was forgotten.

"Well, Mr. High-Stepper here, he was the last of the trio we rounded up. Breaking into Casa del Mar as we said—"

"I told you lamebrains what I was doing!" Gentleman Number Three spat back.

"Yeah, playing dress-ups. That's what your kind always says. Only usually, it's girly glad rags instead of a goddamn Prince Albert."

"Jesus," Gentleman Three groaned, then sank into an unoccupied chair before the Mullers had time to drag him away from the table.

"Not there, darling." Elinor grinned with an expression that had begun to resemble that of the proverbial cat guarding the canary. "Marion put you next to Jack . . . and the costume is simply stunning. You were right, as always, dearest."

As Principessa changed seats, she pulled off her hat and coat. A tumble of yellow hair fell on a broad-shouldered, wide-lapeled men's suit that had been specially crafted for her voluptuous figure.

"See what I mean, dummies?" she demanded, although her good humor was rapidly returning. She shot an appraising glance in Barrymore's direction, then poured herself into the chair Neylan held for her and calmly asked if any dinner was left.

W.R. cackled wildly. "Great getup!" he chortled. "And what about our other visitors? Did we net two harem girls in disguise?" Hearst's stern rule about tardy guests and a prompt dinner hour seemed to have vanished beneath his Henry VIII robes. It was as if he had become that despotic monarch and was now ready to dispense his favors with a regal smile.

"No, Pops," Marion answered while she eyed Gentleman Number One. "You should have telephoned. Abigail and me, we was plenty worried. And we went to the trouble of seating this blasted dinner, too, and you don't even have the decency to bring Nell!" If deeper emotions were at work than those of a rebuffed hostess, W.R. missed them entirely.

"Tom Harper Ince!" he yelped. "As I live and breathe! So it is! Well, this is a pleasant surprise."

Exuberant greetings echoed along the table. A director and producer celebrated as a "star maker" was certain to gain favorable attention, and the crowd gathered in the Refectory hurried to rectify any unpleasant first impressions.

Pickford and Negri scrambled up words of praise, stumbling over each other's remarks in their efforts to prove welcoming, as did Barrymore, Valentino, and Fairbanks. Only Gilbert remained silent, but his black eyes looked as murderous as the depths of alcohol would allow.

Negri and Valentino began peppering the new arrival with questions about his most recent acquisition: the film rights to Kathleen Norris's best-selling novel, *Christine of the Hungry Heart*. No one mentioned the impending and widely publicized deal between Ince's studio and Hearst's Cosmopolitan Pictures; their host had peculiar notions about privacy.

"It is so nice to see you again, Tommy," Greta purred after the initial cheers had died down.

"And without Nell," Barrymore pretended to muse. "How very convenient, Tom."

But W.R. had tired of the nightlong sexual innuendos. "How'd you get here, Ince?" he demanded; the voice was businesslike and brisk, a sound the great man employed when discussing stock options or pork futures.

"Bill flew me up in his Spad." Ince slapped the lanky aviator on his broad and bony shoulders. The young man, his grin wide and disarmingly wholesome, looked more like a college student than a war hero, the kind of person who should have been outfitted in a raccoon coat, saddle shoes, and a six-foot scarf sporting his team's colors. Wellman stared at Jack Gilbert, then realized the uniform was a fake; his face registered disgust before shifting to a guarded curiosity.

"Bill and I left from Santa Monica airport. I'm sorry not to have arrived yesterday, but I had to run some new figures on *The Marriage Cheat*. Ended up working half the night, and my prior engagements completely slipped my mind, I regret to say. The flicker did better than originally projected; the money boys in New York are going to be very happy. Cosmopolitan Pictures should be pleased as well, W.R. . . . Oh, and Nell sends her best to you—and her apologies. She's been laid up with a bad back . . . or maybe it's sciatica. I'm not much good with this medical lingo."

Confident, with the lazy ease that accompanies total self-assurance, Ince tossed his coat and hat to Freddie Muller, then prowled the length of the table searching out his place card. He ran a hand through his wavy, Irish hair; the gesture was vain and proud, the display of a Hollywood magnate in his prime.

"You're over there, Mr. Ince . . . next to Miss Pickford," Abigail ventured. She wondered if she should stand and show the new arrival to his chair, but a glance at Marion told her Tom Ince would have to find his way alone. The director Marion had begun

referring to as a "no-good lady-killer" would be consigned to the doghouse for some time.

"Mrs. Ince was supposed to sit beside Mr. Neylan,
and Mr. Wellman, you're next to Mrs. Chaplin."

"Thank you. I'll be sure to tell Nell what an illustrious dinner partner you had planned for her." Tom
turned a glowing smile on his new champion, and Abigail decided that every one of her boss's remarks were
not only unfair but unfounded. In his slightly rumpled
tweeds, oxford shirt, and conservative necktie, the director looked as uncomplicated and kindly as a history teacher.

"Look out, folks! Tommy's making whoopee!" Barrymore chirped, but no one laughed.

After that, Bill Wellman was officially introduced,
and his tales of flying himself and Tom Ince north
from Santa Monica were repeated, questioned, and
gawked over. Younger than the rest of the group, Bill
described his military service during the Great War
and how he'd run sorties in France with the Lafayette
Flying Corps. He'd been a member of the Chat-Noire
group, operating out of Lunéville, a garrison town
near the German border.

He shrugged off his escapades, however, with behavior that was part humility and part youthful pride.
His spare, angular face matched his words, and his
restless glance skimmed the table continuously as if
he were making momentous decisions.

"I was nineteen when I went over." He smiled,
drumming impatient fingers on the refectory table.
"They took you up in a Spad a few times, then they
told you to wait on the ground till your time came.
See, we didn't have enough planes, so the guy ahead
of you had to die before you got your chance. Some
fellas only lasted a week or two; I was lucky."

Marion grew goggle-eyed, and her stammer became little-girl innocent. "Golly," she whispered, and, "Oh, jeez, how terrible!" She was doing a creditable job of turning herself into a twenty-year-old postdeb, and Wellman appeared fooled by the deception.

He began directing his comments almost exclusively to her, while she, in turn, started ignoring Chaplin, her former favorite. W.R. watched the interplay between these three while the other diners snuck continual glances at their host. Despite Wellman's alliance with the film world, he was an outsider, a "kid," a "loose cannon"; an affair between the young man and Marion seemed unthinkable to the worldly crowd.

"Then I came home. I'd met Doug before the war, and he said if I ever made it back, to give him a ring. So I flew my Spad up to his house in Beverly Hills, and he got me a job as an actor—something I hated with a passion. I looked like an idiot in those fancy wigs and all that lousy camera makeup. No offense, Doug, and you, too, Mr. Valentino, and any other actors I've missed, but I never wanted to be mistaken for a girl."

Marion giggled noisily while W.R.'s owlish stare feasted on her face. But the former Ziegfeld dancer and good-time girl was impervious. "Jeez!" she burbled. "You must be one brave fella! Us showgirls didn't know much about the war; all we worried about was making a buck."

Wellman gave his hostess a glance at once encouraging and compassionate, while Marion smiled an adoring "I never met a flier before I met you." The tension traversing the table was so palpable one could have stabbed it with a fork.

"Anyway, after I quit acting, I took up directing . . . started out with Bernie Durning doing fast-paced melodramas like *The Eleventh Hour* and *The Fast*

Mail. I shot all the flying sequences solo. No one wanted to go up in a plane with me . . . said I was too much of a daredevil . . . but I wasn't doing anything near as dangerous as I'd done overseas.

"What I really want to do, though, is make a flying flicker—something about my experiences in the war. I want to show what it's like to enter enemy territory, the dogfights, you know, and the ground fire ripping apart your propeller blades. . . . Some people in this country still don't understand about the war . . . or they think we should forgive and forget—lousy advice, if you want my opinion—those goddamn Krauts killed my best buddies—"

"Shall we adjourn to the Assembly Room for coffee?" W.R.'s tone was stony as he interrupted Wellman's monologue.

The sound seemed to startle the young aviator turned director, and he frowned as if suddenly remembering a crucial fact. Then his impatient fingers thrummed the table, and he stared at his host, shoving aside his half-eaten dinner plate with an angry "I guess I've had enough of this grub."

Marion protested, "But, Popsie, Bill hasn't finished."

W.R. overrode both voices, with an austere: "Everybody? Shall we go?" The questions were commands, not suggestions, and the guests jumped from their chairs and filed back into the Assembly Room like schoolkids dragged to the headmaster's office.

"Why don't you go straighten up the little girls' room," Marion whispered to a maid refilling the coffee cups. Abigail recognized the order; it meant that a glass of gin would be left for the mistress of the house so that Marion could emerge after powdering her nose carrying something that looked as innocuous as water.

"Yes, ma'am." The maid curtsied with the barest of bobs.

W.R. noticed the servant's abrupt departure, but Marion greeted his stare with an airy wave, then warbled noisily:

"Here's to my Popsie. The best kind of daddy-cakes a girl can have!" By now, her speech was so slurred it was difficult to understand, and she wobbled unsteadily, reaching a haughty hand toward the columns supporting the fireplace mantel as if they had suddenly lurched to one side. "Everybody, listen up! Raise your glasses and give old Pops a toast!"

Conversation stopped, not that there'd been much of note. Following the abrupt conclusion of dinner, the guests had huddled in small groups, talking quietly among themselves as if waiting for some catastrophic occurrence: the death of a moneyed patriarch or the reading of a contested will.

"The king is dead. Long live the king," Marion cackled, although she was the only person to find the jest amusing. "Get it?" she chortled, grinning from face to face. Her attempt at humor nearly bowled her over.

"See, the old king's kicked the bucket, and the new guy's waiting in the wings . . . it's an expression they use in merrie olde London towne . . . and I should know . . . I'm goddamn Anne Boleyn." The speech vanished in a tumble of misshapen consonants while Marion beamed lasciviously at Bill Wellman. "You get it, Billy Boy, don't you?"

And Wellman, who was matching his hostess ounce for ounce, hooted a brash "You bet!"

"Marion?" W.R.'s tone was as cold as death, but Marion was having none of Pops's interference.

"Aw nuts!" she screamed, and stormed out of the room, barking as she disappeared into Casa Grande's stone shadows, "I'm going to powder my goddamn nose—that is, if San Simeon's lord and master permits!"

Marion had been gone for some time, or so it seemed to Abigail. She knew the Chief was fretting over his mistress's absence as well, because he kept referring to his gold pocket watch, pulling it out of a voluminous pocket, polishing the crystal face with a folded linen handkerchief, then squinting at the Roman numerals and replacing the mechanism with a sigh that was half rage and half grief.

Abigail approached the overstuffed settee where the Chief sat alone, intending to ask if she should retrieve the wayward Marion, but Lita beat her to the punch.

"What a pretty watch," the second Mrs. Chaplin enthused, seating herself beside her host. The words had a painfully proper tone, as if Lita were reciting words she'd memorized. Despite her growing belly, she looked no more sophisticated than a convent-school sophomore, a girl/child in desperate need of a friend.

Charlie, Principessa, and Elinor were sharing reminiscences at the far end of the room; Doug, Mary, Pola, and Rudy were huddled over a card table; while Greta and a barely conscious Jack were in the midst of a silent and private battle. Clearly, Lita felt she had no one to turn to. She didn't want to risk gabbing with John Barrymore again; Charlie had warned her to stay away from Louella (he'd called her a "brown-nosing snoop"); Tom and Ernst had stared straight down her bodice; Abigail was hired help; and Bill Wellman seemed to be off-limits. Sixteen or not, Lita knew the score.

She pluffed up the cupid pillows and wriggled closer to her host. "I like gold watches," she announced.

"Charlie says platinum's nicer, but me, I like gold. I guess I'm what you'd call old-fashioned." The remarks didn't have a hint of manipulation. They might have been delivered by a precocious seven-year-old.

"And *are* you old-fashioned?" W.R. beamed, gradually focusing on the pretty child at his side.

"Well, Charlie says I am, so I guess he's right."

"Nothing wrong with being old-fashioned, Lillita. I've been accused of the same thing myself."

"Oh, have you?" The joy in Lita's young voice was so pure, it made W.R.'s eyes fill with moisture, and he took her pale hand in his big, brown paw.

Abigail looked away; she couldn't help Lita; she'd have to struggle through her own mistakes. Abigail surreptitiously glanced at the grandfather clock while Bill Wellman chose that moment to walk toward her.

"I guess you must be new in town. An actress, right? Come see me when we get back to H-wood. I can probably throw you a bit part or two."

Out of the corner of her eye, Abigail saw disaster coming. It was in the shape of Marion, staggering forward and hearing what she assumed was an assignation.

"She's no pro, you jackass; she's a goddamn prissy-assed servant! A goddamn finishing-school nobody!" Marion wailed as she stumbled across the Roman mosaic pavement of the Main Vestibule, then slipped on a Persian carpet just inside the Assembly Room's marble doorway and sprawled in a heap—Anne Boleyn pearls, cap, lace collar, and all. The glass in her hand leapt from her fingers and scattered its contents far and wide as the crystal shattered in a hundred pieces.

"Aw shoot," Marion mumbled while the stench of spilled gin wafted upward.

She tried to gather her legs under her, but she didn't have time to stand or even rearrange her toppled costume because W.R. was beside her in a flash. For a man his size, he could move with disconcerting speed.

"You're drunk, Marion!" Fury hissed through the words; W.R. seemed capable of striking his mistress or dragging her bodily from the room. Abigail knew he'd never laid a hand on Marion; it was a fact she liked to boast about, as if physical restraint were proof he was a "gentleman." Nonetheless, Abigail's first reaction was to wince, and her behavior was mirrored in each of the guests' startled faces.

As if suddenly aware of his audience, W.R. softened his stance, attacking with words instead of blows. "It's time for the 'Little Princess' to go to her tower," he ordered.

"Aw shucks." Marion sniffled, then dissolved in a bout of hiccuping tears. "You're never going to let me forget that damn guy, are you?"

"You're the one who chose to throw him in my face, my dear! 'Mr. James Deering and his lovely villa in Florida': those were your exact words—in case you've forgotten. 'He decorated a suite just for me, named it the Little Princess Room.' "

"I was just a kid, Popsie, thirteen or fourteen . . . hell, I don't know, maybe I was only twelve . . . just starting out in show business . . . with that damn Chu Chin Chow and his phony-baloney 'Ballet.' " By now, the tears were thick and furious; Marion seemed to choke on each one. Her nose was running, and her mascara made globby, black streaks on her swelling cheeks.

"You don't earn much when they put you in the back of the pony line . . . and my parents, you know, they didn't have much."

"So, Deering paid you, did he? Well, you know what that makes you, my dear."

"No, Pops!" Marion had begun sobbing in earnest;

the noise ratcheted through her chest, shaking her shoulders and pounding her spine.

"It wasn't like that. He invited a bunch of us chorus kids down to his house. We went on the train, and he sent his chauffeur to pick us up. It was real proper. Mama Rose came with us and everything. . . . It was the first time us girls had ever left New York . . . and Jim . . . well, Mr. Deering, he had this real nice villa, right on this big blue lagoon, and a swimming pool with a marble boat in the middle."

"And what did you and 'Jim' do out on that secluded marble boat?"

"Aw, Popsie, please don't make me tell you again. . . . It was just funning, you know. . . . It wasn't serious like you and me."

"What about your little fling with Paul Block? I suppose that wasn't 'serious' either . . . or that goddamn, snot-nosed blue blood from Philadelphia!"

Marion tried to stand, but caught her heel in the hem of her Tudor gown and collapsed again, murmuring an almost silent: "You've got a wife, you know . . . and kids . . . and I never say boo about them."

But W.R. heard the forbidden words. "Leave Millicent out of this," he seethed. "And my boys, too. You know you're not permitted to mention their names. Ever."

"Leave her alone." The words were so forceful and the tone so striking that both Marion and W.R. looked up simultaneously—as did every other person in the room. Bill Wellman strode forward, marching directly to his host as if he intended to punch him in the jaw. Instead he reached a hand to Marion and lifted her to her feet.

"Aw shucks, Billy," she muttered, while W.R. ordered, grim-faced, "See here, young fellow."

"No, you see here, 'Pops.' I hate bullies; I always

have, and you're the worst kind 'cause you've got plenty of dough. Wining and dining all these nitwits, buying friendship with a pack of knucklehead sycophants. Guys like you are a dime a dozen." Wellman's hectoring had the self-righteous sound of a college junior who's suddenly discovered that his fellow humans lack altruism. What the tone lacked in stature, however, it made up for in strength, and his fellow revelers shrank away, sharing shocked and furtive glances with one another.

W.R. gave an almost imperceptible nod toward Neylan, who, in turn, gazed meaningfully at the Mullers. The brothers had entered the room the minute Wellman began his defense of Marion. Abigail turned around, and a lamplit corner suddenly darkened with their hulking figures.

"Well, Bill, I'm not sure how I can be a 'dime a dozen' type when you're also accusing me of being richer than Croesus. I guess you'd better make up your mind—or lay off the sauce." The tone was deceptively fair-minded, but Wellman wasn't fooled.

"I'm not drunk. I may not have your fancy language, Mr. High-and-Mighty Hearst, but I know how to call a spade a spade."

The Mullers tensed forward while the filmland guests receded. Shoulders and necks hunched in while arms that had draped themselves on chair backs and half tables and statuary slithered to their owners' sides. No one had ever witnessed such a fearsome breach of etiquette; using that kind of language with the great William Randolph Hearst was unthinkable. It was almost suicidal.

But Wellman had only begun. "Hearst . . . that's kind of a German name, isn't it? Seems to me, I remember reading a lot of tripe about you before the war . . . some rot about your not wanting us to fight

Germany." As if he'd taken his cue from his host, young Bill Wellman sounded like reasonableness itself.

"You can't believe everything you read in the papers, Bill."

"Why not? You print 'em, don't you?"

"I publish some of our nation's newspapers, Bill, but not all, I regret to say."

"And those papers you do publish, the dailies and Sunday editions, the magazines and so forth, they reflect your point of view, don't they?"

"I certainly hope so." An easy laugh accompanied this statement. W.R. looked to Neylan for corroboration, and Neylan nodded smug encouragement.

"Well, then, maybe you can explain how come you were burned in effigy during the war, or why distributors made bonfires of your papers, or why your newsboys had to wear American flags to keep from being attacked. And what about those anti-Hearst rallies and the Hearst-Pathé newsreels that dropped your name when the movie-palace audiences starting hissing and booing every time they saw it? What do you think of them apples, Herr Wurst?"

A collective sigh shivered through the room; meaningful looks shot from one guest to another; eyebrows were raised and heads were shaken; but Hearst and Wellman remained impervious.

"Sometimes being pro-American has its price, Bill. I didn't believe the United States should enter a war I felt certain it would lose." W.R. continued to attempt a honeyed tone, but the effort was beginning to sound ragged around the edges. Real anger had started to leak out, and, as always, a sense of menace wasn't far behind.

"Pro-American or pro-German?" Wellman demanded.

"I think the record shows I was as good a patriot as any."

"Well, I don't agree with your doctored records!" Unfortunately, Wellman had begun shouting.

"Who is this guy, Neylan? A stooge for that pseudo-journalist Horace Glendenning?" W.R. intended the remarks as a jest, but not a soul laughed.

"A lot of my pals died over there . . . died fighting for the Allies. I told you some of those boys didn't survive a week . . . farm kids, a lot of them . . . never even seen a city and they croaked before they learned to *parlez-vous* . . . while here you were, Mr. Kraut Lover, getting pats on the back from the goddamn kaiser and drinking pilsner with a bunch of German spies—"

"If you're referring to Bolo Pasha or Count von Bernstorff, young man, my name was cleared of all charges. I think you'd better get your facts straight."

"I have my goddamn facts straight!" Wellman roared. "And after that lousy fighting was over, after me and a sorry bunch of survivors crept home, you didn't have the decency to support the League of Nations! I guess you figured the League would hurt your German buddies if they ever tried raising Cain again."

"That's enough, Wellman!"

"No, it's not! You used your goddamn newspapers to take sides. You tried to poison the American people's brains. You might as well have murdered—"

"I said that's enough!"

The Muller brothers' strong hands were attached to William Wellman's armpits before he knew what had happened. Then the former aviator and war hero was marched from the room.

No one made a move; no one dared breathe. The grandfather clock ticked, and the fire that W.R. had so solicitously provided for continued to blaze and crackle, sending out mini-explosions that perfumed the air with singed cedar and eucalyptus and pine and oak, but those were the only noises present.

After a moment, W.R. stalked out. He didn't bother to say good-night, nor would he wish his dumbfounded guests "God speed" the following day.

14

"EXTRAORDINARY!" CATHA BURKE WHISPERED AS she stared at the newspaper clippings, letters, ancient guest lists, table assignments, menus, and photographs spread across her motel-room bed.

"Abigail Kinsolving . . . working for W. R. Hearst. What an amazing discovery! I wonder why my mother never mentioned the fact?"

Catha straightened her spine and stretched her legs over the motel room's quilted burgundy bedspread. Her skirt was a disaster, a lumpy wad of wrinkles, and her back and shoulders felt no better. Catha looked at herself with disgust. Unfortunately, the bed faced a mirror almost as broad as its own king-size girth, and she had no choice but to confront her image or return to the artifacts scattered on the expanse of glossy, polyester quilt.

She decided to stand up, that way avoiding both mirror and bed. Catha grinned with a fair amount of inward pride. No one would ever fault her resolve or stamina when it came to hunting historical clues.

"Okay," she announced, "so what have I learned?"

But her feet, which had fallen asleep, began tingling so unbearably she flopped back down on the rumpled mattress, beginning a mini-avalanche of papers. Abigail's letters (written at Marion's behest) slopped into the two- or three-line zingers Marion had scribbled herself; Ethan's methodically typed police report slipped from the pillows; a few brittle news clippings fluttered in the air, and Catha's own notes collapsed onto the floor, a shuffle of lined legal pages the associate professor hadn't yet bothered to number.

"Oh, hell's bells!" Catha yelped. Thoroughly annoyed at her sudden lapse of professionalism, she bent down, recovering the sheaf of yellow paper, and swearing that when she became a full professor, she'd have a research assistant—and never work in spaces that didn't have proper desks and decent lighting.

Then she walked to her tiny balcony. Despite the cigarette-size holes in its grass-green, indoor-outdoor carpeting and the splotches on its stuccoed walls, the balcony was a cheerful place. Its view (if you ignored the motel's parking lot) revealed the double stand of stately royal palms lining Santa Monica's Ocean Avenue and the wide, sculpted park edging the city's bluffs. The Pacific Ocean filled the rest of the scene, stretching north toward Malibu and south to Palos Verdes, an expanse of flawless blue that never let you forget you were in California.

Bicyclists cruised the meandering park, getting a last-minute glimpse of the brilliant sky before the sun began its disappearance westward. Sunset watchers had already started gathering near the concrete benches, couples mostly, tourists decked out in sandals and shirtsleeves. Catha felt momentary disgust with her solitary existence.

Well, Win's definitely out of the picture, she reminded herself, returning to the curtained darkness of her room and yanking open the drapes. The yellow light of a waning, autumnal sun billowed onto the bed, turning San Simeon's stationery and invitation cards a creamy tan. Catha watched the metamorphosis, caught, for a moment, between the two distinct worlds of modern Santa Monica and the Hearst castle in 1924.

"I wonder how I would have felt living up there," she murmured. "It was quite a place. It still is." Then, with habitual speed, Catha's thoughts changed directions, and she was back on the subject of Win Reid.

New friends and associates found this habit disconcerting; Catha's quick brain often juggled several conversations at once, and she responded when criticized, "I'm sure I finished the sentence—didn't I?" as if the explanation helped listeners who'd been left behind. But then Catha also claimed she could decipher her own handwriting.

"It's better this way," she insisted now. "If I'd been able to see Win off on his sabbatical, it would have given us both a false sense of losing something we never had. The man had his good qualities, but I have to admit that spontaneity and warmth were never among them.

"So, okay, let's return to the subject at hand—my newfound grandmother, Abigail Kinsolving." Catha began reshuffling her notes and riffling the scribbled pages:

"Newspaper clippings . . . a fleet of Cadillacs for Thomas Ince's studio . . . the film adaptation of Elinor Glyn's *Three Weeks* . . . Ince and wife, Nell, in their home in Benedict Canyon, previewing his new film, *The Marriage Cheat* . . .

"Rumors about a married Rudolph Valentino and Pola Negri . . . Chaplin and Lita Grey . . . the obituary of an unnamed filmland biggie . . . but no murder." Frustration made Catha want to shout aloud.

"Okay, so maybe there wasn't a murder. . . . Maybe it was a rumor . . . somebody dies under mysterious circumstances, etc. . . . No, that's no good. Ethan conducted an investigation for the sheriff's office in Cambria. Even if the entire event were hushed up, someone believed there were dirty deeds afoot.

"Donnie certainly thought a murder had occurred, otherwise why would he have started describing it in the San Simeon tour bus? And, clearly, Ethan had—and still has—his own suspicions. . . . Plus, if a story lasts this many years, it's got to be founded in truth.

"So dispense with an accident." Catha made another furious note on her legal pad. "It was a murder, pure and simple . . . but of whom—and by whom? Because I absolutely refuse to believe Abigail Kinsolving was capable of a violent act like that—even if Ethan insisted she had plenty of 'gumption.' "

Without giving her actions a second thought, Catha grabbed up the phone and put in a call to Lucas Purnell.

"He's got to have more information—or maybe his uncle hid a few more clues," she murmured while the vampirette at Lucas's law firm answered the phone and put Catha on hold for what seemed like three days.

Only when she was informed that Lucas had "left for the remainder of the weekend" and that she would be transferred to voice mail did Catha's heart do a quick flip-flop.

Of course, she'd forgotten it was late Saturday afternoon; of course, she hadn't prepared a concise message, and the memory of Lucas's serene smile produced a garble of "maybe" 's and "um" 's that ended in a none-too-eloquent "Call me—please?"

"Oh, shoot!" Catha groaned as she dropped the receiver into the cradle. "Why couldn't I have simply left my name and number as I do when I check other academic sources?" Inadvertently, her eyes leapt to the ubiquitous mirror and registered every flaw in her face and body. "Maybe brown lipstick," she muttered under her breath, "and a blouse that's a little more clingy."

With no Lucas, and no means of knowing when (or even if) he'd return her call, Catha realized she'd have to call it quits for the evening. First thing tomorrow, she'd head for the research library at UCLA. Not only could she track down the mysterious obituary in their microfilm collection, but she'd be back on terra firma—a university campus. She'd be in her element once again.

To say that the University of California at Los Angeles was a change after the small New England school Catha had been accustomed to would have been a major understatement. Wesleyan's petite campus with its ivy-covered quad and pristine Greek Revival houses was a striking contrast to the vast accumulation of Moorish architecture, brick walks, fountains, pergolas for outside dining, and sun-swept sculpture gardens that composed the educational facility known by the acronym UCLA. Catha decided it was the biggest university she'd ever seen.

Finally snagging a parking space in one of several mall-like structures, she navigated her way toward the cavernous building's exit, stepped over the authoritarian treadles, wondered what had become of kids relying on their trusty bikes, then got the full blast of southern California campus life—on a Sunday morning, to boot.

A steel band was set up along Bruin Walk, and a nearby barbecue was in full swing, spread out on industrial-strength grills that seemed capable of feeding five hundred at a go. Charcoal fires leapt skyward, carrying the sizzling aromas of ribs and chicken legs. Some students were dancing and eating simultaneously; others, on Roller-blades, were skating to the beat as they wove in and out of the scented smoke.

The entire student body seemed caught up in the party. Catha was tempted to stop and join the fun; dancing placed high on her list, but she realized with a sudden gulp that she was no longer nineteen.

The shock was one of those peculiar epiphanies that happen at odd moments, like repeating a word until it loses its meaning. Of course, Catha knew how old she was; if anyone had asked, she would have answered, "Thirty-two," at the drop of a hat. It was simply that she didn't feel thirty-two or twenty-eight or any age in particular.

"This is horrendous," she murmured. "Here I am, growing older, and I don't even feel mature yet." She watched a couple of girls bopping along the path; they were nineteen or twenty, at the most, and both wore incredibly short skirts. Catha noticed their legs weren't nearly as shapely as her own, a discovery that delighted her.

"As soon as I'm finished with the microfiche," she promised herself, "I'm going to zip back into Westwood and buy myself some new clothes. I'm tired of looking like a frump."

Because of the party, the microfilm library was deserted. Catha had the place to herself, which was fortunate as signs above the machines warned users that a maximum of ten minutes was permitted when the library was full.

"Ten minutes!" Catha protested as a rabbity, female assistant with red-rimmed eyes and a twitching mouth produced films from both the Los Angeles *Daily*

Times and *Daily Examiner*. "Who could accomplish in-depth research in so little time? What kind of a library is this anyway?"

But the microfilm drove all other thoughts from her brain. Catha had started sequentially, cross-referencing dates and names, and the first entry to appear on her screen was a half-page photo of Thomas Ince, reclining in a wheelchair following an automobile accident.

The date was May 12, 1915; the newspaper, the *Daily Times*. Projecting equipment surrounded the director/producer, and the upper left of the picture had an insert, a still from his newest film. The caption stated that the boss of "Inceville" had been forced to preview the film at home before sending it to New York.

"Bingo," Catha whispered as she punched a magnetic card into the copy machine, printed an impression off the screen, then zapped the rewind button and threaded another reel.

This time the year was 1918, the day November 22, and the story concerned a fatal accident at the Inceville Motion Picture Studio. Two carpenters had been killed outright when a scaffolding collapsed, hurling them forty feet to the studio floor and breaking their necks. Two other men were listed as "probable" fatalities, and five more were "seriously" injured. Alvin Riggs and William Graham were the deceased. The set had been intended for use in a "street scene."

"My God," Catha said.

Then came a 1919 article about Thomas Ince signing a contract with Adolph Zuckor and First National Pictures, then another reference to the director—this time in a new picture deal on September 5, 1921.

Catha squinted at the page, scanning up and down, magnifying the words and then reducing them. A photograph lay tantalizingly half-hidden on the screen. She rotated the page sideways and the picture appeared: Charlie Chaplin sailing for Europe aboard the *Olympic*.

The actor was waving to a crowd of well-wishers, the sun splotching his curly hair and turning it a deeply contrasted black and white. A woman accompanied him, but her face was lost in the shadow of a deep cloche hat, and the caption didn't identify her. It did, however, note that among the "festive bon voyage party" were Mr. Chaplin's "great, good friends" Douglas Fairbanks and Mary Pickford.

"Copy," Catha ordered aloud, grabbing another stack of films. These she raced through, searching for and discarding possible tie-ins. The last tape in her selection contained a duplicate of one of Ethan's clippings:

Marion, the "Queen of the Screen," "talking" to England via radio. The date was April 18, 1924; apparently, Marion had begun her speech with a gentle "Hello, can you hear me?" Naturally, the newspaper was Hearst's own *Daily Examiner*.

On a whim, Catha decided to look up Billy Bitzer, D. W. Griffith's famed camera operator. She cross-referenced the camerman's activities with work she considered propaganda in nature. Sure enough, G. W. "Billy" Bitzer was mentioned in a *New York Times* article.

The date coincided with the Spanish-American War; the event had been Navy "war games" fought near Newport, Rhode Island, and Fishers Island, New York. Bitzer had filmed the action—including a "surprise interruption" by the Duchess of Marlborough cruising Block Island Sound on the Astor yacht.

"I guess W.R.'s newspapers scared the entire na-

tion," Catha marveled. "Even the New England coast-
line was preparing for attack from Havana."

Fort Wright, on Fishers Island, which suffered the
training session's only casualties, was deemed "defen-
sible" despite the gunners killed when one of the
twelve-inch guns exploded prematurely. The body of
a Pvt. Edelard Roy was torn "limb from limb" in the
blast. A fellow soldier was "seriously wounded by a
blow" from Roy's severed right arm.

"Jesus," Catha muttered. "What a waste." She
glanced at her watch; a half hour had passed, and she
still hadn't found any reference to murder. "Maybe I
should go check and see if Lucas returned my call,"
she argued aloud as she handed back the film basket
and waited for another allotment.

By now, the assistant was regarding her with down-
right suspicion; the nervous, red eyes had begun dart-
ing fearful glances at the door.

"Is there a problem?" Catha demanded with her
best professorial scowl, and the girl scurried off to fill
the request.

On the last reel, Catha found what she was looking
for. The information was in a small article near the
rear of the *Daily Examiner* dated December 21, 1924.

Advertisements for resorts in Yosemite, Hawaii,
and Big Bear Lake; scheduled sailings for the Los
Angeles Steamship Company's "Super Liners"; a
larger-than-life-size drawing of a can of "Gebhardt's
Chile Con Carne Con Frijoles"; and a curious account
of a "purported gunman" found "slain on a deserted
highway near Colma" almost obscured the story Catha
had been searching for.

But there it was in black-and-white newsprint!
Catha panned in, magnifying the letters. INCE RUMORS
DENIED, the tiny headline stated, quoting several

"semiofficials" who announced there would be "no further criminal investigation" despite the fact that the director's death had been "alternatively reported" as "acute indigestion" or "heart failure." Ince had collapsed while on board William Randolph Hearst's yacht, *Oneida*. The date had been Sunday, November 16, 1924. He'd succumbed the following day.

"Oh, my God," Catha whispered. "That was the funeral clipping Ethan saved . . . the one with the missing page. THRONGS PAY FINAL RESPECTS TO FILM WORLD LEADER . . . quotes from the widow, photographs of film stars and the flags in Hollywood flying at half-mast . . . it was Thomas Ince's funeral the paper was describing. He's the Hollywood honcho Abigail is supposed to have killed."

15

IT WAS THOMAS HARPER INCE!" CATHA FOUND herself shouting into a pay phone in the basement of UCLA's Powell Library while a nearby watercooler rumbled a deafening gurgle.

". . . No, Lucas . . . Ince is the nameless person in that funeral article. The one your uncle saved . . . from the clippings in the box you gave me. . . . What? . . . No, I can't hear you. There's some stupid water fountain making Niagara Falls noises down here. Hold on, I've got the information right here."

Yanked up short by a minuscule length of shiny pay-phone cord, Catha fumbled with her briefcase and a sheaf of photocopies from the microfilm library. She knew she'd begun her part of the conversation badly, that enthusiasm had flung words out of her mouth before she'd thought them through, and that she hadn't introduced herself properly, on top of it.

Lucas had been forced to ask her name twice before finally realizing his caller was "the teacher." Catha could hear amusement zinging through every syllable of every question, and her response was sudden chagrin. She realized she was being unreasonable, but that didn't alleviate the problem.

"Here . . . listen to this: THRONGS PAY FINAL RE-SPECTS TO FILM WORLD LEADER. Ince's name doesn't actually appear until later in the article. . . . What do you mean, 'Who's Thomas Ince?' . . . Well, I just assumed, being a native Californian, that you'd be familiar with industry lore. I mean, you know the current members of the film world . . . Meryl and Jayni and all those other names you mentioned in your office yesterday."

Catha sighed while the water fountain repeated its attack. Damn, she thought, here I've made this fabulous discovery, and I'm reduced to sharing it with a broken watercooler and an environmental lawyer who doesn't care. Frustration made her stand up straighter while her voice took on the authoritative tone she reserved for her professional life.

"Actually, I'm surprised you don't know the name. I would gather from the amount of microfilmed articles that Ince was extremely well known during the silent-film era. So, what I need to ask"—she tried for less demanding sound—"is do you have any more of your uncle Ethan's effects? . . .

"Well, when do you suppose you could look? . . .

"Not till then? I was hoping you'd say this afternoon. I realize it's Sunday, but I've got to return to Connecticut, and thought I could finish my amateur sleuthing . . ." Hearing an edge begin to creep into her voice, Catha decided to back off.

"I'll buy you lunch," she suggested, while Lucas's warm laugh came in suddenly loud and clear.

"The movers and shakers of L.A. don't 'buy' each other lunch, Catha," his voice chortled. "They 'do' lunch. If you and I are going to discuss these wheeler-dealer types, even ones who lived during the twenties, you've got to get the lingo straight."

"So?" Catha relaxed into the same easy spirit.

"So, meet me at my house in forty-five minutes. . . . No, better make it an hour—I've got a few more calls to make."

Then he gave his address in Venice Beach, followed by a tangle of directions about "the 405 freeway on Sunday," "alternate routes," "side streets," and "possible" neighborhood parking spots. Catha scribbled catch-up notes; she felt as if she were conversing with a technician at NASA.

"Ozone Court?" she teased when he'd finally paused for breath. "You're kidding! You live on a street called Ozone Court? Are all the environmental lawyers housed there, or are you the only one?"

Lucas didn't have an answer for that, and Catha hung up the phone smiling to herself. Then she hurried out of the building, raced across the campus, bounced into her car, and made one brief stop at a boutique in Westwood where she purchased a sheer, fuchsia-colored silk shirt, a (very) short skirt of ever-green-hued crepe that complemented the brilliant green of her eyes, and a sexy pair of suede heels. In a final act of rebellion, she told the salesgirl to add the skirt's matching jacket to her purchases, and to toss her old outfit in the garbage bin.

Lucas's craftsman-era bungalow was a complete surprise. Catha had expected streamlined glass or a tubular, turquoise-accented wraparound that passed for "California style." She hadn't envisioned Lucas as caring about his home; she'd thought "condo," "rental," "bachelor share," but what confronted her after she'd finally secured a legal parking place (Lucas had been correct; Sunday in Venice Beach wasn't intended for amateur drivers) was a lovingly restored cottage, painted in nature-inspired colors that added a touch of whimsy to a solid, timeless building. In a city of "teardowns," Lucas's home revealed a good deal about its owner.

"I bet he has copies of the original deeds, too." Catha smiled to herself. "Who would have imagined it? A closet historian. Inside that macho athlete's body lies the soul of a thoughtful man."

A narrow brick walk led through an arbor trailing white and magenta bougainvillea. Again, the effect was comforting yet stylish; the flowers' vibrant hues contrasted perfectly with the sea tones of the veranda's trim.

The bungalow's interior was another matter altogether. Catha scarcely managed to keep from gasping aloud when Lucas opened his door. Wall-to-wall clutter greeted her eyes.

The living room looked like a combination locker room and student's cram session. The space was a jumble of discarded running clothes, battered take-out pizza boxes, an empty juice carton lolling on a cast-aside squash racket, puddled towels, forgotten newspapers, and a bare minimum of college-dormitory-style furniture—a type once known as Danish modern. Male hormones had obviously run unchecked here.

Lucas followed Catha's openmouthed stare and made a stab at tidying by kicking a single running shoe under a couch covered in orange plaid Herculon overlaid with a pair of raggedy, gray exercise sweats, then bluffed, "I don't spend much time at home . . . I mean, I haven't gotten around to decorating or . . ."

Lucas's lionlike eyes gazed helplessly at the room. The casually rolled shirtsleeves, horn-rim glasses, and square jaw grew more boyish and insecure by the moment; it was as if he were finally seeing his living quarters in all their true horror. Then he became aware of Catha's transformation, taking in the chic new clothes, hairdo, and self-possessed stance. The effect seemed to add to his distress.

He swiped a bunched-up towel from a leatherette chair and stuffed a squash racket under the couch. "Besides"—he tried to laugh—"they say this Scandinavian stuff is making a comeback."

"I sincerely hope not." Catha grinned. Then she dropped her purse on the only unoccupied table and told herself that Lucas Purnell had met his match.

The garage (where Lucas believed he'd "stashed another of Uncle Ethan's treasure boxes") was as much a pigpen as the house. Law books spilled over the floor, jockeying for position with cartons of unmatched china and cookware that were clearly hand-me-downs. A mountain bike hung from the wall, both tires decidedly flat. There was no room for a car; there hadn't been for some time, and a dusty, poster-size photo of an elderly black Labrador retriever leaned against the unused garage door.

"That's Charlie," Lucas said, but the tone was different; it had turned thoughtful and a little sad. Catha looked up into his face, and her superior smirk vanished.

"He was my wife's dog. Prince Charles. She named him when she was a kid. Said she'd always wanted to be a queen. . . . Charlie was a great old guy. Then he went blind. Deaf, too. Labs don't like to outlive their usefulness; they try to sneak off to die. We were living in someone's guesthouse then . . . you know, law school students paying minimal rent till we nailed our first decent jobs. We had a hell of a time keeping old Charlie confined. Finally, we had to put him to sleep."

Oh, how sad, Catha started to say, but Lucas's silence stopped the words in her throat; they seemed superficial and shallow. Lucas continued to stare at the dusty portrait as if he were running down a list of private decisions.

"My wife died a year later," he stated simply. "Cancer. That's what we're doing to ourselves, you know, with this crap we're throwing into our air and water. Electromagnetic fields, steroids in processed cheese . . . You name it; there are pollutants everywhere. . . . She would have been a good lawyer if she'd lived."

Catha found this sudden revelation deeply moving. The Lucas Purnell she'd interviewed in his sleek Century City office hadn't appeared a man of deep emotion. Now she realized she'd been mistaken.

But before she could summon an appropriate response, Lucas shrugged and affected a dismissive smile as if making a concerted attempt to expunge the difficulties of the past.

"Ancient history," he insisted. "I'm sorry to badger you with my personal battles." Then he returned to the array of unmarked boxes as if they were of paramount importance.

"So, let's see . . . Uncle Ethan's treasure trove. I'm sure it's here somewhere. . . . I know he gave me two boxes . . . wanted them kept 'separately' . . . 'just in case.' Uncle Ethan can be quite adamant . . . as you know."

Lucas prized open a couple of liquor-store cartons. "Nope . . . undergraduate memorabilia . . . high school diploma . . . track team photo."

He reached for a cobweb-drenched container balanced within the garage's rafters, and an avalanche of baseball cards came tumbling down. Rectangular slabs of colored cardboard dotted the floor; the effect was like confetti cut for a giant.

"I guess you think I'm kind of a pack rat." Lucas smiled sheepishly while Catha answered an encouraging: "Lucky you! I'm compulsively tidy."

By the time the elusive artifacts were found, they'd taken on a minimal role in Lucas's and Catha's lives. Both professed joy at retrieving Ethan's hidden horde, but both had begun to put historical research on the back burner. The box remained unopened on the grungy garage floor.

"What about lunch?" Lucas suddenly asked. "You hungry?"

"I'm always hungry!" Catha said, beaming.

The fish-and-chips joint Lucas had chosen was on Venice Boulevard, within sight of the ocean, but not, as he'd explained it, "next to the crazies with the chain saws. You don't want to expose yourself to that situation on a weekend."

"I'd rather not run into a lunatic with a chain saw even on a weekday," Catha had countered, but she glanced through the restaurant's windows and down the street while she spoke.

"Oh, the guy I'm talking about is harmless, Catha. He juggles chain saws, that's all."

"Juggles them? While they're whirring around?"

"Yep." Lucas's smile was a ripple of perfect, white teeth.

"You Californians really are nuts, you know that?" This time it was Catha's turn to grin.

"Would you rather spend your life in Middletown, CT?"

"Good point." Catha wiggled her newly freed mane, then caught sight of her reflection and blushed.

"Your hair looks better without the braid, if that's

what you're wondering. The new outfit's not bad, either."

"A compliment, I assume," Catha shot back—and didn't blush in the slightest.

By the time the food arrived, Catha and Lucas had dispensed with personal stories and moved ahead into a discussion of William Randolph Hearst. Their talk followed a relaxed pattern of interruptions, non sequiturs, and verbal double takes.

"No, that was the exact phrasing of Hearst's editorial, Lucas. . . . The one following President McKinley's assassination. . . . Even from our present standpoint, I can't imagine writing more inflammatory. . . .

"Of course, Teddy Roosevelt excoriated the publisher. Said he was advocating anarchy." Catha dunked a french fry into a gob of ketchup, then began to nibble it lengthwise, intoning between bites:

" 'If bad institutions and bad men can be got rid of only by killing, then the killing must be done.' Fighting words, don't you think? And to run them in a newspaper? Especially right after the president of the United States has been murdered! What a scary guy Hearst must have been . . . 'then the killing must be done'—"

"Do you always eat your food in such a provocative manner?"

"You should see me with butterscotch Krimpets," Catha answered without thinking. "By the way, the newspaper was the *New York Journal*. It was the second paper Hearst owned, and he was locked in a bitter circulation battle with Pulitzer, his onetime boss and mentor. Both wanted absolute control of the so-called sensational press—"

"So, what's the skinny on this guy Ince?" Lucas interrupted, returning to Catha's research at UCLA.

"I have some vague recollection of Uncle Ethan mentioning a homicide that involved the illustrious San Simeon crowd, but I'm afraid I put his ravings down to old age and didn't pay much attention. The elderly sometimes imagine themselves more important than they actually were. . . . I take it you believe Ince was murdered?"

"Absolutely! If he wasn't, why has the rumor persisted all these years—especially when certain people were desperate to see it disappear?" Then, true to form, Catha jumped back to her previous thought.

"Sometimes I keep a package next to my bed," she murmured. "That way I don't have to walk all the way into the kitchen if I wake up hungry. The smell when you open the wax paper is out of this world."

"Are we on microfilm reels now or Ince or Charlie Chaplin or what?"

"Butterscotch Krimpets." Catha's face wore a child's look of impatient innocence. She had a difficult time understanding how often she left her listeners in the dust.

"I don't know." Lucas smudged a large piece of fried flounder into a puddle of tartar sauce and vinegar. "Frozen Reese's peanut butter cups are hard to beat—"

"In bed?" Catha's tone registered shock.

"Sure, why not?"

"But don't you get covered in chocolate?"

But before Lucas could continue, Catha had swung back to a rundown on Ernst Lubitsch, Jack Gilbert, and her discoveries at the Microfilm Library.

"So, what do you think?" Catha demanded when she'd finished her monologue. "Let's face it, Tom Ince must have angered more than a few people. He was a producer and director, for one thing, and we all know how actors feel about that particular breed. Writers, too. Glyn wasn't always happy with the film adaptations of her work.

"Plus, Ince was on the rise. If the deal had gone through with Hearst's Cosmopolitan Pictures, the man would have had almost unlimited financial clout. . . . Besides, remember the fatalities at his studio. . . . I think he must have had some determined enemies."

"But murder, Catha? The paper stated the investigation had been terminated—"

"That was Hearst's paper! He owned the *Examiner*—as well as twenty-two others in seventeen cities. There wasn't a section of the country that didn't have a Hearst publication! He could decide which facts to print and which to delete. Granted, editors on papers beyond his control made their own decisions, but the mighty Hearst empire carried a good deal of weight. Obviously, the investigation was too hot to obliterate entirely, so the boys in the city room chose the second-best approach: they buried the article next to an advertisement for canned chili. It was all I could do to find it. The microfilm catalog from the twenties is written in longhand, an old-lady, librarian script. At first, I assumed someone had made a mistake—"

"Are you going to eat the rest of your fries?"

"Yes." Catha scarcely paused for breath. "No, you can have them." Plates were exchanged without Catha's noticing the trade. "So, what I'm thinking, Lucas, is that something awful happened on board the *Oneida* . . . the man's poisoned—or stabbed, maybe . . . then he collapses, is carted ashore where he dies the next day."

"Wouldn't someone have witnessed this supposed attack?"

"That's a problem, I admit, but the yacht was huge. Two hundred feet plus. I bet a would-be murderer could find time alone with Ince . . . an unoccupied stateroom . . . I'm sure there were plenty of clandestine goings-on."

"Okay, I'll play along for now."

"Anyway, the yacht's out for an afternoon spin, and this catastrophe happens. Ince is carried away comatose, and the next thing you know, he's dead. . . . The whole affair is hushed up, which leads to rumor and speculation. One report claims the producer died of 'heart failure'; another asserts it was 'acute indigestion.' Conflicting stories like those seem highly suspicious."

"Well, maybe it was bad booze, Catha. That contraband stuff they imported during Prohibition was often potentially lethal."

"Then why list a 'probable' cause as 'heart failure'?"

"A typo?"

"Lucas! Get serious! Don't you find planted newspaper articles in your line of work? Public relations efforts intended to fool the public?"

"All the time."

The waitress appeared, dessert menus in hand, but Catha seemed to stare straight through her. "Coffee," Lucas mouthed without waiting for a response.

"So, I believe it was murder. A murder very cleverly disguised to look like something else . . . or maybe it wasn't disguised . . . maybe Hearst was so powerful he simply quashed the reports. . . . Your uncle Ethan began an investigation; there was a Dr. Steinbeck listed as well as Hearst's private physician, Dr. Goodman. Two medical men examine the deceased . . . but the next thing you know . . . *whhhhft*, the whole problem vanishes."

Two cups of coffee were placed on the table, along

with a sugar bowl and creamer. Lucas waved both items in Catha's face, but she didn't respond.

"I want to know why that investigation faltered," she insisted instead. "Was it simply because whoever—or whatever—killed Tom Ince occurred on Hearst's yacht? Was he merely protecting himself from bad publicity? Or was he shielding a murderer? Did he know the truth and order his city editors to drop the story?"

"Do you want cream or sugar?"

"Because I simply can't believe my grandmother was involved. Why would Hearst have protected her? She was a nobody, Lucas, an orphan whose blue-blood relatives had sent her to 'finishing school' and then pulled the financial plug. I assume that when she journeyed to California to start her job, her only assets were a pair of white cotton gloves and a dinky seed-pearl choker."

"Do you think, Catha, that you may be the tiniest bit prejudiced in this opinion?" Lucas's query was gentle, but Catha answered a quick and defensive: "Absolutely not! Until Friday, I didn't even know the woman existed."

"But perhaps there's a reason for that. Perhaps your mother knew Abigail's story and felt ashamed. It happens, you know."

Catha reflected a moment, and a look of pain and doubt shadowed her face. Lucas had an intuitive sense she was trying to remember something her mother had once told her. "Maybe," Catha mumbled, drawing the word out, "but I don't think so." Then the troubled expression turned to one of resolve. "I believe Abigail was innocent—and that some sort of conspiracy was involved. Blame the person who can't defend him- or herself; it happens all the time.

"On October twenty-third, 1924, Abigail had been

working at San Simeon a little over two weeks. When Ince died on the seventeenth of November, she'd been a Hearst employee for six weeks only. If Abigail had killed Ince, she would have been turned over to the authorities on the spot. Hearst was a loyal man, but only with people who paid him in kind. With the rest of the world, he could be a brutal son of a bitch." Catha's tone was passionate with conviction.

"Read Ferdinand Lundberg's *Imperial Hearst: A Social Biography* if you want a truly damaging portrait. The book was published in 1936 and dedicated to Haywood Broun and the American Newspaper Guild . . ."

If Catha had been paying attention, she would have noticed an indulgent smile creeping around the corners of Lucas's eyes. The smile spread to the mouth, then the cheekbones and nose; soon Lucas was positively beaming

"What?" Catha demanded.

"I was just thinking how attractive you are—especially when you're passionate about a subject."

Catha stared at the crumb-flecked table. "Coffee," she finally said. "Oh, good."

After lunch, they walked Venice Beach. Daylight was creeping toward evening, and the heat of the southern California sun was gradually deserting the sand. Catha stepped out of her new shoes and felt how cool the beach path had become. The dry sand felt nearly wet with chill.

The air was the same, although the sensation was pleasantly refreshing. It's like springtime at home, Catha thought, a sun that's climbing toward summer and a breeze that remembers the gusts of winter.

"Do you ever miss the change of seasons?" Catha asked.

"That's what all Easterners wonder." Lucas laughed. "You don't realize California has seasons, too."

"You don't have snow."

"And you don't have roses blooming in December."

"Or seven years of drought eradicated by a three-day deluge that makes a monsoon look like a water shortage," Catha said, laughing in return.

"That's because L.A.'s been overbuilt. We're a community created from desert land. We irrigate artificially, creating a falsely lush landscape—"

"Thus your famous roses in December."

Conversation then jumped to Lucas's struggles with the wetlands project, the lobbying groups promoting development and the grassroots organizations attempting to battle big business.

"Oh, absolutely!" Catha interjected almost every other sentence. "It's always fiscal considerations that win in the end. That's why the environmental movement needs to create financial goals. If money could be made from developing ecologically sound products or harvesting natural resources without decimating the source—"

"Precisely!" Lucas interrupted. "I take it you noticed the oil rigs off Santa Barbara—"

"Who on earth approved that folly!"

In complete harmony, the two rabid conservationists talked all the way back to Lucas's house.

"Well, don't you want to open Uncle Ethan's box of goodies?"

Catha was sitting at one end of the now cleared couch, her feet drawn up beside her, while Lucas perched nearby on the (also clutter-free) leatherette chair. They were so close, their knees almost touched.

"You know, I'd almost forgotten that's why I was

here." Catha attempted an offhand laugh. "I guess I was having too good a time."

Hearing herself, Catha's face grew suddenly serious. Late afternoon had given way to evening. The room, which had been recently suffused with the red-gold glimmer of sunset, was now turning dusky as a fox's den. She could see the outline of Lucas's jawline and the contour of cheekbone and forehead where his hair curled over his ears.

"What are you thinking, Catha Burke?"

"I'm thinking I had a wonderful afternoon," she answered thoughtfully, "and also that it's time for me to make a graceful exit. . . . Why don't I take your uncle Ethan's artifacts back to the motel . . ."

"And why don't I open up a bottle of wine, and we'll sort through Ethan's horde together. Maybe order some Chinese take-out. . . . I'm pretty good at hunting for clues, you know. We could both get to the bottom of this mystery."

Neither of them made a move, however, and the sun continued its slow exit, passing out of Lucas's living room as if it were tiptoeing away. Catha heard a car door bang and a doorbell chime; the sounds seemed the most comforting in the world.

"This is a nice room . . . a nice house," she finally said. "It suits you."

"The exterior or the interior?" Lucas's tone was amused. He shifted on the chair, drawing nearer to the couch, and Catha could feel warmth emanating from his body. "You should have seen your face when you walked through the front door."

"Well, I hadn't expected dormitory-style living. Not from a top environmental lawyer." Both Catha's remarks seemed dangerously reminiscent of the past. I'm sorry, she wanted to add, I didn't mean to remind you of your wife. But the words stuck in her throat.

The room grew dimmer, and the corners began to disappear in shadow; then whole sections of the floor vanished, and the ceiling where it turned the corner and drifted toward the kitchen. It felt to Catha as though the universe were growing smaller, small enough to encompass only two.

Lucas stirred slightly and their knees finally touched.

"I really should be going," Catha whispered.

"If you want." Lucas moved to the edge of his chair, and Catha closed her eyes and waited. I can't let this happen, her mind began arguing. I can't let this happen. I mustn't. I won't.

But she stayed stock-still, aware of the neighborly noises creeping into the house, the return of families from Sunday outings, the happy shouts of kids and parents, the gleeful barkings of dogs, and the slow sift of Lucas's trouser legs stretching across the chair.

"I think I should leave," she said.

"Well, I disagree." Catha heard the tenderness in his tone so clearly it might have been a smile spreading over his face.

"Lucas," she repeated, while he slid to the couch and wrapped her up in his strong, sure arms.

The kiss when it came was wonderful, a moment of passion mingled with gentleness. Catha knew in an instant that she loved the taste of Lucas's mouth and the cozy, vanilla scent of his skin, that his curly hair was wonderful to twist her fingers in, and that his ears were the sexiest on the planet.

"You're really something, you know that?" she murmured. All traces of Connecticut schoolmarm had vanished.

"And you hate to keep your mouth shut."

They remained in that serene place for several long minutes, the world that exists just after the first declaration of intention and before the ineluctable decision to move ahead into the heedless depths of lovemaking.

It's a lovely world, full of slow, mild thoughts and breathless palpitations. Hope is everywhere, and a kind of crazy comfort that makes each second seem better than the last. Catha's stockinged toes tangled in Lucas's now shoeless feet; her legs felt how sturdy his athlete's body was while his arms caressed her back, and her hands felt the heat of his flesh under his starched, cotton shirt.

"We've got to stop," she finally murmured. "We're going too fast. Besides, I . . ."

"I know, you've got a husband waiting at home, and five little kiddies clamoring for their supper."

"Don't joke, Lucas. I'm being serious. I'm trying to take this situation seriously." There was sudden hurt in Catha's voice.

"I'm sorry. You're right. I guess I'm not accustomed to experiencing these pangs of emotion anymore. All I have is my workday—and a minor flirtation tossed in every once in a while."

"Flirtation?" Now it was Catha's turn to tease.

"Well, you know what I mean."

"You're too shy to say the word *sex?* That certainly comes as a surprise."

"Look who's joking now."

"I should go," Catha repeated slowly, moving to the edge of the couch and planting her feet on the floor.

In the sudden glare of lamplight, she straightened her fuchsia-colored blouse and olivine skirt. She didn't feel self-conscious in the slightest. On the contrary, she felt more alive than she had in a very long time. "Your hair looks much better all tousled like that," she said, smiling.

"I can't say the same for yours. You'd better brush it or the neighbors will talk." Lucas grinned.

Then they both grew quiet as Catha finally remembered Ethan's still-sealed carton and picked it and her purse up and then stood hesitantly beside the front door.

"Will you call me?"

"Of course," Catha answered too rapidly.

"I don't mean about this obsessive investigation of yours . . . or to return Uncle Ethan's treasure trove. I mean, will you call so we can go out again . . . see a movie or something . . ."

"I'm not sure, Lucas. Everything's moving so quickly. I'm a long way from home right now, and I'm not altogether certain this is the right thing to do."

Then she hefted the box and her purse and walked down the garden path toward her rented car.

Ensconced in her motel room, Catha finally decided to open the box. There was nothing else she could do with the remainder of the evening, and to sit there mooning and grousing was an inordinate waste of energy.

"Damn," she repeated for probably the one hundredth time. "Why can't life be easy! Why do I have to fall for some guy from L.A.? What's wrong with New Haven or Hartford, for God's sake? I mean, hey, I'd even settle for New York or Boston . . . or Poughkeepsie . . . there's a decent university there!"

While Lucas, across an expanse of streetlights and asphalt, was considering the very same problem—and finding as few solutions.

"Damnation!" Catha ranted. Then she slid Ethan's box to the center of the king-size bed, plopped herself beside it, wrenched open the packing tape, and peered inside. The usual confusion of papers was tumbled together, mixed in with a small black packet of photos and several more painstakingly folded newspaper articles. Catha reached inside the carton, touched something rectangular and surprisingly solid, and drew the thing out.

She was on the telephone before she had time to monitor her response. "Lucas," she said the moment he picked up the phone. "You're not going to believe this. I've found my grandmother's journal."

16

"WILLIAM WELLMAN WAS THROWN OUT ON HIS EAR after the fiasco following the masquerade dinner," Abigail's journal stated. The style was so candid and direct, Catha felt as if she were conversing with her long-dead grandmother. I bet I would have liked this spunky lady, Catha decided. We would have had a lot in common.

He wasn't even permitted to spend the night, because the moment Mr. Hearst left the Assembly Room, the Muller boys grabbed Wellman's elbows, marched him through Casa Grande's main door, down the front steps, across the terrace, and out to the drive. As if by magic, one of the Cadillac limousines was waiting in the shadows.

All the guests followed this eerie parade, although no one dared say a word. We stared at the ground like a bunch of guilty children. Finally, the Muller brothers threw their prisoner into the rear seat, slammed the door, and then climbed into the

217

chauffeur's compartment. They moved in such perfect unison, they looked like windup soldiers.

Mr. Barrymore stood next to me; Mr. Gilbert, Miss Garbo, Mr. and Mrs. Fairbanks, Miss Parsons, the Chaplins, and the other guests were there, as well. Marion had also trailed along, but she never opened her mouth. I guess we must have created a fairly bizarre spectacle—all of us in our masquerade costumes: Madame Glyn still wrapped in her tiger skin, Mr. Chaplin in his Napoleon rig, John Barrymore dressed as Beau Brummel, and me decked out as the Revolutionary War maid, etc.

In less than five minutes, the disgraced Bill Wellman had been whisked off into the night. Then the somber group disbanded and drifted away to the guest cottages. Marion's party was definitely over.

Catha read her grandmother's succinct description a second and third time, imagining a hundred thoughts and phrases that might have been deleted. It was clear Abigail had eliminated her own response to the incident, that she feared someone might discover her journal. But who that person was, Catha didn't know. Was it Marion? Or W.R.? Had Joe Willicombe been instructed to search the servants' private possessions—or the Mullers?

Catha fingered the journal. It was a cheap affair: a black cardboard cover stamped to look like pigskin, lined pages that had turned musty gray with years, and a spine gone brittle with use. Several entries were missing, and an entire section seemed to have been ripped out. But the book was Catha's only hope. What Abigail had chosen to describe or what she'd hidden between the lines would provide the sole clues to the Thomas Ince mystery. With a studiousness approaching reverence, Catha opened the journal again:

The day after the party was simply awful! That was October 26. Marion never quit her diet of bootleg booze following the confrontation with W.R. and the subsequent removal of Bill Wellman; and she insisted I sit up with her. We remained in her suite like two moles caught in a gardener's trap—Marion writhing restlessly on her bed, and me tiptoeing around or dozing in a chair.

Nothing I did was right. I was too "loud" when I opened the windows; I didn't speak "distinctly enough"; my voice sounded like a "pregnant hyena's." She even threw a slipper at me, but then started to sob afterward. I felt so distressed I forgot to be angry. In fact, I nearly started crying myself.

This situation lasted all of the twenty-sixth and well into the twenty-seventh. Marion didn't touch the meals the maid brought up on a tray and one time tossed an entire dinner onto the floor—all over that priceless Persian carpet! I doused the stains with table salt, but I'm not convinced the trick worked.

For both days and nights, Mr. Hearst refused to see my boss or even talk with her via the intra-house telephone. Every time she tried to get through, Mr. Neylan would answer and tell her the Chief had gone for a walk or that he was in discussion with Miss Morgan or studying the "dailies" or conversing with one of his executives down at Cosmopolitan Pictures in Hollywood.

It was an unhappy time; I kept having this fear that Marion and I were awaiting execution (my boss had dressed up as Anne Boleyn), but I never let on. We heard the guests depart during the afternoon of the twenty-sixth, but their voices were so muffled, it was impossible to distinguish one person from another.

219

None of Marion's friends said good-bye. Not even Mr. Chaplin, although maybe that was just as well. It would have been typically bad luck if the Chief had decided to finally pay Marion a visit only to discover her laying a farewell smooch on Charlie's lips!

At the end of the second day of her punishment, Marion turned frantic. Began bawling like a baby, vowing she'd never "loved anyone but Mr. Hearst," said she kept "failing him" because she was "young and stupid." Then her mood shifted and she became reckless and loud, shouting a lot of things she shouldn't have. Finally, she ordered me out of the room, and then immediately called me back. I've never felt so sorry for a person in my life.

Catha put down Abigail's diary. She felt a strange queasiness at this glimpse into Marion's troubled existence as well as compassion for her unsuspecting secretary. Within a month, someone would kill Thomas Ince, and either that person was Abigail—as rumor had it—or the true murderer would remain undetected, shifting the blame to an innocent young woman who had no champions in a dangerous house.

"Abigail! Abigail, answer me when I speak to you, God damn it!"

"Yes, ma'am," Abigail murmured. She was dog-tired and felt light-headed with the lack of fresh air in the suite. Marion had kept her up for two nights running now, refilling the glass with gin, then more ice, then flushing the entire mess down the toilet when her boss got the heaves. One moment, Marion would weep like a child; the next, she'd turn angry as a hornet.

"Abigail, God damn it! What's the goddamn time?"

"Nearly nine, ma'am . . . in the morning. . . . It's October twenty-eighth."

"Don't you 'ma'am' me, you snooty, little Miss So-and-So! I'm not some old hag like Julia Morgan, and don't you forget it! I know the difference between morning and night." Then Marion's tone flip-flopped; the boss-lady act became a lonely mumble. "It's the twenty-eighth?" she whispered. "October twenty-eighth? How did that happen?"

Abigail couldn't think of a tactful answer. Instead she moved to Marion's bed and began straightening the pillows. When her father lay dying in the hospital, Abigail had watched the nurses employ the same activity; it had seemed to have a calming effect.

"Jesus H. Christ," Marion muttered, "I feel like death warmed over. . . . No, that's wrong . . . death ice-cold—that's me." The attempt at humor seemed to brighten her momentarily, and Marion suddenly demanded a mirror, hairbrush, and lipstick, then thought better of the idea and barked a fierce:

"Forget it! I know what this sad sack's going to look like. Every time I go on a bender, I see the same ugly mug—and then I want to puke some more. Gin'll kill you, Abigail. The stuff's not mother's milk—not even my Mama Rose's.

"She's the reason I became a showgirl in the first place . . . did I tell you that? Mama Rose knew what it takes to get the fellas drooling. . . . They come to me for handouts, you know . . . on account of I got so much dough." Marion began to weep again, then clutched desperately at Abigail's hand.

"Don't you ever do it," she warned. "Don't you ever fall for some fella just 'cause he's young and cute and sexy. A girl's gotta think about her pocketbook. Good lays are a dime a dozen, Abigail. And I should know." Here Marion's tears turned into chest-heaving sobs. "But now I've screwed it up! Popsie'll go back to Millicent; I know that's what he's thinking . . . 'Society Page' Millicent and her grown-up sons. Those boys are ashamed of me, I know. That's why Popsie never lets them visit. I guess I broke the family apart just like people say."

Abigail was about to observe that W.R.'s decision concerning when and how to see his sons was his own choosing, but she held her tongue.

"You haven't spoiled anything, Marion," she answered instead. "Mr. Hearst is just busy. All those newspapers and mines and cattle ranches and the movie business, too! It's a wonder he can keep everything straight."

"He's got Neylan."

"Well, yes." Abigail's response was wary. "He does have Mr. Neylan. But they say successful businessmen do their own decision making; that would mean Mr. Hearst would have to know more about his business affairs than Mr. Neylan—or Mr. Brisbane or any of the newspapers' city editors. Why, that kind of knowledge requires tremendous concentration—and a lot of time."

"You're a good kid," was Marion's wan reply, then her tone turned edgy with fear. "You know something, Abigail? It's a secret, so you gotta promise you won't blab."

"I promise."

"Do you, kid? Do you swear you won't tell no one?" Marion clutched at Abigail's arm, pulling her close within the confines of the shrouded, silky nest. Abigail smelled alcohol mingled with the acrid scent of panic.

"I mean, you won't . . . you won't breathe a word to . . ?" Marion obviously couldn't bring herself to implicate her lord and master; instead her bloodshot eyes filled with tears, and great dollops of warm salt water began tumbling down her swollen cheeks.

"I mean, you won't go blabbing to . . . to . . . Neylan or Joe Willicombe. They don't like me, you know . . . they'd like to see me 'escorted' the hell out of here—just like poor Bill Wellman.

"Neylan and Willicombe, they think I'm just some tramp on the make . . . a floozy chorine with dollar signs in place of a brain. . . . But I been loyal, you know . . . and it hasn't always been easy. Sometimes his doctor says we gotta lay off the fun and games . . . you know what I mean . . . and I can't keep up with all this art talk, so—"

"You can trust me, Marion," Abigail interrupted, then immediately questioned her decision. What if Marion has something horrible to confess? Abigail wondered. What if she tells me she's "jazzing" Charlie Chaplin or Bill Wellman or even Thomas Ince? What if those men are the "better lays" she was talking about? What do I say then? It's Mr. Hearst who pays my wages, and I guess I owe him more than I do Marion.

But, all at once, Abigail realized she didn't like Mr. Hearst. She didn't like the way he was treating his mistress; she didn't like his manipulation or his ruthlessness. Marion was wholly dependent on the man, and because of that she was vulnerable. If he tossed her out, she'd end up losing her career as well—and then what would she do?

Sympathy ripped through Abigail's heart; she found herself becoming angry, protective, and hurt all at the same time. Marion should be down in Hollywood where she belongs, Abigail told herself. My boss is young and pretty; she should be dancing at fancy nightclubs, and painting the town red with her acting buddies—not trapped in some mountaintop mausoleum waiting for a marriage proposal she won't ever get!

"You can trust me, Marion," Abigail repeated. Her tone was newly resolved. She'd stick by Marion no matter what.

"I believe you, kid," Marion whimpered, "I believe you're telling the truth," then inexplicably she began moaning again. It was as if her secretary's promise had released a flood of self-loathing. "All my life, I been a failure," she sobbed. "Acting in pictures or dancing with Ziegfeld's troupe . . . And you know something else . . . that stuff Popsie said about James Deering, how I was his 'Little Princess' and all?"

"You don't have to tell me anything you don't want, Marion." Her boss's confessions were beginning to make Abigail positively nauseous.

"It wasn't just me, you know. Deering liked to have a bunch of us show kids visit. . . . He'd set us up, sort of . . . invite single gents, and a few ladies, too. . . . Mama Rose said it was a good idea . . . got our names known, besides introducing us to the finer things in life. . . . And I don't care that Popsie knows! That's what keeps him running! He's afraid I'll find some other guy . . . just like I'm afraid of Millicent."

"It's all right, Marion," Abigail murmured, but she might as well have been talking to herself.

"I just don't know why I get so hateful! If Mama Rose was here—or Papa Ben—they'd slap me a couple of times and tell me to wise up. . . . I mean, how could a kid born in Brooklyn's Eighth Ward—with all those saloons and two-bit hookers—how could that kid end up with all this . . . this splendor?

"I just don't know why the goddamn place has to be red. Look at it, Abigail! Drapes and pillows and chairs and even that damn antique rug! 'Cause I ain't no whore! I've never been a whore in my life!"

With Marion sleeping peacefully at last, Abigail tiptoed from the bedroom and pulled the door shut. She took stock of the sitting room as she passed through it, the russet-toned painting of Saint Catherine, the sixteenth-century settee swathed in scarlet damask, the Renaissance chairs backed in carmine velvet, even the monastic Spanish doors seemed imbued with a crimson hue. Abigail realized she'd never before noticed such a concentration of a single color. Marion was right; the effect was like a slap in the face.

Abigail narrowed her eyes, tilted her chin pugnaciously, and hurried across the hall separating Mr. Hearst's suite from Marion's. Noticing that the door was ajar and the rooms empty, she squared her shoulders and marched toward the back of the house and Hearst's private Gothic Study.

"Neylan, I won't repeat my demands a second time. Either Horace Glendenning acquiesces and publicly apologizes or he'll find himself in a most unfortunate position." W.R.'s threatening words tumbled into the hall, but Neylan's answer was more circumspect. None of his response seeped through the closed door, although Abigail heard the jangle of ringing phones as San Simeon's switchboard operators tried and failed to put through calls to the great man's mountaintop office. The Gothic Study was the heart of Hearst's publishing empire when he was in residence. Sometimes Arthur Brisbane or the various city editors would drive up for meetings, and on those occasions the long, polished table reflected the fears and insecurities of a good many men. Each was expected to bring the Chief a small but expensive gift to enhance his prodigious art collection, and how that offering was received meant the difference between having a job or not.

Abigail had only been in the room a couple of times. The vaulted ceiling with its low, stone ribs and dark murals, the high-backed medieval chairs, and the ceiling lamps that swung ominously on long, silver chains reminded her of a dungeon tribunal.

"It's not an idle threat, Jack. I know how to handle men like Glendenning. I've done it before—as I'm sure you recall."

Abigail shrank back within a shadowy alcove. She had a sudden fear that the study door would fly open or that Joe Willicombe would round the corner, accusing her of eavesdropping and demanding why she wasn't working. She considered sneaking back to Marion's suite or scurrying to her own tower room, but then wondered if the creaking wood floor might betray her.

"But what about your political ambitions if Glendenning refuses? Or worse, if he blabs to Pulitzer?" Neylan's question deteriorated into a garble of words Abigail didn't fully understand. There was something about the League of Nations as well as several references to a gubernatorial race in New York; finally, the methodical query was cut short by Hearst's violent outburst.

"Don't ever mention Al Smith's name again! That son of a bitch refused to share the ticket with me two years back—and in public, no less! Claimed I'd 'taken up with a blond actress,' then leaked the news to Pulitzer and the others. To say nothing of the snub I received when I trotted out Millicent and the boys at the convention this year. Organized a dance for six hundred stalwarts at the Ritz-Carlton, invited FDR and Eleanor, and William Jennings Bryan, got Will

Rogers to perform . . . and Al Smith rains ice water on my parade.

"Oh, I made certain my newspapers crucified him, all right. 'Suggested' his methods of graft and government corruption were responsible for the 'murder of tenement children.' . . . You remember some of my editorials . . . headlines, too! Al Smith and his Tammany gangsters—and Horace Glendenning: they claim I publish 'lying, filthy newspapers'; those are fighting words, Jack! And I'm not a man to forgive my enemies' transgressions."

Conciliatory noises emanated from Neylan. Abigail couldn't make out words, but whatever the response, it brought an almost hysterical laugh from W.R. "I don't know how you get away with it," his squeaky voice yelped. "You're the only adviser who dares argue with me. I could have canned you a million times, but I never do."

Abigail breathed a sigh of relief and was reconsidering tapping on the door and requesting that the Chief visit his abject mistress when another outburst sent her ducking for cover.

"Save your breath to cool your porridge, Jack! I'll continue calling the goddamn Chinese and Japanese the 'Yellow Peril' as long as I live; and you and Artie Brisbane and the rest of my city editors better leave my editorials alone. A newspaper is a powerful weapon; a hundred is like owning an army. Look at the way I used the printed page to attack McKinley. Or those banner headlines I ordered during the Spanish-American War! 'Avenge the *Maine,*' I shouted, and the nation obeyed! If you don't like my politics, you can pack your bags and leave.

"Now, let's get back to business. There's a contract between Cosmopolitan Pictures and Thomas Ince we need to discuss. The fellow's known as a 'maker of stars,' and I want him to work his magic on my girl. I want her to be as big a star as Pickford or the Gish girls. If it weren't for that gate-crashing, pissant Wellman, we would have gotten the problems ironed out when Ince was here for the costume party."

Abigail realized this was no time for an interruption; instead she began creeping away from her alcove, but before she'd reached the safety of the stairway, another explosion burst out of the study door.

"He's been doing what?" Hearst roared. "Who told you that? What I mean to say is, were there any witnesses to this . . . this activity?" The words were punctuated by the shattering of ancient wood as some priceless object broke apart under Hearst's enraged hands. Guilt-stricken silence followed. Abigail could hear her heart beating with fear. When the Chief succumbed to one of his temper tantrums, all the household staff suffered.

"Now, look what you've made me do!" the Chief finally screeched. "God damn it! Look what you've all made me do!"

"There was nothing I could do after that incident except go up to my bedroom and wait for the air to clear," Abigail wrote. "I couldn't risk incurring Mr. Hearst's wrath, even for Marion's sake."

Another week went by; by now my boss was up and around but feeling terribly lonely. W.R. locked himself away with his work, only permitting Mr. Neylan, Miss Morgan, or Joe Willicombe to enter his sanctuary. Marion and I passed the time riding in the pergola or swimming or endeavoring a lackluster game of tennis, then she'd stare at me with those enormous blue eyes of hers, but you could see that it wasn't me she was seeing. The Hearst "dailies" were flown in every morning to the private airstrip at the bottom of the hill, and we'd get news of the rest of the world. Well, we'd get the stories those papers printed.

In all this time, Marion never again confided in me, and I was relieved she didn't, but I guess I also felt a little sad. Not that I'd ever expected a famous person like Marion Davies to be my friend, but it seemed strange to be suddenly demoted. You could tell that Mr. Hearst was the only person she cared about, that everything she thought or did revolved around him, and that every waking moment was spent trying to worm her way into his good graces.

"I've been thinking," Marion announced, but Abigail knew better than to answer. The two were strolling the zoo, making a desultory parade when Marion stopped in her tracks in front of the black bear's cage. "I'm going to throw another party. But this time no one's allowed to make life difficult for my Popsie. We'll have a smaller, more exclusive group, and I'll tell the kids they'd better park their Hollywood battles at the door."

Enthusiasm had produced a new glow in Marion's face; her eyes glittered, and her speech hurried along in a breathy rush as if the words couldn't tumble out fast enough:

"John B. can come—Pops thinks he's 'tony' on account of his stage credits—but he's got to bring a dame this time, otherwise he gets randy as a goat. Charlie and Lita, of course. Did you notice how sweet that little kid was to my Popsie at the costume affair? If I didn't know them better, I'd say my old man was soft on the kid."

Abigail opened her mouth, then shut it. She had a

very different recollection of Marion's previous party, but she knew her boss would never listen.

"Let's see . . . Elinor, I guess, 'cause she's writing for Popsie's papers . . . and that dragon, Louella. . . . I swear I don't know what Pops sees in her. It's like she's got some weird power over him. . . . We'll nix the Fairbankses, which is a crying shame since Doug's such a doll, but I can't stomach her nibs again. . . . Likewise Garbo, which is fine 'cause Jack got so soused at our last dinner; and if there's one thing Pops can't tolerate, it's a drunk."

Not even these words gave Marion pause. In her mind, she was discussing John Gilbert's shameful behavior and nothing more. "So who are we missing?" she demanded. "From last time, I mean."

"Miss Negri, Mr. Valentino, Mr. Lubitsch," Abigail offered, tacking on a hurried, "Also Mr. and Mrs. Ince . . . and Mr. Wellman."

Marion's face clouded, but she pretended not to hear the last three names. "Forget Ernst," she decided on the spot. "I'll mull over Pola and Rudy. I kind of like having them around even though they're quiet. Rudy's got a wife, you know—like my Pops—and Pola's a—" Here Marion interrupted herself with a quick, infectious giggle.

"We'll go out on Popsie's big boat!" she said, beaming. "The *Oneida* and a picnic supper aboard! A yachting party—that's it! And we'll get gussied up in sailor suits! Let's see . . . the kids get here Friday . . . we have a cozy dinner mountainside . . . and then take to the briny on Saturday. . . . Get cracking, Abigail! You've got work to do!"

17

I'D LIKE YOU TO INCLUDE THOMAS INCE FOR YOUR
yachting party, Marion," W.R. ordered. His pale,
milky eyes were unwavering and unusually cold. Marion sensed trouble ahead, but decided to bluff her way
out of it.

"Aw, Popsie, I don't care about Incie making me a
star. Honest I don't. You don't have to drag him into
Cosmopolitan Pictures for my sake. Besides, I'm mad
at that dumb cluck. First off, he never called to say
he'll be late for our last shindig, and when he did
show, he left Nell behind."

"I would have imagined that kind of behavior would
thrill you."

"Having a guy turn up late? You know me better
than that, Pops." Marion attempted a gentle swat at
W.R.'s beefy shoulder. Both were sitting in lounge
chairs beside the Neptune Pool, although Marion was
clearly the more at ease in the hot afternoon sun. Her
black bathing costume showed off a tanned and lan-
guid body, while W.R.'s white arms and whiter legs
were the color of library paste.

"I was referring to your obvious enjoyment at having a flock of gentlemen admirers in attendance."

Marion didn't answer. She sensed the remark was a trap for which there was no correct response. She couldn't very well contradict Popsie, and to deny she liked flirting would be opening a bigger can of worms. The safer choice was to ignore the observation entirely.

"You make the rules up here, Popsie, and I like to see the kids stick to them. If you say 'be on time,' your word's law." Marion grinned an ingratiating smile, but her sunglasses diminished its brilliance.

"Take those things off." W.R.'s voice brimmed with rage.

"My cheaters?"

"And don't use that cheap expression. They're eyeglasses—with dark lenses to block the sun's glare."

"Cheaters is what they call them on the lot," Marion grumbled.

"Just because your filmland . . . companions employ a term or behave in a certain manner doesn't mean you have to mimic it."

Marion translated the criticism as a comparison to Millicent's high-toned ways, and her heart fluttered in sudden panic. She never stopped to consider that her lover's words might conceal a darker intent.

"Sure, Pops," she soothed. "I get lazy, I guess, talking to those bozos. But Abigail, she's been teaching me."

"And where is Abigail now?" W.R. jumped up from his chair, then paced to the water's edge and back again.

"You going for a swim?" Marion was immediately beside him, as eager to please as a child. "I'll race you to the deep end!"

"No, Marion, I don't feel like taking a dip at the moment."

"Oh . . . Oh, all right, Popsie." Disappointment dashed across Marion's face, but she made certain to keep the concealing sunglasses in place. Every ounce of her body told her something was wrong, but she couldn't imagine where that problem lay.

"You been working too hard, Popsie. You need your little Marion to give you a pick-me-up! What do you say we head down to those new bathhouses of yours? We could christen them good and proper. All those nice towels and mirrors and stuff." A good deal rested on this proposal. Marion hadn't been permitted in W.R.'s bed since the debacle with Bill Wellman. "We could even do it in the shower! Standing up! We never done it like that!"

"I'm afraid I'm too busy at the moment."

Marion bit her lower lip until her teeth left a mark on the rosy flesh. The pain kept her from crying. How the hell do I get Pops to quit the deep-freeze act if he won't let me do what I'm good at? she demanded silently. Frustration made her breath bump along in random gasps.

Hearing the splotchy pants, W.R. felt momentary pity. The ruthless publisher who'd once urged war with Spain turned weepy when confronted with tales of destitute widows and orphans. Then the man's crueler nature resurfaced.

"Perhaps you need other companionship, Marion. Someone closer to your own age."

Marion failed to hear the sexual innuendo. As far as she was concerned, Pops had forgotten about love-making entirely. "I got Abigail," she mumbled.

"Oh, I was thinking about someone a little more lively. A male companion. A person like your friend Tom Ince, for instance."

Marion stared at W.R., pulling off her sunglasses as she studied his face, but his response was a noncommittal grin. "So let's get back to your plans for this yachting festivity, Marion. That seems a most interesting proposition. And you will include your friend Incie."

"I mean, do you think he could be hinting at something?" Marion demanded.

"Like what?" Abigail's answer was cautious.

"I don't know . . . something." Marion scuffed at the dirt with her riding boot, and a small cloud of powdery dust coated the polished toe. The two women stood beneath the shade of the pergola, the only place Marion had deemed "safe enough to gab," but confidences given in a sober state were clearly uncomfortable—even with two bay geldings snuffling the nearby earth.

Abigail's hesitancy matched her boss's. She knew she was treading dangerous ground in learning too much about Marion's private life. "I'm sure Mr. Hearst would say whatever was on his mind, Marion," Abigail answered slowly. The scene in the Gothic Study jumped into her thoughts: Hearst's relentless rage at his enemies, followed by the strange explosion over Ince.

"Sometimes," Marion answered cryptically, "and sometimes not. He likes playing games."

Her boss didn't elucidate, but Abigail knew she wasn't referring to activities "behind the barn." "I wouldn't worry, Marion," she said gently.

"Why not?" Marion almost shouted, and the noise shook the horses out of their pensive torpor. One whinnied and shook himself; the other stared with doleful eyes. "If you was me, you'd be worrying. I got that damned Millicent breathing down my neck, and she isn't no goddamn English riding horse.

"But you know what I think?" Marion hurried along, talking to herself as much as anyone. "I think this little deal's got something to do with Incie. Like, why would Popsie insist on having him here again? I think he's setting me up. Wants to catch me misbehaving. Maybe all that hoopla about Cosmopolitan Pictures and Ince is just a come-on. Popsie wants to see me get hot and bothered. The actress and the director. You know the score. The famous casting couch and all that other malarkey. Popsie's like that, you know. It turns him on that I had other guys. Sometimes, I think he wished he could have been there watching."

Abigail looked away and began stroking her horse's neck. She needed something other than Marion's words to concentrate on.

"Incie's like that, too, you know," Marion suddenly giggled. "You can't tell no one, but he rigged up this secret gallery in that new house of his, so when he's got overnight guests, he can spy on them. Sex is a peculiar bugger, when you think about it, isn't it?"

Abigail had turned slack-jawed. "How do you know all that?" she finally managed.

"About sex?" Marion chortled.

"No. About Mr. Ince."

Marion was immediately coy. Two conflicting desires were at battle within her: the one a need to boast about her triumphs, the other, the necessity for survival. "I don't remember," she hedged. "Rumor, I guess. . . . Or maybe Incie showed me. I don't recall. . . . Maybe John B. mentioned it. Or Charlie . . . Charlie could have spilled the beans. Those two are thick as thieves, you know."

"Well, perhaps Mr. Hearst heard about this house

tour," Abigail insisted, overriding Marion's excuses. "Maybe that's why he's become jealous."

"I don't know who'd blab about me visiting Incie's home," Marion countered. "Even if I did, I mean."

"A thing doesn't have to be true to find believers, Marion."

The house began massive preparations for Marion's "yachting party." The date was set for November 16, and the captain readied the Oneida. Cases of liquors and wines and champagnes were carted down the hill. Given Mr. Hearst's abstinent nature, the activity would have struck me as peculiar, but I'd learned my employer was a man of conflicting personalities.

I sent the invitations, then made certain all the guests were aware of the schedule. Marion was insistent on promptness, as well as certain ground rules. Mr. Barrymore was glad to acquiesce. He answered my call by asserting he'd be accompanied by a Mademoiselle X; he didn't grace the lady with another name—a clandestine approach that made me more than a little nervous, but Marion didn't mind in the slightest. "A would-be starlet, is my guess," she said.

Whatever problems had existed between my boss and W.R. seemed to have evaporated. I won't say they gushed like newlyweds, because Mr. Hearst appeared unusually reserved, almost angry. But Marion was happy, and her joy became infectious. I decided his problems were due to difficulties with Horace Glendenning and nothing more.

"So we're all set, Abigail?" Marion shouted as she paced nervously along the *Oneida*'s long pier. The 220-foot steam yacht shimmied in the Pacific Ocean rollers; her brass gleamed, and her teak planking and rails looked as though they had been varnished that morning. She was a ship accustomed to travel; when W.R. was in residence in New York, she was moored in the Hudson River; when he returned overland to California, she made the passage through the Panama Canal. Although only occasionally in use, the *Oneida* was outfitted like a seagoing palace. Maritime oils in heavy gilded frames graced the public salons. The many guest cabins were accoutered with all the comforts of home: pressed linen sheets and flowers in crystal vases, antique tables and overstuffed chairs. The dining saloon was a smaller version of San Simeon's silver-laden luxury, while the deck was an idler's haven of wicker lounge chairs arranged for sun and shade.

But the postcard-perfect picture didn't dispel Marion's uneasiness. She took one more turn of the pier, walking with rapid, skittish steps. "Well, I guess that's the best I can do," she muttered. "Anchors aweigh, bon voyage, and all that other seafaring claptrap."

Abigail followed dutifully behind. Her boss had been in a tense mood for two difficult days; Abigail was beginning to view the yachting party as an ordeal instead of a treat. She was convinced something calamitous was about to occur.

" 'Farewell to college joys / We sail at break of day,' " Marion's edgy voice broke into song.

"We haven't assigned the guest cabins yet," Abigail cautiously interrupted.

"That's the Navy song," Marion announced by way of answer. "I used to sing it when I worked for Flo Ziegfeld. I was all gussied up in a sailor's suit: bell-bottom trousers, middy blouse, the works. Pops thought I was a boy when he saw me, thought Flo had forgotten to put me in the show."

"Don't you think we should?" Abigail repeated. "Assign the cabins, I mean."

"Those were the good old days. We were in New York, Pops and me. Millicent was there, too, of course, in the big mansion uptown or out on her Long Island estate, but Popsie was real different then. Cock of the walk and kind of boastful—like he was getting away with murder."

"At least we could assign cabins for changing into swimming costumes or whatever," Abigail persisted. Her boss's strange mood was affecting her as well. "Then if you decide to stay out for the night, everything will be taken care of."

For answer, Marion turned on her secretary with a surprisingly vicious snarl. "I told you no one's sleeping on board! We're off for an innocent, little cruise and nothing more. There's no hanky-panky allowed. I can't risk getting in Dutch with Pops again! And if you slip up, Abigail, or if you let one of our guests get away with something he or she shouldn't, so help me, I'll . . ." Marion left the threat unfinished. "Now, let's rumble up to the hilltop and get this show on the road."

As if Marion's unhappiness were an airborne plague, everyone seemed to have caught it. Arriving in San Simeon's limousines, the stars were tense and their smiles overbright. Elinor Glyn barely spoke to Principessa; Lita's upper lip was swollen and she cowered each time Charlie approached; Louella took copious notes, hiding her pencil and pad only when the Chief appeared. Tom Ince arrived stating that his wife, Nell, was "indisposed," and Pola came without Rudy, then hurriedly added that he was "working."

When Louella asked what "work" the great Valentino was engaged in, Pola lunged at the columnist. The only moment of levity was the appearance of Barrymore's date, Mademoiselle X, a voluptuous girl of sixteen with a happy-go-lucky laugh and a way of interspersing every statement with an awestruck "Golly gee!" She seemed to be having the time of her life, although no one was able to discover her true name. "That's for me to know and you to find out," she'd say, grinning as if she'd invented the expression herself.

Marion took stock of the situation and told Abigail to approach each guest privately and warn them to "wise up." "Tell those sons of bitches this'll be their last invite if they don't watch their p's and q's. Oh, and you'd better add I could make life real sticky when it comes to Cosmopolitan Pictures. They'll get the drift. There isn't a person on the hilltop who isn't dependent on Pops in some way."

Abigail did as she was told. It was an unpleasant task; even little Lita eyed Abigail as if she were a spy. Tom Ince was the sole exception. He invited her to sit down while he unpacked, then chatted pleasantly as he moved about the room. Both Mr. and Mrs. Ince had been assigned Casa del Monte's most spectacular room, and Marion had been unable to renege when Nell didn't appear. Abigail felt herself relax. She looked at the canopied bed with its gilded columns and velvet hangings, at the coffered ceiling that seemed to sparkle like a hundred silver trays, and then at the view of the undulating mountains, and she decided the guests at San Simeon were the luckiest people alive.

"So what happened next?" Ince was asking. "After your father died, I mean."

"I lived with my great-aunt for a short time, but it

239

turned out that she didn't like children, so I was sent to a distant cousin of my mother's. She and her husband had a home in Rhode Island. I tell people I did a lot of traveling as a child, but really I only moved from relative to relative." Abigail laughed here. She'd never shared her life story before, and it was a remarkably pleasant experience.

"But what about summers?"

"Oh, here and there. Some years were all right; some weren't." Abigail began noticing the cozy scent of Ince's after-shave lotion. It reminded her of new leather automobile cushions, and the smell of the earth after a spring rain.

"And school chums? I suppose you must have gotten fairly lonely with all those transitions."

"Oh, I learned to keep my own counsel."

"Keep your own counsel! That's an odd phrase for a young girl."

Abigail felt suddenly confused. She had to admit an attraction to Tom Ince, but the sensation began mingling with a fear that he might be manipulating her. That thought made Abigail angry enough to stand.

"I'm not a girl," she said, and began backing toward the door.

"No one could ever accuse you of that, Abby," Ince answered with the smoothest of smiles, and Abigail felt her skin go cold.

"Charades, everybody! That's what we'll play!" Marion's nearly hysterical voice struggled to galvanize the after-dinner crowd. She'd been drinking more than she'd intended, but the party she'd put so much faith in was turning into a major flop. It seemed as though each of her guests were nursing a private grudge. Incie and Elinor had argued over an author's credit on a photoplay; Principessa had cattily suggested John was robbing the cradle; Lita had jumped to Mademoiselle X's defense, earning a glowering glance from Charlie, who had then turned on Ince, accusing him of "getting too big for your director's britches." Marion couldn't tell what her Popsie thought about these rude shenanigans; she'd only glanced in his direction a few furtive times, and at each of those moments he seemed to be staring at Mademoiselle X's curvy bosom and the sheer white evening dress that barely concealed her manifold charms.

"Jesus H. Christ," Marion muttered under her breath. She felt like sitting down and bawling her eyes out. "Abigail," she whispered with a nervous stammer. "Tippy-toe off to the little girls' room, will you, honey bun. I need a glass of 'water.' "

Abigail knew she couldn't refuse; nor could she call attention to her task without risking the ax. Sick at heart, she walked away to fetch Marion's clandestine glass of gin.

"Charades!" Marion then sang louder.

"Okay by me!" Mademoiselle X wriggled to the center of the group, and all eyes followed. Principessa's formfitting, black, sequined sheath was no match for the younger woman's revealing silk. Principessa glared; Elinor smiled an I-can't-wait-to-see-what-happens-next grin; Tom Ince trailed the would-be starlet as if she had him on a chain; and Barrymore moved in as though he were about to challenge the director to a duel. Only Pola and Lollie seemed impervious to the chaos.

"But I don't know how to play," Lita mumbled, while Charlie groused loudly, "No kidding!"

"Then you come sit by me, Lita," W.R. announced. It was one of the few sentences the great man had spoken all evening, and everyone stopped midmovement and swiveled their heads in chagrined disbelief. The words flung them back into reality; they were Hearst's guests, after all. By the time Abigail returned with Marion's forbidden gin, the Hollywood crowd had assumed their sunniest poses, and Marion was busy drawing up teams for the game.

Little Lita had clearly captivated her host. Despite the exhortations thundering from the game's participants, neither Hearst nor Lita had stirred from the sofa facing the fire. In fact, with each noisy barrage, the two seemed to burrow deeper into their pillow-laden nest.

"It was *War and Peace!*" Elinor cheered in the distance, while Charlie cackled, "Oh, I thought you were doing Warren Harding."

"This sure is a nice house, Mr. Hearst," Lita whispered as her husband and Elinor continued to hold court on the other side of the room. "I like visiting it. I'm sorry I'm no good at games."

"You don't have to apologize, Lita. You're perfect just the way you are."

For some unfortunate reason Marion happened to overhear this remark, and though she wasn't drunk, she was tipsy enough to have dropped her guard. "Charlie and me's gonna go next," she hissed loudly.

Tom Ince immediately interjected, "I thought you and I were partners, Marion."

"No, it's Charlie and me. I changed my mind."

"You can't do that midgame! No fair!" were the raucous objections.

"I can do anything I want!" Marion insisted. "It's my party, so I make the rules. Now, Charlie and me, we gotta go into the Billiard Room and come up with some new tricks. You folks cool your heels, pop a couple of champagne corks, why don't you. Charlie

and me will be back in two shakes of a lamb's tail."
Marion's eyes were on W.R. throughout this speech,
but he appeared impervious, murmuring pleasantries
to Lita, who beamed shyly in response.

Inebriation caused Marion to misinterpret her Popsie's intentions toward the younger woman. In retalia-
tion for what she imagined she was witnessing, Marion
grabbed Charlie by his belt and began marching out
of the room. "You two bosom buddies on the couch!"
she bellowed. "If you need anything, just holler for
Abigail over there!"

As W.R. watched his mistress disappear with Chaplin,
his response was to turn and stare at Ince. Then Hearst
resumed his conversation with Lita; his face bore the
most dangerous smile Abigail had ever seen.

The night wore on; sex was in the air, as pungent
as perfume. The charades players began slipping away
to other rooms, to the pool, the garden, even to the
house's enormous kitchen and larder; partners reemerged, changed, and disappeared again. By now
W.R. and Lita were gone, but only Marion seemed
to care.

"I'll make him eat dirt," she spluttered in a voice
thick with tears. "He can't take me for granted like
that. I've given up a lot for him. Marriage and kiddies
and all that other fairy-book baloney."

"I know you have, darling," Principessa answered.
Her arm was draped protectively around Marion's
shoulders.

Abigail decided it was time to leave. As she passed
through the Billiard Room on her way to the stairs,
she almost fell into John Barrymore and Tom Ince,
who lay sprawled in two chairs, a bottle and bucket
of ice between them. The room was unlit, although
neither man seemed to care.

"Every woman, I'm betting you, Jacko! Every single lady in the entire establishment!"

"Not my little piece of hot, buttered toast."

"I haven't made up my mind, yet."

"Well, I'm making it up for you, friend."

Both men were drunk as skunks, although their words were remarkably lucid. Abigail was about to apologize for intruding, but a sudden fear made her hold her tongue. Neither Barrymore nor Ince seemed aware of her presence, however, and Ince continued vehemently, "So what do you say, Jackie boy? Are you a gambling man?"

"Do lions have manes?"

"Well, I repeat my wager. I bed every woman here before the weekend is out—all except the little brood mare, Lita."

Barrymore appeared to weigh the odds. "Every damsel except Lita—and my homing pigeon. And let's speed up the process. All your . . . ah, courtship has to be consummated by the time the *Oneida* returns to shore."

Abigail hadn't touched a drop of wine at dinner, but she felt drunk and nauseous and dizzy with anxiety. The weekend was a disaster, and she knew she'd be blamed. She felt tempted to pack her suitcase and sneak down the hill; instead she pulled out her journal and started what she believed was her last entry from San Simeon.

It's now two-thirty in the morning, and the guests are still going strong. All the lights in the Assembly Room and Refectory are blazing, and there's a group gathered in the kitchen, singing and banging pots and making a terrible mess. I don't know where Marion is or Mr. Hearst either, and

*I don't want to find out. I guess I'll get the sack
tomorrow. Marion will blame me because I'm convenient, and Mr. Hearst will back her up for the
same reason. I probably won't even get a letter of
reference, but to tell you the truth it's just as well.
I don't think I could stand to live here another
week. There's someone banging on my door. It's
probably Marion with some ridiculous demand.
I'd better go before the whole hall wakes up.*

Abigail opened her door to find Tom Ince tottering
there. He lurched into her room before she had time
to protest.

"Old party poop, Abby," he mumbled. "The former
'girl' turned woman."

Abigail said nothing. In an ill-considered attempt to
keep the noise from the other servants, she closed the
door. The action was as wrongheaded as any she'd
taken.

"Glad to see me, I notice," Ince smirked as he
stumbled toward her writing table, spotted the open
journal, and began pawing through it. "I'll write my
name here, Abby." He grinned. "You'd like that,
wouldn't you? Famous director signs star-struck secretary's diary. . . . Lots of girlies are happy with
far less."

"Please, Mr. Ince, there's nothing for you here,"
Abigail started.

"Oh, but there is, Abby. There's this gorgeous view,
for instance." Ince walked to the window, and his
drunken shamble turned surprisingly lithe. "Quite a
vision, Hearst's spread. Come on over and show
Tommy your favorite sights."

Abigail couldn't have said what impelled her to
move to his side: a doomed sense of failure, perhaps,
or a recurring bout of loneliness. Whatever the mo-

tive, she did as she was told, then stood there as his clumsy embrace began enfolding her. This is wrong, she told herself while he grasped her neck and arms with hot, sticky hands. She stared at the darkened glass while the hands started groping her, and only then did she spring to life.

"No!" she ordered, but Ince was too strong for her. She tried to push him away, but found her hands pinned to her sides. "Stop!" she wanted to shout, but shame kept the words in her throat. "Please, Mr. Ince! Please go away," she whispered instead as he ripped the bodice of her dress, then thrust a hand between her legs. "All the girlies like this," Ince insisted, while Abigail whimpered:

"Please, Mr. Ince! I won't tell. I promise I won't."

"And you're no different, are you, Abby? You're a whore just like the rest."

With her hands finally freed, Abigail swung at him. Her first blow sliced the air, but the second hit its mark, and Ince recoiled slightly, struck hard on the side of his face. He glared at her and at her still-clenched fists while Abigail backed away, realizing the battle was far from over. Ince's flushed face was contorted with rage.

"So you like to play rough, do you, girlie?" he sneered through tight teeth as he nursed his cheek.

"I'll hit you again, Mr. Ince."

"You have me shaking in my shoes."

Ince's left hand shot out and grabbed Abigail's wrist, wrenching one hand downward while the other clawed futilely at his face. Then he landed his own blow, catching Abigail almost squarely in the mouth and splitting her upper lip.

"Oh, God," she muttered while blood spattered her jaw and torn dress. "Please, Mr. Ince. Please don't do this." She lashed out again, but he caught her fists and twisted them against her back before they could do further damage.

"Nice and easy, Abby, honey," he breathed against her swollen face. "I promise I won't tell."

Leaving Abigail weeping on the floor, Tom Ince walked through the now silent house. He didn't feel the slightest remorse. Hadn't the girl almost begged for it? Barging into his room with some phony-baloney excuse about a message from Marion? The kid's East Coast aloofness was no more than a come-on. Abigail wasn't any more refined than the starlets hunkered outside every studio door. Dime-a-dozen kids whose chief appeal was that they were cheaper than hookers. Besides, Ince realized, now I've won Barrymore's wager. And with time to spare.

The director entered the hall that led to the third-floor Lobby and Gothic Study. He began measuring his steps; he didn't want to risk getting caught by the Muller boys—especially near Hearst's and Marion's private quarters. When Ince reached the Lobby area, he poked his head around the corner, then descended to the second floor and the Library. The light was particularly bad on this part of the stairwell; it cast peculiar shadows across the stone and made navigation difficult; Ince gripped the iron rail as shafts of this dusky lamplight fell across his wavy hair, turning it white while leaving the rest of his face in murky shadow. The man appeared weaker, smaller in stature, and the physical change seemed to affect his bravado as well. Ince was a different man.

In his anxiety, the transformed director failed to see his host emerging from the Library door. Hearst ducked back inside as this mysterious shadow passed in a panicky rush, then stood staring as the footsteps vanished from the house.

"Chaplin!" W.R. muttered to himself, wholly mistaking one man for the other. "My goddamn rival's that idiot Chaplin! Neylan's spies were wrong. It isn't Tom Ince at all."

18

CATHA DROPPED THE JOURNAL. SHE FELT ANGRY AND sickened at the same time. "Abigail didn't have a prayer!" she swore. "Even if she'd called for help, who would have believed her? Hired hands don't accuse famous directors of rape!"

Protective rage bounced Catha off her motel bed. She rushed into the bathroom, dashed cold water on her face, then returned to the bedroom and stared at the ominous journal. "Abigail would have been fired if she'd opened her mouth," Catha announced with grim certainty. "Marion was only interested in saving Marion."

Without considering the time (it was almost 2 A.M.), Catha grabbed the phone and dialed Lucas. Only after a seemingly interminable wait did she realize how late it was.

"Hello?" Lucas's voice was hazy with sleep.

"I woke you up. I'm sorry, I wasn't thinking." Catha's anger drained away in an instant, leaving her feeling hollow and vulnerable.

"No, you didn't." Lucas's tone was gentle. "I make

a habit of staying up till dawn. I find it makes me more clearheaded at work. What's up? I hope you're calling to say you've changed your mind."

"My grandmother was raped by Ince." Catha forced the words. Half of her wished she'd never picked up the telephone; the other half desperately needed Lucas's soothing influence. "The night before the yachting party. Nearly the entire household was asleep. He burst into her room. Abigail thought it was Marion with some bizarre request."

"Oh, my God," was Lucas's shocked response.

"She never had a chance, Lucas. A young woman like her . . . what could she do in a situation like that? She needed the job, needed a good recommendation. . . . Women had only obtained suffrage four years earlier with the passage of the Nineteenth Amendment. It was considered a novelty for members of 'the fairer sex' to defend their rights, and they were castigated for it. Held up to ridicule and worse. There were probably more incidents like the one Abigail endured than anyone cares to admit."

"Do you want to come over?" Lucas said after a long, quiet minute.

"No . . . I don't think so. I need to be alone for a while. Sometimes kindness is too hard to take. For me, anyway." Then, attempting to close the conversation on a less revealing note, Catha repeated her apology for calling so late.

But Lucas wasn't fooled by the effort. "Don't be too tough on yourself. And remember, I'm here if you need me."

Catha sat staring at the phone. She was a bundle of raw emotion. Lucas's sympathy had only served to open old wounds; everywhere she looked she saw a litany of inadvertent cruelties: lovers and friends she'd been too busy to understand, a mother she'd never loved enough, and now a grandmother whose daughter had disowned her.

She picked up Abigail's journal and forced herself to turn to the next entry, marveling at the change in style between one day and the next. The words had turned leaden and halting—a schoolgirl's dutiful description of events too confusing to comprehend. The lively, bright-spirited Abigail had vanished, but her chronicle continued.

Berthed at her pier, the steam-powered yacht *Oneida* was a dazzling sight. Her brightwork shimmered like liquid gold; her mahogany and teak glowed under layers of crystalline varnish, and the paint on her white hull was as blinding as the sun. The yacht's many-colored flags stirred in the freshening, morning breeze, and the noise of canvas slapping halyard and mast perfected this aura of perpetual grace. Crew members, preparing for another Hearstian extravaganza, hurried aboard carrying delicacies procured especially for the cruise: Long Island oysters bedded in ice, Dungeness crabs shipped down from the Pacific Northwest, mammoth hothouse strawberries and sickle pears nestled in straw-filled boxes.

Abigail gazed at the spectacle, but she neither smiled nor frowned. Her split upper lip was swollen and livid, and the skin near her mouth had become a puffy purplish green. "Morning, Miss Abigail!" one of the stewards called. "Boy, you must have taken some tumble last night!"

"Yes," she mumbled as she traversed the length of the pier. "I fell on the marble steps outside Casa Grande." Then Abigail stepped up the *Oneida*'s gangway and walked aboard.

"The motorcade will assemble at San Simeon at

eleven-thirty," she informed the yacht's captain while trying to keep her wounded mouth in shadow. "After that we'll proceed directly down the mountain. Mr. Hearst wishes to cast off at noon on the dot. Any stragglers are to be left behind."

Abigail's appearance as well as the mechanical sound of her voice surprised the captain. "Are you feeling all right, miss? That's some bruise you're sporting. Maybe Doc Goodman should take a look at that cut on your lip." The concern in his voice made her suddenly want to break down and cry.

"I'm fine," she responded quietly. "I had a slight accident, that's all. I hardly feel it." But the words were a total lie.

As promised, the motorcade arrived on time; and with much hoopla and snapshots and shouts of "Bon voyage!" the luncheon cruise set forth. The mood of the revelers had shifted dramatically since the night before. The wild hysteria had been replaced by a cozy, almost familial camaraderie. Elinor beamed at John; Pola linked arms with Principessa; Lollie and Charlie chuckled together; and Tom Ince was so expansive he might have been mistaken for the host. He even joked off a bruise darkening his right jaw, declaring that he'd had a "run-in with a certain stone statuette."

The glaring exceptions to the pervasive gaiety were Marion, whose hungover stomach and pounding head concealed an almost incapacitating terror; Mademoiselle X, who complained sotto voce that John wouldn't let her "get near Tom Ince"; Lita, looking nervous as a cat; and W.R., whose lowering brow and stormy face kept his guests at bay.

He'd pulled a pearl-handled target pistol from a round and velvet-lined case specially constructed to hold six matching weapons and was now attempting to scare away a flock of seagulls by repeatedly firing into the sky. When Chaplin jokingly suggested that his host simply shoot a couple of the offending birds, W.R.'s expression turned villainous: "I'd never harm an animal. You should know that, Charles—with all the times you've visited. But if I did decide to eliminate these creatures, why, you can be certain I wouldn't hit merely one or two. I'm an excellent marksman. I could kill the entire flock with as many bullets, if I chose."

"Can I try?" Lita interrupted, unsure what W.R. and her Charlie were squabbling over, but intuiting that it was time for feminine intervention.

"Of course, my dear!" Hearst's stony countenance became warm honey. "You can do anything you want. And anytime, I might add."

"Me, too!" Mademoiselle X spoke up, untangling herself from John, whose boozy body seemed in danger of collapsing under its own weight. "I want to play, too. John can be such a stiff sometimes."

"Two lovely girls," W.R. intoned loudly. "Now, which of you beauties wishes to go first?"

This exclusive threesome only deepened Marion's fears; she walked toward the group irresolutely, then backed away, looking to her secretary for help, but Abigail stood rigidly at the rail. Her back was to the crowd clustered on the deck, and she seemed to be staring longingly into the sea. The stance infuriated Marion, who felt Abigail had deserted her in her moment of need.

"Who wants chow?" Marion growled. "I'm hungry enough to eat a horse." Charlie Chaplin's broad wink at that remark made Marion turn as pale as a fish's scales, a reaction W.R. immediately noticed.

"Is something bothering you, Marion?"

"Oh, no, Popsie. I'm just hungry is all."

"My little girl has a big appetite."

"I . . . I guess I do, Pops." Marion hadn't the slightest idea where Hearst's questions were leading. "I guess I like to eat same as everyone else."

"More, I would imagine."

Marion fared no better at the outdoor luncheon. The long table on the yacht's aft deck seemed specifically designed to distance her from her Popsie. While he indulged himself with the simpering attentions of Lita and Mademoiselle X, the other guests' smug anecdotes left Marion in the dust. Everyone was smiling; everyone was laughing; they tapped playful, demonstrative fingers on each other's hands and arms and repeated familiar stories ad infinitum. Marion felt old and desperate and wholly unloved. It didn't help that every time she glanced at her Popsie she caught Charlie's devilish eye or that twice she saw Tom Ince ogling Abigail or that her once loyal secretary now appeared as remote as a cigar-store Indian.

"Bunch of snakes," Marion muttered under her breath. "I'll show them! No one tosses Miss Marion Davies aside."

Luncheon continued and the autumnal sun began to wane, suffusing the diners' faces with color or obscuring them in shadow. None of the guests looked the same as when he or she had boarded the *Oneida*. Ince's face was cherry red with alcohol; Chaplin's wavy hair had been ruffled by the breeze until it duplicated Tom's unkempt waves; Pola was wearing Elinor's veil-covered picture hat; Principessa had donned Mademoiselle X's cast-off turban; Lita had acquired a man's nautical blue blazer that transformed her pregnant frame into boyish innocence; and John had managed to slip below during courses and return in a terry-cloth robe and swimming shorts.

"You look as if you're ready for bed," Lollie quipped.

John assumed a playful leer. "I just might be, Miss Parsons, honey. That is, if you know where I'm bunking."

W.R. surveyed the scene, then pushed his chair back from the table and bellowed heartily, "Target practice."

The announcement was greeted by an equally enthusiastic "I brought fireworks!"

"Did you, Tom?" Hearst responded jovially.

"It's not Tom . . . it's Charlie, sir."

The change in W.R.'s demeanor was instantaneous; he looked as if someone had punched him in the softest part of his belly. "So it is, Charlie," he almost sneered. "A trick of the light, I imagine. I never realized you boys bore the slightest resemblance to one another . . . either in work or life."

Only Marion heard the menacing note in W.R.'s voice. I'm a cooked goose, she told herself. Popsie's got the goods on me for sure. I wish I knew who blabbed. "Oh, let's not play target practice this afternoon," she wheedled with her most innocent smile. "This little girl's too sleepy. She's got to take her a teensy-weensy snooze." The speech was intended as a come-on, but W.R. refused to play.

"I'm sure you are tired, Marion." His face was unsmiling. "You've been entertaining a good many admirers. None of them would begrudge you a few moments' sleep, I'm certain. Not after last night."

With that statement, everyone at the table fell into an awkward silence. Then, as if the attack had been intended for the guests instead of the hostess, each began imperceptibly pulling away from Marion.

"Fireworks! What fun!" Principessa drawled, while Lollie cooed a sycophantic: "I'd love you to teach me to shoot, Chief."

"Well, why don't we open my set of pistols again and put a practice range near the stern rail. Follow me, boys and girls. You'll have to take turns, but I don't believe there's a man or woman here who isn't accustomed to sharing."

No one could have explained what had happened to W.R.'s stringent two-cocktail rule. As if shipboard life had altered his persona, the prissy policies and behavior of San Simeon vanished with the tide. "Drink up," Hearst urged his guests. "That's fine whiskey . . . excellent gin, as well. None of that Mexican rotgut for me. I get my booze straight from Canada. Smooth as ice cream, so the bootleggers tell me. The best that money can buy. I won't be duped into paying for shoddy." The hollow laugh that accompanied this last declaration went unnoticed. In everyone's estimation, W.R. had suddenly become a hell of a lot of fun.

"You're one terrific guy!" Charlie swore, throwing a diminutive arm across the great man's shoulders. Hearst flinched slightly, but then masked his disgust with a broad and phony grin. "Sharing all this . . . this wealth with us, I mean." The comedian's cockney accent was laid on thick. "A real sport, yes, indeed."

"There are some things I like to keep to myself, Charlie. Certain possessions a man should never permit another man to touch."

"You're right there, sport! I couldn't have put it better!" Chaplin waggled one of W.R.'s pistols in the air, took aim at a seagull, and missed by a good five feet.

"Your turn's up, Charlie." Hearst beamed the coldest smile Abigail had ever seen, then turned to the secretary and proferred the weapon. "What about you, Abigail? Want to give it a go?"

Abigail hadn't opened her mouth during luncheon, nor had she joined in the raucous deck games. "I don't think so, Mr. Hearst." She forced the words, but they were hollow and monotone.

"Are you feeling all right, Abigail?"

"I'm fine, Mr. Hearst. I had a small accident last night," Abigail lied. "I guess I'm still feeling a little wobbly."

"Old Charlie knows what pretty girls need. What do you say we take you down to one of the cabins for a quiet siesta?" Chaplin attempted to take hold of Abigail's arm, but W.R. stepped between them.

"Leave her alone, Chaplin," he ordered. "One conquest is enough for the weekend. Besides, you don't want to risk insulting your friend Marion, do you?"

Afternoon gave way to early evening, and the revelers grew more reckless as well as a good deal more drunk. Ince dove into the water, then Charlie followed suit, and the Oneida's captain was forced to bring the yacht around so that the two spluttering swimmers could be fished out of the water. "More whiskey," Tom bellowed as he was hauled aboard, while Lita celebrated her husband's rescue by repeatedly firing a pistol into the air and yelling, "Duck, Charlie!" each time she pulled the trigger. For some reason, W.R. thought this was the most amusing spectacle he'd ever witnessed.

Then a still-sodden Charlie lit more fireworks while W.R. opened another box of ammunition, and the deck grew hazy with sulfur and gunpowder. Everyone choked and coughed, but no one wanted to stop the fun.

"He knows, you son of a bitch!" Marion hissed to Ince in the midst of one of the noisiest explosions.

"Knows what?" Ince demanded, immediately clear-headed as he shivered in the dark.

"About us, you sleazy-eyed bastard. What we did down in the bathhouse last night."

"If that's the only time he's gotten wise to you and me, I've given the old goat too much credit. Besides, there's always Charlie—or do you think you've kept those little escapades secret as well."

"You dirty creep! You blabbed, didn't you?"

"I know who's got the butter, Marion, and who owns the bread."

"Because if you ever do, Tommy, if you ever tell him, I'll wring your goddamn Irish neck."

"Temper, Marion. I doubt those dainty hands are big enough to do the trick."

"Don't underestimate me, you bastard!"

Standing unnoticed and still as a ghost, Abigail overheard this exchange. She grabbed the rail and vomited into the sea.

Then evening became night, and the *Oneida*'s mast lights and lanterns sprang to life, creating vivid patterns in black and white. Faces and limbs and bodies appeared and then vanished. There were shouts of "Supper aboard!" and "Mutiny! Let's take this tub around the world! No more moving-picture shows for me!"

W.R. egged on the wild behavior; he seemed delighted to be at the center of such a bacchanalia. He sent a cabin boy below for yet another box of ammunition, reloaded the empty pistols, and ordered the captain to steam in slow circles while dinner was prepared and then consumed. "After that, we'll see." He winked with his owlish eyes. "Maybe we will shack up on board. To hell with tomorrow. To hell with rules and the good, old U.S. of A.!" To celebrate, he fired off a round into the starry night.

Suddenly Tom Ince groaned and toppled forward, sinking to his knees near the port rail. Marion rushed to his side, but Abigail had gotten there first; Mademoiselle X was close on their heels.

"Oh, gee, the poor guy," the starlet gushed as the three women dragged the nearly insensate director toward a deck chair. "Too many cockytails . . . that stuff'll nail you sure as shooting." The genuine concern in her voice was overshadowed by disappointment. Mademoiselle X had been trying to get a private moment with the director ever since they'd both arrived.

"Whew," Ince muttered in an almost inaudible whisper, "I don't feel so hot. My stomach's a mess . . . on fire, like I . . . I guess it's too much sauce." Then he blacked out completely.

"Oh, jeez!" Mademoiselle X wailed louder. Neither Marion nor Abigail spoke.

The news of Ince's illness took a few moments to penetrate the inebriated crowd, but when everyone had been apprised, a shocked silence overcame the guests. Drunkenness was acceptable; passing out in public was not. Then, as if Ince's prone body were emitting some lethal contagion, his fellow partygoers began sifting away from it. John straightened his jacket; Charlie shook out his waterlogged trousers; and each lady took furtive stock of her own respectability.

"I warned him," Elinor was heard to murmur, while Principessa agreed forcefully, "You can't play around with booze. I don't care where the stuff is manufactured."

W.R. took the most decisive steps; he canceled dinner, ordered Ince's huddled form be carried to a stateroom and the captain return to shore immediately. Then Hearst gathered the guests and informed each that Ince's "incapacity" was "under control" and that stories of the director's "overindulgence" must "never be repeated." If there was one thing the publisher couldn't abide, it was unfavorable press.

"Don't you worry, Chief," Lollie soothed with her slyest whisper. "I won't breathe a word. And neither will the rest of the gang. Tom had a marvelous time. It's just too bad he caught a case of stomach flu. Or maybe his problem was mal de mer."

"As the ocean's dead calm, I believe we'll opt for the former," Hearst answered, then added a wistful: "Tom's a marvelous director. I hope this mysterious illness doesn't endanger his partnership with Cosmopolitan Pictures."

19

Night at San Simeon wore on; no one paid attention to the time. A plate of sandwiches and thermoses
of coffee and tea sat on the Assembly Room's central
table, but not one guest touched them. Ever since the
hasty docking and evacuation of the *Oneida,* followed
by the race up the mountainside with the stricken and
groaning Ince, all thoughts had been focused on the
director.

"Shouldn't we call a—" Pola Negri now murmured,
but Elinor interrupted vehemently, "Mr. Hearst will
decide what's best! He told us he'd telephone his own
physician in the morning—that is, if the patient
doesn't improve," stopping Pola's final word before it
could escape.

"I heard Tom mumble something about 'indigestion' before they took him to that infirmary room upstairs," John ventured, approaching the problem with
his habitually rakish tone. "I guess that's his way of
admitting he was drunk as a two-headed skunk."

"Maybe he needs a bicarb," Charlie joined in, but
the two men's joking efforts failed to alleviate the

gloom pervading the room. Marion, her guests, and Abigail sank deeper into their separate chairs. W.R. was not among them; he'd long since gone to bed, but his spirit remained—as overbearing and judgmental as if he were hiding in the shadows.

"I can't stand it," Mademoiselle X finally announced. "I'm going up there. The poor guy shouldn't be alone when he's feeling so punk!" She glared criticism at Marion, but her hostess refused to fight back. "If being famous makes you an old meany, I'm glad I'm a nobody."

"Watch out for the guy," Barrymore quipped. "He may have a sick tummy, but that's only one organ out of commission."

"I think you're all a bunch of low-life cretins!" the starlet shot back as she flounced out of the room.

Another fifteen minutes or so passed; Abigail couldn't be certain. Small talk erupted from the clustered chairs and then died an unremarked death. A stifled yawn was followed by a nervous sigh while the members of the group wrestled with uneasy consciences, and even more tangled excuses. Each person devoutly wished himself long gone from San Simeon's stout walls. Although he was known for his newspapers' antiprohibitionist editorials, W.R.'s political aspirations would be doomed if news of a drunken spree leaked out.

"We've got to stick together on this one," Charlie muttered through clenched teeth, while Lollie's merciless "You certainly do!" brought a chill to every spine.

Suddenly a scream split the hostile air. It was followed by another and then a third and a fourth. By the time the third scream hit its peak, everyone in the Assembly Room was on his feet and running toward the sound.

* * *

"He's dead!" Mademoiselle X moaned. She was standing in the fourth-floor hall outside the infirmary door, her body glued to the far wall as though she'd been blasted from the room. "I came up just to look, you know . . . see how he was doing . . . maybe have a little powwow . . . but his eyes were open, like . . . like you see in the flickers."

As Marion and her guests continued to stare, Mademoiselle X added miserably, "I didn't do nothing . . . didn't touch him or nothing."

"Anything," Marion corrected with sudden vigor, causing Abigail to turn and stare hard at her boss. "*Nothing* isn't proper English. If you want to succeed, you've got to know the score. Winners don't make mistakes." Marion looked past her secretary and the rest of the huddled group. It was clear she was rehearsing some momentous scene.

"We've got to wake Pops," she continued evenly, "and Joe Willicombe and Neylan. Neylan handles all W.R.'s messy situations." Marion was running a private list in her head.

"Abigail, you get W.R. I'll handle Willicombe." The new, take-charge Marion wasn't prepared to face her lord and master just yet. "Joe can deal with Neylan. The rest of you yokels sit tight. I'm sure Popsie's doctor will have questions. Just make sure you remember your lines . . . a stomach bug . . . maybe someone could claim Incie wasn't feeling too hot when he arrived."

"Tom and I had a long chat last night," John volunteered, while Abigail involuntarily shuddered. "I can tell the sawbones Ince admitted being under the weather before we even boarded the *Oneida*."

"Perfect," was Marion's succinct response.

"But what about me?" Mademoiselle X whimpered. "What should I do? I don't want to stand here all night. . . . You should see him . . . his face is all splotchy and white. He looks like that vampire guy."

Marion gave the starlet a glance of absolute contempt. "Shut her up, John," she seethed, "or I'll do it myself! This is no joking matter, this bootleg hooch. Those damn prohibitionists will raise a stink if they learn Popsie's been ladling out booze."

Hearst's private physician, Dr. Goodman, spent only a brief time examining the corpse. As he reappeared in the crowded hall, his metallic-gray eyes searched every face. There was something inhuman in the expression, and the guests recoiled as if a spotlight had been aimed at their faces. "An intestinal malady?" he asked the Chief, whose brooding presence underscored the severity of the situation. "Is that what Mr. Ince claimed when you brought him back from the yacht?"

"It was last night actually," Barrymore immediately interjected, "when Tom first mentioned feeling ill. We were sharing a . . . a private moment in the Billiard Room when he complained of stomach cramps and whatnot."

Dr. Goodman's eyes bore through the speaker. "Did you witness Mr. Ince stumble at the time—or could he have been struck by anyone?"

"What does that mean?" Barrymore was beginning to lose the thread of his fabricated tale, and his voice became defensive and edgy.

"I'm attempting to ascertain the cause of that nasty bruise on his cheek."

"Bruise?" the actor repeated as if he'd never heard the word before.

"The deceased has severe discoloration on the right side of his face. I assume he must have been in a fight."

But Hearst stopped the interrogation with a hurried "Ince's illness can be corroborated by the others. As for the mark on his face, he told us he barged into a statue—an understandable accident in a strange house at a late hour."

"I'll have to send for another physician," was Goodman's curt reply.

"For God's sake!" Hearst exploded. "Why do an asinine thing like that? Neylan and I told you what happened."

But Goodman stared down the Chief. "Because the man was shot. A small-caliber bullet. Probably a .22. The type of ammunition common to a target pistol. The bullet passed into the abdomen, and the wound cauterized immediately. There was almost no noticeable mark in the fatty, exterior flesh. Without medical care, internal hemorrhaging occurred. To put it simply, your guest quietly bled to death, and I believe the mark on his cheek may be an indication of a prior feud. Perhaps your Mr. Ince was concealing an enemy."

Dawn arrived, and then another glorious mountain morning, but the sun beamed down on a dismal house. In the Assembly Room, the curtains were still drawn from the night before. Whenever a maid tried to open them, one of the exhausted guests would mumble a protest from deep within the room's many chaises and chairs. No one had been to bed as yet; following Dr. Goodman's terrifying pronouncement, a local physician had been called in, a Clarence Steinbeck, the nearby town of Cambria's sole practitioner.

Dr. Steinbeck was a grizzled and bowlegged man with decidedly communist sympathies. He disliked the exclusive San Simeon crowd, but he was known for his thoroughness and honesty; his opinions could neither be bought nor sold. His assessment of the situation concurred with Goodman's: Ince had been killed by a .22-caliber bullet lodged in his abdomen. The bruise was also duly noted, leading to the supposition that the murderer had attacked Ince on a previous occasion.

At Steinbeck's insistence, a law enforcement officer was notified. Neylan (mouthing W.R.'s words) had suggested that the metropolitan police force in San Luis Obispo be "excluded from the investigation until Nell Ince is apprised of her husband's demise." The crusty communist was suspicious of the request; concern for a fellow mortal didn't jibe with William Randolph Hearst's capitalistic policies, but the doctor also understood the Hollywood crowd's fear of adverse publicity. San Luis was a midsize city; gossip would reach Los Angeles before the telephone receivers turned cold. Without being fully cognizant of the machinations guiding him, Steinbeck agreed, and Cambria's young deputy marshal was sent for. That man was Ethan Purnell.

20

No, THERE ISN'T ANY MORE INFORMATION, LUCAS."
Catha clenched the telephone, afraid Lucas's secretary
would interrupt with yet another piece of pressing
business. The distractions hurt despite Catha's efforts
at unruffled composure. "Abigail's journal is finished,
kaput. Either she ripped out the remaining pages or
somebody did it for her—"

"Hold on a sec, Catha." Lucas put his hand over the
phone's mouthpiece, returning a moment later with a
harried "You were saying?"

Catha's former self would have ended the conversation with a wounded and brusque "I'll fill you in later.
You're obviously too busy to talk," but a night of
soul-searching had changed that rote response. "I was
hoping we could drive up and see your uncle Ethan
together," she chose instead. "I didn't realize how
jammed your schedule was—"

The secretary broke in again, and Catha's newly
constructed persona almost cracked apart. Frustration
made her grip the receiver even tighter.

When Lucas returned, it was his turn to be irritated.

"God damn it. Of all the days! I've got a meeting in ten minutes. Another half an hour after that . . . preliminary work on this wetlands hearing that can't possibly be postponed."

"I'll go see Ethan on my own," Catha offered with forced nonchalance. "If you don't mind calling him first and paving the way . . ."

"I'd like to drive up with you, but I can't reschedule these interviews. I'm not the only person involved."

The line remained mercifully quiet while both Catha and Lucas assessed the situation. Both had a sense of being in the wrong place at the wrong time. Catha stubbornly maintained she wasn't ready for another romantic entanglement, while Lucas reminded himself of the distance between New England and California—in miles as well as careers.

Catha finally broke the silence. "It's nice of you to offer though." She meant it.

"Look, I'll tell you what. You go and see Uncle Ethan this morning. He'll probably talk to you more than he would to me anyway. An attractive young woman . . . Ethan was quite a ladies' man in his younger days."

"Like his nephew, I assume," Catha tried to joke.

But Lucas wasn't about to accept the glib remark; he'd seen the pain beneath it. Instead he moved into the next phase of his plan. "So you drive up to Uncle Ethan's now . . . and I leave the office by six, hop the commuter to San Luis . . . which should put me in Cambria by nine. There's a nice inn there and terrific restaurant. Can you wait that late for dinner?"

Propped up in an uncushioned, ladder-back chair, Ethan's unyielding bones and fierce eyes seemed transformed. From the ramrod-straight physique to the shock of ferociously brushed white hair, the frail body almost quivered with impatience.

"It's good to see you again, Mr. Purnell," Catha began, stepping into the room and shutting the door behind her.

"Call me Ethan," was the barked order. "Even if it weren't for Lucas's heap of compliments, I feel like we're almost kin. I met your mama right after she was born."

"Abigail's daughter," Catha prodded gently. "I read the journal."

Ancient sorrows flickered around the old man's eyes, becoming as livid as new scars. "Course you did," he stated with a show of bravado. "Lucas told me." But then the bluster faltered, and the proud shoulders slumped. "That wasn't the entire story, you know."

Catha didn't answer. Ethan seemed to be wrestling with some deep-seated burden; she wondered if perhaps it wasn't cruel asking him to relive the past, and cursed herself for making him dredge up long-buried secrets.

"I was in love with her," Ethan finally continued. The tone was matter-of-fact, an attempt at escaping unpleasantness and grief.

"You've guessed that, I'm sure. . . . A smart lady like you . . . a professor. I was nothing but a hick cowpoke back then . . . never mind that fancy deputy marshal's badge. I knew I wasn't good enough for Abigail in spite of everything she claimed . . . such as people with pedigrees and big bank accounts being phonies. . . . She said that later, of course. In the beginning, she hardly spoke a word."

Ethan paused here, straightening his spine and lifting his porcelain-pale jaw. It was as if he were trying to slip inside his former self, and Catha could almost see him: a rawboned youth with large, expressive hands, and shoulders that seemed too wide for his slim body. His smile would have been shy but steady—a heartbreaker when you got beyond the deferential manner.

"Twenty-two and a half years old, I was, and green when it came to women. Especially a young lady like Abigail. I'll never forget the first time I seen her. Old Doc Steinbeck called me up to the castle, said some Hollywood fat cat had gotten himself murdered; you could tell the doc was pleased as punch. He hated those rich folks, insisted they were parasites and worse."

"And Abigail was among the guests when you arrived?" Catha interjected as delicately as she could.

"She had on a yellow dress. It was the color of buttercups, and all I could think about was walking through a field with her beside me."

"Aside from the dress, was there anything else you remember? Her behavior, or how she and her boss were getting along—even Mr. Hearst's conduct? Was there anything suspicious in their interaction? Or among the other guests?"

"If you mean did Abigail act like a murderer," Ethan fumed, "no, she did not."

"Then why was she blamed—"

"You read her journal—or what was left of it after Marion finally handed it over." Ethan's black eyes flashed.

After Catha had nodded hesitant agreement, he continued loudly and insistently, "Well, I'll tell you how it was, missy. If you want to pull up a chair and take a load off your feet, I'll explain exactly what I learned about your grandmother's case." But before continuing the tale, the old man interrupted himself, with a rapid-fire: "Feisty! That's what Lucas told me. . . . Just like Abigail, I said to myself. A woman's nothing without a spine." Lost in his memories, Ethan didn't see how deeply Catha was blushing.

"This is Deputy Marshal Purnell. He'll be in charge of the investigation. I realize you're all in a state of shock and disbelief, but Mr. Hearst has promised that each of you will cooperate to the fullest of your abilities." With Neylan's brief introduction dispensed with, Ethan was on his own. It was ten o'clock in the morning; he knew he'd remember the hour because it seemed so peculiar to see draperies drawn as if it were still night. Ethan decided that moving-picture people were mighty odd and wondered if the cause wasn't spending too much time in a make-believe world. Then he considered William Randolph Hearst's hilltop palace, and the art and antiques stacked to the rafters, and realized the Hollywood crowd didn't have a patch on their host when it came to separating fantasy from reality. This investigation is going to be as difficult as persuading a steer to swim to Oakland, Ethan told himself while he cleared his throat and stepped forward.

"I have a filming schedule that can't possibly be altered," Pola began before Ethan could open his mouth, and the others immediately chimed in with their own watertight excuses. Everyone had "a prior commitment," "a vitally important meeting," or "script to peruse." Even Mademoiselle X invented "an audition for a starring role."

"I won't keep you any longer than necessary," Ethan assured them, but his age and clearly inferior status conspired against him.

"And how long might that be, young man?" Elinor demanded, using her haughtiest British accent.

"Madame Glyn is a famous novelist," Principessa

added, as Lollie threw in, "And, of course, you recognize Mr. John Barrymore and Mr. and Mrs. Charles Chaplin." Marion concluded the remarks with an imperious and suddenly stutter-free: "We're only too happy to help, but none of us saw or heard a thing out of the ordinary. One minute dear Tom was the life of the party, the next he was doubled over in pain. We assumed he had a nasty case of indigestion. Mr. Hearst's table is known for its excellence, and Tom, I'm afraid, was equally renowned for his appetite. The idea that someone would shoot such a stalwart friend is simply too ghastly to consider."

"Hear, hear," John tossed out for good measure, and the revitalized crowd pulled closer together.

"But someone must have heard gunfire," Steinbeck grumbled. He hated seeing a boy like Ethan railroaded by a lot of fancy names. "A noise like that is hard to miss. I don't care how much booze you'd been swilling." Then he added an aside only Ethan heard: "You'll have to check each of those target pistols. Run a ballistics test."

"I'm sure you're aware, Doctor," Elinor stated in her frostiest tone, "that some of the guests were experimenting with fireworks while others amused themselves with target practice. I can assure you that the sounds produced by those various explosions—as well as the sulfurous smoke—quite eliminated all other considerations. We could scarcely see our hands in front of our faces."

Marion interrupted again. Her lips were curved into a smile that lacked even a residue of warmth. "As for alcohol, Doctor, I'm surprised at you. The purchase and consumption of spirits is illegal; I'm sure Mr. Hearst's private physician, Dr. Goodman, can attest to the fact that our cruise was a dry one."

Holed up in an oversize chair and nearly invisible in the shadow cast by the Refectory door, Abigail raised her head and looked long and hard at her boss. She'd never heard Marion use such high-flown language—hadn't even considered her capable of it. She must be a terrific actress, Abigail told herself, then studied the doyenne of San Simeon as if she expected further surprises to pop out.

Marion returned the glance with a smug smirk. "We're in this together," the expression seemed to say, "but I'm the lady who's calling the shots." Abigail closed her eyes and shivered, and at that moment Ethan noticed her.

She seemed so defenseless sitting there in her yellow dress, her long legs tucked under her and her wavy hair brushing her sleeveless shoulders. The dress fluttered around her; its thin, gauzy material seemed to bathe her in light, creating a golden and hallowed place all her own.

Ethan took up his pencil, held it over his notebook, then realized his hand was trembling and returned the useless props to his side. "And what about you, miss? What did you see?"

Feeling his appraising gaze, Abigail had opened her eyes. Her expression was impossible to read; it might have been withholding secrets or crying for help.

"My last name's Kinsolving," she stated in a clear and unhurried voice that Ethan immediately recognized as "quality," "but you can call me Abigail. That's how I'm referred to here."

"Abigail's my private secretary. She's from the East Coast and has been in my employ for approximately six weeks," Marion interjected. "I'll answer any questions on her behalf."

"I'd prefer Miss Abigail speak for herself," Ethan

responded, then added a heartfelt: "You must have taken a nasty spill, miss. Lucky you didn't knock out a couple of teeth."

"She fell on the steps leading to the garden," Marion again intercepted, while Abigail's swollen lips formed the loneliest smile Ethan had ever seen.

"I saw nothing until Mr. Ince collapsed. Miss Davies is correct. We were too involved in other occupations."

The preliminary questioning concluded almost immediately after that. Steinbeck attempted a couple of strong-arm tactics, growling disbelief at both Chaplin's and Barrymore's statements, but the accusations were met with the bemused condescension reserved for a member of "the great unwashed." The group was determined to stick to its story: Tom Ince had been suffering from some type of gastric complaint. No one saw any liquor consumed; no one heard or witnessed anything out of the ordinary. But not one person could account for the whereabouts of the target pistols when Ince fell to his knees, and here the various accounts began to unravel.

"I smell a rat," Steinbeck muttered to Ethan as Marion and her guests filed out of the Assembly Room. His none-too-secret pronouncement was met with a sidelong glance from Elinor, who then hooked her arm through Principessa's and giggled a stage whisper: "I wonder if communists sleep with women or if they consider sex a vice invented by capitalists?"

The remark set off a chain reaction of self-laudatory titters; Pola, Lollie, and even Lita joined in. The women and their male companions were the high and mighty; Steinbeck was a "hack and a quack," and Ethan was that "pathetic boy playing policeman." As far as the guests were concerned, the unfortunate event was over; they'd been loyal to each other and to their host; like true troupers they'd performed as directed; now it was time to go home.

Only Abigail remained behind in the Assembly Room with Ethan and Steinbeck. She hadn't stirred from her chair and was so curled in upon herself that she seemed to be suffering from cold.

"Are you all right, miss?" Ethan asked.

"Abigail," was the hollow answer, but her eyes continued to shine into his as though they were begging for reassurance.

"That's more like it." Steinbeck's craggy face agreed with the semblance of an approving nod. "A woman of the people! So, Abigail, which one of these parasitic insects shot the man?"

But Abigail only gazed at Ethan, and Ethan at her.

"Oh, I see how it is," the doctor finally chortled. "Well, I was young once, too. . . . But, Ethan, don't go forgetting your duty. You've got to hound those people. Follow them down to their fancy houses in Los Angeles, and to their studio bungalows, too. You can't trust one of them. They're all under Hearst's thumb, and he's as crooked as they come."

Ethan would have bristled at this injunction; he considered himself the sole person in charge of the investigation (his first murder case and almost the first in Cambria's history), and he didn't like taking orders from a small-town doctor. But Ethan told himself that true authority meant appearing unfazed.

"Of course. I'd already decided to make that area my next stop." He never once took his eyes off Abigail.

"You won't be questioning Marion anymore?" she asked.

"Not unless you give me reason to."

"Then you won't visit La Cuesta Encantada again?"

Ethan's response was painfully slow in coming. "I'm not certain . . ."

"I'm leaving," Steinbeck interrupted. "Those two goons are going to drive me back into town. Better call in the cavalry if I wind up missing. I wouldn't trust those boys not to toss me in a dry gully somewhere." A bitter chuckle accompanied these words. "Of course, I've already let the cat out of the bag, so I guess disposing of me wouldn't do any good. On the other hand, Ethan, if both you and me vanish, no one but Abigail here will be the wiser. And, of course, she's only a secretary—who'd believe her side of the story?"

Left alone, Abigail and Ethan continued to study each other.

"May I sit down?" he finally asked. By this time the Ince investigation had almost vanished from his mind. In answer, Abigail moved in her grand chair, allowing room for him, too, but Ethan decided perching beside her would not only look foolish with so many pieces of unoccupied furniture nearby, but would also seem the height of presumption. He chose a chaise, then leaned as close to Abigail as he dared.

"How long have you been working for Miss Davies?" he began more for conversation than information, but Abigail merely clenched her teeth and then began to weep silently.

"It's a terrible situation—having a man die like this," Ethan soothed, reaching out his hand in comfort and then immediately drawing it back. "And I'm sure living here is no church picnic. . . . These are flighty folks; I bet they don't make your job any too easy."

Abigail's tears increased and she buried her head

in her raised knees. "It's all right, miss," Ethan murmured. "If you saw something . . . or heard anything unusual, your secret's safe with me."

Abigail ceased crying and gave Ethan a look he couldn't fathom. "I can't help you," she finally answered.

21

WHAT HAPPENED TO DR. STEINBECK?" CATHA couldn't help interrupting. Ethan's tale had become so engrossed in its description of Abigail that he'd left that important element of the story dangling.

"What's that?" the old man demanded, jerked back to the present and his unhappy status as nursing-home resident. "Who's that you're yammering about? Some doctor? We got plenty of them here. . . . You look fit as a fiddle, though, if you want my opinion."

"No . . . Steinbeck, the local practitioner from Cambria." All at once Catha was afraid she'd destroyed Ethan's narrative. Lucas warned me about these lapses, she reminded herself, and so did Donnie. Why didn't I listen? "Steinbeck . . . the man who called you up to San Simeon."

"Oh, he died," Ethan answered airily.

"That day?" Catha gasped. "You mean the Mullers killed him? Weren't they caught . . . or sent to prison?"

Ethan focused on Catha's face. "You're so much like your grandmother," he marveled. "Almost her

278

double. And you're blind to the evil around you, too, same as she was." Then he shifted course abruptly, returning Abigail to tantalizing darkness.

"No, Steinbeck lived another fifteen years or so. Got to be a crazy old buzzard. He never stopped hating Hearst or accusing him of 'conspiracies,' insisted that he twisted the truth to suit his 'schemes.' Even during the Depression when the town of Cambria would have dried up and blown away if it weren't for the jobs up at San Simeon. You see, the doc had never been inside the castle before Ince was shot. My guess is that seeing the place was too much for him . . . all that money spent on paintings and such when the world was filled with hungry children. . . . And then there was all that misery surrounding your grandmother."

Catha didn't speak. She sat in her rigid chair facing Ethan and listened to the muted sounds thumping through the convalescent home's plasterboard walls. "What misery?" she wanted to ask, but a small voice inside her warned her to keep quiet.

"Unwed mothers were a scandal in those days, and Abigail had to visit the doc secretly. She'd decided she didn't want anything to do with Hearst's guy, Goodman—even though Marion tried to pressure her—so one of the Mullers would drive her down to the village for her checkups. The whole procedure was hushed up; Abigail wore a big picture hat with a long, dark veil and one of Marion's coats. For a while, there was a rumor afoot that the pregnant lady was Marion herself, and the curious would idle outside on that old plank sidewalk we had, waiting for a glimpse of the movie star as she climbed out of her chauffeured limousine. Then one lady claimed the 'sinner' was one of San Simeon's upstairs maids, and another insisted the 'fallen woman' worked in the scullery. No one ever got the story straight. But then that was how Marion wanted it."

"What do you mean?" Catha finally broke in. "What did Marion have to do with Abigail's pregnancy?"

"Lucas is sweet on you, isn't he?" was Ethan's surprising response, then he stared at the blank, white wall of his cubicle bedroom as though he were seeing an animated picture of times gone by.

A chill wind and a sudden, squall-filled rain lashed at San Simeon's bulky turrets. Ince's funeral had taken place the day before—on a sunny November 22 in Los Angeles. Marion hadn't been permitted to attend, and it was questionable when she'd be allowed to escape to Hollywood again. Ince's death had affected W.R. strangely; he'd become moody and withdrawn as if he were chewing on an unsolvable problem. In his self-exile, he insisted Marion remain at his side. Or perhaps the reason was a total lack of trust.

Marion's response to her imprisonment was equally peculiar; she vacillated between vindictive spates of recrimination and fawning servility made worse by insecurity. Neylan had become her "enemy"; Joe Willicombe was "Satan's monkey"; the Mullers were "in league with the devil"; while Julia Morgan had turned into "the whore of Babylon." Following Ince's death, Marion's speech had reverted to the Catholic epithets she'd heard as a child. Her reminiscences were stuck in those early days as well; Abigail heard more about Mama Rose and Papa Ben than she wanted, and often the tales were so conflicted she wondered which were true and which fabrication.

Then there was Marion's problem with the bottle, although this she managed to keep secret from W.R. "On pain of death!" she ordered Abigail. "If he finds out, you'll wish your only punishment was losing a job!" Abigail felt as though she'd been consigned to the ninth circle of hell.

The days wore on, and November came to a bleak and suddenly frigid end. Sometimes the mountaintop appeared totally removed from the rest of the world. Icy cloud cover often enshrouded it, chilling Abigail to the bone. She was also in the throes of morning sickness, and between that and the cold she often wished she'd never been born.

Her only consolation was Ethan; he came to San Simeon every other day or so, summoned by Neylan at the Chief's behest. The "official" investigation had been delayed while Neylan conferred with W.R. and then, via the telephone, with the weekend's guests as well as some faceless attorneys in New York. There were ample excuses for the postponement: Nell Ince was reported to be "in deep mourning," Chaplin was "filming," Elinor was "in New York delivering a series of lectures on romance and marriage." If Ethan felt frustrated at the myriad excuses, he didn't show it; he remained respectful of San Simeon's lord and of his mistress, although he reserved his true chivalry for Abigail. For reasons he couldn't comprehend and didn't fully trust, Marion conspired to put the two young people together as much as possible. And they were always left alone.

"Why do you suppose that is, Abigail?" Ethan asked. The two were walking through a gully halfway down San Simeon's undulating hillside. A dense, white fog covered them, wetting their clothes and faces and turning the springy spikes of field grass the color of sea foam. The sight reminded Abigail of snow.

"You mean Marion leaving us alone all the time?"

"Forcing us is more like it."

"What a prude you are, Ethan! I suppose you're scared of being on your lonesome with a wanton woman like me." During her many walks with Ethan, Abigail was a different person from the frightened, introverted one he'd first met. She laughed and joked about her childhood, did impersonations of Marion, W.R., and Neylan. Only when returning to the castle did she revert to the guarded, silent Abigail who existed within the compound's walls.

"Why do you think she's doing it, though?"

"Are you being a detective now or is this a real question?" "Real questions" were the only ones Abigail permitted during these private moments. The yachting party and the dinner the night before were never mentioned, nor was Thomas Ince.

"Real." Ethan grinned. He had an almost irresistible urge to touch her, but knew it was forbidden; Abigail had shied away like a terrified yearling the first time he'd tried to take her hand.

"Marion's probably being nice, Ethan, that's all. Or maybe she's getting rid of us so you stop needling 'Popsie.'" Here Abigail batted her eyelashes, simpering a rendition of her boss's coyest stutter.

"You don't think she's trying to hook us up?" Ethan tried to sound offhand, as if the idea were a jest and not ready for serious consideration. His shirt and dungarees were soaked through, his sun-bleached hair slick with water; he felt as if he and Abigail were swimming through breast-high waves instead of walking. He kept reminding himself that she was too good for him, that the best he could hope for was friendship, but all the same he wished life could be otherwise. "On account of your not being married and all," he added in an almost inaudible voice.

"No," Abigail said firmly. "Marion doesn't waste her time worrying about my future." With that, she turned away and started up the long hill that led to the mountaintop.

"So you weren't aware that Ince had raped Abigail?" Catha asked, and was surprised at how quickly Ethan made the transition from memory to the present—and his existence in the old-age home.

"I only knew the man had been murdered. I didn't find out what he'd done to Abigail until much later . . . near the time your mother was born. Marion told me. . . . Of course, my investigation had been officially closed by the governor's office in late March of that year, so the information was useless."

"But the rape might have provided Abigail with a motive for shooting Ince . . . ?" Catha's face was crisscrossed with confusion.

"There were other considerations," Ethan answered cryptically, then added an equally puzzling: "Besides, Marion never did anything without having a reason. She was a smart cookie—especially when it came to protecting her own hide."

"But didn't you wonder who the baby's father was?" Catha persisted, attempting to make sense of the conflicting pieces of the story.

Ethan appeared to ponder the question; his answer was slow, as if he were only now examining his own motives. "I guess I wanted to think Marion had hired Abigail knowing she was in the family way—sort of a lady bountiful gesture. Marion liked to do things like that once in a while . . . hampers of food delivered to folks in the village . . . that type of thing."

"But didn't you ever ask?" Frustration was beginning to gnaw away at Catha's patience, and Ethan responded to the change in tone with a stubborn: "No, I did not."

"You just assumed you'd never be good enough for

her, and so you let this crucial issue slide? That's like loving only half a person—the part you find acceptable!" Catha was taking Ethan's confession far more personally than she cared to admit.

"Hold on there, missy!" Ethan's temper had also flared. "You can't go accusing people when you don't know the whole picture. Those were different times back then. We didn't talk about sex like you young people do today. Hell, we were hardly allowed to think about it!"

"A lot of good that did!" Catha snorted, and Ethan gave a sudden and glee-filled laugh. "You are a firecracker," he cackled. "I hope my nephew knows what he's in for."

"So you didn't suspect Abigail of murder," Catha continued, skirting the subject of Lucas. "What about Marion? Were you suspicious of her?"

"Not at first. I only imagined she had something brewing when it came to Abigail and me. . . . Oh, hell, I don't know. Maybe I believed I could wear Abigail down with my pestering—make her agree to marry me. If Marion kept dragging us kids together, who was I to say no?"

"But I don't understand! Marion protects Abigail, who ultimately gets blamed for Ince's death. What about the other guests? Where do they fit in?"

"I'm coming to that," was Ethan's crotchety reply, but before he had time to resume his story, Donnie swung open the door with a falsely cheerful "Suppertime!" while he wheeled in a dinner tray of lead-gray beans, ashy-hued potatoes, and junket the color of bubblegum.

Ethan's eyes sped from the cart to Donnie, and the young man inside him vanished completely, leaving a wiry shell and ancient hands clutching the chair's hard sides.

"Ethan?" Catha asked softly, but the reply was a deadened facade that seemed incapable of thought. Ethan stared at her as if he'd never seen her before.

"Just like that," Donnie gloated. "I told you. The old coot can be a regular leaking faucet or go dumb as a horse. You never know what you're going to get."

"Should I wait?" Catha murmured, shocked at Ethan's metamorphosis as well as Donnie's callous acceptance.

"I wouldn't bother if I was you. You can try again tomorrow if you want. Maybe you'll get something out of him, but then again, maybe you won't."

In response, Catha rested a reassuring hand on the old man's rigid shoulder, then bent down and searched his face as she gently squeezed his ancient hand. "It's okay, Ethan. I'll come back."

The cozy restaurant was lit only by candles and a fire flickering in the hearth. An autumnal scent of pumpkin pie and apple flan echoed the crisp November night, the golden moon, and a sky luminous with stars. "Look at that, Catha," Lucas marveled as they stood on the Victorian porch, pausing in the cold before the room's cheery warmth drew them in. "Orion and the Dippers." Crowned with a gingerbread arch and lit by the firelight spilling from the window, Lucas seemed a person from an earlier era. Catha imagined a small New England village, and a life that began and ended within the reassuring perimeter of a close-knit family and lifelong friends.

"I hope you'll consider coming back East and visiting sometime," she said. Lucas didn't answer; he simply took her hand.

"So tell me more about Middletown and the Connecticut River Valley." Lucas poured the rest of the wine while the waitress removed the dinner plates. "And Ivoryton—was that the name of the village?"

"It's a sleepy little place now—except for that knockout restaurant I told you about—but the town was a commercial hub during the early 1800s. Ivory piano keys were manufactured there, and combs and . . . You can trace the area's entire history in its domestic architecture." Catha halted her headlong rush of words. "You have to see for yourself, Lucas. In the winter, in the snow . . . icicles and pine boughs bending under a mantle of white. . . . We could drive down the coast as well . . . to Leetes Island and Guilford. That's another ancient settlement."

"I suppose you wouldn't be happy living anywhere else," Lucas suggested.

Catha's face turned suddenly serious. "Why don't we take it one moment at a time."

During coffee, Catha brought up her interview with Ethan. "That's everything he told me," she said, shrugging her shoulders after a brief description of the afternoon. "I didn't tell him you were coming up tonight because . . ."

"That's all right," Lucas smiled. "I was planning on calling him tomorrow. I wanted to devote the evening to you."

Catha glanced at the tablecloth and then across the room. "Tomorrow may be no better, Lucas. I hope it wasn't my fault . . . wearing your uncle out. I should have known better, but I get so . . . so . . ."

"Wound up?" Lucas laughed. "I warned Uncle Ethan. He knew what to expect. Besides, he's no weakling—despite what Donnie says." Then Lucas grew silent while his legal brain went to work.

"So, according to Ethan, everyone was a suspect," he concluded after a moment.

"That's how far we'd gotten when Donnie blew in with that revolting tray. Your uncle's official investigation hadn't even begun, however. I gather it was kept on ice as long as possible . . . thus Ethan being summoned instead of the big boys in San Luis."

"And Abigail was eventually blamed," Lucas mused, then focused on Catha, adding a quick, excited: "But never found guilty."

"Not according to any records I've found." Catha's words were slow and methodical. "In September 1926—two years after Ince died—one H. P. Bee, editor of the *Culver City Call,* came forward, claiming to have inside information on the fatal party aboard the *Oneida.* After Bee testified, 'unofficial sources' debunked him, insisting he was involved in a graft scandal elsewhere in the state and could therefore be ruled out as a 'responsible source.' There were no further inquiries into the death; and the Ince investigation was dropped."

"This is according to research you did at UCLA?"

"Yep. I've got the photocopies from the *Daily Times* in my car."

"So you're saying there's nothing in print that mentions or even suggests murder."

"Nothing." Catha took a sip of her coffee, then cradled the cup, letting her fingers absorb the heat of the china. The burning logs in the hearth at her back crackled and snapped, perfuming the air with the homey aroma of wood smoke. "So do you think you'll visit back East?" she asked, suddenly more interested in the present than the past.

But this time it was Lucas's turn to be distracted. "No murder charge," he mused. "And yet the rumors persist."

"Where there's smoke there's fire?" Catha offered,

reaching across the table and grazing the tips of Lucas's fingers.

"Run this by me again." He frowned in concentration while sliding his hand over hers in a movement both comfortable and natural. "From your first encounter with the murder theory to your research at the microfilm library."

And Catha did, detailing the delayed accounts in the newspapers and the conflicting reports on causes of death. "Ince was reputed to have died of acute indigestion,'" she said, summing up her discoveries. "Then the story was amended to 'heart failure brought on by indigestion'; there was also some question as to whether or not he was aboard when he collapsed. Even that tale varies from paper to paper."

"Could Hearst have been powerful enough to quash the truth?" Lucas leaned forward, gripping Catha's hand as he spoke.

"What do you think?" she asked.

They drove back to the seaside inn through deserted streets. A few lamps lit the roadway, but where the piney woods encroached, the landscape turned black as new pitch. Catha pulled her coat collar tighter against the cold night air; she didn't ask what sleeping arrangements Lucas had made or what the next morning would bring. Her circumspect life as an associate history professor seemed a long way in the past.

"I'm really happy, Lucas. Not just tonight . . . I mean, happy knowing you."

This time Lucas didn't tease her for being tongue-tied. He merely answered, "I am, too, Catha."

They made love in the light of a small fire glowing within the bedroom's rough stone hearth. The smoke had a salty tang of driftwood, and as the embers shifted and fell apart, they sent reflections of themselves spinning over the ceiling. Catha thought the room and the bed and Lucas beside her had the quality of a lovely dream. She was afraid she might waken and find herself alone in her campus apartment with a sheaf of uncorrected papers stacked on the floor.

"I think I've fallen in love with you," she said at last. Lucas lay beside her in a comforting tangle of sheets, and she gazed at him with peaceful eyes. "I didn't mean this to happen . . . living on opposite sides of the continent and everything."

"I know." Lucas's answer was thoughtful and slow. "I didn't intend to fall for you either . . . didn't believe anyone could matter after my wife died."

Catha didn't speak; instead she touched his naked shoulder and smiled gently at his darkened face.

"That must have been a difficult time," she finally murmured.

"It was. But it's over. It really is over, Catha."

For a while neither of them stirred. The room was silent save for their hearts beating and their measured breaths. Catha listened to the nearly inaudible sounds and realized she felt closer to this man than she had to any other person in her life.

"Where do we go from here?" she asked.

"Maybe you should tell me."

They fell asleep without answering the question, then woke to the sound of surf below the cliffs. The windows were black and the fire had been reduced to rosy ash.

"Are you ready to start again?" Lucas laughed.

"I'm ready for anything," Catha grinned.

The sun's pale, early rays flickered over their faces. Catha opened her eyes to find Lucas already awake and staring at the ceiling. She nestled her face against his shoulder, mumbling a soft: "I wish you didn't have to go back to L.A. this morning."

Lucas dodged the comment with a tenacious and supercharged: "Okay, so you're telling me Abigail and Ethan didn't have sex . . . didn't even talk about it . . . that's what you said. . . . I mean, what kind of weird existence was that?"

"How long have you been awake?" Catha laughed, propping herself up on her elbows.

"Just now."

"And I wasn't the first person that popped into your mind?"

"Yes . . . and no. It's just that I hate riddles that can't be solved."

Catha smiled inside until the warmth of her feelings flooded her face. "So do I." Then she returned to Lucas's question. "Why couldn't Abigail and Ethan have cared deeply about each other without having a physical relationship?"

"As opposed to you?" Lucas joked as he slid a pillow behind her back, then moved so close their bodies seemed attached from shoulder to hip.

"I didn't have to go to bed with you, you know."

"Oh, no?"

Whatever Catha's response might have been, Lucas stopped it with a lingering kiss. Catha felt her chest beat and her skin grow hot. "You don't know everything," she mumbled through smiling lips.

"That's not what you told me last night."

When they broke away again, Lucas grabbed another pillow and scrunched it up behind his neck. "Business before pleasure, isn't that what they tell us?"

"I guess." Catha looked at Lucas with a doting expression she couldn't have prevented even if she'd wanted to.

"What I can't understand is why Ethan didn't ask about Abigail's pregnancy. . . . Okay, let's say it didn't show. She could have been in her first month or her third . . . which would make the good-hearted-Marion theory entirely plausible."

"Maybe Ethan was being delicate," Catha suggested. "It was a different generation, after all. He wouldn't have asked who the father was, and Abigail couldn't name Ince without becoming a suspect in the murder. The situation seems entirely normal."

"But what was Marion's role in all of this? Why did she wait so long to tell Ethan about Ince? What did she know?"

Catha turned serious; the reaction seemed unusual given her nakedness, but she felt as relaxed and free as if she and Lucas were sitting side by side sharing a late weekend breakfast. "I guess the only person who can answer that question is Ethan."

22

Despite Donnie's dire warnings, Ethan was not only back on track but delighted to see Catha. "They keep you locked up in here like newborn kittens," he grumbled. "It's not healthy . . . the same gobbledy-goo to eat every day . . . the same whiny, pretend-happy voices . . . everything gets jumbled . . . like those things I saw pictured on the TV . . . you float around in bathwater and forget what day it is."

"Sensory-deprivation tanks?" Catha offered, repressing a smile. Ethan had indeed lost track of the years.

"Fancy words for losing your marbles," he groused. "They should try getting old." Then he launched full force into his next subject. "So I drove down to Hollywood," he announced without waiting for Catha to pose the question. "That would have been during the second week of December. I told you how Mr. Neylan kept stalling me."

Catha nodded assent, but Ethan's narrative had already moved past her. "We had a sudden dry spell; the roads weren't as good back then as they are now, and I guess the automobiles weren't much better, but I took advantage of the clear skies and headed south. We used to get fierce mud slides along old Highway One—there weren't any of your fancy freeways in those days—and I didn't want to get caught away from home, or Abigail.

"It took me near the whole day to make the trip; I drove down that big hill into Malibu at about three o'clock in the afternoon. Some of the film stars had started to build big spreads out there, but the village was a long way off from the studios—almost like being in another state. There were fishing shacks clustered along the roadway, real impermanent structures that looked like they'd been tacked together with colored paper and string . . . and then all of a sudden there'd be this fancy house with electric lights, stone patios, and a garage big enough to hold a fleet of limousines. Those places were my first taste of what you might call Hollywood excess."

This time Catha didn't interrupt; instead she pulled off her coat and sat as quietly as she could while Ethan continued to spin his tale.

"I'm afraid I can't help you, old boy." John Barrymore turned his majestic profile to Ethan as he spoke. They were in the star's wildly Spanish-inspired home high above Tower Road in the new development known as Beverly Hills. Clementine, Barrymore's pet monkey, alternately posed upon her master's tweed-covered shoulder or chased around the gigantic aviary where the actor's English butler had left a handsome serving tray of "liquid refreshments" before silently withdrawing. Clementine dispensed with the crystal decanters, aiming her pranks at a tame vulture named Maloney. Ethan eyed both the bird and the primate with suspicion, garbling his questions and losing his place in his notebook.

"No, there's simply no more to be said. Tom complained of stomach distress the night before we set sail. I assumed it was overindulgence at our host's bounteous board, and I'm afraid I didn't take his complaints seriously until he collapsed the next day. As to murder, who would want to assassinate a director and producer as successful as Tom—unless, of course, he refused to hire you." Barrymore knocked his pipe against a stone urn, then relit it with the fluid grace of a British gentleman possessing a large inheritance.

Ethan was scribbling furiously and trying to keep from noticing Clementine gnawing on his bootstraps.

"That was a jest, old man, a bit of thespian badinage."

Ethan hadn't a clue what Barrymore's words meant, but he spelled them out phonetically as best he could. Abigail could help him translate the actor's elaborate language.

"Ah, well," the great man sighed. "Those who've never trod the boards cannot comprehend the Machiavellian connivings of the performer's brain. Death by target pistol is too kind a demise for many an impresario. I've plotted far more diabolical ends, although regretfully never experienced the pleasure of realizing my dreams."

"How did you know it was a target pistol?" Ethan jumped back to the previous page in his notebook.

"Dear boy! We were all there when Dr. Goodman passed judgment."

"That's right. It was your lady friend who discovered the corpse." By now Clementine had nibbled her way through one strap and was beginning on the second boot. Ethan pretended to ignore her, but Barrymore proclaimed a mock-pious "My little angel's in love. She's washing your feet with her tears."

"Can you tell me where I might find this . . . this Mademoiselle X?" Ethan persisted, but Barrymore deftly changed the subject, insisting on giving the deputy marshal a tour of the house's spacious grounds.

"I look down upon Hollywood from all sides," he confided as Clementine leapt to her master's shoulder, and the men left the aviary and Maloney behind. "You have no idea the solace I take in that fact."

Ethan saw the gun room, the trophy room, the rathskeller with a mahogany bar imported from the Klondike, and a gunslinger-size cuspidor from Virginia City, the bowling green, tennis courts, skeet-shooting range, the vast azure pool, and the terraced gardens landscaped with fantastical topiary shapes. Every room and vista looked like a stage set, and Barrymore rattled off descriptions of his collection or the creation of his estate as if they were lines in a play he hadn't yet fully memorized. But every time Ethan turned the conversation to the whereabouts of Mademoiselle X, he was met by determined silence.

"I'm afraid I can't supply you with the young lady's name or address, old sport," Barrymore finally said as his very British valet appeared to escort Ethan to his car. "Gentleman's honor and all that. Besides, I made certain the girl never spoke to Tom. She doesn't know a thing."

By the time Ethan found his way to Rudolph Valentino's Falcon Lair on Benedict Canyon Drive, it was eight o'clock, the time most of the film world's glamorous denizens were ensconced at their dinner tables. The house had been difficult to find; the road had only a few, secluded residences, and it wound upward through uninhabitable scrub that comprised the main section of Beverly Hills. John Gilbert was Valentino's neighbor, living a mile or so away, but Ethan decided not to stop and ask directions there. Abigail had described the first weekend at San Simeon, and he decided against tangling with another swashbuckling actor; Barrymore had been enough.

After the deserted roadway and its thicket-filled canyons, the wrought-iron gates at Falcon Lair were impressively high and regal; they were also sur-mounted by lethal-looking spikes. Ethan told him-self he was there on official business and rang the buzzer. At the sound, a chorus of growls and snarls and yips burst from the house as a service door was flung open and two enormous mastiffs bounded out followed by a man wearing a torn sweater and rum-pled trousers.

"Stop right there," the man ordered in a bastardized Irish accent Ethan guessed hailed from the lower depths of New York City. "His Highness is entertain-ing. No visitors allowed."

"I'm looking for Pola Negri." Ethan stood his ground while the hounds rushed the gates, whimpering and yelping when the iron bars stopped them short.

"Well, you won't find her here. The missus, neither. His nibs is entertaining the boys tonight." The man's laugh was dismissive and smug. "It's a stag soiree, so you'd better beat it."

Just then the mansion's arched door swung open, and Valentino appeared. He was wearing a gauzy shirt and white chef's apron that looked incongruous against the ornately brocaded hangings draping the doorway. Ethan caught a glimpse of a round, bronze shield hanging on the wall, as well as a large collection of swords and lances. The entire room appeared full of ancient weaponry.

"Is there a problem, Mickey?"

"No, sir, just scaring away some snoop." Mickey grinned, showing teeth as yellow as the dogs' as he began swaggering toward Ethan.

"I'm a deputy marshal in Cambria, sir," Ethan shouted. "I'm here investigating Mr. Ince's murder. Could you tell me where Miss Negri is."

Laughter erupted from the house. "She's not here," a voice from behind Valentino giggled, but the actor squelched the interruption with a weary: "Quiet, Arturo."

"Like I told you," Mickey repeated. "The lady's not in residence."

"I need to speak with her," Ethan insisted while the dogs pawed at the ground and shook their foam-speckled muzzles.

"Mickey can give you Pola's address," Valentino called back, slowly closing the door on his private world. "He's a policeman like you—or at least he was until I found him. As for me, I'm cooking spaghetti." With that, the world-renowned lover was gone.

Pola was no more help than Barrymore; in fact, between her thick accent and wildly vacillating emotions, Ethan found it hard to understand half of what she was saying.

"You did see him . . . my *querido?*" she kept insisting while she twisted around in a gold-colored chair. But when she was questioned about Mademoiselle X's discovery of Ince's body, her eyes froze.

"A tramp. A nothing. She only desires a part in the films. She went to find Thomas because she wanted him all to herself."

"Did you ever mention the lady to Mr. Valentino?"

Pola pulled herself erect. "Why would I do this stupid thing?" she demanded.

Ethan slept in his car; the eerie wildness of Beverly Hills' empty miles discouraged him from unrolling his bindle bag and camping under the stars. Deer crept through the underbrush while the constant yipping of coyotes approached and then receded, but those noises were nothing compared to the low grumble of mountain lions prowling the inhospitable terrain. Ethan wondered why the likes of Barrymore, Gilbert, and Valentino lived in such a remote and inaccessible spot. If he'd had their means, he would have bought himself a ranch among the verdant orange groves of the beautiful San Fernando Valley.

In the morning Ethan resumed his search, driving to Charlie Chaplin's studios, which, even in the distance, looked like the idealized English villages that decorate chocolate tins. The buildings had sharply peaked roofs and half-timbered walls, but the fantasy was marred by the palm trees lining the dusty road and the snow-capped elevation of the San Gabriel Mountains rising in the cobalt-blue east.

"Mr. Chaplin's too busy to see you," Ethan was told, then another assistant ordered him to wait while a third reiterated the first man's curt advice. Ethan decided to sit tight. He'd made an appointment to visit Nell Ince at her home, Dias Dorados, but wasn't due there until after lunch.

Ethan passed the time studying the comings and goings around him. He guessed the people hurrying by were actors and actresses hoping for an audition; not one of them smiled or spoke. They scarcely acknowledged one another as they jostled through the hall, and everyone kept a furtive eye trained for the comedian and director himself. The frenzy reminded

Ethan of a barnyard full of chickens waiting for the day's scattering of feed.

"You're Purnell?" A voice above him broke the reverie. "Follow me." Ethan struggled to his feet, then noticed that one had fallen asleep as he began hobbling after the disappearing assistant.

Charlie Chaplin himself opened a narrow side door, allowing Ethan to slip in before the bustling throng noticed. "Casting call. The torments of the damned." But that cryptic pronouncement was the extent of Chaplin's chat; the rest of the abbreviated interview was a series of monosyllabic noes and yeses. Charlie's story was no more enlightening than the others'. No, he'd neither seen nor heard anything unusual; yes, they'd all had a turn at the target pistols; yes, he'd produced a box of fireworks; and no, he hadn't witnessed any consumption of alcohol. The bruise on Ince's face was equally mysterious; Chaplin didn't remember when he'd noticed it, then repeated Hearst's excuse about a dark house almost verbatim. As for Mademoiselle X, the comedian's remark was unexpectedly loquacious:

"If you find the kid, send her over. I may be doing additional hiring."

And then Ethan was back on the street.

Entering the dead man's house gave Ethan the unpleasant sensation of trespassing. He half-expected the maid to tell him Mrs. Ince had changed her mind; instead he was shown into a long living room with low, dark beams and flooring that looked like a ship's planked decking. A huge model of a sailing yacht sat on a table in front of leaded-glass doors, but unlike Barrymore's home or the brief glimpse Ethan had had of Valentino's aerie, the remainder of Ince's home was sparsely furnished. Dias Dorados was a male retreat; there was not one feminine touch.

"Good," Nell Ince said as she marched down the three steps that led from the foyer. "You're on time. Now, let's get this over with."

Her brisk and decidedly unmournful manner so unnerved Ethan that he forgot his prepared list of questions and blurted a tactless: "Do you know anyone who would have liked to murder your husband, Mrs. Ince?"

"Oh, a good many people." She laughed as she threw herself into a fat, velvet chair. "Myself among them. Of course, I wasn't there, so I'm off scot-free." Nell Ince's eyes were merry, but at the same time malevolent; they reminded Ethan of a cat at play, and he didn't trust cats in the slightest.

"Shall I run down a list of Tom's critics?" she continued breezily. "We could start with those fatalities at Inceville when it was still based on a tract of land where Sunset Boulevard meets the highway heading up the Pacific coast. Twenty thousand acres, Tom had. No doubt you've done your research and are aware of the stagehands killed when the scaffolding collapsed?"

Ethan nodded, but Nell had already moved ahead. "Or perhaps I should go further back—when dear, old Tom was shooting one-reel oaters. There was an actor who was ruined financially because of Tom. You still see him around town, panhandling and falling down drunk."

"You're taking your husband's death remarkably well, Mrs. Ince," Ethan managed to say. "Mr. Neylan led me to believe you were in mourning and couldn't be approached yet."

"Oh, W.R.'s shown the utmost concern." She smiled with her cat's glinting grin. "He's insisting I keep the

Culver City studio running to capacity. . . . You know Mr. Hearst and my husband were in the midst of arranging a deal between their two production companies?"

Ethan nodded. His stomach was churning, and his mouth tasted sour. He told himself that he hadn't eaten since morning, but the sensation didn't feel like hunger.

"I'm thinking of buying myself a present . . . a nice, little yacht. That is, if Mr. Hearst . . . well, enough said about business. . . . Let me show you around. If you're investigating a murder, I should imagine you'd want to know the man who had the starring role." Nell jumped out of her chair and bolted up the steps, pausing in the foyer to let Ethan catch up. "You're even younger than Mr. Neylan led me to believe," she said, beaming. "He made a clever choice."

"What happened after that?" Catha couldn't contain her curiosity a second longer.

"Mrs. Ince showed me the house." Ethan's response seemed guarded; Catha had the distinct feeling he was withholding information.

"And?" she prodded, but Ethan didn't answer immediately, and a wealth of possible scenarios passed through Catha's brain. What did Nell mean by 'young' and Neylan's making a 'clever choice'? she wondered. And what about the yacht idea? Did Nell eventually purchase one? Where did the money come from? Finally, there was the last big question: Was there a connection between the studio in Culver City and the editor of the local newspaper—the man who'd claimed to have "inside information" on the case? But Catha kept those riddles to herself, sitting anxiously on her nursing-home chair as she waited for Ethan to collect his thoughts.

"Dias Dorados means Golden Days," Ethan finally mumbled. "I guess it was a nice house . . . but the compound wasn't my style."

"What happened there?" Catha asked softly.

"I told you I wasn't feeling so hot, and trooping all over this thirty-acre spread didn't help. There were thirty-five rooms and ten big bathrooms . . . a banquet room, a bakery, a beauty parlor for the missus, a trout stream, pigeon tower, a swimming pool built to look like a lake, a roller-skating rink in the basement, a shooting gallery, theater, and a projection room painted like a South Seas island."

"And?" Catha interjected, convinced Ethan was hiding something.

"And this secret gallery that circled the guest rooms," he finally admitted. "Mrs. Ince told me her husband liked to watch what their friends did . . . you know . . . at night."

"I see." Catha leaned back in her chair.

"That shows you the sort of person he was!" Ethan burst out angrily. "If I'd known then what he'd done to Abigail, I would have turned in my badge on the spot . . . told myself a guy like that deserved to be shot."

"But you didn't know," Catha continued, mulling over Ethan's story. "You didn't learn about the rape for many months. And so you continued your investigation. . . . Was there anything else you remember about the day? Any other peculiar moment?"

Ethan thought a minute. "A photograph of Ince. I'd never seen a picture of him before . . . saw him dead, of course, but folks look different when they're no longer breathing. . . . There was this big photo of the man in the projection room . . . stood on a table with a special light. I thought it was a studio still of Charlie Chaplin; the fellow had the same wavy hair and squared-off jaw, even a similar crook to the nose . . . in that funny light, the two men looked identical. I mentioned the fact to Mrs. Ince, and you know what she told me, Catha . . . told me lots of people noticed the resemblance, but that she didn't see it herself . . . said Chaplin was a much 'nicer' man."

23

THE TELEPHONE CALL COULD NOT HAVE COME AT A worse moment. Just as Catha had begun urging Ethan to elaborate on the similarity between Chaplin and Ince, the door flew open and Donnie yelled a disruptive: "Phone for you, Catha. You'll have to take it at the nurses' station. Our system's on the fritz." True to the pattern patient and orderly had earlier established, Ethan went dumb on the spot.

"I won't be a minute," Catha murmured, but the old man showed no spark of recognition.

"Damn it, Donnie!" Catha argued as the two hurried toward the phone. "You could have knocked! A scare like that is liable to induce heart failure or something." Catha's equanimity had vanished. She felt like grabbing the orderly's pudgy shoulders and giving them a hearty shake. "Don't they give you training in dealing with the elderly?"

"I didn't think you'd want to keep the fellow waiting," Donnie answered, unrepentant.

"What fellow? I don't know anyone who lives around here."

"You'll see." Donnie's answer was less than friendly.

"Catha Burke," was the irritated announcement Catha delivered into the phone, but her displeasure vanished when she recognized the caller was Lucas. "Oh," she gulped, "I didn't expect . . ."

Seeing Donnie lurking nearby, she cradled the receiver and turned her back on his curious ears. "Me, too," she whispered. "I had a wonderful time, too," then bolstered her official status by adding a louder, "Your uncle Ethan and I were just discussing the physical similarities between Charlie Chaplin and Thomas Ince. A new twist on the case, I should think—"

But Lucas interrupted her. "Can you save it for tonight? I thought we could make a repeat of our evening in Cambria. I'm getting addicted to commuter jetting."

"Oh, I'll think about it," was Catha's teasing answer.

It wasn't until she was halfway to Ethan's room that she suddenly realized what had been nagging at her brain. "Barrymore," she'd been mumbling subconsciously. "Barrymore in his new house on Tower Road . . . English butler and . . . Oh, my God, that's it!" Catha was back at the nursing-station phone before she realized she'd moved at all.

"The funeral home!" Catha shouted the moment Lucas answered. "Quilman Brothers! Where Mother's funeral service was held. There was a book . . . a register . . . Lita Grey's assistant would have signed it and John Barrymore's valet. . . . I know what you're going to say," Catha interrupted herself before Lucas had a chance. "The man at Quilman's was Barrymore's last valet—he didn't work for the actor in 1924. But those names are our only leads!"

"Hold on there." Lucas finally found an opening. "What have two mourners at your mother's funeral got to do with a murder at San Simeon?"

Catha explained the connection as patiently as she could, but her mind kept leaping ahead and her words kept pace. "So I think one of them must know where she is—or was!" she concluded in a breathless and confusing tumble of words.

"Who?"

"Mademoiselle X!"

"Slow down, Catha. I'm lost here. Why is this unknown woman important? If Ethan never found her, what makes you believe she knew anything?"

"But that's exactly the reason, don't you see?" By now Catha's raised voice had created a stir in the nurses' station. Several worried heads were raised, followed by a round of disapproving glances. "Sorry," Catha whispered, then forged ahead with her argument.

"If Mademoiselle X didn't have some potentially damaging information, why didn't she come forward?"

"And what is it you want me to do, Catha?" The words were tinged with disappointment. Catha realized Lucas had begun to feel her search was interfering with their relationship, but she felt too close to a solution to stop.

"Go to the funeral parlor. I know it's in Santa Monica and you're in Century City, but if you just head out Santa Monica Boulevard, or maybe—"

"I hope you're not planning on giving me street directions," Lucas rallied, and Catha heard the smile return to his voice. "Okay, so I go to Quilman's and then what?"

"Look up their names. They were the last two

306

mourners to arrive. Ask Mr. Quilman's assistant to help you . . . her name's Dawn . . . or no, no . . . it's Fawn! Fawn will be thrilled to help you!"

"I'll bet," Lucas chuckled. "And then what?"

"Call me back!" Catha smiled into the phone. "You know where to reach me." Then she beamed magnanimous reassurances at the nurses' mute faces and returned to Ethan's room.

"I've been thinking," Ethan began as Catha opened his bedroom door. The vacant stare was gone, but in its place was a quieter version of the old man who'd greeted Catha that morning. The dimming effect reminded her of a three-way lightbulb: some memory or event succeeded in cutting the wattage, and when the weary brain flickered on again, it was difficult to foresee how brightly it would glow.

"Have you!" Catha answered too cheerily, then realized she sounded exactly like the nurses she'd just left.

But Ethan didn't seem to notice the vapid remark. "About this resemblance between Ince and Chaplin," he continued slowly. "I never made the connection until today. Do you suppose Ince was killed by mistake? That someone was gunning for Chaplin? It was dark, remember, and there were all those fireworks . . . not to mention the booze they all swore they hadn't been swilling. Hell, it could have even been Lita. . . . You know they got divorced a few years later . . . a real nasty case . . . it made all the papers. She accused him of all kinds of terrible things. . . . Maybe Ince didn't have an enemy. Maybe all that folderol about a bruise on his face was intended to throw me off the track. . . . Remember, it was Dr. Goodman who remarked on it first. Could he have been protecting someone?"

"I suppose it's possible," Catha admitted, with half her thoughts still on the elusive Mademoiselle X.

"Sure it is!" Ethan's pale face sprang to glowing life again. "And that nonsense Marion began spouting later, why, that must have been a pack of lies, too—except for Ince raping Abigail, I mean."

"What sort of things was Marion saying?" Catha perched herself on a hard-backed chair.

"Why, about Abigail confessing. . . . I told you all that baloney, didn't I?"

Ethan's statement dropped Catha in place with a bang. Her preoccupation with Mademoiselle X and the two mourners at Louise Burke's funeral disappeared before the calm simplicity in Ethan's voice. So there's no mystery after all, Catha found herself repeating numbly; Abigail admitted shooting Tom Ince. My grandmother confessed to Marion. Catha's thoughts had the surreal quality of words reiterated until their meaning is lost.

"No, you never mentioned Abigail's confession." Catha's tone was sluggish and weary. "Perhaps you'd better tell me now."

"It was terrible up there at the castle, but after I returned from Los Angeles, things went from bad to worse. Every day got grimmer. Old man Hearst wanted to clear up the case, of course; there were crazy rumors spreading all over the state, stories about how Marion had shot the director out of jealousy and that Hearst was covering up for her—even tales that W.R. had killed the man himself.

"But the folks up at San Simeon knew Ince's death couldn't be officially listed as murder; the scandal would have finished Hearst's political hopes and maybe his publishing empire, too—even if he hadn't pulled the trigger. 'Acute indigestion' as a cause of death began to look pretty bad. Prohibition had the country running scared, and a public figure serving up booze . . . Well, you can imagine the outrage that information would stir up. W.R. hadn't discounted moving into the White House one day.

"I was called up to San Simeon more times than I can remember. I guess the reason for my presence was to keep the gossips at bay, but I think Hearst and Neylan genuinely needed help. . . . That was about the time they decided to come up with their 'heart failure' theory. I guess the scheme was Neylan's brainchild; he'd been masterminding a lot at the castle—on account of the Chief being in such a funk; and the story seemed plausible. . . . Ince was known as a high-stepper, and a temperamental man when it came to work . . . a 'perfectionist,' they said; and we all know that type of behavior takes its toll. . . . Pretty soon all the newspapers had an amended version of Ince's death. Goodman was the physician quoted . . . Steinbeck was never consulted. . . . And as for me, what could I say? I'd come up blank on every lead. Not one of the folks who'd been on board the yacht was willing to talk.

"Maybe the old man was relieved to have the disaster behind him; maybe he needed distance from the scene of the crime; or perhaps he was harboring a grudge against Marion for dragging him into the entire fiasco. Whatever the reason, he took off, went back to his wife in New York, and Marion was left behind. It was a couple of days before Christmas. I don't know if he'd told the Mullers she wasn't to leave the property or if she decided to go into hibernation on her own, but she stayed up there in that huge house, rattling around like a ghost. Abigail was the only person she'd talk to—when she was sober enough to speak.

"When Hearst left, I went up fairly often to see how Abigail was doing. The compound was almost shut down; with the boss away, Julia Morgan's work had come to a halt, and the scaffolding on Casa Grande's towers turned dusty gray from disuse. They looked pretty near to collapsing.

"At first Abigail was real happy to have me visit. With the boss back East with his wife, Marion had become a bundle of nerves. When she wasn't soused, she was crying or screaming she'd get even; and when she tried to cheer herself up, it was almost worse. She'd make Abigail sit up with her all night, playing cards and telling stories Abigail could never repeat.

"But as the months dragged on, Abigail got more and more distant . . . told me there were things I'd never understand and equally peculiar stuff. But you know what was really strange, Catha? Marion hardly ever left us alone together anymore. She was always lurking around a corner . . . like she was eavesdropping.

"Abigail accepted the situation, and that made me mad. She never left San Simeon except to visit Doc Steinbeck, and when I'd try to tell her she wasn't Marion's prisoner or that I'd stand by her when the baby came—she'd clam up and tell me her decisions were none of my business.

"Oh, I kept on traipsing up the mountain, bringing wildflowers when spring began and poppies in early summer. For a while I told myself Abigail was acting like any pregnant lady, getting secretive and kind of hiding away, but I don't think I ever believed it.

"It was in the beginning of August that Marion told me Abigail had confessed to Ince's murder, but like I said earlier, the investigation had been officially closed in March. . . . Besides, Marion was so drunk she could hardly stand."

"Tell me about it," Catha finally breathed.

"Get over here, Ethan!" Marion bellowed. She was enthroned in the dimly lit Assembly Room, propped up in her Popsie's favorite chair as if she were keeping a vigil. Empty bottles of Booth's gin littered the carpet; Marion had decided to keep count of her "dead soldiers." "My private army," she'd croon when a maid came to take them away. "Little Marion needs all the help she can get." The staff lived in terror that W.R. would unexpectedly appear, but as no one knew when—or if—that might occur, Marion's silent legion remained.

"Get over here!" In the shadowy gloom (Marion refused to have the lamps lit) Ethan's tall form looked unexpectedly heavy as well as a good deal older. Marion's next order died in her throat, and she stared at the figure hesitating near the entry-hall door. "Popsie?" she quavered in fearful surprise. "Is that you? I thought you was someone else."

"It's Ethan, ma'am," came the answer from the mosaic floor, but Marion was too far gone to listen.

"Oh, Pops, I knew you'd come home! . . . I been waiting here every day . . . faithful Maid Marion." The words were badly slurred and accompanied by a case of hiccups that served to heighten her stammer. "And I told Abby, too . . . said my Popsie wasn't an old meanie . . . that he loves his itsy-bitsy girl. . . . Course she doesn't know everything else I told you . . . and I'd never blab, Pops. Honest I wouldn't." Marion peered into the shadows. "Come here and give your baby doll a big, sloppy kiss."

Ethan didn't move: He imagined that by remaining

rooted in one spot, Marion would exhaust her bizarre ramblings and recognize him.

"Aw shucks," she whimpered as her chin slumped against her chest, making her speech even more incomprehensible than before.

"Still mad . . . ," Ethan heard, followed by, "The guy was asking for it, though . . . like I told you and Neylan . . . thought I was free for the taking." Then the words were further blurred by a sudden spate of tears. Marion was a wallow of grief and remorse.

"But you been good to me, Pops . . . through thick and thin. 'Nobody touches my Marion!'—that's what you said . . . remember? Before you left. . . . Said it was 'bad for business'?"

Marion raised her head suddenly and stared straight into Ethan's frozen eyes. "You're looking good, Pops," she stammered. "Younger . . . thinner, too . . . maybe being around Millicent did you some good . . . maybe Marion's tricks wear her Popsie out." Then the voice turned suddenly harsh. "You're not thinking of ditching your little girl and going back to that old cow, are you, Pops? 'Cause if you are, I'll get me a pair of scissors and cut off your goddamn balls!

"No, I don't mean that, Popsie." Marion forced a lugubrious laugh. "I'd never hurt you. . . . You know Marion's only joking. . . . And I'll tell you something else. . . . I got what it takes to keep my man jazzed all night. . . . I'm the best piece of ass you'll ever get."

Ethan hardly allowed himself to breathe. He was aware of every noise in the house, and of the August heat settling into the room's cavernous corners. Outside, the noonday air had seemed sun-fresh and scented with hay; inside the house, the same smell turned fetid and rank.

"Come on over here and let your little girl give you a quickie on the couch."

Ethan didn't move, and Marion began unbuttoning her blouse. "Just like the old days, Pops, a quickie on the davenport . . . that's what Mama Rose called the sofa, remember? At our house in Brooklyn? . . . She liked them fancy words after she met you." The reverie curtailed all movement. Marion sat in her chair with her fingers pinned to her unbuttoned blouse. "Mama Rose taught me everything I know," she mumbled to herself. "Told me how to please a man."

Marion's eyelids drooped, and her head jerked downward in the quick nod of sleep. Ethan allowed himself a gulp of air, then shifted forward on his feet, preparing to skirt the Assembly Room and sneak toward the back of the house where he assumed he'd find Abigail. But the noise or the motion disturbed Marion and she was awake in a flash.

"What are you doing here, Ethan?" she hissed. "Are you spying on me?"

"No, ma'am." Ethan had no idea how much Marion might remember, and so he opted for an innocent approach. "I just walked in the door, ma'am. I'm looking for Abigail."

"You'd like to make time with her, wouldn't you, Ethan?" Marion snapped. "But I'm going to make certain you don't."

Why would you care? Ethan was about to demand when Marion suddenly let out a scream. "You were standing there pretending to be my Popsie!" she shouted. "Wearing that big hat and looking kind of bashful and shy. . . . You were hoping I'd fess up, weren't you, Mr. Deputy Marshal? Tell you how I snuffed Incie just like I told the Chief! Popsie said to keep my eye on you—said you weren't as dumb as you looked."

By now Marion had staggered to her feet. Her blouse was hanging open, and she'd unfastened the top of her skirt as well. "You're trying to catch me, aren't you? Pin the murder on little Marion . . . but you'll never be able to, 'cause Pops is protecting me. . . . He got all his goddamn lawyers and advisers on the case . . . said he'd never let anything bad happen to his little girl . . . said he loves me better than anything else in the world."

"I wouldn't be so certain of that, Marion." Ethan couldn't have said what had changed within him. Maybe it was the knowledge that Marion was deliberately keeping him away from Abigail, or maybe it was Marion's habitual cruelty. The woman sickened him; he realized he'd felt that way since the beginning.

"If W.R.'s so hot on you, why did he run home to his wife?"

"You creep! You goddamn, low-life, kiss-ass creep! Get out of here before I call the Mullers!"

But Ethan was suddenly unafraid of either the Mullers or their Chief. "And what would those boys do? 'Escort' me down the hill like they did Bill Wellman?"

"They don't need to toss you out," Marion gloated. "Popsie and Neylan already made certain you didn't have any balls. Cambria's deputy marshal—Mr. Crime Investigator. What a laugh."

The self-assurance in the words took Ethan by surprise, and he slowed his own attack momentarily. "What do you mean by that?" The tone was dangerously vulnerable; Marion sensed Ethan's confusion in an instant.

"You goddamn dope! Why do you think you were called when Incie croaked? Why didn't we get a real team of cops, instead of some backwater slob? And a kid to boot!"

Ethan didn't answer; he was trying to fit the pieces together, and the picture he began seeing looked frighteningly like the one Marion was describing.

"And that weird, old commie. Jesus! What a pair of assholes!"

"Save the ladylike speech for Popsie." It was the only answer Ethan could summon. His powerlessness felt overwhelming. The entire investigation had been a hoax; Marion and probably Abigail, too, had been laughing at him from the start. "Pops may appreciate that kind of language, but I don't."

"Don't you dare mention his name!" Marion screeched. "W.R.'s got you wrapped around his little finger."

"Your old man's got himself a slut for a mistress, Marion—that's all he's got. And I wouldn't count on that divorce you keep yapping about. My guess is that he's sticking to his wife."

Marion gasped at this accusation, then began tottering forward. Her opened and rumpled blouse slid over her breasts, and her skirt skidded across her hips. She looked like a woman with nothing left to lose.

"Yeah, well, you're dumber than I thought," she croaked. "Popsie can't leave me now—or ever. I made him think I killed Ince, and he's too scared to let me go. He can't turn me in 'cause I'm his gal, and he won't smell too sweet with a convicted killer for a mistress."

"But you didn't shoot Ince?" Ethan's question was deceptively simple. He was beginning to see a way of redeeming himself. If Marion was lying, she might know who the true murderer was.

"Of course not, you cluck. Why would I want to shoot Incie? He was going to put me in all his pictures—besides being an excellent lay, I might add." Feeling herself again in control, Marion turned smug, and she shimmied her way across the room, discarding both the skirt and blouse as she moved. By the time

315

she reached Ethan she was wearing only a stained satin slip.

"Little Miss Perfect whacked him . . . on account of his boffing her that one night. What a chump! One miserable lay, and she falls apart . . . told me all about it . . . big, weepy confession. . . . Jesus! Virgins! They're all alike . . . think the world ends when they pop their cherries. . . . Course I won't let on to Popsie . . . and neither will you, Ethan honey." Marion was laughing so heartily at her cleverness she failed to notice Abigail enter from the Refectory.

"A young hunk like you needs a dame with experience, not some finishing-school novice." Marion guffawed. "I could make your hair stand on end, and I don't mean the stuff on your head." She slithered her bare arms up Ethan's chest while Abigail stopped in her tracks, recognized the scene for what it appeared to be, and ran out of the room. Ethan heard her footsteps hurrying over the stone staircase long after she had gone.

"My God," Catha said. "What did Abigail say to you after that?"

"I never saw her again," Ethan answered. "She gave birth to your mother shortly after that, but I didn't see the baby until after Abigail died. Your mother had been left in the orphanage by then, but I felt kind of useless when I visited the place. . . . I guess I told you all that before. . . . Louise wasn't an easy baby—or a forgiving adult. . . . She didn't want any part of me.

"But to get back to Marion and that horrible scene . . . She ordered me to keep my 'trap shut' about what she'd said up there at San Simeon, said she'd make my life 'miserable' if I 'screwed the pooch and told on her.' Said she'd 'get even' with Abigail, too. Those were the words she used."

"So who did kill Ince?"

"I've always figured it was Marion." Ethan seemed weary with reliving the past. The little color that had flushed his ancient cheeks was now completely drained. "Who else could it have been? That tale about Abigail confessing sounded like a crackpot scheme. As for her being raped, well, I didn't want to believe it. It took the journal to finally convince me—his name in the book—I could almost see him pawing her. . . . But by then the case was officially closed. There was no touching Marion—guilty or not. And after Abigail's car crashed, what was the point in dredging up the past?"

"When did that happen?"

"Two weeks or so after the baby was born. Maybe a little more or less. I got real fuzzy with time in those days. All I could think about was what Abigail had seen when she'd walked into the Assembly Room. From her point of view the situation must have looked mighty bad."

Ethan shut his eyes, recalling the moment. "She trusted me, you see, and she must have figured I was as bad as all the rest. I never got a chance to explain. She refused to see me. . . . And then she ended up lying dead in a gully."

"Did you ever run that ballistics test?" Catha asked as much for her benefit as Ethan's.

"Oh, sure, but it turned out one of the pistols was missing, so the tests were inconclusive. The Mullers claimed the fancy matched set of six wasn't complete when the yacht set sail—that one weapon had vanished a year before—but who'd believe anything those two goons told you?"

24

CATHA STARED DULLY AT THE NURSING STATION phone, willing it to ring and then wishing it wouldn't. The deeper she delved into her grandmother's story, the more plausible Marion's drunken accusations appeared. I should call Lucas and tell him to forget the guest register at Quilman Brothers, Catha tried to tell herself, but never reached for the receiver. Somewhere there was still hope for Abigail's innocence. There had to be.

When Lucas's call finally came, Catha was so engrossed in her convoluted thoughts that the nurse who answered the phone had to repeat "Catha! Phone!" twice before getting a response. Unwillingly, Catha took the proffered receiver.

"I've found the names!" Lucas announced, and the buoyancy in his voice began to slowly dispel her gloom. "Replete with addresses. Your friend Fawn had the entire situation under control. In fact, she was ecstatic to be 'of service.'"

"I told you so." Catha ventured a smile.

"A Mr. Osgood Rowlands of Pismo Beach and a

Mrs. Edina Denson residing in Studio City. Very posh handwriting in both cases, I might add. Lots of starchy flourishes. I can see why you found those two intimidating."

"I've heard of Studio City, but where's Pismo Beach?"

"It's a retirement community half an hour south of Morro Bay."

"This Rowlands guy drove all the way down to L.A. for my mother's funeral? That's what I call dedication!"

"Perhaps your mother was more intertwined with this pair than you realize."

Catha didn't answer at first, but Lucas's polite silence finally prompted a quiet and introspective: "You're right. Mother had an entire life's history she didn't share. And I never bothered to ask. I always assumed the reason was because her story was too ordinary to matter."

The sadness in Catha's voice caused Lucas to add a quick, "So I'll tackle Edina before flying back up to Cambria, and you drive down to Pismo and interview old Osgood. Maybe your mom was a lot more interesting than you realized."

Osgood Rowlands's condominium complex was among a sea of nearly identical retirement "facilities" erected with the aim of maximizing an already crowded view of the Pacific Ocean. Buff and sand and beige were the primary colors, and the determined unobtrusiveness was bolstered by discreet plantings of noninvasive green. Past street names like Enchanted Way and Shangri-la Circle, Catha wove through the complex looking in vain for a distinguishing landmark before finally spotting Osgood Rowlands's nondescript home.

"It's so thoughtful of you to stop by." The door to 632 Enchanted Way had swung open before Catha had time to knock. "I regretted not spending more time after the funeral, but I'm sure you recall how dreadful the weather was that day—definitely not a season conducive to long-distance journeys."

Osgood Rowlands was exactly as Catha had remembered him: an impeccably clad ex–gentleman's gentleman in a navy blazer and charcoal slacks. His oxford shirt had been starched to within an inch of its life, and his subdued paisley necktie looked as if it had just been removed from a dry cleaner's hanger.

"Thank you for seeing me on such short notice." Catha extended her hand and was surprised at the warmth of Rowlands's grasp. His genuine concern seemed at odds with his pristine appearance.

"As I say, I truly regret not having had an opportunity to talk with you at long last. Especially after Louise's proud tales of your many accomplishments."

"My mother talked about me?" Surprise popped the words out of Catha's mouth before she had a chance to gauge how rude they might sound. "To you?"

"Of course. Don't all mothers prattle on about their offsprings' prowess?"

What did she say? Catha wanted to ask, but was suddenly afraid the answer would reintroduce emotions she'd been trying to bury. Instead she stuck to her original plan, asking "Have you ever heard of a Mademoiselle X?" before she had an opportunity to change her mind.

"Oh, my dear, there's a tangled tale," was Rowlands's airy response as he led the way toward his incongruously chintz-filled "front parlor" and a "proper British high tea."

* * *

"She only used the pseudonym, you know, never permitted another appellation. Even my predecessor at the Barrymore estate couldn't recall hearing the lady's true name. There was a good deal of backstairs gossip over the fact, but you know how quickly rumors fly through the servants' wing . . . ?"

Catha didn't, but she kept the thought to herself, accepting another cup of delicately scented Earl Grey tea and a third triangle of cinnamon toast.

"Perhaps it was because the woman continued to live so outrageously, allowing that huge, strange house of hers to grow more and more dilapidated as the years went by. . . . You should have seen it, a recreational-size bedroom overlooking the beach in Playa del Rey, and a sitting room the size of two of my condominiums. . . . Of course, daylight poured through gargantuan holes in the roof, and that marble bath of hers leaked water all over the kitchen ceiling. Her cook had a dreadful time of it, I can tell you—"

"But you said Mademoiselle X never became a film actress," Catha interrupted. "Where did she get enough money to build such a grand residence?"

Osgood Rowlands paused, then answered indirectly, "I was informed that the lady's days of seeking cinematic employment ended with the debacle on Mr. Hearst's yacht. Her financial backing came from other sources." After delivering that tantalizing information, he helped himself to a scone from a handsome silver serving tray, then continued as if Catha's indiscreet query had never been raised.

"When I first came to Mr. John's house, there was a good deal of gossip about Mademoiselle X being frightened by some event in her past—that she'd chosen not to use her real name out of concern for her siblings' safety. By then the poor woman was rather persona non grata at the Barrymore residence, I'm afraid."

"Do you know what that event was?" Catha couldn't contain herself any longer.

The ex-valet turned momentarily cagey. "Not while Mr. John remained among the living, I didn't." Rowlands flicked two crumbs onto a starched damask napkin. "More tea, Catha?

"It was only after the actor departed this life that the Mademoiselle and I became friendly. Edina, as well. . . . The two of us took her under our wing, so to speak . . . the poor woman seemed so frightfully lonely. We even introduced her to your mother after she returned to California. We felt it would be nice for Louise to meet someone who'd been acquainted with her mother."

Again, Catha felt the sorrowful constricting of her heart. Edina, Osgood, and now the mysterious Mademoiselle X: apparently, each of them had known her mother better than she.

"I suppose it was getting to know Louise that completely unhinged the woman . . . why she finally decided to unburden her soul . . . and I must confess the moment was horribly awkward. None of us had had a clue until then . . . of course, the circumstances surrounding the death of Thomas Ince had long since been forgotten."

"What did Mademoiselle X say?" Catha interjected with as much restraint as she could muster.

"We were sitting in Louise's apartment in Santa Monica . . . having a spot of tea and chatting over inconsequential things—Edina, the Mademoiselle, and I—when the poor dear suddenly stood up and announced, 'I saw Abigail throw that gun overboard.' Just like that, she said it! Your mother couldn't have been more shocked, or Edina or I, for that matter—"

Rowlands might have continued his tale, but Catha cut him short. "What was Mother's response?" she demanded. In her mind's eye, Catha pictured the horror of the scene: the long-dead Abigail accused of murder and her daughter confronting her own heritage. "How did she react?"

"Oh, with her habitual stoicism. Your mother really was a remarkable woman. Edina always felt her composure was the result of those many years in the orphanage following Abigail's suicide, but I believe character is inherent. If not, how could she have coped with everything Mademoiselle X told her that day—"

"What suicide?" Catha burst in; by now tears had filled her eyes and were threatening to spill over her cheeks. "I was told Abigail's car crashed into a tree. There was no mention of her taking her own life."

"Well, the note was there, plain as day, my dear. Some fellows named Muller found it at the scene of the wreck, and then had the intelligence to bring it to St. Anne's. That's where Abigail had been, you know. . . . She'd just left your mother there. . . . That was well before my time, of course. Louise was a mere infant . . . less than two weeks old—"

"And where is this suicide note now?" Catha burst in.

"Well, your mother never wanted it—of that she was most adamant. I assume the wretched thing's still at St. Anne's."

Catha was in her rental car again racing toward San Luis Obispo and the place Osgood Rowlands had described as a "greatly diminished St. Anne's." Her brain was whirling and her lungs heaved with every grieving heartbeat. She tried to concentrate on the road, but her eyes kept flooding with tears. She yanked at the steering wheel, swerved onto the shoulder, and let her head fall forward with a wrenching sob.

She wept for Louise and for Abigail, for the bond they'd never had, and the love they'd never shared. And finally Catha cried for her mother and herself.

25

S<small>T. A</small>NNE'S BORE NO RESEMBLANCE TO THE DOUR image Catha had constructed for herself. The weathered wood building with its faintly Victorian porch and sharply peaked dormer windows looked cozy rather than austere, and although the once fine garden and playground had been sold off to make way for a minimall and parking lot, the nearby church with its adjacent elementary school remained. The difference was that the former home for orphaned girls now served as the parish rectory.

Catha rang an antique doorbell that echoed through silent halls, then pushed open a creaky and seldom used front door and stood in what had once been the orphanage's busy reception hall.

If it was possible for stucco and tile and wood to retain their history, St. Anne's had done so admirably. The exposed beams of the ceiling were dusky with age; the floor tiles were chipped and scuffed; and the wood chair rail was marred by years of furtive name scribbling. Catha imagined finding her mother's name carved in a discreet corner, then suddenly wondered what young Louise Kinsolving had been like. Had she had a happy life here, surrounded by other children? Or had her mother's suicide and her own homeless state created a forlorn and timid creature?

Catha tried conjuring up the former, seeing a buoyant seven-year-old Louise roar down the hall that led from a communal dining room. Her hair was braided in untidy pigtails and her institutional pinafore speckled with jelly. She wheeled around the corner and charged up the stairs, followed by a pack of giggling classmates, who scraped the walls with less-than-tidy fingers. Catha could see the blurry line those years of children had left. It bumped its way to the second-floor landing and disappeared down a corridor whose many doors were now locked.

Catha dragged her eyes back to the present, noticing a glass-partitioned reception desk and a blue-haired lady hunched over an ancient typewriter. She was pounding methodically on sticking keys and mouthing words as she typed. Catha waited until the woman took a break from this clearly odious task.

"I wonder if you can help me."

The noise startled the typist, but her answer was a cheerful, "If I can, dear." Then with a myopic smile she struggled to bring Catha into focus. "Let me put on my other specs. I have to use two pairs now, isn't it frightful? That's what age does to you, and I refuse to wear bifocals. They make you look like such an old lady!"

Catha smiled. A blue rinse over white hair didn't exactly disguise the years. "You could get invisible bifocals," she offered.

"Oh, but I'd know the truth! And every time I looked in the mirror I'd see this ancient crone staring back at me! It's bad enough as it is. I don't feel a day over forty. It's very hard to accept the fact that I'm well past seventy."

"My mother was brought here as a child," Catha interrupted gently.

"To visit or to stay?" Seventy plus or not, the woman was sharp.

"To stay. I'm hoping you might still have some record of her. She arrived in 1925. In August."

A sympathetic sigh was followed by a brisk rustling around as the receptionist left her office cubicle, locked the door, and joined Catha. She slid the glass divider shut and put another key in the window's lock. "Isn't it frightful?" she announced. "All these precautions? And us supposedly a house of God!" Then her quick steps led Catha up the stairs.

They passed along the corridor; the place still smelled of children: years' and years' worth of finger paints and library paste and graham crackers.

"As you see," Catha's new friend remarked as they hurried up another stairway that led to an attic, "we no longer take in foundlings. St. Anne's is considering selling off the building; the upkeep is prodigious, and we don't need the space."

Catha glanced at a vine-choked window beneath the attic's eaves. This place was once my mother's home, she told herself. Someday it will be nothing but concrete and glitzy storefronts. The thought made her immeasurably sad.

"I'm not even sure we go back that far, dear. A good many of our records have been lost or eliminated; and, of course, many of our 'graduates' take them when they leave." Catha was confronted with hampers and baskets and boxes of artifacts: framed photos of basketball teams, graduating classes, and faculty members. The years were jumbled together; a picture of a swim meet in 1935 was next to a blurred

1947 photograph of nameless youngsters at a picnic. The children's various histories seemed to be interspersed among the age-spotted prints.

"I have to get back to my post, dear, but you have a look around. Does your mother want anything in particular?"

"My mother's dead." The words were lonelier than Catha had intended. "I hadn't heard of St. Anne's until today."

The effort at businesslike detachment failed to fool the blue-haired lady. "I see." The tone was full of comfort, and the quiet nobility that evolves over a lifetime of helping others. "Well, you take all the time you need."

Catha had been seated among the dust and cobwebs for over an hour. Midday had become afternoon, and a wintery breeze had picked up. Catha could hear it riffling the vines along the roof and scrabbling at the eaves with dried twigs. The noise was a pleasant accompaniment to her task; it was like having a real grandmother and a family home to explore. Catha pulled another wicker hamper toward her; so far her search had been fruitless, and she'd opened over half the boxes. There wasn't much more time, either, despite the receptionist's assurance. Lucas would be waiting for her in Cambria.

Catha smiled, imagining him zipping up and down the state, jumping on and off commuter planes just to be with her. Then the smile turned into a self-deprecating grimace. What am I thinking of? she demanded. I have a job and security on the East Coast; Lucas lives in California. This is crazy. There's no way we can manage a relationship. But no sooner had those angry feelings been vented than other emotions surfaced. Who cares about security, Catha decided. What's life without a little risk taking now and then?

At that moment she found her mother's file. A brittle black-and-white photograph, glued to a form containing the baby's history: Louise Kinsolving. Mother, Abigail Kinsolving. Father, unknown. Child born, August 17, 1925. Admitted, August 30. Catha stared at the muzzy photo and faded lettering. She was surprised to find she was crying.

The remainder of the file was a hodgepodge of instructions from Marion, a copy of a bank statement naming Marion as the principal depositor and Louise Kinsolving (aged eleven) as her beneficiary, a typed letter from John Barrymore mentioning an overdue birthday gift (for Louise's "eighth anniversary celebration"), and two Christmas cards from Lita Grey.

"They all knew!" Catha gasped as she tore through the pages. "I wonder if they visited as well . . . and how their glamorous appearances affected the school—and Louise."

The rest of the folder was painfully thin. There were no notices of disruptive behavior or excellence in sports. No Library Club or Debating Society, no scholastic heights or extracurricular activities; the report cards were a compilation of middling grades that marched through the years without improvement or decline. Louise had hidden her light under a giant basket. Inside one of these studiously lackluster report cards, Catha found the suicide note. The paper had been opened, perused, and refolded many times.

There was something odd about the message from the start. Catha stared at the handwriting, a scrupulous effort at penmanship that didn't seem to match Abigail's previous flair. But the letters resembled her grandmother's, and the paper matched the pages in the journal:

I'm sorry about the baby. I'm sorry for a lot of things.

Not quite Abigail's style, but Catha reasoned the writer was under extraordinary stress.

I told Marion everything. She promised to look after little Louise. I can't live with my horrible secret anymore. I'm sorry for what I done.

Catha examined the last line again. Were there missing letters following the *I?* Had the years erased them; was the error a lapse in Abigail's careful grammar? "I'm sorry for what I done," Catha murmured as the attic door swung open with a bang and a bubbly voice called up the stairwell:

"Gentleman to see you! We're getting to be a regular traffic jam in here!"

Lucas loped up the stairs, taking them two at a time. "I called Osgood Rowlands hoping to find you still there. He told me you might be here—and why. Look, Catha, don't you think you've jumped through enough emotional hoops—"

"It's a fake," Catha interrupted without bothering to hear Lucas out. "The letter's a fake."

If Lucas was either surprised or confused by Catha's pronouncement, he didn't show it. Instead he took the limp and tattered note out of her hand. "How do you know?"

"The grammar for one thing. Abigail never would have made an error like that; I don't care what state of mind she was in. . . . And then on closer examination, it's not my grandmother's handwriting at all. Look at the way these *y*'s loop . . . Abigail was much freer-spirited."

"What are you thinking?" Lucas's voice was gentle.

"That someone forged the note, pretending it was Abigail. It's a pretty clever job, a piece of paper torn from her journal . . . a good, if overly exact, rendition of her script. Obviously the hoax fooled everyone—including Louise." Catha's tone grew quiet here as she tried to comprehend what her mother must have felt staring at this horrific missive. No wonder the letter was so creased and rumpled; Louise must have reread it countless times over the years.

Catha pulled her attention back to Lucas. "My grandmother never committed suicide. She was made of stronger stuff than that. It's too bad her own daughter never believed it."

"Do you think you're clinging to a fantasy here, Catha? According to Edina, everyone accepted the fact—her boss, Lita Grey, included. Apparently, Marion was 'inconsolable' over her secretary's death."

"But who found her body?"

"The Muller boys?" Lucas's statement was more question than answer.

"Exactly!" Catha pounced on the name. "The Mullers! There's no need to look further than that creepy duo! Obviously one or both of them devised a way to get rid of Abigail. She must have become a major liability to Marion's scheme for keeping Hearst's protection. Maybe the whole phony suicide bit was Marion's doing. Or maybe the order to 'dispose' of Abigail came down from the great man himself."

Lucas didn't say a word, and Catha failed to interpret the sorrowing look in his eyes. "Don't you think you're jumping to conclusions? Accusing the Mullers of killing Abigail—and by extension implicating Marion and maybe even Hearst himself?"

"Why couldn't Marion have masterminded the whole thing? Shot Ince herself and then handed the pistol to Abigail and ordered her to toss it overboard.

I mean, who cares what Mademoiselle X claims she saw. She doesn't seem such a reliable source to me! You should have heard the way Osgood Rowlands described her living arrangements."

In answer, Lucas only said, "Let's look at your discoveries again. Maybe there's something you haven't noticed." The words were so soft they were almost inaudible.

Stubborn and defensive, Catha flipped open the file folder again. "Report card, report card . . . diploma graduating Louise Kinsolving into upper school . . . Why didn't my mother take this stuff with her? . . . Another bank statement listing a now thirteen-year-old Louise as beneficiary . . . Marion must have ladled a good deal of money on Abigail's child. . . . That's it, Lucas! Hush money! Marion was feeling guilty as sin! She did it! She shot Ince!" Catha's eyes were shiny with triumph. "Where there's a will there's a way!" she almost shouted. "Let's drive back to Morro Bay and tell Ethan. I can't wait to see his face! My grandmother was innocent."

"I think you and I should have a little talk first, Catha."

The tone caught Catha by surprise; her shoulders sagged slightly, but she pinned them back in a straighter line. "I didn't expect this to work out, Lucas." She tried to smile. "It was nice of you to come all the way up here to tell me."

"What are you talking about?" Lucas looked equally dumbfounded and hurt.

"It's okay, really! No hard feelings and all that other junk." Bravery was becoming a difficult act, but Catha was determined to finish what she'd begun.

"What the hell are you talking about?"

"Aren't you breaking it off?"

"Jesus, Catha! No! I love you!"

332

A long silence embalmed the room at that moment; it fell on the stacks of forgotten and discarded letters, on the photographs no one had wanted, on the broken lampshades stacked in a corner, the mismatched iron bedsteads and trunks of flimsy linens: the detritus of transitory lives.

"Then what did you come here to tell me, Lucas?" she asked softly.

"Mademoiselle X's story—what Osgood Rowlands told you about her witnessing Abigail toss that pistol overboard." Lucas paused. At first he didn't look Catha in the eyes; his glance roved around the room as if searching for any means of escape. "There's more to the tale, and my guess is that your habitual impatience stopped Rowlands before he could finish. . . . Hell! . . . This is even harder than I thought."

"What else did Mademoiselle X say?" Catha's tone was quiet and proud; if Lucas hadn't known better, he might have imagined the words contained no emotion.

"According to Edina, Mademoiselle X had been too terrified to come forward and tell the truth. Apparently two 'German gentlemen' had shown up at her house four times in one month . . . and Marion had ordered her 'to keep her trap shut' as well—"

"And?" Catha interrupted; her voice had turned querulous, but Lucas heard heartache within the simple question.

"Mademoiselle X saw Abigail shoot Ince."

"Where was Marion when the shot was fired?" was all Catha could respond.

"Close enough to make her own deception appear plausible."

"Then couldn't Marion have been the one to pull the trigger?" Catha mumbled, trying to drive away the awful news. She'd invested too much in her grandmother's innocence to have it vanish so abruptly.

"That doesn't make sense, Catha. Why would she need to lie to Hearst if she'd truly committed the crime? My guess is that those drunken ramblings Ethan heard were correct. Abigail had confessed, and Marion was terrified the fact would leak out."

"But Ethan didn't believe her. He said so himself."

"Ethan was in love with Abigail, Catha. Men do strange things under those circumstances."

Catha mulled over this comment, then rallied with a renewed attack. "But what about the Muller boys? What was their role in all this? Clearly, they were up to no good, 'discovering' a suicide note and then rushing off to St. Anne's with their prize. . . . Besides, why didn't Ethan tell me Abigail had committed suicide?"

"Maybe you didn't give him enough time, Catha. Or maybe he was hoping you'd never uncover the truth. He didn't know you'd tracked down other sources, after all. I think he was trying to spare you unnecessary pain."

"But I was with him all morning—as well as yesterday afternoon," Catha continued, grasping any excuse that allowed her to avoid acknowledging Abigail's guilt. "The only reference he made to my grandmother's death was to say she'd died before he could explain that scene with Marion."

"Doesn't that seem natural to you, Catha? That his presiding emotion is remorse?"

"No," Catha answered defensively. "I'm convinced there's more to this than Edina, Osgood, or even Ethan knows." Despite her insistence, she'd slumped down on a battered steamer trunk.

"Let it go, Catha. You can't help Abigail, or your mother, either."

"But the Mullers may have murdered my grandmother! Tinkered with the car's steering mechanism . . . or weakened the brake cable in some way.

Hell, I'm no mechanic! But you can bet those two gorillas were!"

"And if they did sabotage the vehicle?"

"Well, don't you see, Lucas! That would account for the crash! . . . The Mullers are waiting . . . maybe hidden in that dense brush beside the ravine. Abigail's car comes tearing up the hill . . . there's something in the road—maybe one of Hearst's zebras or elands let loose on purpose. . . . Abigail swerves to avoid it . . . the brakes fail or she can't regain control of the steering wheel, and down the car plunges. When they decide it's safe, one of the Mullers approaches the wreck and plants the phony suicide note while the other runs to the castle, pretending to call for help even though he knows Abigail's dead. . . . And maybe Marion's there waiting!"

In answer, Lucas moved to Catha's side and put his arm around her shoulders. "How would you go about proving this, Catha? Nineteen twenty-five is a good many years ago. Even if you could open an investigation and claim that your grandmother's death wasn't due to suicide, how would you go about making your case?"

"I don't know," Catha admitted slowly. "I don't know."

"If Ince's shooting was reinvented as 'acute indigestion resulting in heart failure,' then what are your chances for uncovering new information on the Mullers? Do you believe you'd find one shred of evidence linking them to the scene of Abigail's crash?"

"And so we let these people get away with murder?"

"I realize you're angry and disappointed, Catha, but think for a moment about what you're saying. Didn't Abigail escape prosecution in Ince's death? Wasn't her crime concealed, as well?"

"You know perfectly well why Marion chose to play the part of the criminal!" Defensive, almost desperate, Catha's green eyes burned bright. She stood, still clutching the letter, and Lucas was forced to step back a pace or two. "My mother's life was ruined because of this deception—and Abigail's, too. They never had a chance!"

"And what about you, Catha? Do you think you'll be helping them or yourself if you try to reopen an ancient investigation?" Lucas's voice was as steady and calm as his presence. Catha felt a comforting peace exude from him like warmth from a fire. "Don't you think you've been through enough already?"

Catha allowed Lucas to move close again and slip his arm around her waist. "And so we simply forget it?" she asked.

"Yes, Catha, we forget it. We go on with our lives."

Catha stared at the letter, and then at dusty floorboards and gray windowpanes. My grandmother, she told herself, and my mother. Both of them left tiny pieces of their souls within these walls. Catha closed her eyes momentarily and allowed the sounds and smells of the forgotten room to work their way into her memory. How many other stories are hidden here? she wondered.

"We go on with our lives," Catha murmured, opening her eyes and giving Lucas a grateful smile. "You're right. It's what my mother was trying to do. I never gave her enough credit."

Catha dropped the fraudulent letter into the file, and returned it to the overflowing box; and together she and Lucas walked out into the growing night.

Bibliography

Aidala, Thomas R. *Hearst Castle, San Simeon*. New York: Hudson Hills Press, Inc., 1981.

Brownlow, Kevin. *The Parade's Gone By*. New York: Alfred A. Knopf, 1968.

Carlson, Oliver, and Ernest Sutherland Bates. *Hearst, Lord of San Simeon*. Westport, Conn.: Greenwood Press, 1970.

Chaney, Lindsay, and Michael Cieply. *The Hearsts, Family and Empire . . . the Later Years*. New York: Simon & Schuster, 1981.

Chaplin, Lita Grey. *My Life with Chaplin: An Intimate Portrait*. Brattleboro, Vt.; Bernard Geis Associates, 1966.

Chase, Ilka. *Past Imperfect*. Garden City, N.Y.: Doubleday & Company, Inc., Doran, 1942.

Coffman, Taylor. *The Builders Behind the Castle*. San Luis Obispo: San Luis Obispo Historical Society, 1990.

———. *Hearst Castle, the Story of William Randolph Hearst and San Simeon*. Santa Barbara: Sequoia Books, 1985.

———. *Hearst's Dream*. San Luis Obispo: EZ Nature Books, 1989.

337

Davies, Marion. *The Times We Had: Life with William Randolph Hearst.* Eds. Pamela Pfau and Kenneth S. Marx. Indianapolis: Bobbs-Merrill Company, Inc., 1975.

Etherington-Smith, Meredith, and Jeremy Pilcher. *The "It" Girls: Lucy, Lady Duff Gordon, the Couturiere, "Lucille" and Elinor Glyn, Romantic Novelist.* San Diego: Harcourt Brace Jovanovich, 1986.

Fowler, Gene. *Good Night Sweet Prince: The Life and Times of John Barrymore.* New York: Viking Press, 1944.

Gabler, Neal. *An Empire of Their Own, How the Jews Invented Hollywood.* New York: Crown Publishers, 1988.

————. *Winchell: Gossip, Power and the Culture of Celebrity.* New York: Alfred A. Knopf, 1994.

Glyn, Elinor. *Three Weeks.* New York: Duffield, 1917.

Guiles, Frederick Lawrence. *Marion Davies: A Biography.* New York: McGraw-Hill, 1972.

Hearst, William Randolph. *Selections from the Writings and Speeches of William Randolph Hearst.* Ed. F. I. Tomkins. San Francisco: privately printed, 1948.

Hearst, William Randolph, Jr. *The Hearsts: Father and Son.* Niwot, Colo.: Robert Rinehart Publishers, 1991.

Lundberg, Ferdinand. *Imperial Hearst: A Social Biography.* New York: Viking Press, 1936.

Murray, Ken. *The Golden Days of San Simeon.* Garden City, N.Y.: Doubleday & Company, Inc., 1971.

O'Donnell, James. *100 Years of Making Communications History: The Story of the Hearst Corporation.* New York: Hearst Corporation, 1987.

Parsons, Louella. *Tell It to Louella.* New York: G. P. Putnam's Sons, 1961.

Robinson, Judith. *The Hearsts: An American Dynasty.* New York: Avon Books, 1991.

Schatz, Thomas. *The Genius of the System: Hollywood Filmmaking in the Studio Era.* New York: Pantheon Books, 1988.

Swanberg, W. A. *Citizen Hearst*. New York: Charles Scribner's Sons, 1961.

Swing, Raymond Grom. *Forerunners of American Fascism*. Freeport, N.Y.: Books for Libraries Press, 1969 (reprint of 1935 Julian Messner edition).

Tebbel, John William. *The Life and Good Times of William Randolph Hearst*. New York: Dutton, 1952.

Wadsworth, Ginger. *Julia Morgan: Architect of Dreams*. Minneapolis: Learner Publications Company, 1990.

Walker, Alexander. *Rudolph Valentino*. New York: Stein and Day, 1976.

Winslow, Carleton M., Nicola L. Frye, and Taylor Coffman. *The Enchanted Hill: The Story of Hearst Castle at San Simeon*. Los Angeles: Rosebud Books, 1980.